1

moonbase columbus

The helium-3 processing plant looked like a lunar rover thrown together by a committee of abstract artists.

Standing two hundred meters away, Jason Dvorak recognized the large wheels and the heavily shielded nuclear power unit. Huge triangular heat radiators jutted up and out at an angle, giving the impression of a stegosaurus lumbering across the crater floor. The front of the He-3 processor opened up in a cylinder of diamond-tipped teeth used for scooping and grinding the top layer of regolith; at the opposite end, a jumble of hot debris was deposited like excrement.

As the leviathan crawled along the surface, swallowing regolith, Jason felt pressure on his spacesuited arm. He turned and, in a habit he could not seem to shake, looked at the reflectorized spacesuit visor of his companion before glancing down to the namepatch. *Never look at the face to recognize someone outside,* he kept telling himself. After a year, you'd think he'd be used to it.

Cyndi Salito's contralto voice came over his speaker. "You haven't moved for minutes, Jase."

"Can't help it." Jason turned back to the mobile processor. "I can't believe it's finally working. You beat your deadline by a week. This'll really look good for us. Especially for me—two weeks in command and already I have a major milestone to show off." *And it's a miracle the base hasn't fallen apart,* he added to himself. He still couldn't

11

Celeste rocked forwa ... t
the arms of her chair. ... t
sample. Before it gets loose."

"It's inside a lead-lined vault." Dvorak looked puzzled.

"Now!" she said. "Lead won't stop them. Once they finish taking apart the regolith sample and the debris from the recovery canister, they'll start dismantling the inside of the shielding wall, atom by atom, to keep reproducing."

General Pritchard stepped into the transmission area and raised his voice. "Dvorak, you saw what happened to your hopper and to those three people—and if those things can dissolve an entire spacecraft, they sure as hell can eat through a lead wall!"

Celeste's voice felt cold in her throat. "And it's not anything we developed. Nothing from Earth."

———

"The authors have a fine grasp of character and a slick writing style."—SCIENCE FICTION REVIEW

"Quite frankly, this book has everything . . . can only be described as an absolutely stupendous read, a worthy successor to LIFELINE *and* THE TRINITY PARADOX.*"*—William Barton, co-author of IRIS

"If ASSEMBLERS OF INFINITY *doesn't make you think, you're brain dead!"*—David Brin, author of STARTIDE RISING

"Anderson and Beason are the heavyweight tag-team of hard science fiction!"—Allen Steele, author of LABYRINTH OF NIGHT

Assemblers of *INFINITY*

Kevin J. Anderson
and Doug Beason

M191056936

SPECTRA ™

BANTAM BOOKS

NEW YORK • TORONTO • LONDON • SYDNEY • AUCKLAND

This novel is a work of fiction. Names, characters, places, and incidents are either the product of the authors' imaginations or are used fictitiously. Any resemblance to actual events, locales, organizations, or persons, living or dead, is entirely coincidental and beyond the intent of either the authors or the publisher.

ASSEMBLERS OF INFINITY
A Bantam Spectra Book / February 1993

SPECTRA and the portrayal of a boxed "s" are trademarks of Bantam Books, a division of Bantam Doubleday Dell Publishing Group, Inc.

An abridged version of this novel previously appeared
in *Analog* magazine

ISBN 0-553-29921-2

Published simultaneously in the United States and Canada

Bantam Books are published by Bantam Books, a division of Bantam Doubleday Dell Publishing Group, Inc. Its trademark, consisting of the words "Bantam Books" and the portrayal of a rooster, is Registered in U.S. Patent and Trademark Office and in other countries. Marca Registrada. Bantam Books, 1540 Broadway, New York, New York 10036.

PRINTED IN THE UNITED STATES OF AMERICA

RAD 0 9 8 7 6 5 4 3 2

dedication

For CINDY BEASON, for being there and supporting
my dreams throughout the years.
(Doug Beason)

For REBECCA MOESTA ANDERSON, with her sharp
eyes, sharp pencil, and loving heart.
(Kevin J. Anderson)

acknowledgments

Writing *Assemblers of Infinity* required knowledge and
expertise in many areas. For their invaluable assistance,
we would like to thank Dr. Rod Hyde and Lt. Gen. Tom
Stafford's *Synthesis Group,* Dr. Jim Degnan, Dr. Bel
Campbell, Michael Meltzer, Clare Bell, M. Coleman
Easton, Dan'l Danehy-Oakes, Lori Ann White, Michael C.
Berch, Thomas Ryan Nelson for Aiken and the caviar,
Lt. Col. Tom Walsh, Eric Fukumitsu, Jeff Kidd, Kathleen
M. Dyer, Leslie Lauderdale, Rebecca Moesta Anderson,
Cindy Beason, Betsy Mitchell, Heather McConnell, and
Richard Curtis.

dramatis personae

Columbus Base
Trevor "Can't Wait" Waite—Maintenance specialist
Siegfried Lasserman—Telemetry specialist and hopper
    pilot
Becky Snow—Electronics engineer
Jason Dvorak—Commander of Columbus Base
Margaret Dvorak—His wife, back on Earth
Lacy Dvorak—His daughter, back on Earth
Lawrence Dvorak—His son, back on Earth
Dr. Cyndi Salito—Mining engineer
Lon "Big Daddy" Newellen—Communications expert

Collins L-1 Waystation
Bryan "Zed" Zimmerman—L-1 to Moon shuttle pilot
Dr. Bernard Chu—Director, L-1 Station

Washington, D.C.
Celeste McConnell—Director of United Space Agency
Major General Simon Pritchard, USAF—Special assistant
    to McConnell
Albert Fukumitsu—Duty manager, United Space Agency
    Mission Control
Lt. Col. Eileen Dannon—Bernard Chu's predecessor on
    the Collins

Antarctica
Kent Woodward—Astronaut
Gunther Mosby—Astronaut
Dr. Erika Trace—Nanotechnology researcher
Dr. Jordan Parvu—Nanotechnology pioneer
Sinda Parvu—His wife, an anthropologist
Timothy Parvu—His son
Dr. Bingham Grace—Astronaut and commander,
    Simulated Mars Mission

Alpha Base, Wendover AFB, Utah
Major Jardine Felowmate, USAF—Alpha Base commanding officer
Francine Helschmidt—Liaison, International Verification Initiative

Other Locations
Dr. Maia Compton-Reasor—Stanford nanotechnologist
Dr. Maurice Taylor—MIT nanotechnologist, Erika's PhD adviser
Rico Portola—Astronaut on the ill-fated Grissom
Dr. Piter Sommerveld—Belgian nanotech researcher
Julia Falbring—News reporter
Clark McConnell—Celeste McConnell's husband, killed on the ill-fated Grissom

prologue

daedalus array: lunar farside

For all practical purposes, Daedalus Crater was the most remote spot in the solar system. Centered 180 degrees away from Earth and only 4 degrees below the lunar equator, Daedalus never saw or heard Earth, never received stray radio waves that might diffract over the lunar horizon and ruin delicate astronomical measurements.

Here in the orbital shadow, Daedalus Crater was the perfect spot to station a VLF—Very Low Frequency—array to study portions of the radio spectrum that on Earth were drowned out. Massive dipole antennas sprawled kilometers across the flat floor of the crater in a Y-shaped array encircled by the crater walls, making the site look like a giant Mercedes-Benz emblem.

Because of its remoteness, the VLF site had to function autonomously. All instruments had been designed to run by themselves, to fix themselves with modular replacement parts, to be inspected by telepresence repair drones. With the unchanging nature of the Moon, the VLF should have operated for decades without human intervention.

Until absolutely everything went wrong.

Trevor "Can't Wait" Waite drew a stale breath from the cramped cabin of the lunar hopper as they approached the site. The hopper had been launched from Moonbase Columbus on an investigation and repair mission, and Waite fidgeted until he could go outside and have a look

1

for himself. The scientists Earthside were screaming about their interrupted VLF data, and Can't Wait Waite could troubleshoot faster than anyone else on the base.

Unfortunately, even with ninety-five percent of the hopper's systems automated, outdated safety regs still demanded a full crew of three, with one person to remain inside the vehicle and two required on every extravehicular activity. Waite figured he could have taken care of the problem himself in an hour or so; he was convinced that Sig Lasserman's caution and Becky Snow's neophyte bumbling would triple the time required.

The hopper approached the lunar surface on the upper rim of Daedalus Crater. It was difficult to see in the lunar night. "I am taking her down slowly," Siegfried Lasserman said. He spoke in a clipped German accent as he worked at the lander controls.

"Of course you are," Waite mumbled. He checked over his suit, anxious to be outside and tinkering with the malfunctioning antennas. *Let's get the show on the road!*

He hated to waste time sending a human to do a robot's job, but all the automatic sensors on the VLF had gone screwy, all the maintenance routines had failed, and no one could figure out just which branch in the endless fault-tree had been responsible for the breakdown. Two of the array's dipole antennas had blipped out within an hour of each other; a third quit less than a day later. The three defective units stood in a row, possibly signifying that the malfunction was spreading sequentially. And even worse, the repair drones would not respond.

Moonbase Columbus couldn't even get a visual of the Daedalus site. Waite wondered if something as major as a meteor strike could have wrecked a portion of the array—but all the seismic sensors had been silent as fossils.

"Why is he setting us down up here?" Becky Snow asked, interrupting Waite's thoughts. "This wasn't briefed in the preflight." Her black eyes were wider than they should have been; perspiration glistened on her ebony cheeks and forehead.

Lasserman's attention didn't waver from the controls. "To protect the array from any dust the hopper will kick up. The upper rim of the crater has an access road down to the floor. We'll be close enough up here."

"You'll see the array even in the darkness once we're down the access road," Waite said. Becky Snow had never been to the Farside before and had been on the Moon itself only five weeks. He hated being somebody's on-the-job training instructor.

Lasserman set the hopper down on the landing area blasted flat behind the crater rim. He switched to a different set of controls, powering down the methane engines, as Waite and Snow twiddled their thumbs until their own work could begin. They wore their EVA suits though the hopper cabin was fully pressurized. Waite felt claustrophobic in the hopper, even with his face mask flipped up. He wanted to be outside.

Lasserman crouched by the hopper's instrument panel; his suit was linked to computers that projected data on a heads-up holographic display shimmering in front of him. "I am still getting anomalous readings from the EM sounder. It shows something large and artificial out there, more than just the VLF. And the infrared response makes no sense. Much too high. It's been dark for ten days now—everything should be very cold."

"Maybe our dust is scattering the signal." Waite clicked down his faceplate and switched on the suit radio, impatient to solve the problem. Why talk about it anymore when they had come all this way to do a hands-on?

Lasserman hesitated. "Dust should have settled by now," came his voice over the radio. "That cannot be the explanation."

Waite finished checking his suit and moved toward the hatch. "Well, as soon as Becky's ready, we can go outside and have a look for ourselves. If nothing was screwy, we wouldn't have come all the way out here anyway." *If you weren't willing to take any risks, why did you come to the Moon in the first place?*

Startled, Becky fumbled with her own suit. Out of the corner of his eye, Waite watched to make sure she went through the proper checks.

Lasserman nodded in response to his controls, adjusting his throat mike. "I am informing Mr. Dvorak that we have arrived and are still receiving anomalous signals. I will rig it so that they can observe the mission in realtime."

"Right," Waite said. As if the moonbase commander didn't have anything else to do. Or maybe he didn't. Jason Dvorak had been in command of Columbus for only a few weeks, and his promotion had surprised himself as much as everyone else, especially Bernard Chu, the former commander. Maybe Dvorak did want to watch the repair activities.

"Ready," Becky said.

"Rog. We're going out now. Deploy the rover." Waite sealed the airlock and squinted at the blocky buttons on the control panel. A green READY light blinked at him. Pushing his spacesuited thumb against the panel, he immediately felt his suit stiffen as the air bled out of the lock. A rush of warm air diffused through his suit as the heaters kicked on. Beside him in the cramped chamber, Becky Snow stood completely still.

"We'll get this straightened out in no time," he said for the benefit of the moonbase audience who would be watching the transmissions, and no doubt the hackers on Earth who loved to tap into boring moonbase jabber. The special-interest comm-channel, United Space Agency Select, had long ago stopped broadcasting news about routine mission activities.

When the hopper's outer door unsealed itself, Waite climbed out of the airlock. He held out a hand to steady Becky as she climbed down the ladder, but she kept her own balance.

Turning, Waite paused to assess the distance to the VLF. The rover would kick up some dust, but that little bit shouldn't cause too much of a problem for the dipole antennas. Even in the darkness, through a breach in the crater wall, he could see the wide and crumbled access road left behind by the construction vehicles that had installed the array five years before. It would be a quick drive down.

"Don't spend too much time gawking at the scenery," Waite said to Becky. He turned to see that she had already

4

begun disengaging the rover vehicle from the hopper chassis. Lasserman had deployed the package while they were still in the airlock. The lunar rover bounced once on the moon dirt, or regolith, and began to unfold.

"All right," she answered and waited for him to get into the rover.

"We're heading out, Sig," Waite said.

"Roger that. I am reading everything from your suit cameras. You are relaying directly from the rover up to L-2."

"Isn't realtime great?" He just hoped that the moonbase people wouldn't muck around with his job out here. He was the one on Farside, and he would make the decisions himself.

Lasserman would have preferred to sit wringing his hands until Dvorak or somebody else told him what to do, or maybe even until Celeste McConnell made a decision back on Earth. If he had to wait for them, Can't Wait would die of old age before they got around to choosing the "most judicious course of action."

Waite paused while the rover's steering wheel popped out, then seated himself on the vehicle's framework. The light banks came on, spilling out across the path ahead of them.

The Moon at night was full of shadows, but starlight undimmed by any atmosphere glimmered down like ice-cold points. As soon as they passed over the lip of the crater, bouncing along the access road on the rover's wide tires, Waite saw immediately why the VLF array had ceased functioning. "There's something very wrong here," he transmitted, keeping his voice steady.

"I can see that. Unbelievable!" Lasserman's voice came into his ears. "I've already checked in with Columbus. Somebody is going out to get Mr. Dvorak right away."

That seemed unimportant to Waite. He stared down the sloping crater wall to the floor of Daedalus. Behind them a line of their own fresh tire tracks serpentined back toward the hopper.

Beside him, Becky leaned forward. "None of the archival photos looked like this."

"That's because the archival photos were two years old. You go ahead and gawk all you want."

In the starlight, he could see that two arms of the Y remained intact, but the third looked as if it had been bitten off. Directly next to the crater wall, a pit like a gigantic mine shaft plunged downward, a kilometer in diameter if it was an inch. It yawned like a giant mouth swallowing the floor, the VLF array, and every sign of human presence. Waite could not see the bottom.

Spreading out in translucent strands, a wispy structure extended up from the pit—ghostly arches of fishline, support frameworks, silvery lines like a faded but complicated architectural drawing that had been mostly erased.

Becky Snow whispered, "It looks like the lair of one of those tunnel spiders. You know, with the spider waiting in the hole, and the web stretching out in all directions."

The sensors in his suit flashed warning lights to display his suddenly increased blood pressure and breathing rate. Scrubbers worked double time to deal with the rush of sweat that had just burst from his body. Waite bumped on his chin mike, surprised to hear how steady his voice remained.

"Sig, can you see this?"

"Only from your transmitter. I cannot see it from the hopper."

"That's because you're too far up, on the other side of the crater wall. You'd better make sure my transmission is getting to Columbus."

"Roger. Your stereochip is still broadcasting to L-2. This is—"

Waite cut him off. "I'm going to follow the access road for a while, go around the side to get a different perspective."

"Be very cautious," Lasserman said.

"You can bet on it," Becky answered for Waite.

Waite eased the rover forward down the slope, which took him farther away from both the hopper and the structure. He wet his lips and looked down again to survey the hole. It was uncanny. He knew there hadn't been anything like this on the satellite recon photos, last taken years ago with the lunar orbiters. The Moon was geologically dead—there wasn't supposed to be any need to keep mapping the surface.

"How could you excavate a hole like that without making the seismographs yammer for days?" Becky asked.

"No way. You can't do it. The geologists should have been able to pinpoint the source to within a few meters. They're a pain in the butt, but they're not *that* incompetent." After he had spoken, he realized he was "hot mike," transmitting everything back to the moonbase. *Oh, well.*

As the rover continued its descent, Waite turned his attention to the other portions of the array, erected there by humans a few years before. The "spiderwebs" extended to the fourth dipole antenna on the array, draping the dipole.

Lasserman's voice burst into his ears again. "Columbus advises that you do not go too close to the pit."

Waite was aggressive, but he wasn't stupid. "No problem."

He steered past truck-sized boulders and tried to keep out of the deepest shadows. With all the strange stuff going on, no telling what might jump out at him. The headlights shone ahead of him, calling too much attention to the rover. He felt like an intruder in a very dangerous place.

"I am beginning to lose you on IR," Lasserman said. "The background of that whole area is warm, quite a bit above normal."

How the hell can it be warm? Waite muttered to himself. Night on the Moon was so cold that it had taken years for spacesuit designers to come up with any systems that could cope with it. Before a long-term colony could be contemplated, NASA, ESA, and later the United Space Agency had to find new designs to tolerate the cold.

But the low temperature of the nighttime had nothing to do with the shivers running down Waite's spine.

Waite stared across the crater at the enormous pit. It reminded him of a strip mine that had appeared overnight, with no construction tracks, no seismic traces, and no debris. Still trying to convince himself it must be some kind of impact scar, he searched for ejecta, fissures, the

7

swelling of a lip. But the hole was deep and black with an edge as sharp as a knife. It was simply . . . *there*. But who had dug it? And in only two years, max?

Extending from as far down inside the hole as Waite could see, the diamondlike threads rose into the lunar vacuum in symmetric arches around the orifice. Two of the nine arches met in the middle, a good kilometer above the surface, like the petals of a gargantuan glass flower. A thin film of wispy material seemed to be filling the gaps between the lines. The rest of the arches still seemed to be under construction.

"Trevor," a new voice came over his suit radio from the moonbase, "this is Lon Newellen. I'm trying to track down Dvorak right now. You'd better not get any closer to that thing."

"Fine with us, Big Daddy," Waite said. "You think this is going to be on Agency Select? I'm wearing my good spacesuit." It was a joke to fend off his growing uneasiness. Nobody watched newsnet stories about moonbase daily routines anymore.

The attempt at humor sailed past Newellen. "What's your distance?"

Waite looked around and guessed. "About half a kilometer from the edge of the thing."

"Okay, let me figure this out. If I can't find Jason, I need to check Earthside. Director McConnell should know about this. Let her make the final decision. For now, why don't you go back to the hopper. Don't take any more chances."

Waite didn't argue, other than to grumble about who should be making his decisions for him. He found a wide spot on the access road, backing and filling until he managed to turn the rover around. Becky Snow kept her faceplate to the structure below.

Waite pushed the rover's maximum speed, rolling on the balloon tires toward Lasserman and the waiting hopper, now five kilometers away. The access road was steep and winding, but getting farther from the crater floor and closer to the hopper made him feel safe. As they rose over the lip of the crater ten minutes later, the sight of the hopper eased his tension.

"Ah, Trevor? Columbus?" Lasserman said. "I am getting some trouble readings here ... a lot of them. My— my sensors are going wild!"

"What kind of—"

"Oh, my God! I've got microleaks all over the place! Where are they coming from?"

Waite increased the speed of the rover, as if that would do anything. Newellen at the moonbase transmitted again, asking for Lasserman to confirm his readings. *Stupid!*

"My cabin pressure is dropping!" Lasserman's voice jittered with panic. "Hull integrity is—this whole thing is—disintegrating! I don't have my helmet on!"

"Sig!" Waite shouted into his suit mike just as Lasserman screamed.

In front of their eyes, Waite and Becky watched as the hopper's body split open, gushing white frost as the ship's atmosphere exploded outward. Rocking from the force of the blast, the hopper teetered on its spindly legs. The hull crumbled, as if the metal had somehow turned into powder. The main body sagged and collapsed.

Becky was yelling. Waite shouted over the commotion. "Columbus! Big Daddy, did you get that!" In the back of his mind—the part not deadened with shock—he kept thinking, *How are we going to get back? We're stranded out here on the Farside of the Moon. How long will it take them to send another hopper over? How much air do we have?*

He shook as he checked the rover's communications dish. The laser communications telescope still pointed to the L-2 relay satellite keeping vigil overhead. "Columbus. Columbus Base. Mayday, Mayday!"

Becky kept shouting, but it was not mindless terror. "Trevor, I've got a puncture somewhere. My suit's leaking! I'm losing pressure—" She slapped at her suit.

He could see the red telltales on the outside control pack. Every one of her suit systems was malfunctioning. She was standing up in the rover, flailing her arms, pawing the chest control pack with her thickly gloved hands. "Trevor! My God, help me!"

He couldn't react quickly enough. How could everything go wrong at once? Then he noticed the metallic surface of her suit seething, boiling. He stopped himself from reaching out to touch her.

She made a choking noise over the radio, then suddenly a splash of blood splattered her faceplate. Explosive decompression killed her as vacuum breached her suit, dropping the pressure enough to make her head pop. Lifeless, sagging, she slumped over the side of the rover.

"Becky?" Waite's voice cracked. The horror froze his guts. He had to make a conscious effort to blink his eyes, to keep breathing. *My God,* he thought. This couldn't be happening. Everything around him looked perfectly quiet and still.

All he could hear was the sound of his panicked breathing; somewhere in the back of his mind someone was yelling at him over the radio. The hopper was gone. Lasserman was gone. Becky was gone. Some impossible structure had appeared in Daedalus Crater with no hint as to its origin. Becky had compared it to a spider waiting in its lair.

Then five telltale red lights winked on in his heads-up display, bathing his face in a glow like blood. Bitchin' Betsy, the voice-programmed chip, screamed, "Warning— your outer seal has been breached. Your suit is leaking at a rate of—" He stared down at his sleeves, watching the silvery coating foam as if someone had poured acid on it. Microleaks by the thousands sprang up through the suit, growing larger. His inner sealant systems made a valiant effort, but his entire suit seemed to be falling apart. Someone was screaming over the radio. . . .

Air rushed past his ears, and in an instant his eardrums burst. His chest pounded as his breath exploded into the vacuum, collapsing his lungs. Waite opened his mouth and a sheet of thin ice and spatters of blood covered the inside of his helmet. He tried to scream but then his visor dissolved.

He didn't even see himself falling to the lunar surface.

moonbase columbus

The helium-3 processing plant looked like a lunar rover thrown together by a committee of abstract artists.

Standing two hundred meters away, Jason Dvorak recognized the large wheels and the heavily shielded nuclear power unit. Huge triangular heat radiators jutted up and out at an angle, giving the impression of a stegosaurus lumbering across the crater floor. The front of the He-3 processor opened up in a cylinder of diamond-tipped teeth used for scooping and grinding the top layer of regolith; at the opposite end, a jumble of hot debris was deposited like excrement.

As the leviathan crawled along the surface, swallowing regolith, Jason felt pressure on his spacesuited arm. He turned and, in a habit he could not seem to shake, looked at the reflectorized spacesuit visor of his companion before glancing down to the namepatch. *Never look at the face to recognize someone outside,* he kept telling himself. After a year, you'd think he'd be used to it.

Cyndi Salito's contralto voice came over his speaker. "You haven't moved for minutes, Jase."

"Can't help it." Jason turned back to the mobile processor. "I can't believe it's finally working. You beat your deadline by a week. This'll really look good for us. Especially for me—two weeks in command and already I have a major milestone to show off." *And it's a miracle the base hasn't fallen apart,* he added to himself. He still couldn't figure out why the Space Agency director, Celeste McConnell, had named him—an architect, of all people— commander. He was still getting used to the title.

"If it's working," corrected Cyndi. "The ten metric tons of dirt it's processing should yield a hundred milligrams of He-3. If the wizards back dirtside keep their part of the bargain, we could have a working fusion plant by early next year. We're also due to receive another proton transmission from the Nevada Test Site next month."

"I'll turn this place into a resort yet." Jason laughed.

"That's why you're up here, Jase," Salito said. Jason hated to be called by the nickname, but he never bothered to correct people. She nudged him back to their rover. "Come on, demonstration's over. If I was ten years younger, I'd take you out to dinner."

"You're just trying to make points with the boss," he said.

Salito made a sound like static on the suit radio. "Won't need to after next month."

"Columbus won't be the same without the fifteen of you," he said. "I'm going to miss you and the other old-timers."

Salito snorted. "Old-timers! We haven't been up here much longer than you have."

Jason stepped over a rock as he climbed onto the rover's passenger seat, trying not to grip anything. Even at 4.5 psi suit pressure, the gloves still bit into his flesh. It was a common complaint. *Fifty years of spaceflight and you'd think they could solve a simple problem of constant-volume suits*, he thought. For months he'd put up with rubbing his hands raw each time he pulled off his gloves.

Salito started the rover and turned for Moonbase Columbus. "Don't you look forward to getting back to your wife and twins when it's your turn to be rotated home?"

"Of course," he said. That's what Salito expected him to say. But Jason's wife Margaret had filed for separation a month ago, before he had even been gone a year. Some devotion! Talk about twisting in a knife from 240,000 miles away. And his children Lacy and Lawrence hadn't seen him except on video transmissions since they were three years old. He was not looking forward to returning home. Being so far away put a little distance on the pain.

He tried to sound upbeat, for Salito's sake. "Hey, someone's got to put in that second level of habitation modules and make this base livable, not a crummy boot camp. Can't trust a bunch of physicists and astronomers to get their hands dirty, digging tunnels and piling regolith. I watched how much trouble Bernard Chu had getting you all to put together the Sim-Mars base!"

Salito grunted over the radio; Jason had the frightening feeling that she saw right through his small talk.

Four groups made up the sixty-person base, and everyone worked and socialized within their own group. Every six months a group rotated off the Moon, and a new one came on. After a six-month apprenticeship under Bernard Chu, who had transferred up to the Collins station at L-1, Jason had suddenly found himself the new commander of Moonbase Columbus. The change in assignment had surprised him as much as it had Chu. . . .

As the rover continued, Mare Smythi unfolded to reveal Columbus Base. The Earth hung low over the crater wall, like a big blue drop teeming with life. The tip of the base's sixteen-meter telescope was barely visible behind the embankments of the buried living modules. From this vantage point, Jason couldn't see the optical interferometer, the gamma-ray telescope, and other astronomical equipment.

One of his first troubles as commander had been to placate the Earthbound astronomical community by assuring them that the seismic vibrations from the wandering He-3 processing plants would not disturb any of the sensitive astronomical devices. It wasn't as if someone using a Disney telepresence link would be driving these monstrosities; the Disney corporation used only miniature robotic rovers in a compound hundreds of kilometers away.

Jason had done that himself once, before he told anybody his dream to come up here. He remembered sitting behind the controls after waiting five hours in line at Disneyland, marveling at how he could be sitting on Earth and driving a real rover on the Moon, just for the fun of it. He smiled as Cyndi Salito continued to drive to the moonbase.

As if a switch had been thrown, radio chatter filled Jason's helmet as they came into line of sight. "—not sure what happened. We lost contact with the hopper just before Waite's signal ended." "Get a hold of Dvorak yet?" "Still trying! L-1 can't raise him—"

Salito turned toward him, but Jason was already using his chin mike to break into the discussions. "Columbus, this is Dvorak. Big Daddy, what's going on?"

"Jason, am I glad to hear you! We were just going to send someone out to find you —"

Jason cut Lon Newellen off. "Okay, I'm back. What's going on?" He barely noticed Salito increasing speed.

"Trevor Waite's hopper—we haven't been able to raise it."

"Did the communications link fail?"

"No, that's not it. They ... they were broadcasting from the VLF. Waite had gone with Becky Snow down into Daedalus Crater and Lasserman was relaying the information from the hopper—" Newellen fell into an uncomfortable silence. Jason was about to press him when Newellen spoke again.

"There's something more. You'd better get in here and see the visuals yourself."

Two meters in diameter, the transparent holotank took up the center of the hemispherical control center. Jason placed a hand on the shimmering image and let out his breath. "Whoa. What in the hell is that?"

A faint shimmer could be seen between translucent spindly arms growing up from an impossibly deep hole. The rest of the object seemed to be under construction.

The enormity of the scale made Jason take a step back when he caught a glimpse of the hopper landing zone outside the crater. The hopper itself was destroyed. Trevor Waite, Becky Snow, and Siegfried Lasserman were dead. The first deaths on the Moon in years. And they were his responsibility.

But the mystery of the artifact kept grabbing his attention. The thing was huge—and no one had even suspected its presence.

"Flash up the most recent orbiter picture of that site." A cube dilated in the holotank and rotated. It showed the identical scene—without the hole and ghostly infrastructure. "When was this picture made?"

"That's from LO-3. That orbiter went down two years ago. Those pictures were taken just after the VLF went operational."

Jason stepped close and squinted at the images Waite had transmitted, but the tank's resolution got no better. "I can't make out any vehicle marks, except for Waite's rover."

"There weren't any."

Newellen brushed off his powder-blue jumpsuit and moved with balletlike grace in the low gravity toward the holotank. The heavyset man seemed out of place in the lunar environment, but Newellen's beefy frame was held up by some of the largest bones Jason had ever seen. People didn't appreciate the nickname of "Big Daddy" until they met the man up-close.

Newellen jabbed a chubby finger into the shimmering 3-D image. "Way over here you can see plenty of rover tracks—here, here, and even here. These are all from when the VLF array was built years ago. You can even tell where some of the folks went off joyriding. But except for this isolated spot by the . . . the thing"—he outlined the volume with a chubby finger—"the regolith is undisturbed. See." He punched at the holotank and the entire view collapsed to the spot he had outlined some seconds before.

Cyndi Salito pushed closer to the image, standing shoulder-to-shoulder with Jason and Newellen. "How come we didn't detect any of this before? What could have built that thing in the past two years without leaving any footprints? Has the regolith around the hole been swept back to cover tracks?"

"No way." Newellen magnified the image even more, and the ground took on a jumbled appearance. "We already ran a Mandelbrodt simulation—we got the same distribution as what you're seeing here. The ground is essentially undisturbed."

No one spoke as he pulled the view back to encompass the entire structure. Jason kept staring at the image. "So what you're saying is that something the size of a football stadium just appeared out there, without any sign of construction, no by-products? That doesn't explain a damned thing!"

Newellen just shrugged. "Abracadabra."

"And Hopper-1—no idea of what happened? Or that last transmission from Trevor Waite?" Jason scowled and ran a hand through his dark curly hair. "Come on, dammit! Skyscrapers don't just start growing on the lunar surface!"

When nobody spoke for several moments, Newellen reran Lasserman's video transmission, relayed from Waite's stereochip. He stopped at the close-ups of the gossamer structure rising up from the pit.

Cyndi Salito finally broke the silence. "I'm not going to be the first to say the 'A' word."

Newellen rolled his eyes. "Right. Alien construction corps invades Moon. That'll rank right up with that statue of Elvis we're supposed to find on Mars."

Jason looked around to the other people in the control center and narrowed his eyes. "I'm not going to be a laughingstock. But three people are dead, and we'll damn well find out why. Put me through to Director McConnell on Earth."

united space agency—washington, d.c.

The general was in his element. Celeste McConnell could tell by his animated gestures, the emotion on his face as he strode in front of the sprawling holographic tank. He focused Celeste's attention on images of the asteroid as it tumbled toward Earth, an unstoppable island of rock nearly a mile across.

"Icarus is on an intercept course," said Major General Simon Pritchard. "It hasn't come this close to Earth orbit since 1968. These views are from the wide-field-of-view cameras on the orbiting Leansats." The window showed a potato-shaped Icarus rotating as it approached. It grew larger as the frames changed.

A picture of Earth filled another window as the general moved his fingers over the computer's controls. A moving bull's-eye scanned the Earth as the asteroid approached. Right then, the point of impact was crossing Brazil.

"If we use the SpaceGuard orbiting defense system—" Just at the edge of the screen, Celeste could see a missile, streamlined and coasting outward, with the insignia of the United Space Agency perhaps too bright and prominent on its nuclear tip. The proposed SpaceGuard missiles were intended to be directed against space-borne threats.

Celeste smoothed her business suit. She still found it uncomfortable, even after all these years. But Washington, D.C., demanded a strict dress code. People wore ties and three-piece suits while relaxing in front of a fire. She

17

had never gotten used to it. She preferred the comfortable zero-G jumpsuits she had worn as an astronaut, seven years ago now, while on the Grissom.

Pritchard didn't look up as he reviewed the simulation. Two stars were prominent on each of his shoulders. She wondered what he would have been like as a college professor, like most of the other PhDs she knew. Celeste suspected he had groomed himself specifically for her visit. He had set up the meeting weeks in advance.

Pritchard remained focused in total concentration. On the primary screen, Celeste watched a crater the size of a shopping mall appear over the asteroid's terminator as Icarus tumbled on its axis. The SpaceGuard missiles streaked toward the craggy rock.

The situation here seemed surrealistic to her, a two-star general and the director of the United Space Agency alone in this control room. Pritchard had chased the techs and his aide away. He wanted to run the simulation himself; he had spent enough time training on the system.

"Missiles are incoming." Pritchard nodded at the image of Icarus. She could see the rock moving, changing, tugged by the steep gravity well of Earth. The nose of one of the SpaceGuard missiles tilted, and a targeting cross appeared on the surface of the asteroid. On the third viewing window, Earth rotated, placidly unaware of the approaching threat.

"Course correction." Propulsion systems kicked in with a blast of silver-white vapor.

Pritchard's eyes were wide, enraptured by the events. Celeste tore her attention away from the screens to look at him, maintaining a professional expression on her own face. His medium brown hair was tousled, a thin film of sweat holding it to his forehead. Wiry and sharp, Simon Pritchard did not look like a "Blood 'n' Guts" general.

"Ready, ready . . . impact."

Brilliant orange and yellow flared up on the screen showing Icarus as the missiles detonated. "Now, either the yield will be small enough to deflect the asteroid's orbit—" On another screen an orbital diagram appeared, showing the old orbit in red, intersecting Earth's position with an ominous **X**; then a new path in blue projected a more elongated ellipse that carried Icarus safely out of the bounds of Earth.

"—or it will fragment the asteroid into smaller pieces. And *that's* the problem. A lot of tiny chunks could hurt us more than the whole asteroid. The trick is to have the missiles diagnose the asteroid while in flight, then change their yield so that the asteroid is only deflected."

Celeste put her hands on her hips. She stood several inches shorter than the major general. "If you can convince anyone to be worried about the threat in the first place. Seems to me you're just busy doing make-work."

"The probability of an impact is actually quite high," Pritchard said. "Right now, a kiloton of rock hits the atmosphere each year—and that's just a lot of small stuff. Icarus is on its way, after all. Watch."

The screen refreshed, showing an unaltered view of Icarus, still hurtling toward Earth. Celeste watched as the computer-generated views showed the asteroid tumbling end over end. It flared into brilliance like the Sun as it plowed into Earth's atmosphere, boiling steam from the air so that she couldn't see even the vaguest outlines of continents. It vanished into blood red and orange as the model tried to show the impact.

"A couple of gigatons," said Pritchard. "Just like what hit the dinosaurs. We'd all be extinct, wiped out from the shock, from the earthquakes and tidal waves, or at the very least smothered over the long term by massive climatic disruption." His gaze seemed to bore into her. Celeste felt uncomfortable, but she paid attention. Something about Pritchard's technique might be useful when she needed to convince members of Congress to support a pet project of her own.

Celeste folded her hands. She appreciated seeing this in a simulation room instead of enduring some boring lecture that had to be tailored to wide audiences and endless interruptions by aides and pagers.

With a jerk of her narrow chin, Celeste indicated the holography. All of the pictures had gone blank except for one, showing the globe smothered in gray clouds beneath

19

which orange glows could be seen. "Is this a useful simulation, General?"

He raised his eyebrows, thought for a moment, then chose his answer. "Icarus swings close to us every nineteen years. The error bars of its 2025 orbit are almost overlapping our path. An impact *will* happen—if not Icarus, then another one. We've squeaked by over and over again. I guess it just depends on how lucky six billion people feel. Are we prepared if it does happen? Most emphatically no."

Then Pritchard used a tactic she did not resent, though most other people would have been too frightened to bring it up. He said softly, "You of all people, Director McConnell, should not be comforted by the supposedly insignificant odds."

Celeste fixed him with a cold stare. She caught the slightest quiver in one eyelid. If she pushed, he would probably back down and apologize. But Celeste didn't want to do that.

The Grissom station had been wiped out by one such unexpected impact, by "space debris." Two people had died, one of them her husband Clark. Celeste herself and five others had been saved only through her quick thinking and what everyone else had called plain dumb luck. The incident had ruined her life, made her an international heroine, and, propelled her rise through the bureaucracy, and eventually led to her appointment as director of the United Space Agency. Few people were willing to mention that part of her past.

"I admire what you're doing, General. I really do. And in me, you have a sympathetic ear. I especially appreciate your candor. I have to put up with enough bull in twelve committee meetings a week.

"But now I must be honest with you. Regardless of the Icarus threat, whether perceived or real, your SpaceGuard defense system is not something I can sell to Congress. Nobody wants to hear about space-deployed missiles. Nobody wants to even think about them—even if we need to."

The general set his mouth. "*I* didn't calculate the probabilities that we'd be hit, Ms. McConnell. It was your people that approached us for a solution."

Celeste reached across the table, palms up. "I realize that. But in the current political climate, even if the Icarus impact were an undisputed fact, it still wouldn't do any good. Nobody wants to hear about a threat from space. No matter how bad it is."

She beamed a smile at him. "Forget about Icarus, General. According to mythology, Icarus was a fool who lost his wings and crashed into the sea. Daedalus, though, was the interesting one who created dazzling new technologies. Come with me—let me show you exactly how interesting Daedalus has become."

Celeste took Pritchard past the two stone-faced guards into the Agency's Mission Control. The two guards, a young Japanese man and woman, scrutinized Celeste's badge, though they had seen her a thousand times before. But recent terrorist threats by an EARTH FIRST! group had forced increased security. Before either guard could object about the general's presence, Celeste raised her hand. "It's all right. I'll vouch for him."

Pritchard started looking around before the reflectorized booth door closed behind him. Celeste saw his eyes widen. Mission Control was drastically reduced from those in the days of the Shuttle missions. Because of advances in neural networks, distributed processing, and sheer computing power, the United Space Agency did not need a room the size of an auditorium staffed by a small army of personnel to run the various missions; a handful of people in a large meeting room sufficed.

While Pritchard gawked, Albert Fukumitsu, the duty manager, waved her over. "Director McConnell, we've been trying to track you down!" He wiped sweat off his forehead. He had shaggy black hair tucked behind a headband. "Jason Dvorak keeps calling from Moonbase Columbus."

"I had my pager shut off," Celeste said. She had enjoyed her few moments of peace enough to make the headaches of being out of touch worthwhile. "Jason needs to stop panicking and handle a little more himself."

Fukumitsu looked at her with a wry, skeptical expression. "This is a somewhat unusual circumstance."

"Agreed. Did he launch the telepresence probe on schedule?"

"Yes, an hour ago." He waved his hand toward the screens on the wall. One of the technicians, eavesdropping, called up a file that showed the hopper rising up in a puff of methane. "ETA at the Daedalus site in about ten minutes."

"Long enough to get Jason on-line." Celeste pulled up one of the chairs vacated by an off-duty tech and sat down beside Fukumitsu. "He's probably fidgeting like a new father in the hospital waiting room."

She still smiled at how unlikely being in charge must seem to Dvorak, and she certainly couldn't explain to him the reasons behind her unexpected decision to place him in command.

Dvorak was an award-winning, innovative architect; he had grown bored with the mundane on Earth after having designed the impossible a dozen times over. Then he had used his connections to get himself an audience with the director of the United Space Agency. When he sat down across the desk from her, Celeste had had no idea at all why he wanted to see her. But when he began to spill his idea about revamping the entire moonbase, getting it ready for the explosion of inhabitants that would arrive as soon as the Mars mission was a success, Dvorak had won her over. "They are our pioneers," he had said. "Right now they're living in flimsy tents. Let me give them log cabins at least."

She had approved his training and his assignment, and after nearly a year on the moonbase, scoping possibilities, reconfiguring some of the living quarters, Jason Dvorak had already made his mark on daily life up there. Without giving him any preparation time, she had rotated the former moonbase commander, Bernard Chu, up to the Collins waystation at L-1, while sending Collins's former commander, Eileen Dannon, back Earthside, where her frequent disagreements with Celeste could be covered up much more easily.

At first, Dvorak had reveled in his dream-come-true assignment, but at times like this he was proving to be too much of a nice guy to make tough decisions under stress. Maybe Bernard Chu would be better off back down on the Moon . . . ever since the Grissom disaster seven years before, he had supported her in everything she asked.

But no, Jason Dvorak had only been in full command for two weeks now. He deserved more of a chance.

"Let me see Waite's pictures," she said. Fukumitsu nodded to one of the techs, who worked on pulling up the images.

General Pritchard came up beside her, relaxed in his Air Force uniform. "Daedalus—that's where some of your astronomy equipment is stationed on the lunar Farside."

"That's right."

The image of the crater as seen from Trevor Waite's viewpoint appeared. "Zoom in," Fukumitsu said.

The images of the Daedalus anomaly resolved themselves on a large window that blossomed in the center of the wall. Unlike the general's computer-generated graphics, though, these images were real. She felt her skin crawl with an eerie foretaste of what would be in store for the world as soon as they understood what was really happening on the Moon. She had had nightmares about this.

"We're still analyzing the situation," Celeste said to Pritchard, "but I hope we know something new in a few minutes."

On the screens, they saw close-ups of Daedalus, its flat crater floor dominated by pieces of the VLF array and the smooth-walled pit covered with a translucent framework. The general seemed to comprehend that this was something bizarre. "What is this? Where did it come from?"

At that moment, the main portion of the holowall was supplanted by a too close image of Jason Dvorak. His brown eyes were glassy with fatigue, his dark curly hair mussed, but his lips had a persistent upturn that always made him look about to break into a grin. He stepped back into better focus.

"Director McConnell, I was beginning to wonder if you'd be here to witness the probe."

Celeste smoothed her trim business suit and stood into prime focus. She was petite, but carried a powerful presence. Her eyes were dark enough to look like black lacquer. Newsnet profiles insisted on calling her the Ice Lady. She spoke softly, letting her voice carry a chiding tone, but not enough to jeopardize her working relationship with Dvorak.

"Jason, I agreed to be here, but I didn't promise to be early." After a half beat of silence, she continued, "This is Major General Simon Pritchard. He's here to add his thoughts. Perhaps together we can figure this thing out."

Pritchard nodded with surprise, but he recovered quickly. The transmission lag meant that holding a conversation from the Earth to the Moon was a bit like a drunkard's walk: two steps forward, then a pause to catch bearings, another two steps forward again.

Dvorak looked offscreen. He nodded, then said, "Switching to the cameras on the hopper." The view expanded to take in a group of people clustered around him.

A large man next to Dvorak called up a holographic control panel that hung in the air in front of his hands. Other technicians in the cramped control center called out numbers and sent readings down to Earth. The window showing Dvorak's image receded to the upper left corner, while new windows opened to display telemetry, a CAD animation showing the attitude of the hopper, and a rotating globe of the Moon displaying trajectories with a targeting cross over Daedalus Crater on the nightside. The largest window on the viewing wall opened up to show the probe's view of Daedalus. Already they could make out the mysterious gossamer structure of the anomaly.

As the hopper flew over, Dvorak refrained from commenting, which Celeste appreciated. Nobody knew what was going on here anyway.

Pritchard drew in a breath as the hopper's medium-resolution camera showed the arcs rising from the dust, the framework of a huge bowl, impossible lacy girders that seemed to have no support whatsoever. It looked as if some gigantic being had played cat's cradle in the middle of a crater.

"Okay, getting some readings now," Dvorak said. "X-ray backscatter shows the materials are extremely hard and light, not very dense. Like an aerogel, except made out of diamond fibers. Maybe it's like the diamond foam they're trying to fabricate in the orbiting labs."

Celeste nodded. Dvorak's voice took on a trace of alarm. "I'm detecting no sign of my crew. Nothing. Where the hell are they?"

"What is he talking about?" Pritchard asked. Speaking in a rushed whisper out of the corner of her mouth, Celeste filled him in.

"But how did it get there?" Pritchard said without taking his eyes from the display. "Look at that pit—to excavate that would have required a few megatons of energy!"

Celeste had forgotten about Pritchard's background as a scientist. "I know. But we detected nothing. I can show you all the traces. The Moon is a million times less active than Earth, and we should have at least seen something. But there's been no seismic activity near Daedalus."

The hopper flew over the wide pit. *Was this some surreptitious lunar mining operation? Ore pirates?* The thought was so ridiculous Celeste was glad she had not said anything aloud. Even under the dim nightside illumination, the depths of the pit looked as black as tar. If anybody was still working down there, they used no lights.

"Could they—" the general paused. He had balked at the word "they" as if afraid to suggest what he might be thinking; Celeste had already begun arguing with herself about the same thing. "I mean, could your seismic network have been scrambled somehow? The traces erased?"

"Either that," she said, "or they found some way to excavate that pit and erect those frameworks without causing a jitter."

"Impossible, isn't it?"

"General, the entire thing is impossible!"

Dvorak interrupted. The CAD viewing window showed the hopper flying away from the pit. They had opted to use all of the vehicle's fuel to survey the site completely, forgoing a return flight. "Maneuvering fuel is getting low. That's about all the overhead reconnaissance we can manage if we want to guarantee a safe landing."

"Set the hopper down," Celeste said.

"Go to one of those tower structures," Pritchard suggested.

As the hopper settled down on a flat tract of regolith, Celeste could see the sharp-edged tread marks of one of the lunar construction rovers that had erected the VLF array three years before. The base of a ghostly tower rose seamlessly out of the soil, cutting in half the footprint some worker had left behind. Dust from the hopper's landing clouded the black sky.

Spotlights shone up into the weblike arches. In the upper left corner of the viewing wall, Lon Newellen played with the telepresence panel. The probe deployed its instruments.

"I'm getting no motion anywhere. Not a tremor, not a heartbeat, just a few jitters left over from landing. This place is as still as a fossil."

Somehow the image reminded Celeste of the great Egyptian pyramids, or the sphinx, or some long-abandoned temple erected at the dawn of time. But this was not old. She kept reminding herself of that.

Data from electromagnetic sounders, mapping spectrometers, and five other types of sensors scrolled along the bottom of the viewing wall as Dvorak interpreted them. "Not seeing any radiation, no detectable energy surges, but the area temperature is about seven degrees hotter than we can account for. I keep getting ultra-transient blips on the UV detectors. Too brief to contain any information. I would try to explain them away as glitches, but they're confined to a very discrete energy range. That doesn't make sense."

The image on the screen jerked with a blast of static, then refocused. The static returned, worse this time, and the picture did not wholly recover. The image skewed, with video distortion and graininess. Then the camera swung sideways, as if someone had bumped the entire probe.

"I'm not doing that!" Newellen said, holding his hands up as if to display his innocence.

Several of the probe instruments blared error messages. Two went blank.

"Turn the camera to look at the ground," Celeste said.

Newellen's own answer overlapped hers in the transmission lag. "Something's screwing with the electronics. Failures are showing up everywhere." The image jerked, as if some piece had just snapped off the supports. But Newellen managed to swivel the camera around, zooming in on the spiderlike leg of the probe.

The gleaming gold surface showed grainy pitting. As she watched, Celeste saw it fizzing like foam.

"The whole thing is disintegrating!" Dvorak said.

The hopper canted, then toppled over on its side. The image swung wildly to display the silent, gossamer towers stretching toward the stars. Then all the windows on the viewing wall filled with a thunderstorm of static before Fukumitsu closed them, bringing Dvorak's image back into the primary position.

"I don't know what else we can do," Dvorak said. "No radiation bursts, no energy surges. I didn't detect anything that could have caused this!"

"All right." Celeste tried to sound soothing. "I want you to try again. If it's radiating in the infrared, I want an IR flyover. Put a new sensor package into those javelin probes you've been deploying to take remote core samples for the geologists. This time, arrange for a sample-return mission."

"We need a closer look," the general said.

"I'm not going to send a person out there. I've already lost three people, and now this probe," said Jason.

She paused to ponder her options. "No, we can do it remotely. Something in the area itself seems to be disintegrating our machines. We've got to grab a chunk of that regolith, then return. But I don't want to risk contaminating Columbus if it's something in the dirt. You can set up an isolated laboratory in the Sim-Mars module—that should be far enough away to keep you safe."

Dvorak spoke again, sounding formal now, "I don't think I have the facilities here to do much, Director McConnell. We aren't a full-fledged research station, you know."

She sighed. "I'm going to gather a team of experts to help you out. We'll even send them up if need be, but we need to know more before I can choose."

27

Dvorak nodded, still looking overwhelmed, but a bit more relieved. "All right, but I think it's time we go public with this. Waite, Lasserman, and Snow deserve that at least."

"I agree. I have no intention of keeping this a secret," Celeste said. "No intention at all."

After Dvorak had signed off, General Pritchard remained grim-faced. Celeste placed a hand on his shoulder, which startled him. His uniform felt crisp and uncomfortable beneath her palm. "Well, General, how is that for an outside threat? I don't think you need to continue your Icarus scenarios. Do you think we can stir up a little interest now?"

antarctica

The fat tires of the Mars Exploration Rover lurched over the jagged rock outcropping. The thin-walled vehicle bounced as it righted itself, straining against the wind.

Inside the pressurized compartment, Kent Woodward gripped the steering controls with one hand. "Vroom! Vroom!" he chuckled. "I wish this thing went faster than thirty klicks. Maybe the headwind is slowing us down."

Beside him, Gunther Mosby muttered an expression of alarm in German, grabbed his spacesuit helmet, and pulled it back on. "What if this were the true Martian environment out there? You could get us both killed!"

Kent looked out the sturdy pane of the viewport. The vast, white landscape was scoured by snow and wind. A high haze in the sky masked most of the blue, leaving it indistinct from the Antarctic plain. Sharp lumps of brown rock dotted the monotony.

Kent tried to envision it as Mars, the lifeless nothingness of ochre dust, impossibly cold temperatures, and not enough air to breathe. But the illusion didn't work. He saw only Earthbound terrain. "You're going to infect yourself with a healthy neurosis, Gunny, if you keep dodging reality."

Gunther blinked, as if running the words through his mind again. "Excuse me, Kent. I do not understand a 'healthy neurosis.' What is healthy about a neurosis? Is this an imagined problem about being too healthy?"

Kent shook his head and kept driving.

Gunther tried hard to control his sharp accent, which made him speak with such slow precision that it maddened Kent. He had quickly been able to turn Gunther's preoccupation with speaking perfect English into a few jokes of his own.

The Mars practice mission had kept the six-person crew in low-Earth orbit for three months, simulating travel time in zero gravity. Then they had landed in Antarctica—the closest thing to Mars's primal cold and desolation—for a six-hundred-day stay. They had set up the same inflatable habitation modules they would use on Mars, extracting water and methane fuel by breaking down atmospheric carbon dioxide with catalytic converters.

Even their communications via optical uplink to the main control centers was artificially delayed by ten to forty minutes, depending on the current distance of Mars from Earth. They were on a real training mission—they might as well have been on another planet. All six of them had been living under austere conditions for nearly a year now, and Kent looked for any break in the monotony he could find.

"You know, Gunny, if we're successful with this practice mission, the only thing we have to look forward to is doing it all over again—only then for real."

Gunther blinked at him. "Naturally."

Kent sent the exploration rover crawling up a slope. Behind him he left wide tracks, like the first marks on a pristine landscape. He got a thrill out of that. It reminded him of the family vacation when he was ten years old, traveling from British Columbia across the western U.S. The most memorable part had been the Great Salt Desert in Utah, a vast expanse of featureless white alkali. All along the Interstate other people had lined up rocks to make arrows, circles, and their initials. Kent and his sister had spent half an hour gathering rocks to write their names on the blank slate of the desert. Seeing KENT W. spelled out like that gave him a feeling he had never been able to match, but it was cheapened by the fact that hundreds—*thousands*—of other people had done the same thing before.

Kent wanted to make his mark on the world in a way no one else had. He wanted to go where no man had gone before, as the cliché said.

Antarctica was the closest thing he had found yet. Mars would be the ultimate. He wanted to spell out his name in the red Martian sand for everybody to see. Then he would be fulfilled.

He guided the rover across the unbroken landscape, using the Doppler radar to lock in on where exactly he was going. With his background in exploration and expertise in geology, Kent had been the natural choice for exploring with one of the base camp's two rovers. Gunther, with his combined specialty in medicine and aeronomy, was completely at a loss about what they were doing. Kent had once made the comment that his buddy couldn't find north if he were standing on the south pole.

"If you please, Kent," Gunther said, taking off his helmet again. "Could you tell me what our mission is today? You have been so secretive. I saw nothing interesting on the schedule."

Kent cocked a smile. "Why, Gunny, we're out cruising for girls! I thought you knew—didn't you dress up?"

Gunther maintained his serious expression. "Does it have something to do with that flyover and package drop from this morning?"

Kent blinked in shock. Indeed, he had received a priority transmission to go meet a rapid-transport helicopter from McMurdo Sound. "Gunther! I don't know what you're talking about."

Gunther nodded to the interseat compartment. "Then what is in that canister?"

"What canister?" The sealed black container was roughly cylindrical, contained no markings whatsoever, and bore an encrypted interlock keypad. "Oh, that's just a thermos of coffee."

"Coffee?" Gunther said, playing along. "May I please have some?"

"No. It's bad for your nerves. Just relax—Commander Grace sanctioned this."

Gunther fell silent. Kent flashed a glance at him. The

31

German's pale skin had flushed in anger. "I am weary of not knowing what my partner is doing."

Ah, so he was trying the guilt-trip ploy. Kent knew how to divert that. "Still need to work on your vernacular, Gunny. Nobody says the word 'weary.' It's like something out of a Jane Austen novel. Old stuff. You should say, uh, horny. Yes! When you're very tired, just say 'I'm horny,' and then people will get the point."

Gunther nodded. He kept his voice low. Kent could barely hear his partner's words over the rumble of the wide wheels and the hum of the methane engine. "Not knowing what is going on makes me very horny, Kent."

When they reached the top of the rise, they looked down into a rocky depression. The wind howled outside, jetting snow across the opening. Tall crags shielded the area from three of the four sides. They could see the crushed snow path from the other direction. Kent had purposely gone around to the back to deceive Gunther as to their true destination. Now he circled the big outcroppings to reach the path.

In the center of the depression, surrounded by boulders like pillars from Stonehenge, stood three optical satellite telescopes. Glinting in the sun sat the dome and adjacent housing unit of the Nanotechnology Isolation Laboratory. The dome shone with metal and glass, looking completely out of place in the desolation.

Kent waited for his partner's reaction. Gunther stood half out of the seat, his expression twisted with alarm and dismay. His skin flushed a deeper red. "We are not supposed to be going to that place. Mission profile states that it is off-limits except under extreme circumstances."

"I'm just doing a little sightseeing."

"You could jeopardize the Mars mission!"

Kent sighed with a you-caught-me expression. "Special orders. Straight from Director McConnell." He tapped the black canister beside them. Gunther suddenly seemed to realize what the encrypted-lock cylinder must contain and writhed away from it as if it had suddenly changed into a cobra.

"Still feel like having some coffee, Gunny?" Kent asked.

"Do not joke!"

"The rest of this is classified, too. The wind is too high for the Navy helicopters to make the delivery. We're the escorts."

Gunther looked defeated and sighed. He bested his fear. "I wish I had not offered to come along. I do not like that place."

Kent wiggled his dark eyebrows. "What's the matter? Erika Trace is in there, and she's the most available woman on this whole continent."

Gunther Mosby seemed not to hear as he sealed his helmet, for whatever protection that would afford him against the canister samples. "At least they have showers," he said.

Low-angled sunlight pooled through the passive solar heating plates of the Nanotechnology Isolation Laboratory. Dr. Jordan Parvu smiled to himself as he stared at the images of his four grandchildren. They rubbed their eyes and waved to him. Parvu had forgotten that it would be the middle of the night when he called his son, but Timothy had rushed to wake up the children. As busy as he was with his work and with the perpetual daylight here in Antarctica, Parvu sometimes forgot the natural daily rhythms of other people.

The NIL's optical uplinks and the big viewing screen were supposedly used for teleconferencing, data transfer, and occasional telepresence experiments from other nanotechnology researchers across the globe. But no one would begrudge him an occasional personal call. His only assistant, Erika Trace, rarely used her own allotment.

Timothy seemed at a loss for words and didn't know how to keep the conversation going. Parvu himself didn't need to say much—just looking at his family made him feel warm inside.

Parvu could see an image of himself in Timothy's face: the sharp nose, the thick hair that before long would turn to a uniform iron gray, the bushy eyebrows, dark eyes with a fan of laugh lines around them, deep brown skin, and bright teeth in a perfect smile.

33

"Where has your mother been?" Parvu said, "I tried to contact her a few times, but no one responds."

Timothy's expression drooped. "She's in Africa for the whole month. We told you that last month, Dad. Tromping around the Olduvai Gorge again."

"Ah yes. Please forgive me for forgetting." Sinda spent half the year indulging her interest in anthropology and primitive cultures. They had been married for thirty-five years, and their love had passed into a comfortable and relaxed stage. They no longer needed to be together all the time, which allowed Sinda the liberty to travel to Africa, South America, and Australia. Parvu could spend a year in Antarctica with no great hardship.

Erika Trace burst into the teleconferencing room. "Jordan—I mean, Dr. Parvu," she amended quickly, seeing him speaking to his family, "we've got company. One of the Mars rover vehicles." The tone of her words mixed disapproval and anticipation. She wore her blond hair in a serviceable cut, long and plain with no particular attention to style. Her greenish eyes looked darker in the low sunlight.

"Ah, they must be bringing the samples from Dr. Compton-Reasor. Excuse me—" He turned back to Timothy and was surprised to find a disapproving expression on his son's face. But Erika had never shown any sort of attraction toward him—thank goodness!—or even toward the Mars expedition trainees. Passion for her work consumed her. That sort of obsession shouldn't come until later in life, Parvu thought, after one had spent time living. He hoped Erika learned that before she had wasted her youth.

"I must go now, my son, my grandchildren."

"Wave goodbye now," Timothy said. In unison, the four children flapped their hands and giggled. Parvu signed off. The blank screen always made him feel hollow.

Parvu and Erika departed through the set of double airlock doors to the outside living quarters. As he cycled through the second door, he felt the wind stream past him. The air pressure increased by twenty percent through each of the doors to eliminate any chance of nanotech migration.

Astronauts Woodward and Mosby entered the habitation section only moments after he and Erika had gone to wait for them. When Kent removed his helmet, he flashed a grin at Erika. "We've brought you a present!"

Parvu had a difficult time tuning his mind to the chitchat the two young men seemed to expect. Once he saw the black cylinder in Kent Woodward's hand, he wanted to hurry back to the lab and start testing.

Parvu noticed that Gunther Mosby kept shifting his feet as if wanting very much to leave. Parvu wondered if Mosby worried more about contamination from the prototype nanotechnology machines, or about the deadly fail-safe sterilization procedures built into the NIL. Woodward, on the other hand, kept his attention on Erika, obviously smitten. Parvu tried to hide his smile.

Erika flipped her hair behind her ear, lifted her nose in a gesture of impatience, and took the sealed specimen container from Woodward. She gave him only a brief acknowledgment before turning to Parvu. "I'll prepare the nanocore."

Before Parvu could stall her, to get her to talk to these young men, Erika had left through the airlock.

Parvu rubbed his hands together and looked at Mosby and Woodward. Eagerness to analyze the new specimens made him fidget. They had been waiting for weeks. He wanted to contact Maia Compton-Reasor and her team at Stanford, then get in touch with Maurice Taylor's team at MIT. Together, they would begin the first analysis. Combined research had been developing these new specimens for months, but they could not go forward with active automata except down here in the secure NIL.

But the astronauts seemed to be expecting something else.

Parvu breathed a sigh. They always had time for a shower. Even in Antarctica—the most isolated place on the planet—he still found himself playing the host.

"So, young men, would you be staying long enough for a shower?" Both of them nodded quickly.

After the two astronauts had left, Jordan Parvu scrubbed his hands, straightened the towels in the shower cubicle, and changed into warm slippers. He kept everything meticulously clean and neat, but at the moment getting into the central clean-room lab seemed much more important. Erika would be waiting.

He passed through the airlocks into the NIL dome itself. The entire outer third contained the teleconference room along with the main computers, power generators, file storage, a small cubicle containing the test animals, terminals, and working areas. Inside a thick, doubly insulated wall was the main clean-room area.

In the outer ring, Parvu could look through the observation windows at Erika. Garbed in her clean-room outfit, she prepared the black canister next to the cylindrical shaft of the nanocore that rose to the ceiling. She would have checked everything several times and made the initial optical linkup request with MIT and Stanford. Parvu would do the sample transfer himself.

As he entered the second set of airlock doors into the laboratory dome, he stopped to don a plastic cap, lint-free smock, and booties over his slippers. He pulled thin rubber gloves over his sweaty hands, then stepped on a pad of gray stickum before he passed into the lab room itself.

Erika bustled about. She was always so dedicated to him, to their projects. When she had met him, Erika had been one of Taylor's students at MIT, with a background in physics and integrated-circuit fabrication techniques. In her, Parvu had discovered a kindred soul, and they worked well together. Erika had begged him to take her along when he left MIT to work for the Center for High-Technology Materials in Albuquerque. He wondered why he deserved such a devoted acolyte.

"Our astronaut friends have departed," Parvu said.

She ignored his comment. "I've got everything ready. Taylor is out of reach, probably on his way into campus. They've summoned Dr. Compton-Reasor. She was asleep, I believe, but had left word to be called whenever we got in touch."

"We will need Dr. Taylor's code to activate the samples," he said. He could tell by the tone in Erika's voice that she had little respect for her former PhD adviser.

"He's on his way." She lowered her voice. "He always manages to be late, no matter what the situation is."

"Just so," Parvu said, then moved to help her.

She had mounted the sample canister to the access port on the transparent shaft of the nanocore. The seals were locked; all the fail-safe contacts had automatically engaged. If anyone tampered with the seals on the canister, the interior would be sterilized by an incinerating charge.

The nanotechnology samples inside were dormant. A code from Compton-Reasor would initialize them; a second code from Taylor would activate them. Only Parvu could open the seals to let the prototypes into the nanocore.

Rising to the depleted-uranium shield on the ceiling of the NIL dome, the transparent nanocore was filled with a clear resource solution. Within the core were microwaldoes, precision-guided lasers, stereo microscopes, electron microscopes, scanning x-ray microscopes, and a low-energy collimated particle beam. A strong electrostatic current ran on a conductive film just inside the nanocore walls as a barricade against the tiny machines.

The final defense against escaping samples came from capacitor banks beneath the dome; they powered the coaxial conductor running through the nanocore to a high-Z target on the roof. If the automata somehow breached all barriers, the capacitor banks would discharge, sending a magnetized plasma ring through the central conductor to slam against the uranium shield. An immense shower of x rays would flood the entire NIL, sterilizing everything . . . and killing everyone inside.

Parvu had insisted on the defensive measures before agreeing to head the NIL work. All nanotech researchers around the world knew how threatening runaway self-replicating automata could be. Most of the public didn't quite understand yet—which was fine with Parvu—yet he did not want to take any chances.

Oddly enough, Parvu had never thought his major supporter would be the United Space Agency, but when Celeste McConnell had pitched to him her incredible proposal for terraforming Mars, his imagination had ignited with the possibilities. He imagined generations of self-replicating automata seeded on the frigid surface of Mars, spreading out across the iron-rich sands.

Their programming would be simple, with no mission other than to liberate oxygen molecules in the rocks and to shut down when the partial pressure reached a pre-set level. Satellites transmitting an ABORT code could stop the oxygen production at any time, if human command-and-control made that decision.

Given the speed at which the oxygen nanominers could reproduce, Mars could theoretically have a breathable atmosphere in a week. *A week!* Parvu knew that there was another lab, nearly identical to this, waiting on the surface of the Moon if they were successful here . . . but it would be another two years until that became operational.

"Those two astronauts seem like nice young men, Erika," he said. "Kent Woodward seems especially interested in you."

She looked at him with an expression of such disbelief that it made Parvu feel like a child. "He's just looking at me because he's been in isolation for months."

Before Parvu could chide her for her cynicism, the teleconference screen chimed and an image of Maia Compton-Reasor appeared. She was a squat African-American with sleepy eyes and hair cropped so close to her head it looked like felt. "Dr. Parvu? Dr. Parvu, are you there?"

Erika had disengaged the SEND half of the loop, and Parvu toggled it on. "We're here. We've just received the samples. Sorry to wake you."

She dismissed the comment with a wave. "I can sleep anytime. Are you ready?"

"Nearly so. We are still awaiting Dr. Taylor's response."

Compton-Reasor snorted. "We always have to wait for him."

Erika fidgeted in the lab space. Parvu noticed she had slid to the side, out of the screen's field of view. She never wanted to take the credit due her. He would have to insist that she begin acting like his partner instead of an assistant. She deserved that, whether she wanted it or not. He had already put her name as first author on a handful of journal articles, without telling her.

"I think you'll find these are the most promising nanomachines yet," Compton-Reasor said. "If this pans out, it opens a whole new line of development."

For decades, researchers had been attempting ultra-small engineering—using scanning tunneling microscopes to build nanoframeworks, ballistic electron emission microscopy to etch templates for even smaller circuits, and collimated neutron beams to chisel out gears and rods less than a millionth of a meter across. Other researchers worked with protein engineering, trying to program organic machines.

In addition to the Stanford and MIT work, research efforts at Cambridge, Tokyo, and a European consortium in Belgium bought time in the NIL facilities. Parvu often felt himself in the position of the caretaker of a world-class telescope while visiting astronomers squabbled over observing time.

The Stanford team had designed a new organic and mechanical prototype, assembled in tandem with protein engineering and with micromechanical parts. Taylor's team had developed software that could make these machines function as incredible analytical tools. Ideally, they would be able to take apart a sample, analyze it, then broadcast data—detailed to the molecular level—back to receiving computers.

With the new prototypes in hand, Parvu dreaded the thought of an hour of aimless chitchat with Compton-Reasor while waiting for Taylor to show up. Sensing this, Erika moved back beside Parvu. Before they could attempt to make small talk, Taylor responded. The receiving screen divided the imaging area in two and displayed Maurice Taylor's flushed face looking more like that of a football player than an award-winning researcher. He wasted no time.

"Sorry I'm late. We had no idea when the package would arrive." He fumbled at a keyboard off the boundary of the screen. "Well, Erika, nice to see you again. Jordan. Are you ready? I can transmit now."

Compton-Reasor began a sharp response, but Parvu muted her half of the screen and nodded politely. "Yes, if you please. Everything else is prepared."

Erika went over to the nanocore. Parvu waited until Taylor had sent his portion of the activation code. An embedded green light, previously hidden, glowed on the smooth side of the black canister.

"Very well, I will now open the environment to the nanocore." He entered the encrypted key sequence to the self-destruct seals. The canister gave a dull click. Parvu knew that inside, the dormant machines had been flushed into the absolute isolation of the core. He resealed the lock and removed the empty canister. It would be bathed in x rays and then slagged.

"Secure. Now, Dr. Compton-Reasor, would you do the honors please? The second half of the activation code."

Erika leaned close, peering into the curved transparent wall of the nanocore. Parvu could tell by the stabilization readings that the microwaldoes were drifting in a slight current caused by the introduction of the new samples.

"It's sent," Compton-Reasor said. "Everything's under way."

It was all very anticlimactic. The new samples—so small that tens of millions of them could line up and still not cross a centimeter mark—could not be seen inside the resource solution. After days had passed, he and Erika might be able to discern a cloudiness in the fluid caused by so many tiny bodies.

"Congratulations, all around," Compton-Reasor said. "I hope you and Ms. Trace have some champagne with you."

"We'll make do," Parvu said, smiling.

"I'll monitor the progress," Erika said.

"Then I'm going back to bed," Compton-Reasor said. She waved a dark hand and signed off.

"Let us know if anything happens," Taylor said, then his image winked off.

The Nanotech Isolation Lab remained totally silent. Parvu thought he could hear Erika breathing. They were both smiling. Something about these new prototypes seemed promising. He had high hopes for the project, and for the terraforming of Mars.

Inside the nanocore, the tiny prototypes, newly awakened, began to self-replicate, using raw materials from the solution around them. Soon they would go about their work.

4

moonbase columbus

The nightside of the Moon was so cold that the extra seven degrees of heat around Daedalus showed up like a spotlight in infrared. The IR trace was a perfect circle glowing scarlet in false-color intensity.

Centered exactly on the gaping pit, the residual heat in the ground extended three kilometers out. On the holoscreen, black data points showed where Lasserman had landed his hopper, where Waite had driven his rover, where the telepresent hopper had landed. All of them fell right inside the red circle.

"We need a sample of regolith from inside that hot zone, but anything we send there gets eaten up," Jason said. He raised his eyes to the other people in the control center. "Suggestions anyone?"

He glanced over at Big Daddy Newellen. The man shook his meaty head; behind him, Salito stared into the holotank. Nobody met Jason's eyes. "Come on, people!"

"Well," Newellen said, twisting his lower lip with two fingers, "that all depends on the answer to another question. What's really going on? Is there a disintegrator ray out there, zapping anything that happens to trespass on the construction site? Or is the regolith itself impregnated with acid or infested with some kind of bug that's taking our stuff apart? Either way, how do we get hold of a specimen to look at?"

42

"How do you pick up a universal solvent?" Cyndi Salito asked.

Jason raised his hand. "Okay, we went over the readings from both hoppers already. No sign of any kind of energy surge at all. No zap ray."

"At least nothing we could detect," said Salito.

"We need a regolith sample, just like McConnell told us." Newellen's eyes got a faraway look. "What about storing it in a magnetic bottle? That way the sample wouldn't touch anything."

"Dirt?" said Salito. "You gotta be kidding. Regolith isn't affected by magnetic fields."

"But iron is," said Big Daddy Newellen, "and regolith contains ilmenite, which has iron in it. If we had a high enough B field, we might be able to isolate a sample of regolith. We could put a magnetic bottle on the container. The core-sample javelins penetrate into the dirt, grab a chunk, then launch the container back to the pickup point, leaving their outer shell behind. If we move fast and get a small sample, maybe we can hold a specimen long enough to get it into Sim-Mars, use the isolation lab there."

Jason felt enormous relief at finally hearing something that sounded reasonable. Built over the past three years, "Sim-Mars" was intended to serve as a simulated Mars base for the final dress rehearsal of the Mars mission. The outpost was fifty kilometers away from Columbus Base, far enough so that when manned, the Mars mission members would have their semblance of isolation—yet close enough that the astronauts could be helped in an emergency. The self-contained labs at Sim-Mars would be the perfect place to remotely investigate the Farside regolith.

"Sounds like a plan," he said.

In the stuffy closeness of the control room, Jason closed his eyes and tried to slow his breathing. The javelin probe seemed to take forever to reach the other side of the Moon and shoot back. Right now he wanted to take an hour around the Columbus exercise track, where he often did his best thinking.

Before this, his career on Earth had been easy—designing exotic structures using the new alloys and fibers made possible through microgravity engineering, playing around with CAD systems, and pushing the new material properties to their limits.

He could still hear Margaret's voice as he left Earth, telling him that this job was more than he could handle, that he should just stay home with her. *What more do you want?* she had asked. *We already have more money than we can possibly spend.*

Margaret had never understood him at all.

Jason wet his lips. The manufactured air was so dry that he frequently suffered from a nagging cough and chapped lips. He swiveled his chair back to the group in the control center, his people. Red and green lights from the panels reflected from the sheen of sweat on their faces. The control center was heavy with the smell of close-packed bodies.

They all waited for the core-sample javelin to do its work. It had already landed, grabbed a minuscule sample in the magnetic bottle, then rocketed the container back toward Sim-Mars. Now they waited to see if it would remain intact long enough to reach its target, or if the chunk of regolith would eat the container from the inside out.

"Big Daddy, get a teleop rover over to Sim-Mars," Jason said after clearing his throat. "We'll use it to manipulate the sample into the automated lab."

"That'll take one away from Disneyland, Jase. Think of the kids crying."

Jason kept forgetting about so many things, so many details. How had Bernard Chu kept track of it all when he had been the base commander? "I think this is a bit more important," he said.

"Big meanie."

Jason ignored the comment. Looking up, he glanced at the digital clocks flashing the time from points on Earth: WASHINGTON D.C., JOHNSON SPACE CENTER, STAR CITY, PARIS, TOKYO, MILLER. No matter what the various times showed, it hadn't been more than twenty-four hours since the

44

remote hopper had dissolved at Daedalus, two days since the alien construction had been discovered . . . since three of his people had died.

"Heads up," Newellen said. "Sample's coming in." He grinned. "And it's intact."

Cyndi Salito called up another image in the crowded holotank. It showed a dim, cramped room filled with lab equipment that looked too clean, too new. She brought up the lights. "Sim-Mars is on line," she said. "Remote ops."

Newellen hunched over the virtual controls, driving the teleoperated rover vehicle. Reaching the expected impact point, the rover's camera swiveled back and forth, its stereochip scanning for the incoming javelin package.

The telerobot waited, ready to hurry to the javelin and remove the shielded sample as soon as it landed. Back at Sim-Mars, another 3-D receiver also kept watch for the projectile.

Jason wet his lips again. He would have to request some lip balm in the next shipment from Earth.

A splash of dust appeared at the corner of the viewing cube, and the telerobot's camera lurched over to fix the position. Since the Moon had no atmosphere, incoming projectiles did not streak across the sky like meteors.

"Got it," Newellen said. He worked the virtual controls in front of him, as if he himself were in the driver's seat, rolling across the lunar terrain to fetch the package.

He followed the long furrow in the regolith until he came upon the heavily shielded canister surrounded by ejecta. Using robotic manipulator arms, he reached into the impact site.

"Bingo!" Big Daddy held up the specimen canister with the rover's arms. Three-D high-definition television gave viewers back at Columbus the sense that they were actually present. "A real flags-and-footprint mission."

"Off to Sim-Mars," Jason said.

As the telepresent rover approached the isolated training habitat, a quad-armed robot detached itself from the Sim-Mars expedition module and rolled out to receive the sample. Specially designed by Hitachi-Spudis for conducting detailed geological surveys, the robot extracted and deposited its shielded core of regolith into a delivery station, then rolled back toward Sim-Mars.

Newellen peeled off with the telepresent rover, roaring away from the lab. "I'm going to Disneyland!" he shouted.

"Cyndi," Jason said, "let him get twenty klicks away from Sim-Mars, then give control back to the kids." He looked at Newellen, grinning. "The other kids, I mean."

A razor-sharp shadow extended in front of the quad-armed robot as it returned to the Sim-Mars bay. Fine powder covered the robot as dust from the rover's tires fell back to the surface.

The robot rolled around to the service-module entrance and worked the controls to gain access. Through high-definition eyes, they viewed the entry room as it passed through the double doors. Newellen switched over to teleoperating the quad-armed robot just as it finished its preprogrammed sample-recovery procedure.

"We're recording all this, right?" Jason asked.

"Yes," Salito answered. "Agency Mission Control is probably piping it through the newsnets, too."

"Would you guys be quiet?" Newellen said. "I'm trying to concentrate here."

Gingerly, Newellen worked with the quad-armed robot. Lifting the canister recovered from the Daedalus hot zone, he had the robot place it inside a thick lead vault. After the vault was sealed, the robot turned to the center of the room, powered down, and stood dormant as it waited for further orders.

"Ready for external decontamination," Newellen said.

"I'm running it," Salito called from the back of the control room.

At the center of the Sim-Mars isolation chamber, a meter-thick tube ran from floor to ceiling. In vacuum, low-inductance capacitors made no sound as they charged to thirty million volts. An instant later, a milligram ring of xenon boiled into a plasma and accelerated to the ceiling. When the plasma ring impacted the high-Z plate on the roof, megajoules of x rays sprayed through the entire lab room, sterilizing any organism that might have been on the outside of the sample container.

A minute passed. Satisfied that nothing could have survived outside the lead-shielded vault, Newellen powered up the telepresent robot again. Its circuits were heavily shielded against cosmic-ray bursts and hard solar radiation.

The quad-armed robot approached the sample. "Time to open our package," Newellen said.

Jason swallowed a nervous lump in his throat. Daedalus Crater seemed a long distance away, but Sim-Mars was right in their backyard. What if they were about to open Pandora's Box?

Lon Newellen shook his head. Sweat dripped from his forehead, soaking his dark hair. *Damn!* Manipulating the waldoes took getting used to, but he had never been this clumsy before.

"Want me to take over, Big Daddy?" Salito asked.

"Shut up."

Newellen flexed his telepresent waldoes and tried to "touch" the contained sample again. The term "butterfingers" popped into his mind for the fifth time.

"You sure Director McConnell is watching all this?" he asked.

"Yes I am." McConnell's voice responded in two seconds. "I won't make any mistakes then."

Newellen pushed his hand forward and tried to use the waldoes to pinch the largest chunk of rock in the sample, but it slipped from his grasp again. *Double damn!* Beside it, the opened outer shell of the sample container lay in two pieces.

He ran a sweaty hand across his forehead again, then squinted at the rock. The thing seemed to be growing smaller. And how could it possibly be slippery? The metal walls of the javelin's sample container also seemed to be melting.

"Hey, the temperature's rising inside the vault," Salito said. "A lot more than I can account for by the x-ray burst."

Newellen grunted. "Just let me get my hands on this sucker." He had already completed a third of the standard

Extraterrestrial Examination Procedure. So far, except for this problem of holding on to the rock, nothing seemed out of the ordinary.

He dropped the rock a third time. Too many people were crowding around him.

Cyndi Salito leaned into the high-definition hologram, blurring its edges. "Say, what did you spill on the sample?"

"Nothing." Newellen debated unscrewing Cyndi's head from her body, but decided Jason might get upset.

"No, really. Take a look." Cyndi dodged Newellen's elbow and stuck a finger into the hologram. "Here. It looks like some kind of goo."

"Goo? Move your head, dammit!" Newellen couldn't see with all the people in the way. "Well I'll be dipped. There is something on that rock. Let me play that back, get a closer look." He pulled back from the waldoes and punched up the recorder. The holotank blinked, then showed in reverse motion Newellen's analysis effort. In backward time, the goo disappeared and the rock grew larger again.

Newellen stopped the playback. The surface of the sample foamed and seethed. "I think we've brought back something very nasty."

5

mission control—washington, d.c.

Major General Pritchard looked fascinated and horrified at the same time. Celeste McConnell glanced at him, then back to the main window displaying the remote analysis of the Daedalus sample. They had expected to detect some kind of anomaly on the regolith—thermoshocked granules, a change in the crystalline structure, perhaps even traces of exotic chemical residue. But nothing like this. The fizzing sample reminded him of the telepresent hopper that had disintegrated as they watched.

On a separate image, the Columbus control center buzzed with activity. "Are you sure it's contained?" they could hear Dvorak say as he looked at the image of the goo-covered sample.

On Earth, General Pritchard muttered to Celeste, "Of course it's contained. Nothing outside could have survived that sterilization dose, and the sample is behind four-inch lead shielding."

"But what if the contamination can break out?" Celeste said.

She turned to Albert Fukumitsu; all of his techs were staring at the moonbase transmissions. Even the Japanese guards at the doorway had turned to watch. "Albert, are we still on? I want to transmit something."

Fukumitsu tossed long hair out of his eyes and indicated one of the techs as Celeste stepped into the transmission zone. "You're on," he said.

"Jason?" She paused long enough for him to look up. With the transmission lag she tried to plan two seconds ahead of his reactions.

Dvorak turned toward her. "Ms. Director, I don't have a clue what's going on, so please don't ask just yet." His voice was sharp and tired.

"I just want you to consider some drastic actions, in case this turns out for the worst. I want all of your people to be prepared to evacuate Columbus if it becomes necessary."

Two seconds later—"How are we going to implement something like that? Take us up to L-1?" Dvorak sounded weary, defeated. "The Collins could never hold this many people, and there's no way the supply shuttles have the capacity to pull off a rapid evacuation. We're stuck."

Celeste tightened her lips. Dvorak had a point. What good would an emergency evacuation do? He had turned his attention to her now.

"Look, Ms. McConnell, we appreciate your concern, but the people on my base are accustomed to day-to-day threats. Everything's dangerous out here. We're used to dealing with it."

"I hear you, Jason," she said. *Have I just been trying to look good for the newsnets?* she wondered. Celeste had never worried about that before—especially now, with no need to impress anyone. As Agency director, she ostensibly reported to a few international oversight committees and the president of the U.S., but effectively she was her own boss. Over and over, the newsnets had lambasted her for those sweeping damn-the-consequences types of decisions, even though they almost always proved successful.

"Okay, then let's figure out what this thing is and we won't have to worry about it. I've got a hunch I'd like your team to try."

When he nodded, she said, "Whatever's happening there is taking place on a much smaller scale than we can see right now." Celeste drummed her fingers on her chair. "Use higher magnification. I mean *very* high. You might need to try x-ray spectroscopy, but use the TEM first."

Dvorak blinked. "We're still trying to finish the testing protocol. There's a strict sequence of procedures we have to follow—"

"Super high magnification," she said again. "I think I know what this might be. There's a chance you've stumbled onto something we've been investigating down here—"

"Investigating?" Dvorak looked up sharply. She could see the angry boy behind his features. "What do you mean? Is this something the Agency has done? Are you testing something at Daedalus that I don't know about?"

"No, but we're working on some concepts in Antarctica, as part of the Mars project. This might be something similar."

Pritchard looked at her with a puzzled expression. She motioned to him to wait. All he knew about was the simulated Mars base camp in Antarctica.

"And just what is that, Director McConnell?" Dvorak said after the two-second light delay.

"Nanotechnology."

Pritchard straightened. Most of the people in Mission Control didn't seem to know what she meant. Neither did Jason Dvorak.

"Whatever you say," Dvorak answered. He motioned to Newellen, still running his telepresent analysis. In the main window showing the close-up of the regolith sample, the view spun inward, defocused, then resolved through a different sensor to show the view from a Transmission Electron Microscope.

Suddenly the crystalline structure of the regolith sample looked like an enormous city during rush hour. Tiny objects bustled across the screen, swarming and chewing, dismantling the rock, building copies of themselves. Little machines like busy microscopic bulldozers, racing their way up and down tiny structures in the regolith.

A murmur swept through Mission Control, half a second before a similar transmitted undertone reached them from the moonbase.

"Is it a virus?" Pritchard asked, moving closer to the screen. "An infestation, like a plague? Microorganisms—"

"No, not a disease," Celeste said, cutting him off. "They are . . . mechanical. Tiny, tiny machines."

The microscopic shapes were fuzzy, boxlike, with tiny lumps that could be arms and levers, crystalline cores that must hold some kind of controls. There seemed to be half a dozen different designs, modifications in the number of flagella, the size of the core. Larger substations were scattered throughout the structure, like control centers.

Celeste pulled up a chair and rocked forward, gripping the arms. "Jason, you need to destroy that sample. Before it gets loose."

"It's inside a lead-lined vault." Dvorak looked puzzled.

"Now!" she said. "Lead won't stop them. Once they finish taking apart the regolith sample and the debris from the recovery canister, they'll start dismantling the inside of the shielding wall, atom by atom, to keep reproducing."

As Dvorak hesitated, General Pritchard stepped into the transmission area and raised his voice. Good, she saw that Pritchard at least had grasped the nature of the threat immediately. "Dvorak, you saw what happened to your hopper and to those three people—and if these things can dissolve an entire spacecraft, they can sure as hell eat through a lead wall."

Celeste made her voice placating. "Jason, we can't lose Sim-Mars. We need to alter our plan of attack. You can get another sample later—once we've sent you some help. Now at least I know what type of expertise you need. And I know exactly where to get it."

It took longer than the two-second light delay for Dvorak to show his approval. "Okay," Dvorak said. He directed Newellen to flood the interior of the shielded vault with a decontamination burst.

General Pritchard turned to her. "I can see it, but I still don't understand it. How did you recognize this? What are we looking at?"

"Nanotechnology," she said to him again, but she knew Dvorak and the entire moonbase crew were listening as well. "Tiny self-replicating robots that can build or take apart just about anything, one molecule at a time. They're assembling that enormous construction at Daedalus."

Her voice felt cold in her throat. "And these aren't anything we developed. Nothing from Earth."

antarctica—
nanotechnology isolation laboratory

A strong wind whipped snow into the air, obscuring much of the desolate Antarctic landscape. Inside the Nanotech Isolation Lab, Erika Trace blinked, startled, as Parvu brought out caviar and crackers.

"Where did you get this?" she asked. The soft burr of her southern accent grew more pronounced with surprise.

Jordan Parvu busied himself with tiny cans, plastic-wrapped packages, and vials of powdered seasonings. "Personal effects," he said. "I have been waiting for a chance to use this, to tell you the truth. Now, we have cause for a celebration."

Erika sat up straighter and smiled with the success they both shared. Celebrating with Jordan's questionable delicacies didn't sound terribly exciting, though.

Inside the NIL, the nanocore had begun to turn cloudy as the prototype devices assembled and replicated themselves. The nanomachines had functioned better than expected. Taylor was smug upon reviewing the data; Compton-Reasor was ecstatic. Just an hour ago, the prototypes had transmitted their first data to the outside.

Parvu and Erika had proven that they could indeed build functional replicating machines on a submicroscopic scale, machines that could make a simple analysis of their surroundings and communicate back to the macro scale.

Erika watched Parvu open his tin of caviar. "Well, we have been waiting for this a long time." The fish eggs looked black and slimy. "I've never tried this stuff before."

"Then you are in for a treat, Erika. This is the real thing, from the Amur River in Mongolia. Sturgeon eggs, none of those awful perch egg imitations. You will like this." He craned his head toward her. His hair was neat, his eyes bright, his eyebrows too bushy. "With as much as this cost, we cannot afford to have too many more celebrations, so let us enjoy this one."

She nodded, keeping quiet. She would do what Parvu asked. He had rescued her from being a perpetual graduate student at MIT, pried her away from Taylor. Caviar was only one of many things she hadn't experienced.

Growing up in Aiken, South Carolina, Erika had struggled with her out-of-place intelligence in an unambitious blue-collar family. Her father and her older brother Dick worked at the Savannah River Nuclear supercomplex. Both were beer-drinking, pool-shooting rowdies who listened to songs about big trucks, faithful dogs, and cheatin' women. They scorned Erika's aspirations.

But Erika's mother had made all the difference, planning a better life for her daughter. She had put aside a college fund, collecting enough money so Erika could attend the best schools—and her mother insisted that she excel. With her father's and brother's indifference and her mother's pressure, Erika had found herself withdrawing, with no escape but herself.

She had fled to MIT and worked for Taylor, and might still be there, afraid to break or afraid to change since leaving Aiken had been so difficult. Then she met Parvu, and clung to him. Parvu had seen in her the makings of a good researcher, and she had given him her best work out of gratitude. Parvu seemed embarrassed by it all. After she had finished her PhD, he did his best to talk her out of following him first to Albuquerque, then to Antarctica, but Erika insisted with a savage devotion. She had not felt happier or more worthwhile at any other time in her life.

Occasionally, when she stared out through the insulated windows to see the snow and the rocks, Erika longed to be back in Aiken, with the thick forests, fresh air, and the primeval expanse of Hitchcock Woods. Sometimes she just wanted to listen to the birds again. She remembered spring, with its parade of wisteria, dogwoods, and azaleas filling the air with ever-changing perfume. She had watched from afar as rich people rode horses down the clay paths in front of their mansions.

But then Erika remembered what kind of life she had left behind, and those scant hours of enjoyment in the woods did not make up for the rest.

Here, in their cramped living quarters, with Parvu playing classical music over the sound system, Erika knew she could celebrate much more than just the nanomachine success.

"Jordan," she said, "for you I'll try even salty fish eggs."

Parvu removed two crackers from a plastic package, handing one to her with all the reverence due a communion wafer. He scooped out a bit of the lumpy caviar with a small knife. It glistened like tiny black pearls at the tip of the blade.

He spread the caviar on his cracker, then dipped out another portion for Erika. She took a sniff and imitated his gestures.

"Under ideal conditions," Parvu said, "you accompany the caviar with a slice of boiled egg, sour cream, and chopped white onion. Here, we must make do with their dehydrated equivalents."

Erika sprinkled powder on top of her caviar. She wanted to take only a tiny bite, but she took the cracker whole, chewing quickly to be over the first shock of taste. She was surprised to find the caviar not unpleasant at all, salty and juicy, with only a faint fishy taste. She kept chewing, swallowed, and smiled. A real smile.

Parvu withdrew a metal flask and poured a capful of pale liquid into it. It looked like disinfectant. "Here," he said. "Peppered vodka. It is the perfect thing. Cleanses the palate."

Erika took it and sipped, but the alcohol and the pepper

set fire in her mouth, burning away the fishy taste. She felt tears stinging her eyes.

"So?" Parvu said. "We celebrate!"

Just then the communications chime rang through the intercom. Someone was trying to contact them in the conference room within the outer perimeter of the dome.

"Even here we are interrupted!" Parvu sighed.

Erika tagged along behind him, but stayed back, knowing that the communication could as well be from Parvu's family. They passed through the doors into the outer lab area, and Parvu accepted the call over the big screens.

The image focused, startling Erika as she recognized the caller. They had had little contact with the woman directly, merely transmitting progress reports on schedule. Erika had an uneasy feeling. It was the director of the United Space Agency, Celeste McConnell.

Hovering off to the side, making sure she did not intrude upon Parvu's conversation, Erika listened as McConnell described the Daedalus construction and what had happened there. Erika and Parvu had been so wrapped up in their work that sometimes they ignored the newsnets for days on end.

McConnell showed images of the alien nanotech assemblers, more sophisticated than Parvu's wildest dreams. Erika took a step backward, stunned; she could see Parvu struggling to contain his astonishment. All of a sudden, the major progress they had just made in the NIL seemed utterly trivial. They had been knocked down to the lowest rung of a new ladder.

McConnell paused a long time after her last sentence. Parvu, polite as always, waited for her to continue. Erika knew the director had reached her important point.

McConnell folded her hands. "Dr. Parvu, I need you up on the Moon. You are not only one of the foremost experts in nanotechnology, but you are also the only one with any practical experience. This is not a theoretical problem. I need you to figure out this mystery for us."

Parvu held up his hands as if to ward off shock. Erika frowned. *Jordan, going away?* What would happen to her?

What would happen to their work down here, the prototypes? What if Parvu left and they put—who?—Taylor in charge? McConnell certainly wouldn't let him run the NIL, would she? This couldn't be happening. . . .

Parvu recovered from his shock before McConnell could say anything else. "I am afraid that is most impossible, Madame Director. I am old, and I can be of better assistance if I remain here to give advice, okay?"

"Dr. Parvu, we have no other choice. None of the other nanotech researchers have the hands-on experience you do. They have dealt with theories, nothing more. I must insist." Her voice sounded a bit sharper.

"I'm afraid you do not understand—"

"I'm afraid that *you* don't understand, Dr. Parvu. There's more to this than you leaving your research down in Antarctica. Sixty people on the Moon may lose their lives. And the next fatality may be our entire space program."

Parvu stood silent for a long time. McConnell pulled her lips tight, giving time for him to answer. She folded her arms and waited.

Finally, Parvu opened his mouth. "You do have another choice, to tell you the truth." He reached out and took Erika's wrist, pulling her into view. McConnell's eyes widened.

Erika felt her breath grow short, her face redden.

Parvu continued. "Why not take my colleague, Dr. Erika Trace? I have complete faith in her abilities. She has just as much practical experience as I do, and a bit more imagination. And she is physically fit."

"I appreciate your suggestion, Dr. Parvu, and no offense to you, Ms. Trace, but frankly"—she spread her hands wide—"we need an internationally recognized expert—"

"Erika has published more papers than *I* in this area, Ms. Director!" Parvu drew himself upright.

Erika couldn't say a thing for a moment. This was worse than she had feared. She did not want to leave the NIL. Was this supposed to be an honor? She supposed so, but right now it sounded like a punishment.

Parvu patted her on the wrist. "We will discuss this further between ourselves, Director. Thank you for the intriguing information about the Moon. We will review it in more detail, okay?" His words picked up speed, as if he knew Erika was trying to gather her arguments. "I will be back in touch shortly." He switched off.

Erika turned on him, balling her fists. "Thanks for making up my mind for me! Y'all can't just send me away! My place is here. We've got work to do."

Parvu looked at her mildly and indicated the image of the Daedalus construction, which he had frozen in a separate window on the screen. "Don't you believe we can learn more from studying *that* than from any number of years spent here?"

"That's not the point. I don't want to go."

"You are being silly, Erika. With an opportunity like this, you will be the most respected and most envied nanotechnology researcher in the world." He sounded stern and paternal, not at all like her own father, who would have laughed in disbelief at the thought of his daughter being the only person in the world qualified for an important job. He softened his voice. "Besides, it is time, perhaps, for you to leave the nest."

"Sounds like you're trying to get rid of me!" Even back in Albuquerque he had pestered her with questions of why she had no boyfriend, why she did not go to movies, or why she had no social life. Taking it upon himself, Parvu had dragged her off to dinners, forced her to go out to places normally frequented by people her own age—which meant that he himself looked hopelessly out of place.

"Oh, Erika! It is for your own good." Parvu turned away, the matter finished.

Erika did not answer, but instead walked out through the double doors to her own quarters. Their open caviar lay on the table; several crackers had spilled out of the package. She hoped he would feed them to the three lab rats.

The speakers on the sound system began to play another selection from Parvu's CD changer. She recognized it as Mozart's Requiem Mass. Angrily Erika switched it off. The music seemed too appropriate.

■ — ■

Erika rode in silence next to Kent Woodward in the Mars rover. Once again the gusting winds prevented any helicopter from landing near the NIL; the Mars crew had been asked once again to perform a delivery service. Their long Antarctic training schedule left many gaps with time to run errands, and the astronauts did not mind the break in routine.

Erika wished that Parvu had driven her in the EOV. The Emergency Overland Vehicle was delta-shaped, with a cramped driver's compartment and an empty space in the back to haul a passenger.

The EOV had been intended for use if one of the NIL people were injured and needed to be rushed overland the 120 kilometers to McMurdo Sound Naval Station, or even to the Mars base camp—one of those "frivolous" emergency measures that Parvu had not designed himself. He had sworn he'd never use the contraption except in an emergency.

In the rover, Kent Woodward kept jabbering, regaling her with stories—no doubt exaggerated to make him seem wonderful—about growing up in British Columbia, his college days in Arizona, mountain climbing and off-trail hiking, and his aspirations and excitement about going to Mars. He kept grinning at her, showing off his skill in the rover as if it were a carnival ride, zipping over rock outcroppings and snowdrifts that had been packed down for countless years.

But Erika could think only of the comfortable, safe NIL she was leaving farther behind each minute. She would probably never return. Her years-long association with Jordan Parvu seemed ended now; they would become peers, not partners. Why couldn't she be thrilled by the prospect? She'd be the first person to study alien nanomachines! But if she had wanted glory and public acclaim, would she have come down to the bottom of the planet?

She thought of her possessions, a pitifully small package stowed in the rear sample compartment of the vehicle. Did it all mean that little?

"What's the matter?" Kent finally asked. Erika looked pointedly out the window at the bleak landscape. "Are you okay?"

"I don't want to talk about it," she answered. "You're doing enough talking for the both of us." Kent shrugged, then seemed to have no objection about continuing to talk about himself.

Reaching the Mars base camp, Erika looked with a mixture of amazement and nervousness at the tiny, cramped modules half-buried under heaped snow and dirt. She saw two living canisters, one for backup; together, they seemed barely large enough for one person, yet this facility housed six, stacked like sardines.

The crewmembers had lived in such close contact for the three-month flight in low-Earth orbit; now they were simulating the six-hundred-day Mars mission in Antarctic isolation. No wonder Gunther Mosby and Kent went out of their way to take advantage of the NIL showers and living spaces.

Erika, who valued her privacy, wasn't sure she could last even one day in this miserable environment while waiting for the big Navy helicopter to take her to McMurdo Sound.

Kent dismounted from the rover as its methane engine puttered into silence. He put on his best tour-guide smile and clicked the faceplate down. The astronauts were required to participate in the simulation at all times, but Erika herself wore only a heavy parka, scarf, and thick mittens. She wore a radio headphone to communicate.

"Over there, we've got an optical communications telescope."

He gestured to a steaming mound several hundred meters from the base. "Our own megawatt nuclear power plant is buried over there. Provides all our electricity. Boy, oh, boy, you should have heard the environmentalists squawk about 'contaminating the pristine Antarctic environment.' As if it makes any difference around here!" He smiled in the cocksure way that was already beginning to annoy Erika.

The inflatable airlock on the nearest cylinder opened, and two suited figures emerged to greet her. She knew Kent, and Gunther Mosby, and she was familiar enough with the commander of the expedition, a middle-aged astronaut with graying hair and gaunt cheeks named Bingham Grace. But Erika had no idea who the other three members of the Mars crew were, and she would never be able to remember all of their names. She just had to try to be as amiable as she could. . . .

Later, inside the living module with her knees drawn up to her chin and the walls sloping against her back, she still tasted her meal of fresh lettuce grown in the "salad machine." She remembered the sharp, salty taste of caviar during that last special moment with Parvu.

"Come over here, Erika," Kent said, crouched by a tiny table that flipped down from the wall. He sat across from tall and angular Gunther Mosby, who looked not uncomfortable in his awkward position. Kent held up a pack of plastic cards. "You can't be antisocial in circumstances like this. Play a game of cards with us."

"Yes, please, Ms. Trace," Gunther added. "Kent always cheats and I need a second person to watch him."

They tried to teach her *Schaafskopf* for the next hour, but her lack of experience with card games left her at a loss. Instead, they settled for Spades, which Erika won twice in a row.

At eleven o'clock, Bingham Grace summoned them together for a daily wrap-up, gave another little welcoming speech to Erika, and mentioned how nice it was to have company "other than these bozos." He made a special point of looking at Kent and Gunther as he said this, then announced that it was time to go to bed. Erika learned only afterward that their clocks gradually slipped to keep pace with the slightly longer Martian day/night cycle. Antarctica, with its half-year-long days and nights, was the perfect place to readjust the team's daily rhythms.

Gunther stacked the cards and slipped them into a small container below the flip-down table, gave an exaggerated yawn, and nodded to Erika. "If you will excuse me, Ms. Trace. I am going to bed. I am feeling very horny at the moment."

Kent raised an eyebrow at her and grinned. "Well?" She snorted. "In your dreams."

Erika stood alone by the towering rocks and ice sheets of McMurdo Sound. She huddled in a Navy parka, synfur gloves, and gel body-warmers, shrouding her face with a scarf. The cold bit into her cheeks. The tall rocks and gray-blue ocean looked like the gates of the Underworld—and she had been cast out.

The ice shelves extending into the water glowed a cold blue from trapped oxygen bubbles. The seas lurched, as if the ocean itself was shivering. Overhead, enormous albatrosses circled like hang gliders with twelve-foot wingspans. On a series of small islands away from the McMurdo installation, jammed penguin rookeries filled the air with an incredible noise, an incredible smell. It seemed numbingly bleak and exotic at the same time.

Years before, she had left the lush forests of South Carolina to travel to the city of Boston, then to Albuquerque and the New Mexico desert. She had thought that Antarctica was the most barren place she could ever see; but now, she found herself on her way to the Moon, with a hasty stop in Star City, the refurbished cosmonaut training facility near Moscow, to cram in astronaut certification.

Where would they yank her next? Why couldn't they let her be? Too many times, people had done things "for her own good."

In the distance she heard a jet. Squinting, she could just make out the silhouette of the C-141 Starlifter come to carry her back to civilization—for a few days.

Erika felt stinging tears from the wind whipping off the water. As the plane grew near, terror was alive and gnawing inside her—not from fear of space travel, or living on an austere moonbase, or even from the responsibility of being the first person to study alien nanotechnology. Erika felt most afraid to be separated from her mentor for the first time in a decade.

7.

to the moon

Erika wasn't in orbit for more than three revolutions before her single-stage-to-orbit Delta Clipper rendezvoused with the shuttle-tug. Earth wheeled above her as if it were about to drop down on her head, making her dizzy as the vessels approached each other. Coming out of the black backdrop of space, the spindly shuttle-tug reminded her of a Tinkertoy model she had once built. Her brother Dick had broken it.

Once docked, the crew handed her off to the Japanese-contracted tug. Everyone seemed rushed—from the moment she had left Star City, to launching in the Delta Clipper that took her to low-Earth orbit, or LEO. If she had gone the usual route, the trip to the Moon would have taken ten times as long. But the Agency was in a hurry to get her to work.

Combining aerospace technology and solar-electric tugs yielded an efficient and affordable option for frequent trips to the lunar surface. But this route also required a month-long spiraling trip from LEO to L-1, the Lagrange staging area to the Moon's surface. Director McConnell at the United Space Agency couldn't afford to wait that long. It had already taken Erika two weeks just to get the bare-bones preparations for her assignment.

So a specially fitted Japanese tug had been brought on duty at L-1 to get Erika to the Moon in the shortest time possible. Outfitted with relatively inefficient but fast nuclear-thermal propulsion, the tug would haul Erika to L-1 within seventy-two hours.

Numbed by the whirlwind of events, Erika did nothing more than follow instructions, allowing herself to be handed from person to person, strapped into her couch, checked over for safety glitches. She had been too busy to feel terrified, but she knew it would hit her during the three-day journey in which she would have nothing to do. Grudgingly she let her uneasiness about leaving Parvu fade to be replaced by a growing enthusiasm for the challenge.

All those training sessions in Star City still seemed a jumble to her—a mishmash of safety demonstrations, spacesuit fittings, survival techniques, breathing exercises, anabolic procedures, lectures on zero-G and low-G hygiene. A crash survival course instead of the full complement of astronaut-certification training. It had been like taking a drink out of a firehose.

She longed for the peace and isolation of Antarctica, where Jordan Parvu now had the NIL all to himself. Was that how he wanted it? She didn't think so. No matter what, she was still going to need a lot of Parvu's assistance to figure out the nanomachine infestation. A good way to test whether long distance really was the next best thing to being there, she thought.

Erika spent the three days in transit studying tapes of the Daedalus events. Events—not deaths. She couldn't bring herself to keep thinking that three people had died just by getting too close to the gigantic construction. If she got too hung up on the people, the loss of life, she couldn't study it with the proper objectivity. She couldn't let herself feel a grudge against the tiny machines.

Waite and Lasserman and Snow could not be living beings to her, not warm flesh with pasts, and lovers, and some sort of future in mind. Seeing the uproar on the newsnets hadn't helped much: interviews with people the three of them had left behind, hometown funerals, grade-school classrooms decorated with crayon-drawn posters portraying them as heroes.

No. They were simply data points—W, L, and S—complex organisms that had been disassembled, just as the regolith sample had been. Erika had always known that nanotechnology was dangerous, hence all of Parvu's incredible sterilization precautions back at the NIL. But these mysterious nanomachines went far beyond anything she and Parvu had attempted. Or imagined.

She felt like a butterfly collector who had always studied mounted specimens, suddenly thrust into the middle of a dense and uncharted jungle.

Webbed into place in her cramped cabin, Erika called up her stored data on the portable computer. Staring at the virtual display, she slowed down every portion of the regolith disassembly process in the Sim-Mars vault. Frame by frame she observed the sequence, zeroing in each 3-D pixel as the sample disappeared from view.

She went over Waite's last transmission. She saw the moonbase control center images of the telepresent hopper being disassembled at the Daedalus construction site. There seemed so much to study, but it was not enough to keep her mind completely occupied. She understood Director McConnell's need to placate millions of uneasy citizens. When someone wanted an answer fast, the easiest way was to grab a local expert and keep the pressure on until a solution was found. Erika had been dropped smack into the middle of the problem, like being given a hand grenade with the pin pulled and told to fix it.

For three days she pored over the events. The other crewmembers, busy with their own tasks, left her alone. That suited Erika just fine.

She turned her thoughts again to Jordan Parvu. *Why hadn't he wanted to come to the Moon?* If he wanted to study functional nanotechnology so badly, why didn't he jump at the chance? She couldn't believe he didn't want to take the risk. After all, Antarctica was perhaps the most savage spot left on Earth. And the Sim-Mars isolation lab on the Moon certainly could be no more dangerous than the NIL.

No, there had to be something more to it. Jordan did not want to step into the spotlight, but to focus things on her.

She felt a warm lump in her throat and tears welling in her eyes. That was the real reason. She knew it to the core. He had always spoken about how much he wanted her to

Kevin J. Anderson and Doug Beason

succeed. Now she had to live up to his expectations. This was different from trying to meet her mother's demands; she wanted Jordan Parvu to beam with pride over her successes. But that didn't make the monumental pressure feel any less.

"Hello, Dr. Trace, I'm Bernard Chu, commander of Moonbase—" The wiry, intense man seemed flustered, then smiled thinly. "Excuse me, I'm sorry. With so many things going on, I can't even remember my own title! I'm the Lagrange waystation director—welcome to the Collins."

Erika shook the Asian man's hand. "Thank you. And please, call me Erika. 'Doctor' sounds too formal." Her soft South Carolina drawl usually made new acquaintances feel comfortable.

Chu nodded and held on to Erika's elbow to help her float out of the chamber. Webbed netting held boxes, ropes, toilet paper, silvery packaging film, and a hundred other things she couldn't identify, nor could she determine any sort of organization scheme. Since she couldn't tell "up" from "down" in the weightlessness, storing material in the netting made sense.

"Since the shuttle-tug normally takes nearly a month to get here, everyone becomes accustomed to zero-G by the time they arrive," Chu said. "But you have not had time to adjust. Are you feeling all right? Space whoops?"

She did not want to be reminded about the queasiness. "I've managed to keep my food down for the past day."

Chu nodded. "No problem then. You'll be heading to the lunar surface within the hour. We have the shuttle outfitted and waiting, pilot ready to go. Celeste—ah— Director McConnell told us not to waste any time."

"An hour?" Erika blinked her eyes as sudden nervousness rushed up on her again.

"That's the nice thing about being at L-1—we're always in position for a lunar rendezvous. Captain Zed—I mean Zimmerman—is the shuttle pilot taking you down." Chu nodded to a lanky, square-jawed man floating upside down at the rear of the room.

Erika started to greet him, but Zimmerman interrupted

her. "If I were you I'd take a shower," he said. "A quick one." Zimmerman pushed himself out of the chamber.

"He isn't very big on explaining things," Chu said. Erika thought Captain Zimmerman's silence would be a wonderful change after enduring Kent Woodward in Antarctica. "He means for the dust."

"Dust?"

Chu set his mouth and got a faraway look on his face. Suddenly Erika remembered that he had been the moonbase commander until a few weeks before. "Yes, the moondust gets into everything—even the water supplies, no matter how much they try to filter it. So if you want to feel clean for one last time, take a shower here before you go. Our water is limited, but for Celeste's special guest, we can spare some."

The words brought back a vision of Kent Woodward and his sidekick Gunther, anxious to take a shower at the NIL. *Is it something to do with these astronauts?* she thought. "No wonder nobody wants to stay down there for long."

She looked up at Bernard Chu, expecting the man to nod in agreement; but he looked serious, as if something else were on his mind. "Yes, you must be right."

"Fifty kilometers above the ground. Check your straps one more time."

Zimmerman's voice startled her; he had broken the quietness only a few times during the transfer orbit from L-1 to the lunar surface. The trip from the Collins had been one continuous silence, with Zimmerman grunting answers to her questions until she had finally decided to be quiet.

On the interior wall of his craft, Bryan Zed had painted GLORIA—his wife's name. He had told Erika, using only about three sentences, how it was tradition to paint the name of one's wife on the outside of a special aircraft— *Glamorous Glennis, Enola Gay*—but since he had no way to reach the exterior hull of his shuttle, the cabin wall would have to do.

He displayed several images of Gloria on the flight deck next to a plaque given to him by his graduating class at astronaut training. They had awarded him "Mr. Person-ality," but it must have been some sort of a joke. Erika wasn't sure if Bryan Zed realized that.

She fumbled at her straps, but they were already as tight as they could be. Erika felt her face flush with excitement and a bit of fear as she tried to see the televised view of their approach. Below, the lunar surface looked like flash-frozen meringue. Gray and black shapes filled the high-definition screen. Craters, tips of craggy mountains, and vast plains of hardened lava slipped past the screen as the shuttle descended. But the shadow of lunar night masked most of the details.

She spotted a lit-up array of half-buried cylinders in the distance, similar to the Mars training camp in Antarctica. All too quickly the view narrowed to a smoothed landing area.

"Five kilometers." Zimmerman was really on a roll. This must have been twice as many words as he had spoken on the whole journey down from L-1. Erika couldn't see his face as he concentrated on the landing, but he contin-ued, "We usually deliver supply pods by remote piloting, but a human in the loop gives a much greater sense of security." He placed his hands over the override controls.

"I guess it must." Erika forced the words, then closed her eyes.

"Two kilometers—we're down to fifty meters a second."

The lunar shuttle vibrated as the stern engines ignited for a few seconds. The viewscreen showed nothing but a landing pad in the distance. Red concentric circles spread out from the middle of the zone. Set into the ground at a ninety-degree angle, a string of strobe lights intersected the circles, bright on the dark plain.

"Looking good." To Erika's relief, Zimmerman didn't turn around, but he kept up the chatter. "If our angle was wrong, the strobes would look red because of prisms in the rim. We're right on path. Relax."

The ground swelled toward them. The shuttle began vibrating as the engines kicked on, this time to stay. The landing pad's strobe lights disappeared from the screen as dust boiled up, spoiling the view.

"Twenty . . . ten . . . five . . . bingo!" Zimmerman slapped at the controls just as the engines cut off. Erika had never imagined he could sound so delighted.

Erika felt dizzy as she sat up. "The Moon. One small step for mankind, and all that."

Zimmerman gave her a blank stare and turned back to the control panel to switch the view from the landing zone to the lunar horizon. The image jumped from an unbroken plain to the brilliant headlights of an approaching rover, glimmering off plumes of dust kicked up from the shuttle's landing. From the other side of the landing pad a gantry rolled up to Zimmerman's lander. As it approached and made contact, Erika heard a faint *thunk*.

Erika pulled out her lunar EVA suit, ready to go through all the motions she had rehearsed back in Star City. But Zimmerman made no move to secure his own suit. She hesitated. "Aren't you coming with us?"

"No," he said in his flat voice. She expected him to say something like "Just the facts, ma'am." "Not in my purview. It's dangerous out there."

The light above the airlock switched from amber to green as she waited with helmet in hands. Air hissed and Erika smelled the tang of ozone. As the airlock door unseated its seals and pushed open, she felt her hair fly up at the edges; a chill ran down her back as she heard the faint popping of sparks.

A spacesuited man with namepatch DVORAK stepped out of the chamber. The suit looked freshly cleaned, which seemed strange since she had just seen him driving across the dusty lunar landscape.

A voice came over the control panel radio, not from the suit. "Hello, Erika Trace?"

Zimmerman nodded to the stranger. "Mr. Dvorak is the commander of Moonbase Columbus. He's patched through the radio."

"Oh." Erika glanced at the spacesuit but spoke toward the transmitter on the control panel. "Uh, yes, sir, Mr. Dvorak."

"Please, call me Jason unless it makes you uncomfortable." He moved his arms, but his voice coming from the

69

other side of the chamber made her feel disoriented. "We can leave for Columbus once you've finished suiting up."

Erika turned and picked up her helmet. Bryan Zed led her to a cubbyhole across from the airlock. "You know the drill?"

"Yeah. I've practiced this enough."

"Have you? Let me help anyway. There's a big difference between stepping into hard vacuum versus the tub of water they use for simulating space back on Earth. Difference in viscosity, for one."

For a moment, Erika felt a flash of defensive anger again, but from the way Zimmerman went about helping her, she realized that he would have acted the same way no matter who it had been. But Erika was so accustomed to doing things herself, working alone or with no one but Parvu for company, she knew she would have to make a conscious effort to fit in. Otherwise her time spent here would be even more miserable than she feared.

She stood in front of the cubbyhole that held the life-support pack and spent the next fifteen minutes letting Zimmerman secure her connections. Once he tightened the last zipper, he powered up her suit.

She felt a surge of hot liquid run through her suit's inner liner. "I can feel the heater." She jerked her neck to bump the chin control, trying to remember all the memorized checklists. "Everything seems okay. I'm ready for the helmet."

With the helmet on she could suddenly hear Dvorak's breathing over the suit radio. "Mr. Dvorak?"

"Ready?" He struggled up from a mesh net that had served as a chair for the enormous bulk of his suited form.

"As much as I'll ever be." Consciously, she made herself smile to look relaxed, but no one could see her through the helmet anyway.

"Let's do it." Dvorak turned his faceless helmet to Zimmerman. "Thanks, Bryan."

Zimmerman grunted, back to his old ways.

"Let's go, Dr. Trace." Dvorak turned for the airlock.

Erika stepped across the shuttle deck and followed him, immediately surprised at the ease with which she could move. The augmented servos that functioned as the suit's muscles made everything simple. In the crash course she had taken back on Earth, the suit and life-support pack had weighed nearly a hundred pounds; even in the water simulation tank she had not gotten a true feel for what it was like to move around in low gravity.

She squeezed into the airlock and waited for the air to cycle out back into the shuttle's reserve tanks. Dvorak pushed against her suit and motioned with his hand.

"Try not to move too quickly, and keep your center of gravity over your feet. If you start to fall, it'll feel like you're sinking in a bowl of molasses and there's nothing you can do about it. So if you drop anything, either let it be or call for help—but don't bend over. That's an acquired skill."

She felt a little more relaxed with Dvorak's conversation. It was a pleasant change from Bryan Zed's impenetrability. She found herself putting a light tone in her voice. "Sounds like how to survive on the Moon in two easy lessons."

"That's about all that you'll need to know for now. But the main thing is that if you've got any questions, don't be afraid to ask. Believe me, the only dumb question here is, Why did she have to die?"

Erika kept her mouth shut. If there really was anything to this nanotech threat that existed on the other side of the Moon, she had a lot more to worry about than learning how to walk in low gravity.

The airlock opened, and Erika felt like Dorothy opening the farmhouse door in *The Wizard of Oz*. The view sprawled in front of her, the same as had appeared on the high-definition screen inside the lander.

They stepped out onto a gantry platform encircled by safety wires. Above, a shower of stars lit the distant crags in pearly relief. As the platform lowered them to the lunar surface, Erika felt no sensation of movement.

Dvorak helped her into the rover, which looked like someone had added balloon tires to the stripped-down chassis of a junked car. Behind them, the gantry withdrew from the landing pad.

Dvorak moved around to the other side, climbing in behind the controls. He powered on the headlights. "We've got about a ten-kilometer ride to the base, half an hour."

"When can I see the nanotech specimens?"

"We're preparing another sample-return mission as soon as you've been acclimated, Dr. Trace—"

"Okay, please stop calling me Dr. Trace. It's Erika, all right?"

"Fine. But in return you have to promise never to call me Jase. Jason is fine, but I hate nicknames."

She found herself smiling behind the faceplate. "A deal. When will we get a new sample? I've been going a thousand miles an hour for the past two weeks preparing for this. So as soon as you can get me to the lab and have the samples ready, the sooner I can do my job here." *And the sooner I can go home,* she thought.

The rover rolled away from Zimmerman's lander. Erika caught a support strut as the vehicle began to bounce on the rough ground after leaving the compressed landing area. "Am I going to be stationed out at Sim-Mars? How far is that from Columbus Base?"

"Just over fifty kilometers, on the other side of the landing zone. We don't have all the specialized tools for you to use the lab telerobotically, so you'll have to go there in person."

"I never thought I'd get there before the Mars crew."

Dvorak sighed. "We didn't think it would be used so soon either."

Erika fell silent, losing herself in the stark, exotic scenery as they bounced along. The grayness of the entire nightside world looked foreboding. She had been on the surface for only a couple of hours and she already wished she could see some color, smell something other than the antiseptic inside her suit. How about the high desert of New Mexico, or the lush woods of South Carolina? Even the sharp snow of Antarctica and the stench of a crowded penguin rookery?

The silhouetted horizon seemed oddly near, as if she could throw a stone all the way to the edge. As the rover bumped along, she picked out a spot on the horizon and imagined how long it would take to reach it.

Approaching the moonbase, Dvorak pointed out the distant astronomical facilities, the enormous dangling box of the gamma-ray observatory, the sprawling radio telescope, the high-energy cosmic-ray observatory, and the solar telescope. The broad proton-beam collector lay off to the left, ready to receive a burst from the Nevada Test Site on Earth.

She couldn't comprehend the effort it must have taken to assemble and distribute the massive equipment. By starlight, Erika could make out tracks in the regolith, indicating that more activity had occurred here. It made her think of the gigantic Daedalus construction.

Dvorak said, "We're almost there." She saw rounded mounds at the starlit horizon. Erika suddenly felt good about being here.

Moonbase Columbus looked as if a giant had strewn empty beer cans on the ground, then kicked dirt over them. In the center of the base a regolith-covered hemispherical dome—the control center—towered over the buried modules. Other cylinders lay like spokes radiating from the dome. The remaining buildings sat above ground in a random arrangement with connections running from cylinder to cylinder.

Dvorak said, "The original base is the pretty-looking stuff in the center. Everything else is temporary storage for Phase II until we can dig below the original structure."

"An anthill on the Moon!" She suddenly giggled.

"Well, the dirt is for radiation protection from solar flares and galactic cosmic rays."

"Wow cosmic!" She laughed again. *Why was everything silly?* She felt punchy, wonderful. She hadn't felt so good in . . . a long time. She wondered what it would be like to dance in low gravity.

Dvorak abruptly turned to her. She couldn't see his face through the mirrored faceplate, but she could imagine the look he was giving her. She wanted to stick her tongue out at him, teach him a lesson, call him 'Jase' over and over again until he got really upset. . . .

Dvorak's voice burst over her helmet radio. "Erika! Check your CO_2."

"See oh two? See you too. See you later!"

He leaned over to check the diagnostic readings on the front of her suit. "Decrease your oxygen supply."

Oxygen. Erika kicked up the reading on her chin display and glanced at the colored lights dancing on the front of her helmet. Most of the lights were green, but two flashed red. She seemed to remember something at Star City about this—

She felt pressure at the front of her suit. Dvorak had one hand on the wheel and the other groping at her chest. Wow, bodice-ripping romance on the Moon! "Hey!" She tried to knock his hand away.

The thought of necking in a parked lunar rover, both of them in bulky spacesuits, sent her into another fit of laughter, but suddenly she realized it didn't sound funny anymore. She frowned and glanced at her heads-up display. The red lights had turned to amber.

CO_2 partial pressure—1 psi: increasing

O_2 partial pressure—3 psi: decreasing

"Hey, I was hyperventilating!"

Dvorak grunted. "You might want to keep your voice alert on to catch that next time. Bitchin' Betsy, we call it. Zimmerman didn't have you switch it on."

Erika flipped up the suit options and keyed it in. "Thanks." She felt incredibly stupid. *Hyperventilating!* What a way to make a first impression—and with the moonbase commander yet.

"No problem. Happens to everyone." He turned the rover and headed toward what looked like a tent in a plowed-level area. "Well, a few people anyway."

As they approached, Erika made out four other rovers parked underneath the deeper shadow of a silvery awning. "Easiest garage in the world," Dvorak said. "Since there's no weather, all we have to do is keep the sunlight off them during the daytime."

Erika climbed down from the rover after he brought it to a stop. Dvorak led her to the moonbase airlock. "Step up and wait inside for me."

The inside of the chamber was lined with several air vents. The metal walls had a control panel embedded near each corner. The multilingual instruction placard described them as emergency manual backups, in case the control center links malfunctioned.

When they were both inside the lock, Dvorak said, "Stand back from the wall and raise your hands."

Erika took an uneven step backward and placed her hands over her head. She heard a rapid *whoosh* through her helmet, then a sharp *snap*.

"That's our dust buster. An electric charge polarizes the dust, pops it off your suit, and the air carries it out. Between that and the floor suction we manage to get most of it. But you'll find the grittiness will still drive you crazy."

The airlock slid open. An enormous man wearing only a powder-blue jumpsuit stood inside the entrance. He was so large that it looked as if he might not have been able to get into the airlock. He helped Erika take her helmet off, letting Dvorak handle his own undressing. With a burst of air from the inside, the first thing she noticed was a musty, humid smell that reminded her of a room packed full of people on a hot day.

"Hello, Dr. Trace? I'm Lon Newellen. I'll be driving you right out to Sim-Mars, after you've taken a breather here." He started helping her with her suit fastenings.

"Thanks." Erika allowed the beefy man to disengage the life support unit from her back as she looked around. The habitat was a long cylinder packed with supplies. Boxes stamped FREEZE DRIED on the side were stacked all through the room. Nets hung from the ceiling, bulging with additional boxes. At the end of the module, looking like the opposite end of a craggy tunnel, was an airlock.

Dvorak moved around in front of her; he tossed his helmet to the side. A middle-aged woman caught it and gave the base commander a thumbs-up. Other people came to the doorway.

Newellen finished unfastening the unit from Erika's back. "That should give you a little more mobility. Feel free to take off the rest of the suit—we're in double-hulled chambers now. All the comforts of home." Erika thought of her austere NIL quarters and realized he wasn't far off.

Erika turned to Dvorak. Finally, she was able to put a face to the voice that had come over the radio: dark curly hair, brown eyes, narrow features. He stood about six feet tall. His lips curved upward in what seemed to be a perpetual shy smile.

"Welcome to Columbus, Erika." He nodded toward the middle-aged woman. "Dr. Salito is our mining expert; you can share her quarters whenever you're not out at the Sim-Mars lab."

"Call me Cyndi," said Salito, shaking Erika's hand. "We're anxious for you to solve all our problems at Daedalus."

"Sure." She felt overwhelmed already.

"We've got you scheduled to go out to Sim-Mars tomorrow," Dvorak said. "Big Daddy has a break in his duties then."

"When he says tomorrow, he means twenty-four hours," Newellen said. "Since the lunar day is fourteen Earth days long, 'tomorrow' would literally mean about ten days from now—"

"Thanks for explaining that, Lon," interrupted Salito. She took his arm and ushered him toward the airlock at the far end of the tunnel, shaking her head.

Dvorak waited for them to leave before breaking into a smile. "Big Daddy gets a little too helpful at times, but he means well."

"I thought you said you hated nicknames?" Erika said.

"On me, but not on anybody else. They're inevitable up here. After living with these people for months in close quarters, they become a little more than neighbors. The flip side of the coin is that you tend to forget how to interact with new people."

Erika nodded. She could identify with that after being isolated for months, seeing no one but Jordan, unless she counted the rare visits from the Mars trainees. It had been nice—peace and quiet with no one around to disturb her research. And the technical papers she and Parvu had published could speak for themselves.

She started to push back her hair when she realized that she still had the rest of her spacesuit on. She held up the thick glove that enclosed her hand and laughed.

Dvorak looked at her curiously, then shrugged. "Go ahead and get out of that thing. I'll introduce you to the crew."

8

alexandria, virginia

Major General Simon Pritchard felt as if he had walked into a world he had left years before. Out of uniform on a Sunday, he sat at a table covered with a huge sheet of brown paper. From the outside, the crab house looked as if it should have sported a buzzing neon sign that said nothing but EAT; instead, this place called itself ERNIE'S CRAB HOUSE.

Celeste McConnell had asked him to meet her here.

The flecked Formica tabletop underneath the brown paper tablecloth had been popular in the fifties, out-of-date for a few decades, back in fashion again during the nostalgia of the eighties, and now looked old once more. The crab house itself seemed unconcerned with a changing world outside.

A waitress brought him a pitcher of beer and an empty mug. He looked startled since he had not ordered it, but he accepted the mug anyway. When she pulled out her green order pad—a paper order pad!—he held up his hand. "I'm waiting for someone." He glanced at his wristwatch. He was ten minutes early.

"Okay. Give me a holler." Tables sprawled across the floor of the open crab house, offering no privacy at all. A jukebox by the door competed with a television set above the counter. He wondered what Celeste was up to. His old jeans and loose checkered shirt felt comfortable, and he fit in with the other customers. Off in the corner fifteen men

78

had pulled tables together and played a game with the check totals to see who would pay the bill; they could have been blue-collar workers or White House staffers.

He sipped his beer. It had been a long time since he had been in a place like this. He did not belong anymore. This was too strange to him. He wished Celeste would hurry.

Simon Pritchard's father had been a tough *Go Union!* auto worker. His three older brothers—Dan, Allen, and Robert—were well built, athletic, and their father's pride. Simon, the smartest and most persistent son, had managed to secure an appointment to the Air Force Academy in Colorado Springs, then embarked on a career strewn with accomplishments.

His father had died of lung cancer at forty-three, before Simon had demonstrated his military success. Dan had become an auto mechanic, Allen an assembly-line worker, Robert a grocery-store manager. Simon's career left them in the dust, but he did not gloat about it. In fact, he rarely thought of them.

He had returned to Detroit to see his mother once. She was still a housewife, living modestly off her husband's pension and life insurance, doing absolutely nothing with herself. During Simon's visit, she talked about her garden, soap operas, and the neighbors, filling him with trivial details about people Simon had gone to school with, her grandchildren, her other sons and their bowling leagues and hunting trips to Canada.

Simon had wanted to talk about the importance of his job, the way he was helping to shape the nation's future. When his mother had cooked a big family reunion dinner with his brothers and their families, Simon had found it one of the most drawn-out evenings of his life.

He had blazed high with success, but he had lost his family in the process. They had nothing in common anymore. *Why did they stall when I went so far? Am I an anomaly, or are they?*

"I hope you're thinking about something important," Celeste McConnell said as she slid into the seat across from him. "That intent look in your eyes is enough to start a fire."

Pritchard tried to recover himself by waving for the waitress. "Just thinking about this place. Brings up old memories. How did you ever find it?"

She shrugged and smiled at him. "Slumming." She had picked up a mug somewhere; now she poured herself a beer. "Actually, this place was pretty well known for a while." She nodded to the wall where old pictures hung of former presidents, astronauts, and senators who had frequented the establishment.

Celeste had dressed in a loose teal blouse and clinging poly-jeans. She had pinned her dark brown hair back behind her ears in a style that made her look girlish, though she was at least six years older than he. She wore little makeup. The whole effect made her look much softer, less businesslike than the iron Agency director . . . and very attractive.

"What are you staring at?" she asked, smiling.

He straightened and took a sip of beer, feeling his cheeks start to burn. "You look different, that's all."

That seemed to delight her. "And so do you, General. You don't look quite so stuffy and intimidating out of uniform."

"Intimidating?" Pritchard found the thought amusing. "I was thinking the same thing about you. I like this version much better."

"Ditto," she said. "The whole idea was to go where nobody would recognize us. God knows my face has shown up on the newsnets often enough in the last two weeks."

"Then why did we come here?" He looked around at the other customers, at the lack of privacy.

"Somebody's always watching my office. I wanted to make sure nobody saw the two of us together. That could put the wrong spin on everything. We have to be very careful about appearances right now."

Now she had his interest. He met her eyes, then turned away. "I thought you had changed your mind and were leaving me out of the picture. I've been out of the public eye—"

The waitress interrupted them as she took their order.

She then went off as the men in the corner burst out laughing. Someone must have gotten stuck with the bill.

Celeste leaned across the table, clasping her hands together. She looked petite, delicate, and very strong. Her black-lacquer eyes were unreadable, but her voice was mellow and reasonable.

"We have more than just a mystery at the Daedalus Crater, Simon. The sheer fact of the construction and its alien origin has stunned the public. We're not alone in the universe anymore, and we don't know a damned thing about the new kids on the block. What is that construction? How fast is it going to be finished, and what will happen when it is? What if they're not friendly? Could this be an outside threat, an alien invasion?"

She stopped to look at his expression. "Don't look at me like that! I've already read it in the editorials, and it's bound to pick up speed. I'm not sure it's so silly. The construction has proven it can be dangerous—three people dead, two hoppers destroyed. What if this 'circle of death' around Daedalus keeps growing? What if those alien machines decide to disassemble the entire Moon? Turn it into a galactic parking lot or something?"

He nodded, serious now. "I've considered that myself, and you could very well be right—but it doesn't make sense that you're trying to keep me hidden in the closet. Shouldn't I be helping you make your case? With my rank and my background—"

Celeste held up her hand to silence him. She took a long sip of her beer, wiped foam off her lips, then studied him again. "Simon, have you ever seen the old movie *Dr. Strangelove?*"

Pritchard smiled. "Yes. Just last year in fact."

It was one of his favorites; it had caused quite a stir when it had been re-released as the first of the old classics that had not only been colorized but three-dimensionalized as well. Purists had boycotted the exhibitions and generated enough publicity that the re-release had done ten times as well as it otherwise would have. Pritchard had gone by himself to see what all the fuss was about; the movie had lampooned all those military stereotypes.

81

"Then you must remember Colonel Jack D. Ripper, the man who wants to destroy everything that does not fit with his philosophy? And that general—Bloodworth? The gung-ho soldier who wants all the big military toys."

Pritchard snorted. "I still know some people like that. But the world is better off forgetting absurd stereotypes."

Celeste grinned sharply. "But they won't! We think we're beyond that now, and the military just needs to keep watch over Third World hot spots. But as soon as a two-star general like yourself starts warning about alien invasions and campaigning to gear up the weapons complex, exactly what image do you think is going to pop into the public's mind?"

Pritchard had encountered that sort of thinking all through his career. On one hand, he had risen remarkably fast, being in the right place at the right time over and over again. As a colonel, he had led the Air Force into cosponsorship with the United Space Agency and had been surprised by the storm of protests even among highly educated scientists about tainting pure research with connections to "warmongers."

Pritchard had always felt that the military's new role should be focused outward, leading the way in colonizing the solar system—like the military of old, who were the real pioneers of the American West, going out on expeditions like Lewis and Clark, braving the dangers of a hostile environment, and paving the way for the second wave of civilians.

With extremely expensive and high-tech weapon systems dropped out of the budget, the armed forces had contented themselves with advanced conventional weapons, fine-tuning their accuracy and effectiveness. Treaties watched over by the International Verification Initiative had dismantled most of the nuclear weapons, leaving only a handful of warheads in secure installations—mostly as a deterrent against certain Third World countries that were ignoring the nonproliferation sanctions to build up their own stockpiles.

After the European Economic Community had effectively wiped out political borders, leaving only cultural differences of more interest to tourists than army commanders . . . after the old communist powers became preoccupied with internal problems . . . what was left? Who did they need to keep on guard against—except the lunatics? "I see your point," he said.

"I want you to work closely with me, but you must keep a low profile. I believe you and I have the same agenda, and together we can make it happen." She paused. "As co-conspirators. This whole thing can launch our future in space, make colonization and expansion more than a PR show or a few experimental exercises."

Now Pritchard knew what Celeste had been up to all along. It was something he had suspected, but not nailed down until now. "I have that dream myself."

His comment seemed to startle her. "I'd be interested in hearing your dreams," she said, but her words were mumbled, and her eyes looked far away. . . .

Seven years before, on board the Grissom, Celeste had awakened from a dream with the gut terror of falling and falling and falling—the way she often awakened in zero-G. Her husband Clark told her she would get used to sleeping on the space station, but after two months Celeste still could not stop the disorientation.

This had been more than just a dream, more than just a nightmare. One of those dreams that compared to ordinary nightmares the way migraines compared to ordinary headaches. This one had been even clearer than the others, more definite.

Explosions—
Freezing—
Tearing metal—
Screams—
Death. . . .

She saw herself floating to one of the modules. Module 4. The protruding module with the medical lab. Only there would it be safe. She had to get to it.

Swimming away from the rapidly fading images, she remembered with razor clarity seeing the glowing green chronometer on the wall panel. She remembered what time the disaster would happen. *Disaster*. The word itself meant an unfavorable alignment of planets or stars. *How ironic*. Celeste blinked now and saw she had only twenty-three minutes left.

Twenty-three minutes until calamity would strike. And Module 4 would be the only safe place on the entire Grissom station—but how to get everyone there? How could she save them all? She knew none of the details, only that something would happen. *It would happen!* She couldn't tell anyone how she knew. They would laugh at her. She would laugh at it herself . . . if her dreams hadn't proven to be true so many times before.

She was alone in their sleeping quarters. Clark would be on duty in the command module with Rico Portola. She had never told even her husband about the dreams—and he would not understand now. She had only twenty minutes.

How could she divert the tragedy if she did not know what to warn them about? She had to get all eight members into a single module, and in only a few minutes.

She remembered the other times that the dreams had come to her . . . the car wreck . . . her brother drowning. Celeste finally hit the wall intercom, turning up the volume. "All station members. Attention! All station members, that's you, too, Clark and Rico! I'm calling an emergency meeting in Module 4. Right now, everybody."

She did not answer when a few of the members sharing her same sleep period answered with befuddled questions. Clark came on the line, demanding to know what she was doing.

"Just come down! Right now. This is very important."

She had no idea what excuse she would use once they got together. If the disaster did not happen, how could she explain? She might be disciplined, maybe sent back Earthside. *But if nothing did happen, wouldn't that be a small enough price to pay?*

Before exiting the sleeping quarters she shared with Clark, she called up the personnel roster on the wall infopad. Maybe she would get lucky—eight crewmembers, extended families, birthdays, anniversaries. She scrolled down the dates, keeping one eye flicked to the dull green numerals of the chronometer on the wall. Fifteen minutes left.

She found a corresponding date. Good! She scanned the name, committed it to memory, and grabbed for the door frame to pull herself through.

Clark's voice came over the intercom on narrow band to their quarters only. "Celeste, what the hell is going on? We can't leave the control center right now. Rico's found something—space debris, we think, but it has an anomalous return signal. It's going to come close. I need to stay and monitor it."

Even floating in zero-G, Celeste felt her knees turn to jelly. "Clark, that's it! I think it's going to hit the Grissom!"

She heard him snort over the speaker. "Naw, it's got a tiny cross-section and a really screwy orbit—it'll miss us for sure. Probably somebody's screwdriver from an EVA twenty years ago. Not on any of our charts, though, so we need to track it and let Mission Control enter it into their database."

"Clark, swear to me that you'll come to Module 4. Right now. You and Rico! I'm not kidding."

After a long pause, he answered her cautiously, his Texas drawl stretching the words. "All right, hon. We'll be down. Promise."

She pulled herself into the narrow corridor and pushed off from the bulkhead to get to the intermodule airlock. Eleven minutes. She worked her way through the airlock, into the next module, then shot into the vertical lock overhead. The closed door said "4" in bright blue.

Dr. Bernard Chu, a thin and intense young biochemist, joined her as he hurried to the emergency meeting. She couldn't see the chronometer. She hustled Chu into the medical lab. Everyone had arrived—except for her husband and his partner.

The gathered crewmembers looked at her, one blinking sleep from her eyes, another looking angry, and two showing fear. Only seven minutes remained. The module was cramped with their bodies. Drifting without enough handholds or seat straps, the six people kept bumping into each other, murmuring about the emergency meeting.

If Celeste was going to have a cover story when all this was over, she had to state her excuse now. It was a lame reason, even stupid. But she could never survive a board of inquiry if she said simply that she had experienced a premonition.

"I suppose you're wondering what this is about?" She looked at all of them. "Well, it's all because of Bernard Chu."

Chu blinked in astonishment. "Me?" The others flashed a glance at him, immediately pegging the biochemist as the cause for the turmoil. "What have I done?"

But Celeste stared at the chronometer, at the hatch. *Come on, Clark!* "We are cut off from Earth here, and we must make every effort to keep our ties. I called us here together to celebrate the birthday of Bernard's son Shelby. He is eight years old today." She smiled at Chu, who blinked in astonishment. She saw tears spring to the man's eyes.

Several of the other crewmembers grumbled in annoyed surprise. Someone clapped. A voice said, "Big fucking deal."

Celeste hit the intercom on the wall again. "Clark, where are you!"

One minute left. Clark was always late. With his long legs and big frame, many had called him a remarkable contrast to petite Celeste and her intense scurry. The newsnets had called them a "darling couple."

"Still up here," he answered. His voice sounded distracted. "There's something funny about the debris. Can't get a good reading. Never seen anything like it."

Despair burned like acid in her throat. The last number on the chronometer changed. No more time. "Shut the hatch!" she yelled at Chu, who sat nearest to the module airlock. Startled, Chu moved to close it.

Over the intercom, they all heard Rico Portola's voice calling to Clark. "Look out the port, Clark! I can see it!"

"Holy *shit*!"

It was the last thing Celeste ever heard Clark McConnell say.

The entire station rang with a sound like a church bell thrown from a tenth-story window. The impact tossed the six of them about in the cramped module. Two men ended up with broken limbs; four people, including Celeste, had bloodied noses.

Chu had managed to shut the airlock hatch in time.

The lights flickered and went out, replaced by red emergency lights powering up from solar cells mounted on the skin of each module. Screams and shouts filled the tiny medical lab. Celeste found herself huddled against the wall near the arbitrary ceiling, whispering her husband's name over and over again as tears bit the edges of her eyes before floating free. *Why hadn't he listened to her?*

Only static came from the intercom linked to the command module. . . .

Later, after the whole story had come out, Celeste learned that the Grissom had been struck by a stealth satellite made of radar-absorbing material specifically designed to have a minuscule sensor profile. The satellite, as big as a bulldozer, had sheared off the command center and one other module entirely, and had strewn debris that ripped into the other three modules. Most of the life-support systems had been taken out, and the survivors had little air and no food. It would be four days before a rescue mission could be prepped and deployed from Earth.

When it became clear how awful the disaster was, Celeste worked with Bernard Chu to sedate everyone, lowering their metabolisms. That had been the only way they could survive.

And they had lived through it, just barely. By the time the rescue shuttle arrived, most of the air had turned bad; their groggy bodies were near starvation. Even with such an enormous disaster, only two people had died: Rico Portola and Clark McConnell.

Celeste's quick thinking had saved six of the eight on Grissom. Some considered it blind luck that she happened to get them all in the same place at the same time, the only haven on the entire station, for a silly birthday party. But it had been her quick thinking and practical actions during the emergency that had saved the surviving crewmembers.

Seven years ago, the disaster had made her a hero and paved the way for her career in the Agency: first as chief of

Kevin J. Anderson and Doug Beason

the Astronaut Office, then the associate administrator for exploration, until finally being nominated as first director of the unified international Space Agency, basically autonomous and responsible only to the U.N. . . .

"Aren't you going to eat?" Simon Pritchard said, interrupting her thoughts. He pounded a crab claw with a wooden mallet. She wondered how long she had been silent. The waitress had brought them a platter of steaming Maryland crabs.

"I hope you're thinking about something important," Pritchard said with a grin, then repeated her own words. "That intent look in your eyes is enough to start a fire!"

She took a small sip of her beer. "I was just dreaming," she whispered.

moonbase columbus

"Are you sure you're not going to need an assistant out there?" Dvorak said. "Newellen is a telerobotics specialist."

"Yeah," Cyndi Salito interrupted, "since nobody can work with him, he's got to do everything by remote control."

"Oh, shut up!" Newellen said.

Erika shook her head. After a full night's sleep, she felt rested for the first time in a week. "I'm more comfortable working by myself, really. With hazardous stuff like those nanomachines, you don't want me to be nervous. And besides, let's minimize the number of folks at risk."

"If you insist," Dvorak said. "Director McConnell wants us to give you every bit of help we can."

"She's got nanocritters in her pants," Newellen grumbled.

Nanocritters! She liked the term. Erika hid a smile by turning to load her gear into the pressurized rover. The airlock opened directly into one of the supply habitats, making the packing much easier than hauling equipment outside.

Erika threw a bundle of vacuum tape into a pile accumulating at the rear of the rover-van. In the low gravity, the bundle sailed through the air. Already she had packed more things than all the personal possessions she had carried away from the NIL.

The rover-van resembled an Earthbound Winnebago RV, larger than the stripped-down rover Erika had ridden in from Zimmerman's shuttle. She half expected the outside to be plastered with stickers that read:

"HOWDY! MERLE AND BILLY JO EBERT SAY HELLO FROM ALEXANDRIA, LOUISIANA!"

According to Big Daddy Newellen, the rover-van could travel five hundred kilometers from Columbus and stay outside for two weeks, if necessary. It was equipped with a telerobotic control panel for interfacing with geological-survey rovers, and was entirely self contained. The best part was that with the pressurized cabin she would not need to stay suited for the whole trip.

She wiped sweaty hands on her jumpsuit and glanced back at Dvorak. He lounged against the airlock, watching her. She couldn't tell if he was smiling, or if his face always wore that puckish grin. "Could you throw me that next box?" she said.

Dvorak bent and picked it up, turning it over on its side. "Chlorine?" He tossed it to her. It tumbled in the low gravity.

She snagged it and set it with the rest of the supplies. "Those—'nanocritters'—might be organically based, and a caustic solution could be useful. I don't want the specimens to come into contact with any of my germs either. Who knows what kind of information they can pull out of even a virus DNA? Other than those first three people who died, these things have never come into contact with any Earth life. Let's keep it that way."

Dvorak set his mouth, but didn't seem to know what to say.

Erika dropped her hands to her side. "I've seen the tapes, Mr. Dvorak. I know you're thinking how dangerous it is. But you've got to realize that I've spent most of my professional life working with nanotechnology." She headed for the airlock. "So let's get me started, all right?"

"That's what I wanted to hear." Dvorak brushed himself off. Somehow, the fine and gritty moondust managed to creep into everything. "I'll let the Agency know you'll be on your way. Take whatever time you need to study the neutralized samples still inside the vault. We can arrange to launch another javelin to snatch a sample of regolith from the hot zone."

"Thanks. And keep doing a daily IR flyover, to make sure nothing changes drastically." She fidgeted. It was time to get going and be alone again; back at work, back where she belonged.

"Okay, but using IR as a diagnostic is pretty much worthless now while the site is in full daylight. The temperature difference is a lot more apparent at night." Dvorak held out a hand. "We'll do our best. Good luck. Keep in contact."

"I will."

Dvorak turned to Newellen, standing just inside the airlock. "And have fun. Don't let Big Daddy push you around. He's just your chauffeur."

Erika backed into the Winnebago and found a seat amid the stacked supplies. Her spacesuit hung by the airlock, dwarfed by Newellen's frame as he sealed the door.

He grinned at her. "I feel like I'm going on a vacation."

With apprehension, Jason Dvorak watched the rover-van's airlock hiss shut, not sure if he was doing the right thing to allow Erika Trace to go off on her own to face the thing that had killed three of his crew.

But Erika was a grown woman, a professional, hand-picked by Director McConnell as the most qualified person on Earth to investigate the Daedalus specimens.

It didn't help that she reminded him of how his wife Margaret had looked ten years ago. But Margaret always seemed helpless out of her element. Erika didn't have that problem.

Jason thought of what Bernard Chu would have done in that situation. Was it really a good idea to let Erika go off alone? He should not be thinking of Erika first. He should be worried about the inherent risk in bringing more live nanomachine specimens so close to the moonbase.

"What is it?" Erika squeezed to the front of the Winnebago. She stared down at the screen, not out the front windshield.

Guided by Doppler radar and a heuristic homing sensor, the rover-van guided itself to Sim-Mars. Lon Newellen sat back and watched the vehicle pick its way across the lunar landscape as he munched out of a bag of food. He pointed a dehydrated apple to the high-definition TV screen inset in the control panel. "It's a week's worth of IR flyover images. I can pull up a slow-dissolve montage of the last week's readings if you want."

"Go ahead." As she watched the glowing red circle around the Daedalus construction, seeing views from day to day, she saw the intensities fluctuate around some portions of the great structure, but nothing moved beyond the three-kilometer diameter. When the two-week-long lunar day spilled solar heat across the area, the resolution of infrared changes dropped drastically.

Far ahead, unseen in the lunar night, sat Sim-Mars, built in preparation for the final simulated Mars mission. No one could ever have guessed it would be used to study alien technology before the training mission ever got there.

Newellen spoke around a mouthful of dried apple chips, "Personally, I don't trust that x-ray shower. I mean, not with my life. There's just no way to make sure that compact toroid thingie produces enough radiation to kill whatever might have contaminated the lab. These nano-critters have survived who-knows-how-many years in open space with all the radiation you can imagine. How can the measly little puff we give them be all that bad?" He started to put another shriveled apple into his mouth when he turned to look at her. She held her mouth tight and didn't say a word.

Newellen shrugged and tossed the fruit up in the air. It twirled in the low gravity and sank toward his mouth in slow-motion. He stationed himself under it and gulped it down. "But it doesn't matter what I think, does it? You're the one going in there. By yourself."

"Yeah," said Erika. "I know."

The Winnebago docked to Sim-Mars. Once he had idled the rover-van's engines to a quiet hum, Newellen didn't let Erika open the airlock until he had satisfied himself that the isolated lab module had ample air and lighting.

Erika hesitated before entering. Everything in there should have been sterilized. Remote diagnostics ran purity tests of the lab's atmosphere; readouts on a TV monitor showed that the simulated Mars base was ready for humans.

"Don't expect me to carry you over the threshold, Erika. That's not my forte, even in low gravity."

Erika forced a smile for him, then drew in a breath as she entered. The air smelled the same as everywhere else she had been on the Moon—stale with a hint of machine oil.

If all of the nanotech specimens had not been killed after all, she probably wouldn't have time to find out. She'd disappear just like Waite, dissolve into nothingness. . . .

She pushed the thought from her mind, and realized that she was being foolish. She knew that if the Farside sample had contaminated the lab, Sim-Mars would have been changed beyond recognition, with every scrap of metal and plastic dismantled.

She turned to Newellen. "Thanks for the lift, uh, Big Daddy."

He shrugged. "Wish I could stay and help you. I'll be camping out about ten klicks away if you need me."

Before her lay her most dangerous and exciting times, her greatest responsibility. Erika strode forward, unmindful of the airlock closing behind her.

Erika flexed the milliwaldoes, reaching into the bowels of the sterilized vault. She watched the high-def holographic tank as the tiny multidigited extensions moved with her. Although the milliwaldoes were a thousand times smaller than her hand, they duplicated her movements exactly. And she did not need to risk contaminating a single cell of her real hands in an environment containing the alien "nanocritters."

Her head ached. She had been working for five hours with the "dead" sample brought over by the first geological javelin probe, the one that had been studied via telepresence from Moonbase Columbus. Unfortunately, the bombarding high-energy x rays had obliterated nearly all traces of the nanomachines, leaving only hunks of microscopic slag, ruined pieces of the tiny destroyers, a few intact dead shells. She had gathered more information just from looking at the long-distance videoloops.

No, she needed a fresh sample. *A live one.*

She contacted Columbus without hesitation. Jason Dvorak agreed to get her one right away, then dispatched another javelin probe to the Farside.

While she waited, Erika inspected the apparatus available to her at Sim-Mars. Nearly every conceivable instrument for extraterrestrial analysis was crowded into the lab area. Though some people had become skeptics in the half century since Viking had landed on Mars, an important portion of the Mars mission would be to search for evidence of microorganisms in the harsh environment.

Using the dead nanocritters as test specimens, she observed them with transmission electron microscopes, then scanning electron microscopes using secondary electrons, backscattered electrons, characteristic x rays, low-loss electrons. She had good results with Auger/ESCA electron spectroscopy, then even better with a scanning x-ray microscope. By altering the energy level of the bombarding x rays, she had fine-tuned her method by the time the quad-armed robot rolled out of its retrieval dock to accept the second package from the Farside probe.

Now, her milliwaldoes hung fifty microns above the new regolith chunk. The entire analytical apparatus was housed in a depleted-uranium-lined vault in the next room, while the vault itself was shielded with lead. Erika worked under the sensation of actually watching from a spot just above the waldoes, a world on an incredibly small scale.

A voice came from the speaker set in the control panel. Stationed ten kilometers away from the isolation lab—rescue distance, Dvorak had called it—Lon Newellen sounded as if he was in the next room. "We're still having trouble with the video link, Erika. Are you sure you've got all the channels enabled?"

Erika threw a glance behind her at the tri-video camera. It was positioned to stare over her shoulder during the entire sample analysis. A green light blinked RECORD, but two rows down an LCD array read TRANSMIT PARITY ERROR: RESET. Erika smiled to herself. "Uh, doesn't look like anything is wrong here, Big Daddy. It says it's recording."

"How about resetting the parity switch?"

Erika reached toward the disabled switch but stopped short of touching it; when the recording was reviewed later, no one would be able to tell if she had depressed the switch or not. "It doesn't seem to work."

Newellen remained quiet for a moment. "I could come on over and fix it for you—"

"Look, I've got to keep working," Erika said with an edge to her voice. "No telling how much time I have. This is a new facility, remember? It's bound to have some glitches. Don't worry. I'll call as soon as I have anything."

"Oh, all right." He was probably bored with twiddling his thumbs and not getting any picture.

Submitting to the cameras recording her every move was bad enough, though necessary for the permanent record of the nanotech analysis. But Erika could never work with half a dozen people watching over her shoulder, backseat driving in realtime. She would make her own decisions and set her own pace.

"Voice contact will have to do for the first sequence of tests," said Dvorak's voice over the lab speakers.

"Starting the magnification now, from low and working my way up to high." Erika had already moved the milliwaldoes up to the surface of the sample. The view jumped in magnification as the polarized-light microscope kicked in. Computer-enhanced, the image looked weird as false-color coding added to the three-dimensional topography.

Speaking out loud for the benefit of the others suited her fine—she normally talked to herself or Parvu in the laboratory. "I can't see anything unusual at this magnification. The surface of the sample looks viscous, though, like it's liquid. Maybe just Brownian motion. Maybe not."

She checked a diagnostic on the bottom left corner of her virtual goggles. "A good bunch of heat radiating out of it, though. A lot more than you'd expect from an ambient rock. The sample isn't radioactive, and I can't

detect any chemical process. Probably waste heat generated by the nanocritters."

There, she had adopted Newellen's terminology for the
microscopic devices. No doubt it would stick once the
newsnets picked it up.

"Higher magnification?" Dvorak asked over the link.

Erika kept her voice stiff. "I'm still doing an overall
analysis of this chunk. Let me call the shots, okay, Jase?"
She used the nickname on purpose.

"Sorry. I'll stay quiet."

She ran through the standard macro-examination, testing the regolith's mechanical properties, heat conductiv-
ity, pliability, brittleness. She brushed the edge with the tip
of the milliwaldo, hoping to scrape the surface of the
specimen. It seemed to flow away from the tip of the tiny
pincers.

She returned the milliwaldoes to their home base, a
section of thinly sliced ceramic. Just off to the right of her
field of view were the images of larger "precision waldoes"—
devices ten times as large, for fine macroscopic work on
samples.

To the left of the thin ceramic film appeared a dot barely
visible in the holotank. She slowly moved her hands on the
virtual controls. As she approached the dot, she kicked up
the magnification by an order of magnitude.

Smears of chromatic aberration blurred out the details,
but she resolved the dot into a cluster of still tinier waldoes,
able to manipulate objects a millionth of a meter in size.
She left her huge-seeming milliwaldo hanging and slaved
a pair of microwaldoes to follow the now-massive ones she
still controlled.

"Okay," she said into the speakers. "I'm bringing the
micro along to the spot on the sample with the highest heat
readings." She guided the milli back toward the heat
source, bringing with it a tiny set of microwaldoes. "Let's
have a look."

Once over the spot, she guided the giant milliwaldo to
position the micro correctly. Switching controls, she
flexed the microwaldo's digits. The view clicked through
three more orders of magnitude; everything seemed to

rush toward her in the holotank as she now viewed the regolith sample from a viewpoint a thousand times smaller than before, through the eyes of Auger/ESCA microscopy.

"Whoa!" She drew in a breath at the sight.

Stationed just above the regolith sample, the microwaldo's sensors sent back a stereoscopic view: Multifaceted objects scurried around the sample like ants on a stirred-up anthill. She had seen the remote images from the first sample, but now the nanocritters seemed to be right in front of her eyes, in a handful of shapes and sizes.

She was protected only by a wall of lead and depleted-uranium shielding that the nanomachines could probably disassemble anytime they wanted to. Images of Can't Wait Waite and Becky Snow, their suits bubbling and dissolving, passed before her, but she blinked them away and pushed closer to the holotank to make out more details.

She was already at the maximum magnification resolution of the remote lab. No one had ever expected to need to look at material structure on the scale of a billionth of a meter. At that magnification, a simple virus would have looked the size of a house.

And the aliens had been able to put together complicated machines a hundred times smaller.

The nanocritters looked unlike anything else she had ever seen, as far removed from the prototypes in the NIL as a rowboat was from a rocketship. Parvu's attempts had been lumps of machinery jumbled together until the pieces happened to fall into place. These intricate machines looked as if they had been sculpted, designed with an artistic flair in five or six distinct varieties, every subsystem assembled with the precision a model builder used to make a sailing ship inside a bottle. It was incredible.

"Hey, Erika? You still there?" It was Lon Newellen. "Should I come in for a rescue?"

"No. Hang on a minute." She brought her hands down toward the holographic surface in front of her eyes. The microwaldoes mimicked her movements.

Erika could sense her heart beating faster as she got caught up in the excitement. "These critters are so small I'm having trouble even getting a lock on their morphology."

She spoke faster as excitement set in, and her southern drawl deepened. "How can they even function? They're really nothing more than molecules, set in patterns I've never seen before. What's their energy source? I'd guess breaking down chemical bonds inside the raw materials around them. Need more tests, though. Are you all still listening?"

"Wish we could see a picture!" Dvorak said.

Oh, all right! she relented. She pulled her hands from the waldoes and left them stationary. "Let me try emergency repair procedure number two." Blocking the view of the camera with her shoulder, she reset the parity, allowing transmission to commence. Then she made a great show of smacking the control panel with the palm of her hand. "There, does it work now?"

"We've got visuals!" Newellen said from his rover-van.

"Good, now let me keep working."

Now Erika encoded a molecular dynamics program. The code shot off to an array of parallel processors embedded in the matrix of a solid-state cube; the program would perform a perturbative decomposition of the molecular orbits to reconstruct the devices she had seen.

"Seems to be four or five different sorts of devices— some are assembling raw regolith, others are processing it, a third kind is scuttling back and forth between all the others. Is this a coordinator? A supervisor? A reprogrammer?

"There's one type that seems to sit back and do nothing. It's got a completely different shape. I also see bigger islands scattered among all the specimens, like nanocritter shopping malls. Central controlling stations? Boy, there's a lot of hypothesizing going on here."

"Erika, have you figured out how long those things will take to chew up the whole sample and start climbing the walls in the vault?" It was Big Daddy, still talking from his ten-kilometer distance.

Dvorak broke in before she could answer. "Make sure you don't take any chances. We need to destroy the sample before a single one of those things gets out. Director McConnell's people caution four hours max per sample, then it gets sterilized."

Erika glanced at her screen. "Reproduction rate is below critical threshold. Maybe their self-replicating phase is over. Or it's more likely that they need a handful of diverse elements to build more copies of themselves, and they ran out of 'ingredients' in that little lump of moon dirt and they can't get much out of the depleted-uranium chamber walls. That could be why this sample hasn't disassembled yet—they haven't got anywhere to go."

Dvorak said what she had been thinking. "Unless they decide to look for greener pastures outside the containment."

Erika swallowed. "If that happens, I'm not gonna have much time to get out of here."

10

antarctica—
nanotechnology isolation laboratory

Alone in the Nanotech Isolation Laboratory, Jordan Parvu felt like the last customer in a store closing for the night. The lights were dim, the doors secured.

Outside, the wind had set in again, pounding against the wall even through layers of insulation. Erika Trace's quarters were empty. She had removed her paraphernalia from the bathroom cubicle, and Parvu realized that he missed Erika's clutter.

He had forced the moonbase assignment upon her because he knew it would take a major impetus to get Erika to forge her own path instead of following in his footsteps. She was too good to keep working brilliantly in his shadow. Still, Parvu yearned to discuss automata theory with her, as they had done for years.

She had arrived on the Moon three days before. Parvu received the rushed data summaries Erika transmitted to the Earthside researchers, asking for input and suggestions. Though she had not talked to him directly, he was fascinated by her conjectures, how she had classified the extraterrestrial automata into Disassemblers, Assemblers, Programmers, Controllers, and Unknowns. She had done a great deal of work in a short time.

Now inside his quarters, Parvu watched videoloops showing his grandchildren at play, waving to him, smearing themselves with chocolate ice cream at a birthday party. In the silent room, his reflection in the wall's cosmetic mirror looked wistful.

At times like this, he questioned his priorities. *What had caused him to leave everyone behind, to come to this desolate place, rather than growing old with Sinda and enjoying his grandchildren?*

But the pragmatic side of him brought to mind the things he hoped to accomplish, considering how well the prototypes in the nanocore were progressing. He had in his hands the possibility to change the world. . . .

Researchers had been working on nanotechnology for four decades, spurred on by K. Eric Drexler's extrapolations in the 1980s. Drexler had shaken the scientific world with his amazing and frighteningly plausible ideas. Even paging through the old book now, Parvu could still feel the excitement.

Drexler had conjectured automata small enough to work inside a human cell, versatile enough to assemble complex structures—and smart enough to know what they were doing. A single nanomachine could use whatever raw materials it needed to copy itself; the second-generation copy would then copy itself, and so on, in a geometric explosion. With so many tiny and able servants, programmed with the proper instructions, the human race could tackle enormous jobs. A swarm of nanomachines could attack a pile of rubble, separate out the desirable elements atom by atom, and sort them into convenient bins, with no waste and no unsightly mess. Nanomachines could stack up carbon atoms from coal to assemble perfect diamonds.

Inside the human body, tiny scouts could assist white corpuscles in fighting diseases, bacteria, and viruses. Nanodoctors could inspect DNA strands in individual cells, find those that had turned cancerous, then fix any errors and mutations before the patient even knew anything was wrong.

At the time Drexler had proposed his ideas, he had been called a crackpot by some, while others scrambled for ways to invest in nanotech research, only to find that most of the groundwork remained to be done.

Now, thirty years later, with advances in micro-engineering, protein engineering, and artificial intelligence, scientists had finally created the self-replicating prototypes swimming in Parvu's nanocore.

But Parvu's work was hindered by Erika's absence. He had requested another assistant, but with everyone in the field so focused on the lunar automata, the NIL work seemed to have been forgotten. Compared to the discovery at Daedalus, the prototypes in Parvu's nanocore were impossibly crude.

Nevertheless, Maia Compton-Reasor said she was considering coming down to Antarctica herself or perhaps sending one of her best grad students. But those things took time, and Parvu would have to tolerate solitude for now. Piter Sommerveld and the Belgians had made noises about sending a volunteer of their own, but Parvu was somewhat uneasy about their private agenda for research. At Drexler's alma mater of MIT, Taylor's people had been spooked, begging off from the possibility of hands-on work.

Drexler himself had been quick to point out the perils of nanotechnology. A rampant self-replicating machine could create enough descendants to turn the Earth into a ball of gray goo in a matter of days. During college, Parvu had worked in a place that raised white lab rats for research; despite tough controls, rats still got loose from their cages. And a single nanomachine was a hundred million times smaller than a rat.

Even if all controls remained in place and nano-technology was developed without mishap, Parvu tried to imagine the upheaval society would go through if people suddenly had the answer to all pollution, cures to all diseases . . . perhaps even immortality. Since nano-assemblers could make glittering things of value out of any garbage heap, material wealth would mean nothing.

Knowing human nature, how could mankind survive?

But the aliens had somehow overcome those difficulties . . . or had they? Was that why they had sent samples here, as a test? To do their dirty work on a faraway rock to check out the large-scale construction ability of their automata before turning them loose closer to home?

The teleconference chime startled him out of his thoughts and he perked up. Parvu switched off the pictures of his family and fumbled for the screen. When he finally found the RECEIVE button, the screen shimmered and Erika Trace stared at him.

During the two-second delay before she could compose herself, her face brightened visibly when she saw him acknowledge the transmission. Then she looked nervous again, haggard.

She wore a powder-blue jumpsuit; her blond hair was tied back in a ponytail. Her eyes had become weary, with a bit of the innocence polished away. He had put her through much in the past few weeks, but she didn't look bad, just different, stronger.

"Erika! I am delighted to hear from you! Are you well?"

"I'm fine, Jordan. Sorry I didn't call you sooner. It's been a nightmare . . . there's so much to learn. And everybody thinks I know all the answers!"

Parvu stared at the screen, unable to keep himself from grinning. He wanted to ask how her training had been, or her flight to the Moon, or if he could do anything to help. He still had some caviar left, though he had fed the crackers to the three rats during a lonely moment.

Erika looked away from him. With the transmission lag, it never worked to try to hold someone else's gaze. "I just called to . . . I need to go over this. I'm too close to it. I've got the details, but no framework. It doesn't make any sense. I just need another perspective to help nail down the interaction between the nanocritters."

"Ah." Parvu nodded, then sat down in a comfortable chair. "Minor questions, then. I thought you were interested in something important. Very well, let us start from first principles." Parvu ticked off the thoughts on his fingertips. "If an alien race were capable of sending anything to another star system, why would they choose to deliver microscopic automata? If they merely wished to contact us, they could have sent a radio signal."

Two seconds later, Erika interrupted, raising her hand. "That assumes they think somebody's listening and can respond. What if they sent their automata just as probes?

As investigators to see what they would find?"

"Again, I must ask the question—why these automata? Why not send a full-scale probe, if you are going such a great distance? And if they are merely probes, why are they erecting such a huge structure on the Moon? What is it for?"

Erika shrugged, answering the first half of his comment. "Well, maybe nanotechnology is the way they think. Say their society is based on nanotechnology—they wouldn't consider sending massive objects when they can send little probes programmed to build what they want when they get here. But if they're from another star system, then why do they need to build this construction project so fast?"

"Speed!" Parvu stopped, as if a light bulb had winked on over his head. "Of course, speed! Or is it velocity?"

"What do you mean?"

"Speed of travel! Consider—to send a probe from one star to another, it must carry an enormous amount of fuel. It must haul an entire spaceship structure with it, and it would be difficult to boost it to an extremely high velocity. But—" He held up his thumb and index finger, squeezing them together. "A device only a billionth of a meter across is on the order of a particle! Such a machine could be accelerated to all but a fraction of the speed of light. It carries a computer memory equivalent to the old CRAY supercomputer, and when it arrives it can self-replicate. Just think of it!"

Parvu felt his skin flushing, and he sat up straighter. "Suppose the aliens didn't mean to come here in particular, but simply sent out a stream of automata in all directions? Beamed out near the speed of light across the universe, they are bound to encounter a solar system sooner or later. They can traverse the Galaxy more efficiently than if encumbered by propulsion systems and bulky spaceships."

Erika ran a fingertip along her lip. "Talk about 'Go forth and multiply!' And so when one of these scouts happened to land on the Moon, it had programming to start replicating itself and building this . . . structure we can't figure out."

"Yes, indeed! Perhaps alien ships are following behind it, slower vessels plodding along behind their automata. Maybe the scouts are here to set up a—" Parvu shrugged and held his hands out as if to indicate an armload of possibilities. "A transmitting station? A ready-made base for themselves when they arrive? But for what? Just to study other planets, or as a prelude to an invasion?"

Erika looked alarmed. "The nanocritters at that site have already killed three people and dismantled part of the VLF array." She shook her head. "But if they shotgunned nanoscouts out across the stars, there wouldn't be any way to tell which one would hit pay dirt beforehand. I can't believe they'd send ships out after them, just on the off chance they would bump into a habitable planet."

A red border appeared around Erika's image on the screen, with a black mark rapidly encircling it like a ticking clock. "My rest period is up, Jordan. I've got to get back to the lab." She smiled and looked at him with a wide-open face filled with a thousand other things she wanted to tell him.

"Thanks for the brainstorming session. I'll tell Jason Dvorak about this and let him decide whether he should forward your ideas to Director McConnell." Erika scowled as she said that; it seemed she still held a grudge against McConnell for sending her to the moonbase. The black tick mark had nearly encircled the box. "Gotta go!"

"Thank you for calling." Parvu raised a hand, palm outward, then spread his fingers into a V in their joke salute. "Live long and prosper."

The screen winked out before she could respond. Parvu sagged back in his chair, staring at the blank screen for a long moment. Working from the pad on the chair's arm, he accessed images of the automata, different shots of the various "species" Erika had identified. Then he enlarged another window displaying the flyover views of the growing gossamer construction on the Daedalus site. The image of streams of emissaries a billionth of a meter across, pouring into the solar system from across the Galaxy, sent chills down his back.

The Moon itself was just a small rock, a fraction of the size of the Earth. If a wave of microscopic automata had managed to strike the Moon, how had Earth itself escaped? The Earth took up a much larger cross-section of the sky. Could the automata simply have missed? The coincidence seemed too great to accept.

Parvu glanced at the Daedalus construction again. If the automata hadn't missed, how could such a structure go unnoticed on Earth, even in the deepest jungles? Wouldn't satellite photos have detected something so huge? Or could the automata have been trapped in the atmosphere, taking months to drift to the surface? Perhaps they were just now starting their work?

If deadly alien machines were flooding Earth's atmosphere, settling to the ground, what would happen when they began disassembling inhabited areas?

11

collins transfer station, L-1

The Lunar Transfer Vehicle coupled to the seals on Docking Port B of the Collins waystation. The seals made contact, then gripped. Residual air bled out into space.

Floating in the center of the Main Ops module, Bernard Chu felt like a business manager. The telemetry techs read off numbers, kept in contact with pilot Bryan Zimmerman in the LTV, and made sure all pressure points showed proper linkage with the docking port. The crew here had gone through the same routine every month for a year, but Chu watched them like a hawk. He was still new at this.

Glancing at the chronometer on the wall, he scowled, then activated the docking bay intercom from his own panel, overriding the chatter of the techs. His voice remained quiet, but sharp. "I want all cargo pulled off the LTV and stowed within the hour. This operation has a quick turnaround time, so I want twice the usual QC checks: no mistakes, and nothing late!"

That had been Chu's motto whether he managed a small biochemistry lab, research aboard the Grissom station, or Moonbase Columbus. He knew the fourteen people aboard the Collins would be annoyed at him for rushing them through the cargo transfer. There was no real point in hurrying—Columbus was not in dire straits, and a few hours' delay in delivery would make no difference to anybody.

But Chu had been in charge of the Collins for little more than a month now. He took his new post more seriously than any of the other station inhabitants, it seemed. Any deviation from the schedule recorded and transmitted by the Agency felt like a black mark against him, a personal affront. It showed in black-and-white numbers that he couldn't handle the simple tasks of shuttling supplies down to the moonbase or resource packages back up to L-1.

And the unscheduled delivery of Erika Trace down to the moonbase had thrown things completely out of whack. Chu had spoken to Celeste McConnell, and she assured him that she did not expect things to remain unchanged with all that had happened.

But Bernard Chu set his own goals, regardless of how lax others might be. He had learned lessons the hard way, and he had become a hard man.

A tech switched off his link. "Zimmerman has come through the hatch. Everything is shipshape. Teams are removing the resource canisters."

Chu nodded and set his lips in a straight line. Resource canisters. If it wasn't for the containers of solar cells, rare minerals, and geological specimens, there wouldn't be a need to export anything from the Moon. Within the next few years, if the regolith mining operation was successful, these canisters would contain the fusion fuel helium-3, and then the whole damned lunar colony would really start paying for itself. Chu remembered all too well how the moonbase people sweated for the day when they could finally start pulling their weight.

"I'll go to meet Captain Zimmerman," Chu said. "Page me if anything happens."

"Right," the tech said, then turned back to his work, logging in the canisters and hooking up the auto-scanner. The scanner would record each canister as it was moved through the LTV hatch into the Collins. Once set into the loading pod, they would be coupled to the Japanese Inter-Orbital Transfer Vehicle for passage back to Earth.

Bernard Chu had commanded Moonbase Columbus for a year and a half—the longest anyone had ever done so. He had made great strides with improving conditions there. In fact, he took credit for converting the place from an experimental outpost to a permanent human presence on the Moon.

Then Jason Dvorak had come up to do much more than that, and Celeste McConnell—Chu's good friend—had herself told him that Dvorak would replace him. Grudgingly, wondering what she saw in the young architect, Chu had done his best to introduce Dvorak to the rigors of command, the million and one things he would have to watch over just to keep day-to-day living from killing everyone.

Dvorak. Chu had no reason to dislike him. The man was an intelligent, softspoken, reasonably competent, and enthusiastic person. *But he was only an architect!* What business did he have there? As a visiting project manager, maybe, but certainly not as a moonbase commander. That made no sense.

Granted, Dvorak had proven himself to be a skilled manager on Earth, cultivating his own multimillion-dollar corporation, just like some of the computer geniuses who had formed software companies and had suddenly earned more money than they knew how to manage. Dvorak was a wunderkind, no doubt about it. But a moonbase commander? His assignment still seemed odd to Chu.

McConnell, though, had built a career on such unpredictable, surprising decisions. They seemed based on nonsensical intuitions that could not possibly work ... yet somehow always did. Chu couldn't understand it. Yet how could he argue after surviving the Grissom disaster? Chu pursed his lips as he pulled himself through one of the airlock doors toward Docking Port B.

Bryan Zed waited for him in the corridor. His uniform was a crisp medium blue; somehow he had not wrinkled it on the flight from the lunar surface. Clean-shaven, his hair combed, his gaze forward—had the man actually groomed himself before docking?

Chu grabbed a rung with one hand and extended his other in a handshake. "Welcome back, Bryan."

Zimmerman was an enigma—someone with no apparent personality, no sense of humor, square-jawed and built like a rock. He added "sir" or "ma'am" to the end of every sentence. One of the techs on the Collins had mentioned Zimmerman's wife Gloria, whom none of them had ever met, wondering if she was as detached and robotic as he. "Hey, imagine them making love," the tech had said, dropping his voice into a robotic monotone. "Was-it-good-for-you? Yes-it-was-good-for-me."

As Zimmerman pushed along the corridor wall, Chu said, "Would you join me for a break? You must need to relax a bit."

"Yes, sir," Zimmerman said. Tacked onto the end of that seemed to be an implicit "if you insist."

Chu worked his way toward the observation module where the astronomy setups automatically scanned the stars, compensating for the slow rotation of the Collins. Behind them at the docking port a team slipped through the airlock sleeve, hurrying to remove the resource canisters for loading onto transport pods.

Being on the moonbase and firm ground had made him forget for a while, had let him grow accustomed to a solid surface under his feet. But up here, the Collins reminded him how treacherous life in orbit could be.

Of all the Grissom survivors, only Chu had remained in space, working his way up through easy promotions, sympathy assignments, and PR spots. Celeste McConnell had returned to Earth, but she had excelled in the United Space Agency, shooting to the top. All of the others had dropped out of sight.

Somehow, Chu thought that if anything was about to go wrong with the Collins, Celeste would find a way to warn him again.

Bryan Zimmerman said nothing as the two of them drifted into the observation module. Chu floated to a vacant chair, sat down, and strapped himself in for comfort.

Below them, the Moon rose like a great scythe of beaten bronze reflecting sunlight in its gibbous shape. Directly behind, in its shadowed rear, stood the Daedalus artifact, the great alien construction that continued assembling itself.

He supposed Celeste had done him a favor by pulling him off the moonbase before that thing was discovered, before he himself had to worry about an alien infestation. There didn't seem to be any clear-cut answers. But it didn't matter—Jason Dvorak had to handle that now. It was in his lap. *Sink or swim, Dvorak!*

Chu found himself smiling. Beside him, Bryan Zed sat stony-faced. As Chu stared down at the Moon and thought of the voracious extraterrestrial nanomachines, he was glad to be up at L-1—where it was safe.

12

moonbase columbus

Even after running for three quarters of an hour, Jason Dvorak did not feel exhausted. The sheen of sweat dampening his exercise suit soaked into the carbon-sandwich layer in the cloth. He had gone 136 laps around the one-eighth-kilometer underground track, but his feet were too light, his legs too powerful in the low gravity. After eleven months, he still couldn't get used to it.

Optical fibers spilled sunlight across the track, bathing the exercise area in a cool yellow-white. As he ran around the compacted-regolith track, he thought he must look like a ballet dancer, with each delicate and graceful step taking too long to fall back to the surface. He panted through the filter mask, listening to his muffled breathing. Inhaling too much of the ever-present lunar dust could cause bronchitis.

Jason liked to exert himself to take his mind off other burdens. On Earth, he had often gone jogging to clear mental blocks on construction designs, or to brainstorm with himself. It was as if his mind tried to keep pace with his body's exertion.

Everyone at the moonbase knew where to find him at times like this, though few others were using the equipment now. He would have to emphasize that the crew couldn't shirk their mandated exercise routines just because they were fascinated with Erika's "nanocritter" studies. Two men were on the weight machines—a system of pulleys counterbalanced by lunar rocks; a woman pumped on the exercycle as she hummed along with a music ROM on her conduction earphones.

Jason split off from the track and headed to the lockers. He needed a sponge bath, but decided just to towel himself off for now. The allotment of carbonated cleansing water was rationed, but that would change when Cyndi Salito's mining machine geared up to full capacity. He would be in even greater need of a cool rinse after the conversation he was dreading.

It was that time of the week again. He had jogged seventeen kilometers, but he could not run away from everything.

Jason stood in the private communications booth with the door closed and the windows opaqued. Each member of the moonbase crew got a weekly call home, rigidly scheduled by the United Space Agency. Brawls had broken out because some people tried to preempt other scheduled calls, so the rules allowed for no flexibility except under extreme emergencies.

Unfortunately for Jason, the Agency frowned just as much on anyone skipping their scheduled calls. Crewmembers must keep up the morale of the people on Earth as well as on the Moon.

Jason swallowed a lump in his throat as he watched the RINGING designator at the bottom of the screen. It flashed five times before Margaret bothered to come to the phone.

Jason knew what to expect, but he always held a ridiculous, naive hope that she would appear pleased to see him, that she would begin the conversation with a smile and a "Hi, Jason!" That was how he imagined most homebound conversations went, though he knew that many long-distance relationships were badly strained. Several marriages had already snapped—including his own.

Margaret's face was scowling as her image came into focus. She knew the calling schedule as well as he did, but she had not yet gotten up the nerve to refuse to answer. That would come soon.

"I can only talk a minute," she said.

He couldn't see his children in the focal hemisphere. Margaret should have had them available, ready to greet their father. Now, she would probably make him waste some of his calling time while she rounded them up. "Can't you start out by saying hello?"

She heaved a big sigh. "Hello."

Okay, she was making this difficult. He decided not to play her game by getting angry at her. "Where are the kids?"

Pause. "Outside."

"Could I at least see my children?"

Pause. "I'll get them."

Arguments transmitted across cislunar space carried their own checks and balances, with forced pauses to catch a breath and to cool heated exclamations. Margaret's image walked off the screen, leaving him to stare at the large sunken drawing room he had designed. He had spent years dabbling, developing the architecture of his perfect house. It had been a special sanctuary for him, though Margaret had already changed many of his favorite things.

He wondered if he would ever set foot in his home again.

Margaret had filed for divorce. It would be final by the time he returned to Earth. The judge would probably award her possession of the house and enough alimony to support a small Third World country. Sometimes the Moon just wasn't far enough away.

He had first met Margaret at a ritzy grand opening of one of his new buildings in New York. With Jason's success and money, he had to spend a lot of time at social functions he usually didn't enjoy. Margaret, who came from a wealthy, upper-class family in the city, admired his work and his status. She had been rather aloof, but he fell in love with her anyway. She had insisted on a huge wedding—destined to be the "social event of the year"—and she had gotten it. Jason never worried about the cost of things, and he thought it would keep her happy, start everything off on the right foot.

He had been a workaholic all his life—Margaret knew that, and he assumed she knew what to expect. She valued her high-class life-style so much that he had never considered she would begrudge him the time required to earn that kind of income. Perhaps he had been stupid to ignore the possibilities.

Margaret never seemed satisfied, even with a nanny to watch after the kids. He had offered her every opportunity to do what she wanted, to go where she liked, do volunteer activities, get her own job, take classes, attend meetings. Anything she wanted. But Margaret never even knew what she wanted—except, perhaps, that she wanted to be disappointed in him.

Offscreen, he heard the kids coming, and Margaret ushered them into view. She had wasted a full two minutes of his five-minute allotment. *Good job, Peggy!* She hated to be called Peggy as much as he hated to be called Jase.

Lacy clung to her mother's arm while Lawrence scowled; the boy looked tough and protective. The twins had only a vague idea who this man was who called them every week. Children forget quickly. To them, they had no daddy.

"Say hello to your father," Margaret said, nudging them forward.

"Hi," Lacy said, then averted her eyes.

Jason remembered holding them as babies in the hospital, mouthing astonishment to himself. *These are mine! I'm their father! Did we do this all by ourselves?* But he wasn't a particularly good father, and he knew it. Always gone, always busy, he had been a quarter of a million miles away from them for over a year.

Lawrence tugged on his mother's sleeve. "Is Perry coming over today?"

"Yes, honey. He's going to take you to the park."

Jason felt a pain in his chest, not really from any surprise but just that it was out in the open. An odd flatness in Lawrence's voice made him suspect that Margaret had told the boy to recite exactly those words. It was her way of twisting the knife from across the gulf of space.

"Perry, huh?" Jason amazed himself by the coldness in his voice. "That's good. Perry and Peggy—what a cute-sounding couple. Or is he just a fling to occupy you during

Kevin J. Anderson and Doug Beason

those long and boring days when you never bother to do anything else?"

She glared and pushed the children away from his view. "Shut up, Jase! How dare you be judgmental! After what you've done to me, to my life? I'm not a widow and I'm damned tired of living like one."

But over the transmission delay he began talking before she finished her sentence. "After what I've done to you? What the hell are you talking about?" Now he did feel astonished. What could she possibly be thinking of? How could she twist it around and make her weakness his fault? What ever happened to sticking together during the bad times as well as the good?

Out of sight, Lacy started to cry. He wanted to reach out across space and hold his little girl. But the gulf of time separated them as much as distance.

Margaret's doorbell chime rang in the background. Jason had designed the system so that the soft bells could be heard in every room of the house. Now they were working against him. Before she could say anything to him, the red box appeared on the transmission window, ticking down the remaining seconds before his allotted personal call would be terminated.

"I've got to go," she said.

He decided that she must have made sure Perry would come over during his call, just to sting him even more. Such perfect timing could hardly have been an accident.

She ran a hand through her hair. "There's no use arguing about it. You can rewrite history in your mind all you want. It won't make any difference to me." She turned to Lacy and Lawrence. "Say goodbye." Then she reached forward to switch off her receiver before the children managed to utter the words.

Alone in the booth, Jason found he was shaking.

Alexandre-Gustave Eiffel stared down at Jason from a holographic representation in his office wall. Jason had always admired the French architect for his breathtaking bridges and viaduct designs in Portugal and France, the record-breaking eighty-four-meter cupola of the Nice

116

observatory, the inner ironwork structure of the Statue of Liberty . . . and of course the monumental tower in Paris that bore his name.

Eiffel's unconventional successes had been an inspiration in Jason's own career, the way Eiffel pushed his knowledge of materials to their limits and proved that a clever design could surmount nearly every obstacle. Jason certainly needed that inspiration now, if he was to make any progress in deciphering the Daedalus structure.

By burying himself in his work, by studying the nanotech threat, he could purge all thoughts of Margaret, of his lost children, of the choices he had made.

He called up a simulation of the Daedalus construction in the center of his slate holo-dais. The device was designed to digitize schematics of buildings and then build three-dimensional images from them. It allowed architects a virtual reality view of blueprints as they modified various parameters. Now Jason had the computer pull together all the images taken of the alien construction, commanding it to map the entire artifact to the best of its ability.

Staring down at the changing form, the arches, the gossamer strands and support structures, he hoped he could figure out what this thing was about. *What were the nanocritters building out there?* That was his expertise in reverse—instead of seeing a problem and conceptualizing a structure to solve it, Jason needed to complete the Farside artifact from sketchy lines and then extrapolate what it was for.

These blueprints had come from a mind not of Earth, based on preconceptions about planetary gravity, climate, and temperature that were different from everything he worked under. *I just have to make a paradigm shift. Simple.*

Jason Dvorak had made his name as a rule-breaking and trend-setting architect. As a designer, he had made his first million dollars before most people ever got their graduate degrees. Jason's trademark had been to make full use of the material properties of the new super-strong alloys and exotic materials created by microgravity processing. These materials were for the most part untried by architects and engineers other than for experimental tests, but their properties had been measured as fully as simpler materials. Why not use them?

If concrete could be reinforced with strands of fiberglass, he had surmised, then replacing the fiberglass with single-strand diamond fibers extruded in orbit should make the concrete even stronger and more resilient. Jason's "supercrete" provided unheard-of strength and flexibility, allowing builders to construct large-scale shapes and curves that had never before been possible. City skylines began to change as buildings were no longer bound to convention. To him, the St. Louis Arch and the Golden Gate Bridge were trivial exercises.

After five years of fame and awards, though, Jason saw that other architects were imitating him, fine-tuning his innovative designs and building on his ideas. He found this flattering, of course. He had more work than he could personally handle anyway.

But Jason was happiest developing concepts, playing with ideas, brainstorming. He took on large or small projects that captured his imagination, but he had grown dissatisfied. He wanted something different, a new challenge. He got what he wanted by volunteering to redesign Moonbase Columbus.

Which brought him back to thoughts of Margaret and his four-year-old twins. He froze up again.

Lon Newellen lumbered through Jason's open cubicle door. Jason jumped out of his reverie, but Newellen fixed his attention on the holographic model rising from the holo-dais.

"Still staring at that thing?" He nodded toward the image. "Well, I've finally got something that might help us keep a better watch on it, at least at the nanolevel."

Jason noticed that Newellen held a gadget in his hand that looked like an old-fashioned slide projector, the type that had gone out of use in his kindergarten days. "And what's that, Big Daddy?"

Newellen stepped forward, turning the device in his hands. "I've been busy since we decided to leave Erika alone out there. We got here a super-duper camera. A

Scanning Optical Microscope and a transmitter. We want to make a few dozen of these things, load them into the javelins, and shoot one out every few days or so, right into the middle of the building site."

He pointed the probe lens at Jason. "The javelin crunches into the nanocritter-infested regolith. The SOM in the camera here sends snapshots until the critters disassemble it. Each one should last about five minutes, if the remote hopper was any indication. We can get a picture as often as we shoot off a probe, and we got a hundred of those moon-penetrators. Closest we can get to realtime monitoring, and—" He pointed a pudgy finger at Jason. "It's without the risk of returning any active samples. I gotta confess, Jase, those live ones over at Sim-Mars make me nervous."

Jason took the probe camera in his hands and turned it over. It was an impressive piece of slapped-together engineering. "Why are you worried about those samples? Dr. Trace is impeccably cautious, and she's got telepresent teams on Earth double-checking everything she's doing."

"No matter how careful Erika is—those things are smart." He indicated the hologram of the Daedalus construction to prove his point. "If anything does happen, it won't take too long to find out about it. We'll have just about enough time to say 'Oooops!' "

"I get your point. I just don't know what else I can do about it. McConnell is on our backs to find out everything we can. Maybe with your cameras we can get a few steps farther."

"All right. I've got the shop making a couple dozen more. We'll send the first one out tomorrow." Newellen took his probe camera and left.

The image of Alexandre Eiffel scowled at Jason, as if trying to get him to concentrate on the problem at hand. At least he had managed to stop thinking about Margaret. And his children.

He couldn't ignore the nagging question he continually brushed aside—had he ever really loved his wife? He always wrapped himself in his work, pushed himself to higher and higher successes. It had been socially required for him to be "happily married," to have a faithful companion who would help him endure all those tedious functions and take care of the personal stuff he could never be bothered with.

But he had never felt any genuine passion for Margaret. Wasn't his passion used up in his work? Jason recognized echoes of himself in the way Erika Trace buried herself in the problem at hand. He had subconsciously criticized her for ignoring everyone else on the moonbase, but Jason was probably guilty of the same things himself with his life on Earth.

Back to work! Alexandre Eiffel's expression seemed to be saying. Always back to work.

On the holo-dais the bizarre Farside structure glinted up at him, projected in the best reconstruction the computer could fabricate. The pit in the crater wall showed no detail, just a black hole extending underground. Outside, in a circle clearly delineated by waste heat, raw materials had been scavenged one molecule at a time. Three of the dipole antennas of the VLF array had been disassembled. Diamond webs extended to the regolith in nets and taut strands, like scaffolding.

Sloping gossamer arches spread out like the petals of the largest flower in the solar system. The arches did not stand upright, but reclined at an angle of forty-five degrees, held in place by support girders made of the same glittering material. Other struts crisscrossed the main area of the "petals," the gaps between them gradually filling with a translucent material. Diamond foam? That was his best guess.

The structure had changed a great deal in the month since Waite, Lasserman, and Snow had died discovering it. But he still couldn't figure out a purpose or a pattern to the overall object.

"Slow dissolve," he muttered, keying up the initial image sent by Waite's rover, then having the holo-dais reconstruct the Daedalus site day by day as additional probes had observed from a distance. The result was a time-lapse slide show of the changes as billions of alien nanomachines assembled the structure from their built-in blueprints. The petals extended, the arches formed, the superstructure surrounding the pit took shape.

Jason tried to imagine what the thing could be, what the components were meant to represent. He could learn so much about the extraterrestrial builders if he could just unravel the nature of the artifact—how tall the alien race was, possibly the gravity of their home world and the resources available there, not to mention a bit of their point of view. But he had no final blueprint, only sketches.

Alexandre-Gustave Eiffel offered no insight.

Jason let his mind drift in free association to see what he might come up with. It was like looking for an indistinct object out of the corner of his eye.

He had run CAD simulations, asking the computer to project what the structure would turn out to be. No luck. He didn't have enough imagination to figure it out for himself, and the computer had even less.

Jason sighed, waved his hand through the insubstantial image to dismiss it, then powered down the holo-dais. He rested his elbows on the slate surface of the dais and stared at the wall.

The Parvu-Trace scenario—about the aliens sending a near-lightspeed nanotech expeditionary force to set up some kind of outpost here—sounded likely to him, but that didn't help much. Even if that explanation was valid, the purpose of the thing remained a mystery. All this trouble, the huge structure, all the resources used, seemed a bit much just for an alien fact-finding tour. An invasion force? Some kind of stronghold waiting for slower macroships to arrive? Jason didn't know and he needed to find out. All of Earth needed to find out.

antarctica—
nanotechnology isolation laboratory

Jordan Parvu stood in the NIL's teleconferencing room. He had transferred the display screens from the main lab out to here so he could watch in relative comfort, without having to put on the confining clean-suit. Working alone of late, he had grown more and more impatient with the tedium of his strict research protocol, all the discomfort and inconvenience it caused. He no longer had to provide a perfect example for Erika.

Outside the lab, the Antarctic wind picked up, sounding like a frost giant breathing against the walls.

Parvu folded his brown hands in his lap, waiting as the computer searched. High-energy astrophysics was not his field, but he knew what he was looking for. His program scurried through the international database downlinked from satellites to the optical receivers outside the NIL. The next image appeared. Parvu stared at detector tracings taken from the Kuiper-3 airborne observatory, but he found no evidence of a shower of alien automata striking Earth's atmosphere.

"Next," he said to the computer.

For hours, he had been staring at images culled from high-energy cosmic ray experiments, selecting those with huge anomalies in their data. He focused on information from satellite observatories and high-altitude balloons, even from sensitive detectors on the lunar surface. The best images so far had been from the open bay of the aging Kuiper-3 observatory, a C-141 jet that could fly high enough to take astronomical measurements normally spoiled by the thick atmosphere.

He looked at the new display and shook his head again. "Next."

If the aliens had beamed their automata across the Galaxy in all directions, Parvu could not believe that they would hit the Moon and not manage to strike Earth. But if they had indeed reached Earth, why had they not manifested themselves, as they had on Daedalus? Had the automata burned up in the atmosphere? Not likely.

Parvu sighed. He needed another cup of tea.

That morning he had checked on the prototypes in the nanocore. They had continued to study their surroundings, cataloging the microstructure of various samples he squirted into the nutrient solution. One of the images the prototypes had transmitted back—a blocky mosaic of an iron filing's cratered surface—was going to be the cover illustration for an upcoming issue of *Analog*. Of course, photos of the Daedalus construction seemed to be pre-empting everything, and Erika kept discovering new things.

Now, alone in the NIL, Parvu played his music louder on the speakers to make the lab seem less quiet, less empty. He didn't like doing this work by himself. He liked to exchange ideas with someone as he puttered about doing menial tasks. His requests for a new assistant had been repeatedly brushed aside; he suspected it was because most of the qualified people did not want to work under such isolated conditions.

Parvu reclined in the chair in the teleconference room, watching the screen with varying interest. "Next. Next. Next." It wasn't difficult to go through the images quickly. He was searching for something blatant, something that could not be denied even by blindfolded conservatives.

By studying the rate of change in the Farside construction over the past month, Parvu extrapolated backward to determine when the automata must have arrived and started their assembly process. This gave him a window in time for when the stream of machines should have been passing through the solar system. Now he had to find the right kind of detector in the right place at the right time.

"Next." He rose half out of his seat as soon as the following image formed. "There!"

Something too big to be caused by a cosmic-ray shower, and much too small and too energetic to be a micrometeorite, had plowed across the detector like a cannonball through Jell-O. Parvu could barely keep himself from jumping up and down.

With the time frame now firmly narrowed down, Parvu searched through the remaining subset of candidates in the database. He found fifteen streaks from various types of detectors in different locations taken over a two-day period. Almost certainly, these would have been dismissed as mere glitches by the researchers in question, flaws in the recording apparatus or the detectors themselves—but Parvu knew better.

Fifteen data points! Stochastic analysis would be able to pinpoint the nanomachines' point of origin—perhaps that was the most exciting part. They could find, or at least guess, the direction from which the explorers had come.

Back in his own quarters, with Beethoven's bright "Pastorale" playing in the background, Parvu finished the rest of his caviar without crackers, wishing he had Erika back with him to share it. Instead, he gave each of the rats an extra bit of food.

Celeste McConnell squinted her dark eyes, then blinked in surprise as she recognized him. "Why, Dr. Parvu! You don't often call directly, and you certainly don't use the secure line. What's up?" She turned to someone else, a man by his voice, saying that she would be "just a minute."

Parvu composed himself and folded his hands in front of him. "I have discovered something very disturbing to me," he said. "I thought you should be informed."

She frowned. Her small face looked as if it had been chiseled from marble. "Please, tell me."

"You may have wondered how the alien automata happened to travel such a vast distance to land on our Moon, yet managed to miss Earth, which is a much larger target?"

McConnell put two fingers in front of her lips. "That hadn't occurred to me! Do you think the aliens targeted our Moon specifically? Why would they do that?"

"I have another explanation, though it is more troubling." He took a deep breath. "I submit that the alien automata did not, after all, miss Earth. I will provide you with fifteen data points from various cosmic-ray detection experiments confirming that a shower of automata has indeed struck this planet. They are already here."

McConnell looked startled and sat up, straight-backed, away from the prime focus of the viewer.

Parvu spoke again before she could recover. "Now I have a request of you, Director McConnell. I know and you know that every inch of this planet is monitored by a Brilliant Eyes network. I also know that most of the pictures the Eyes take are merely archived unless someone has a reason to suspect something. Now, I suggest that you contact a team of spooks in the government's analysis section and make them scour every scrap of land, looking for something like the Daedalus construction here on Earth, okay?"

He drew in another deep breath and continued, "I doubt the automata would build anything in the ocean, mostly because of the currents—and that eliminates three quarters of the Earth. But there remain plenty of empty spots on mountain ranges, in rain forests, deserts, even here in Antarctica, where such a construction could go unnoticed for a long time."

McConnell nodded. She sounded shaken, but serious. "I agree, Dr. Parvu. I'll get on it right away and let you know what we find."

She signed off abruptly. He knew he had rattled her. Good. The secure link disconnected, displaying a code number on the bottom so that a recording of the conversation could be placed in the National Security Archives. Parvu had no doubt she would give him an honest answer.

If they were to find another construction, he would be the most likely one to study it.

At sixty-seven, Parvu felt like a teenage girl constantly using the telephone. He keyed the proper coded sequence to contact the Mars simulation base in Antarctica, using numbers Celeste McConnell and Kent Woodward had given him. His own optical uplinks went to the designated satellite, overrode the artificial transmission delay algorithm, and he immediately reached the base.

The mission commander, Bingham Grace, was on monitor duty. He patched Parvu to Kent Woodward's rover, which had been deployed for the day on a routine geological survey mission.

"Hey, Doc Parvu!" Kent said upon recognizing him. His own expression was barely visible behind the spacesuit helmet. He flipped up the faceplate to talk better. Beside him, Gunther Mosby, intent on the simulation as ever, kept his suit sealed.

"Kent, how would you like to gather some samples for me, if your duty roster permits? I have spoken to your commander, and this work has Director McConnell's approval."

Parvu already knew the answer. The Mars crew had many practice missions, scenarios they had followed a dozen times for their three hundred plus days in Antarctica. The primary goal of the mission was to make sure they could survive the time with nothing but their limited equipment and their own skills. They were allowed to conduct other useful scientific research in Antarctica while they were stationed there, and the astronauts generally loved the break from tedium.

"Sure!" Kent said. "What do you need and where do we get it?"

"I require random samples of the top layer of snowpack from as wide an area as you can cover. Please provide at least thirty different specimens down to a depth of ten centimeters."

"Am I looking for anything in particular?"

Parvu pursed his lips. "If I tell you what I am seeking, I cannot be assured of a random sample."

"Guess not."

It was a long shot, but the upper layers of the Antarctic snowpack had been little disturbed in the past several months, though the storm season would be coming soon.

"Doctor, I am concerned," Gunther Mosby broke in. "Are we trying to capture something? Did one of your samples escape from the lab?"

"No!" He chuckled. "No, they are fully contained. Please, indulge me in my request."

He heard a burst of static as Kent Woodward bumped one of the radio controls. "Whoa! Didn't see that rock! I could have plunged us right into a crevasse, Gunther—quit distracting me. I'll get your stuff, Dr. Parvu. I've been wanting to go on a road trip anyhow. We'll bring those samples over tomorrow."

"Kent will do it himself," Mosby said.

"Tomorrow, then," Parvu said. He heaved another sigh as he signed off. Time would tell if his fears were well founded.

The pieces of Kent Woodward's spacesuit lay strewn about the floor of the NIL's living annex. It had taken him half an hour to remove every piece of the suit to get ready for a shower.

This time, Parvu was the one pestering him for conversation, torn between his happiness at having company again and his eagerness to begin checking the samples Kent had delivered.

Kent seemed only politely interested when Parvu kept talking about Erika, describing her activities on the moonbase, the training she had been through, the great strides she had made in understanding the alien automata on the Moon.

Kent was more interested to know that she was working in the Sim-Mars lab where the astronauts themselves would be going in a few months' time. Parvu thought this indifferent reaction odd, since Kent had seemed to be madly in love with Erika.

Now, Parvu could hear Kent singing in the shower as he gathered up the forty-five snowpack samples and took them with him into the inner clean-room. Parvu had to stack the containers in the sample-exchange airlock. It could also serve as an autoclave to destroy foreign bacteria, but right now Parvu just needed the samples melted for liquid processing.

Inside the clean-room, Parvu tried to function carefully while clothed in his face mask, rubber gloves, booties, lint-free bodysuit, and hood. His own breathing reverberated in his ears. He had forgotten to put music on in his quarters, but after suiting up he would not go back out for such a trivial thing.

On the sides of each tiny container Kent had scrawled—while wearing heavy gloves—approximate locations where he had taken the samples. Parvu didn't know what he would do if he needed to find the exact spot again.

He had taped a Thank You note to Kent's spacesuit helmet, then set to work gently melting the snow in each sample, pouring the liquid into analysis vials.

The nano-characterization apparatus was a modified blood-cell counter that had been used to sort mutated red blood cells. In the NIL, it was to have been used to scour the nanocore's nutrient fluid for performing a postmortem on any failed experiment. If the prototype automata did not self-replicate, just finding them would be as difficult as the analysis itself. Now, the sorter automatically scanned through vial after vial of the samples.

His electronic message center chimed, informing him that a priority letter had just been delivered to his mailbox. By the electronic address he saw it came from the United Space Agency headquarters.

"Complete search of satellite photos turned up no evidence of another alien structure. Your hypothesis was excellent, though. Glad you kept your head and didn't cause a panic. —McConnell."

He scowled, then stored the message. Did that mean she did not intend to pursue the matter further?

The eighteenth sample turned out positive.

Parvu stared at the micrograph of a nanomachine very similar to those Erika studied at the moonbase. Squarish, fuzzy at the edges, with numerous armlike flagella to move about, to pick up things, to build objects—but this one was motionless, dead or dormant.

Parvu felt a sudden chill pour through him that had nothing to do with the polar winter. If he had managed to find one of the automata so soon, so easily, so close to his own location— He shuddered to think of the sheer numbers of them that must have come to Earth.

Glad you kept your head and didn't cause a panic, McConnell had said. Very well, he would say nothing about it. For now. Though it went against all his instincts about sharing his research with his colleagues, he had to gather more information. He could not cry wolf too soon. Not until he could figure out what to do.

14

sim-mars

Concentrating hour after hour on the nanomachinery was like watching a campfire. The sight mesmerized Erika Trace. She rubbed her eyes and took a deep breath of the air in Sim-Mars, hunching over the display. Her shoulders were stiff and sore, but the problem forced extraneous thoughts from her mind: she had to figure out why this change had occurred.

Jordan would have been amazed to see the alien nanocritters firsthand. She wished he were here right now. He had not been in contact with the moonbase for days, but she knew that when he got an idea into his head he drowned in it for weeks sometimes before finally coming up for air.

Erika kept working at her own studies. She felt no closer to determining what was being constructed at the Farside crater, but she had unraveled a great deal about the nanomachines themselves.

Enlarged in the Sim-Mars holoscopic display, the weirdly shaped automata vibrated with internal energy. The alien critters were versatile, as adaptable as Parvu had said nanotechnology could be. Cures for cancer, immortality, mega-construction, super-microcomputers—all the things people had called wild imaginings when first proposed. Erika wondered what those critics would be saying now.

Nanocritters shot across her field of view. Each machine was long, twisted, and lumpy. She could make out

130

no fine detail because she was observing on the Heisenberg scale: the x-ray photons that scattered off the automata caused a distortion of the surface.

Each machine carried a strand of molecules, like ants bearing tiny clumps of dirt to build their homes. The nanocritters used no appendages; somehow they bonded to each strand to carry it away. Others of the same design, the same *species*—that word better described what Erika could see—connected the strands into some construction only they understood.

The inconceivably small and incredibly efficient Controller substations carried the entire blueprint, the grand scheme of their mission on the Moon. Tiny Programmers or Messengers flitted from Assembler to Assembler, delivering the next step of instructions. Teams of devices that seemed to serve as quality checkers went over the work, making certain that everything fit together perfectly, molecule by molecule. Other nanomachines, identical but with no discernible purpose, sat motionless.

Big Daddy Newellen had so far lobbed two of his supercameras into the regolith surrounding the construction. Both had transmitted beautifully detailed images of the nanocritters at work for about three minutes before Disassemblers had taken all the components apart.

But now, as she continued to study the live sample she kept in the Sim-Mars isolation vault, she found a big difference from the images the supercameras had shown from Farside.

Inside Sim-Mars, all of the Disassemblers had vanished.

She withdrew the microwaldoes a fraction and tried to refocus her field of observation. The scanning optical microscope view pulled back, making Erika feel as if she were hurtling backward. Still no sign of them.

Had they perhaps depleted all the usable molecules in the regolith sample? Without resources available, did the Disassemblers shut themselves down? Did the Programmers change them into another breed? None of the answers made any sense.

Erika pulled her head back from the display and rubbed her eyes. She had remembered to eat a granola bar several hours ago, but it hadn't been enough. In spite of his fear of the nanocritters, Newellen kept volunteering to keep her company at Sim-Mars, but she just wanted to work. Erika refocused her attention on the nanocritters.

The sooner she figured this out, the sooner she could go home.

Ten meters away in the rigged-up nanocore sat the regolith sample, still encased in layers of depleted uranium. Erika knew that it was only a matter of time before the nanocritters would attempt to disassemble the container—if the Disassemblers ever reappeared. Though they did not have enough of the right raw materials to build copies of themselves, nothing would stop the nanocritters from tunneling through the containment if they should decide to escape.

Erika glanced at the wall clock, finding it difficult to concentrate. Another few hours and she would reach the mandated sterilization time limit. *Where had all the Disassemblers gone?*

She hoped Jason Dvorak was ready to provide another specimen immediately after the sterilization. As fast as things were altering, she wanted to find a few answers faster than the questions could change!

What had happened in Sim-Mars to shut off the Disassemblers? In her sample, she now found only nanomachines putting things together, using scraps of material the Disassemblers had already taken apart. But the supercamera images from the Farside site showed the Disassemblers still in full swing. Had she done something during the analytical procedures?

She squeezed her eyes shut. *Two days without any real sleep.* That was stupid, not a good way to take care of herself. In the darkness under her eyelids, vivid colors danced, afterimages from the bright lights of Sim-Mars. Sleep washed over her in an exotic ripple of shapes.

Deep within her head, she imagined she saw the imperceptibly perceptible surface of an Assembler. . . .

Her rest lasted only minutes before she forced her eyes open and struggled upright. Even in the reduced gravity field, she was so groggy that it took an effort to stand.

Parvu would have chastised her for working in such poor physical and mental condition. She wouldn't be able to trust any of her results.

Back at the NIL, Parvu would have brewed some of his incredibly potent tea to keep them both wired for hours. Here, she had access to bad powdered coffee-substitute. Well, maybe if she added two packets instead of one. . . .

Though she could not complete another series of tests, Erika did have enough time to rotate Sim-Mars's optical link to Earth and make a call. She squinted at the control panel. The nice thing about being on the Moon was that you could contact most spots in Antarctica twenty-four hours a day.

In the image in front of her, Parvu leaned back in his chair and tapped his teeth. Though the NIL was more than four hundred thousand kilometers away, she could almost smell the odor of his after-shave, some scent named after a windy sea; she had never liked it before, but now she thought of it fondly. All the air on the Moon was manufactured and smelled like charcoal from the ever-present lunar dust.

Parvu spoke so softly she had to lean forward to catch his words. He seemed very pleased to see her. "Very interesting, Erika," Parvu said. "So, you believe all of the Disassemblers have vanished?"

Erika wondered if she could have missed something that would never have slipped past him. "I've used every search technique without success. I ran the Monte Carlo simulation out to seven sigma. I came up with plenty of all the other types of machines, Assemblers, Controllers, Programmers, Quality Checkers, you name it. Jordan, it just doesn't make sense. The Disassemblers are very distinctive, and it's like they just went into hiding."

"Could they have been modified into a different design? Did the Programmers turn our Disassemblers into Assemblers?"

Erika shook her head. She had gone over this argument too many times in her own mind. "I've identified the roles of the nanocritter species, and they have not deviated one bit. Each machine, once tagged, hasn't demonstrated any different behavior."

Parvu seemed distracted and paused longer than the two-second time lag required. "Erika, you are indeed the very best person for this task. I have watched your reports coming in the past forty-eight hours. Extraordinary work."

Erika couldn't help smiling. In all the years she had worked with the man, Parvu somehow managed to see a bright spot in every dark situation. He always gave her just the proper amount of motivation and encouragement at just the right moment.

Parvu spoke across the transmission lag. "I have run an analysis of the data you've been sending, and you are quite correct. Nothing even remotely resembles the Disassemblers we observed previously. It seems as if something caused them to switch off, perhaps to be broken down for their own raw materials. Did the regolith sample run dry of useful molecules, so the Disassemblers got, well, 'laid off' as the colloquialism goes?"

She sighed and looked at him across the gulf of space. "I don't have the time or the facilities to do anything more, Jordan. I have to sterilize the sample in an hour. And this lab just doesn't have the diagnostics to ferret out the full details. It's like I'm trying to fix a supercomputer with a Junior Handyman toolbox."

Parvu waited two seconds, then smiled. "So, how do you propose to solve this difficulty?" He always approached any difficulty as a problem to be fixed.

Erika remained quiet for a long while. This was the core issue, the one she had been afraid to mention before. The prospect of admitting defeat was behind her now. She no longer cared about what others might think. Parvu had run up against his share of stone walls in the past; he would understand falling back to regroup, to start out fresh, better prepared, with more realistic expectations.

She said, "I need better facilities. More people. It all comes down to whether the Agency is serious about unraveling this mystery or not. Whatever the alien technology turns out to be, there is no way we can adequately uncover its purpose until I get hold of more sophisticated diagnostics."

"Such as?" He was still listening attentively; that was a good sign.

She ticked off points on her fingers. "Gamma-ray lasers for full tri-dimensional holography. Dedicated access to a gigaprocessor to assist with a more realistic realtime simulation. How about a reproduction facility for what we've found so far? And how about some plain old help—"

Parvu held up a hand. "Yes, I get your point. I know what it is to work with no assistant, especially right now, okay?"

She swept her hair back with one hand. The words came out in a rush, but she did not want to appear to be begging. "Can you arrange for me to come back to Earth?" Her reasons suddenly sounded like lame excuses to her. "If I can gather up some more people and sophisticated diagnostics up here, I'll have a better chance analyzing just what it is I'm seeing."

"Why must you return to Earth? It is expensive to ferry people back and forth."

"Not this time. They've supplemented the regular supply shuttle run that goes up to the Collins. I can deadhead as cargo on one of the Japanese transfer vehicles back to near-Earth orbit. I've already checked into it. Pretty much a free return. Besides, it would work best if I were back to handpick the equipment . . . and personnel."

Parvu mulled it over, then he grinned. He seemed to want to bring her back home, but was having trouble convincing himself. "Your requests seem reasonable enough. I would have asked for the same things. But by the time everything is assembled, shipped up to the Moon, and set up at Sim-Mars, it will take over a month. The alien construction could be nearly finished by then, at the rate it is going now."

Erika had suspected as much. "We can project what might happen on Daedalus, but we have no idea what it is, so we can't extrapolate when it'll be finished. But—and this is important—we've seen no evidence that the

135

nanocritters are spreading from the three-kilometer radius. They're diligently working on their own little project. Our first survey crew just happened to be in the wrong place at the wrong time."

Parvu waited longer than the delay to respond. "If it must take this long, it will have to do. I will see if Director McConnell will bring you back home. Temporarily. To arrange everything for your return trip with a full complement of researchers."

"Thanks—"

"I am not promising Director McConnell will agree. But if their supply shipment coincides with bringing you back down, I see no problem."

Erika nodded, already feeling the excitement bring her back to life. "I'd like to head out to Stanford when I get back, see Compton-Reasor and her coworkers. That will help me prepare for coming back to the NIL." She hesitated. "I'd hit MIT, of course, spend some time at the Drexler facility." She thought for a moment. "You know, I was swept up here so fast that I never had a chance to really prepare myself, to run through the labs, talk with some of the researchers. You know as well as I do that consulting over a holotank is just not the same as meeting face to face, interacting. And the only people we ever spoke to were the group directors. It's the worker bees I need to have some face time with—and not just over a holoscreen."

Parvu nodded. "Yes, I do know, Erika. The research assistants usually make the real advances." He smiled once again. "That is the true reason I sent you to the Moon instead of myself."

Erika moved her hand over the light array. The holotank blinked; the receiver in Newellen's Winnebago was already open. She saw the back of the man's head. Just visible in the background was a tiny lap-table strewn with torn-open food packages. He had come out there only a short time ago to keep watch during the sample exchange, but it looked as if Big Daddy had been sitting there for nearly an entire day, eating and waiting for her to call.

"Big Daddy?" she said.

He rotated his chair. His eyes looked puffy, as if he had not had any sleep either. She wondered if he had been nervous waiting so close to the nanotechnology research. He glanced at something outside the view of her holotank. "You done already?"

"No."

"You've got another half hour before I was going to warn you—"

"I know. I've done as much as I can with this sample. The sterilization order, you know. Not enough time to start any other major tests."

Newellen straightened in his chair. "You look tired. I can move in and get you right now. Catch some sleep while they're fetching another sample."

She shook her head. "Please notify Mr. Dvorak I'm coming back to Columbus Base. There's no need at this time to get another sample."

"But you've gotta keep going, lady. What if those things are eating their way through the Moon right now?"

Erika drew in a breath and tried to keep from raising her voice. "There has been a change of plans. Please just come and pick me up."

Newellen shrugged. "Okay. None of my business." He reached forward to switch off the holotank. Seconds later Erika found herself staring into a swirling speckled gray-green mash of interference.

When Director McConnell agreed to the request—after heavy lobbying from Jordan Parvu—Jason Dvorak had not argued against letting Erika return to the Collins. She felt no pangs about leaving the moonbase behind, but Dvorak had made a rather embarrassing show of thanking her for her work.

All the other activity at the moonbase seemed to hang upon her work, on whether she would give them a death sentence. She couldn't blame the crew for wanting her to stay, since this place was their home. She tried to imagine how people would react if an alien construction appeared on the famous polo fields in her home of Aiken, South Carolina.

As the lunar surface dwindled away in the flatscreen before her eyes, the tug of acceleration seemed greater than Erika remembered in the trainer just three weeks before. *Is my body already becoming acclimatized to lower gravity?* she wondered. They would test her thoroughly on the Collins before letting her board the Rising Sun for home. She hadn't expected to feel the changes inside her body so clearly. How much longer before she suffered severe bodily deterioration?

The medical station on the Collins would catalog her metabolic specifics in great detail as part of their ongoing studies of the human body in low and microgravity. The low-G acclimatization affected different people at different rates; and some of those on the Moon might have a very difficult time ever returning to Earth. Erika did not want to be one of them. She thought of Big Daddy Newellen, how much trouble he would have hauling his massive body around in gravity six times greater than what he had become accustomed to.

Although she occupied her mind with other things, the shuttle's burn seemed to last forever. Bryan Zed kept silent during the launch—not much had changed from when he had landed her several weeks before.

Inside the lunar lander, silvery insulation covered the walls. A picture of Zed's wife was taped to the bottom of the middle TV console. Aside from the control panel and acceleration couches, the lander offered little else. It seemed even more Spartan than the Sim-Mars lab or the moonbase quarters.

Erika's body rose up against the seat restraints when the acceleration stopped. Zimmerman ran through a sequence of checks and crisply reported them to the Collins in a corpselike monotone. He didn't turn to check on his passenger.

He flicked the flatscreen view from the still-receding lunar surface to a magnified image of the L-1 station. Erika worked at her straps and struggled free. She bumped against the bulkhead as she approached the quiet pilot.

"Nice view. How long until we leave orbit?"

Zimmerman grunted. "We don't go into an orbit around the Moon. By staging to L-1 we can take a direct trajectory from anywhere on the surface."

"Oh," she said, surprised that Zimmerman had replied in more than a few syllables.

Erika squinted at the image of the supply station ahead. The Collins hung in the center of the screen, unmoving. It looked like a bundle of cylinders wrapped tightly with metal scaffolding to hold the whole thing together. Two spindly shuttles were docked at one end of the cylinders; at the other end were three Hitachi tugs, back from their low-Earth-orbit trip.

The docking was smoother than what she remembered coming up from Earthside. Other than a slight bump and computer graphics showing their trajectory, she only realized they had arrived when Zimmerman began dictating his final trip report to a portable voicescribe.

Erika pushed up from her seat. Spinning, she kicked for the airlock and waited for it to rotate open. Zimmerman finished his report, slapped at the remaining lights that blinked on his panel, and joined her at the airlock. He threw her another quick glance, but remained quiet. She had no idea what he was thinking; perhaps Bryan Zed had somehow managed to obliterate irrelevant thoughts during his flights, conversation with passengers included.

Erika absently reached up to push back her hair. She had tied it back in a ponytail, not wanting to deal with loose strands flying in her way. As she withdrew her hand, she noticed her reflection in a mirror set next to the airlock to allow station personnel to look into the lander. Her face looked bloated and puffy; in weightlessness, her body fluids had redistributed themselves throughout her body. She looked as if she had put on twenty pounds.

A quick glance at her chest showed that her breasts had swelled as well. Compared to how she looked on Earth, even on the Moon, she could probably wear a double-D cup now, three sizes larger than normal for her! Maybe that was why Zimmerman kept stealing glances at her.

As the airlock door rotated open, she wondered how long Zed had been flying the lunar shuttle, and if he was as emotionless as he tried to appear. Perhaps he held all his passion in check only to be released at home. Or maybe he didn't have any in the first place.

Bernard Chu waited for them inside the station. Erika pushed out to meet him; he caught her by the elbow and they both spun slowly around. It felt like dancing.

"Dr. Trace, welcome back. I wish this could have been under better circumstances. I must personally apologize for not having equipped the Sim-Mars lab adequately. When I was commander of the moonbase, we hadn't counted on using the facility for another two years."

"I was thankful for having what equipment I did," said Erika.

Rotating his feet against the bulkhead, Chu pushed out and moved down the corridor. They floated down a polished steel cylinder. Signs posted every few feet pointed to life vessels and air hoods in the event of sudden decompression. Erika followed Chu's motions as he maintained his grip to steady her.

"We heard that you were not able to discover why the alien machines have stopped disassembling things. Or what they are building at Daedalus."

She felt her defensiveness rise up again. "Well, Mr. Chu, I actually did make a bit of progress. I don't think the point was to find out everything about the alien automata. After all, how much do we know about our own experimental nanotech machines? Not a whole bunch."

Chu pushed off the side wall to direct them both down a crosslink. He smiled. "I didn't mean to doubt your ability, Dr. Trace. And by the way, I have my doctorate, too. Biochemistry."

"Sorry, Dr. Chu. I'm not much on titles, and nobody believes I've got a PhD anyway. I look too much like a kid and talk like a hick from the South. But don't worry, you didn't offend me. It's just that . . . well, everyone on Earth expected me to unravel all the mysteries by myself with a few days of research."

Chu nodded and continued to drift. "Ah yes, the public perception of how science can create miracles without having to work at it! Or without receiving any funding!"

He reached out for a handhold to stop their progress. Chu motioned for her to enter the room first. "I suppose you're right, but when dealing with something as strange as this, we must accelerate the discovery process."

"I'm doing the best I can. Look at AIDS research, how much money and effort was poured into that, and how long it took them to come up with even part of an answer. Too many movies have brilliant scientists scratching their heads and scribbling on a blackboard before saving the world over lunch."

Chu lifted an eyebrow. "And do you truly believe risking more people out in the Sim-Mars laboratory may help?"

Erika drew in a breath to keep from getting angry. "With the existing setup at Sim-Mars, one researcher was the optimum solution. As it turns out, we'll need much more equipment and more personnel. I hope I can bring a good team back."

And Jordan Parvu is damn well going to be in it, she thought. *He got me into this.*

"We'll do whatever is necessary to assist you," Chu said. "And that includes being pack mules for getting your equipment in place once it comes up from Earth."

Erika noticed for the first time where Chu had led her. It looked like a small infirmary. Medical garments hung in webbed netting; a case fixed to the far bulkhead held three rows of surgical knives; boxes marked MEDICINAL SUPPLIES were stuck all over the bulkheads; a holotank filled the right side of the room—probably for realtime use in assisting surgery—and a refurbished acceleration couch, complete with straps, served as a surgical table.

Erika's eyes widened. "Looks like a serious medical center."

"Celeste McConnell strikes again," said Chu with a smile. "It was a bone they gave me when they transferred me up here from the moonbase." He waved for her to strap onto the acceleration couch. "As I said, my field is biochemistry. Besides being a waystation and supply depot, the Collins is supposed to serve as a life-sciences facility. Remember the tests they ran on you before leaving Star City?"

Erika nodded. It was the last thing they had done before she boarded the Aeroflot plane for Moscow, then back to the States.

"Now that you're about to head back dirtside, we must calibrate your vitals before you return to full gravity. We've got blood, fecal, urine, hair, skin, and just about every other sample you can imagine of everyone who's been on the Moon. Until we get a statistically significant database, we'll never be able to accurately predict how a human is going to react under long-term exposure to low-G and the enhanced radiation environment. You've been down on the Moon for only a short time, but we still need to see what that few days has done to your metabolism."

Erika eyed a needle that Chu pulled out. She rolled up her jumpsuit sleeve and looked the other way. "You've got it easy," Chu casually remarked as he took the blood sample. "If you were a male, we'd be doing a whole different set of tests."

Two hours before the Rising Sun was scheduled to dock and load her and other cargo bound for Earth, Bernard Chu called Erika into the infirmary, alone. Erika was startled to see how much the man had aged—and it had only been twelve hours since she had last seen him.

He sealed the door behind her.

"Dr. Chu?"

It seemed to take a minute before he turned to her. "Erika—I wanted you to be the first to see this. I . . . I just hope I've misinterpreted something. But I can't see how."

Erika felt a chill run down her spine. Wasn't this the way doctors told patients they were dying of some terminal disease? She shook her head in confusion. "What are you talking about?"

Chu looked as if he had resigned himself to failure. His shoulders drooped and his face seemed ashen gray. He waved a feeble arm at the stereo microscope. "There. Go ahead. Take a look. You of all people should need no explanation."

Erika frowned. She floated slowly toward the twin-barreled microscope. She was so used to working with the microwaldoes, viewing specimens through the aid of a holotank, she hoped she could discern what Chu wanted her to see.

She squinted through the device. She immediately recognized red and white blood cells, bumping up against each other in the display. She started to draw back when something caught her attention just at the limits of her vision. She adjusted the magnification to full and stared hard—

Within the field of view were the unmistakable signs of what she had observed on the Moon, what she had watched for hour after hour until she had been forced to call it quits and head back to Earth for reinforcements—

Mixed in with the sample of blood were thousands upon thousands of nanotech devices—the same alien machines that were erecting a gigantic construction on the Farside of the Moon.

And they were swimming in human blood.

She pulled back in horror. Chu slowly shook his head. "I'm sorry. I'm . . . so sorry. I don't know what we're going to do."

Erika's eyes widened. "This . . . is my blood?"

Chu lifted his head and whispered, "No. And that's why I've asked you to verify what I've found."

He slumped as if he wanted to sit down heavily, but the microgravity held him floating in the air. She noticed that his hands were trembling. He looked at her as he spoke.

"You see, this is *my* blood. A new sample, taken just minutes ago." He swallowed hard. "Your blood looks the same.

"And if I'm right, then everyone on the Collins now has these alien things coursing through their veins."

washington, d.c.

Celeste McConnell woke from nightmares to the insistent beeping of the phone link. She snapped away from sleep and rolled half out of bed. As she fumbled for the set, she saw it was the Stu-5—her secure phone.

She marshaled her thoughts, pulling her attention back from grogginess. Bad dreams had already warned her how important this call must be. A lot depended on her sharp-mindedness now.

Her two dogs, Chuck and Yeager—a black lab and a German shepherd—got up from the foot of the bed, growling, ready to defend her against any intruder. She shushed them as she turned on the "video receive only" channel of the phone link; there would be no pictures this night.

She felt a dreaded eagerness to find out what it was, what the nightmares had warned her about. Then at least she could stop wondering, though she would not know what to do about it.

Celeste finger-combed dark hair out of her eyes. "Hello?"

"Celeste?" Bernard Chu's face appeared. The link was patched in from the Collins.

"Bernard! What are you calling for?"

She remembered watching him frantically sealing the Grissom's Module 4 airlock, knowing their time was running out, knowing the station would be destroyed soon. Celeste still sent Chu's son Shelby a birthday card every year.

144

"Celeste, we have some big trouble here. We've got only five minutes before this call will arouse suspicion. I'm patching in over a private link—I commandeered one of my crewmembers' regularly scheduled calls home so that no one would think anything's out of the ordinary. We've got to do something."

She sat up now, naked on the bed, letting the sheets fall away from her. "Okay, Bernard. Talk to me. I'm listening."

He wet his lips. "We've . . . we've been contaminated. Alien nanomachines!" Chu's voice twisted as if he were about to burst into panic, but he kept it under control. His expression hardened. She saw a man much older than the one she had rescued on the Grissom.

"Slow down, Bernard. What happened?"

"We brought that nanotech researcher back up from Columbus—Erika Trace. We did a routine blood test, as always with people passing back and forth. Celeste—she's got those alien nano-things in her blood. They've infected her . . . and they are in my blood, too! By now they've probably spread to all of us."

Celeste felt blocks of ice falling into her stomach. *The dreams had been right.* "Have you checked anybody else?"

"We just found out ten minutes ago. Erika Trace confirms it. I've ordered blood tests for everybody, including Bryan Zimmerman. I've got to keep fourteen people under control here. The Rising Sun is supposed to dock in half an hour, but I told them we were having difficulties and would have to postpone."

She saw Chu's hands squeeze together and his eyes close for a second, as if collecting his own thoughts, his terror, his anger.

Celeste's thoughts raced forward. *How had Erika Trace been infected?* She had double-checked the young woman's isolation and sterilization precautions herself. Jordan Parvu, Maurice Taylor, and Maia Compton-Reasor had all agreed that they were more than adequate. But somehow the alien nanomachines had broken through.

Celeste thought of the images of Waite, Lasserman, and Snow, as the Daedalus nanomachines destroyed their suits, exposing them to hard vacuum. But why hadn't they disassembled Erika Trace if they were inside her body?

Scowling, Celeste realized she couldn't trust anything the researchers did now. How could they be so cocky to think they could set up a defense impenetrable to alien technology, a technology sophisticated enough to fabricate nanomachines in the first place? Such a civilization could easily thwart any barrier scientists like Erika Trace might set against it.

Celeste remembered, too, Jordan Parvu's suspicions that alien nanomachines had already reached Earth—but thankfully she had seen no hard evidence of that, just a few anomalous cosmic-ray tracings. What would happen if the infestation did get here? What if it spread from the Moon—like a plague?

"What should we do?" Chu insisted, breaking her train of thought. "I wish I could see your face and talk to you directly."

She glanced down at her naked breasts and her thighs, now sparkling with a thin sweat. The illumination seeping through the blinds lit them with a dim gray-blue sheen. Items of clothing lay scattered on the floor, glistening monoweave panty hose, a rumpled dress uniform. "Not now, Bernard."

She waited, thinking. On the screen, Chu fidgeted. "Why didn't Dvorak think to check Erika before letting her board the shuttle? If I had been moonbase commander—"

Silence. Celeste watched him swallow and sit up straighter. She softened her voice. "I don't quite know what to do. Give me an hour to think about it. Don't let anybody leave Collins station. Tell the Rising Sun that the delay is indefinite and find out how long they can orbit L-1 before they have to return to LEO.

"And finish taking blood tests. I must know the extent of this contamination, how far it has spread. I'll call you back as soon as I have more information. Prepare yourself—we may have to take some drastic measures."

On the screen, Chu nodded reluctantly. Celeste needed some time without him watching, to think and to discuss the possibilities out of earshot. "Thanks, Bernard. Keep me informed if anything else happens. I will speak to you soon." She switched off. Her hands were trembling. The dogs whimpered, demanding attention.

Beside her, Major General Simon Pritchard sat up silently in bed. The wiry hairs on his chest looked like metal in the pale light. His eyes were wide, blinking in astonishment. "Oh my God!" he said.

Celeste turned to him. "I was afraid something like this would happen." She couldn't tell him about the dreams. She could not risk having him lose his trust in her now.

Pritchard's face looked boyish. Had it been only a few hours ago that they had been locked together, his arms around her, her legs around him . . . laughing, moving with him, giggling when the two dogs leaped onto the bed, practically causing the box springs to break? Celeste and Simon had drifted off to sleep, contented—but then the nightmares had come to stalk her.

She had been having a lot of bad dreams lately; what frightened her most was that she did not know how to interpret them. Not this time. She could not determine what the dreams were warning her of, but she knew that something terrible must be coming.

It had always happened like this. . . .

Her first "premonition" had been when she was eight years old, living in Quebec. Waking up, she felt as if she were suffocating; everything was dark and murky, and smelled of wet rot. She was drowning! Mud filled her lungs.

The next day, when her ten-year-old brother Christian wanted to go swimming in a nearby quarry, Celeste was terrified and refused to go with him. That afternoon, Christian himself had drowned. The dream-warning had not been for her own sake, but for her brother. She had not bothered to warn him. She had not interpreted the dream correctly.

The next time occurred years later when she was in college. A friend of hers, Peter, had come to visit from upstate. He had stayed late. The weather turned drizzly and foggy, then cold, making for treacherous driving. The night before, Celeste had dreamed of cold, of loss of control, of breaking glass. When Peter turned to leave, she suddenly realized that the dream must have been warning her about him. Uncertain, she tried to get him to stay, but he begged off. She couldn't think of any good reason to give him.

Peter died in a car accident that night.

She was sure she could have saved him; but this clashed with the rational part of her mind. After all, she had a science background, believed in cause and effect, not ESP and pseudo-science. But were the drowning and the car accident dreams just a coincidence? Somehow she couldn't believe that.

And what about the Grissom?

Many lives on Earth, the Moon, and the Collins now depended on whether she could understand those nightmares again. And with Bernard Chu's call, she knew exactly what the nightmares had been preparing her for. Unfortunately, they suggested no solutions.

"We can't let those alien automata reach Earth," Pritchard said. "Even if it means . . . neutralizing the Collins. You see what the things are doing to the Farside crater. What if something like that showed up in the middle of New York City? The three people who first discovered it are all dead. How long is it going to be before the nanomachines take apart Trace and anyone else who's contaminated?"

Celeste didn't tell him about Parvu's suspicions in Antarctica. It could already be too late.

She drew in a breath. "I agree, though it'll be hard on us. We're going to take a lot of flack—but we can get through it." She raised her eyebrows and met his gaze. "It may soon be time to bring your involvement out into the open. We need a strong general, not just a compassionate Space Agency director."

Pritchard pushed out of bed. Both big dogs jumped to him. Yeager reached up and pawed the general's chest; Pritchard distractedly eased him down to the floor and patted his head.

Celeste knew what had to be done. She said it out loud, to get it into the open. "We're going to have to quarantine the Collins station, and the whole Moon—as a first step."

Pritchard nodded as he looked for his uniform and picked up the shirt he had carelessly draped over her chair the night before. His mouth was a grim line. "No one there is ever going to be able to come home again."

collins transfer station, L-1

Strapped to the chair in the Collins observation chamber, Bernard Chu tried to control his breathing. Visible through the thick window on his left, the Earth occupied a good part of the starry sky. Opposite that, the Moon hung stark and unchanging, as if mocking him for having gone back to live in space. He had thought himself safe at L-1.

Directly in front of him the image of Celeste McConnell seemed frozen in the flatscreen. Celeste had not been able to offer him any convenient answers, though at least she was transmitting video now. He wanted to look into her eyes as she told him the bad news.

"Bernard—we all knew there would be risks," she said. "That's why we sent only one researcher to Sim-Mars and kept the rest back here on Earth. I didn't want to take the chance that somebody would get exposed."

Chu tried to mask his frown. "Well, somebody did. And now we all are."

Celeste's face stared back at him as she waited to receive the rest of his words. The two-second light delay made the conversation maddening. Every time Chu interrupted to ask a question, her image would continue to speak, only to stop abruptly and glare foolishly back at him.

"Actually, Bernard, we don't know what would happen if the infestation reached Earth. The nanomachines should have reacted in your bodies by now, taken you all apart."

150

"Don't you think every one of us is just sitting here waiting for that to happen?" He couldn't keep from being angry at Celeste, though he knew it wasn't fair—she had saved him from the Grissom disaster years before, and subconsciously he had always counted on her to give some kind of forewarning before another tragedy could strike. This time she had let him down.

The last time anyone had worried about an extraterrestrial virus was during the first Apollo Moon landings, and even then the precautions they took were a joke. Chu thought of how they had allowed the astronauts to be exposed to the atmosphere before locking them up in quarantine! He knew they had to do it correctly this time, and it was his responsibility not to let the nano-infestation spread farther. He had a good guess what would occur if those machines got loose on Earth.

"—and Erika Trace must have been infected at least a full day before any of you. Yet, you say she has shown no signs of any adverse reaction." Celeste plowed through the conversation, unmindful of Chu's interruption. When she stopped, the delay allowed him too much time to think, to feel sorry for himself.

"It's only a matter of time before somebody gets disassembled. We're all watching each other to see who's the first to turn into a blob of . . . whatever."

Celeste came back gently. "Bernard, I'll give you all the help I can from here, but I'm not sure what to do."

"I'm sure as hell not going to sit here and wait! What's happened to you, Celeste? You never resigned yourself to waiting for the end before! What would have happened if you'd done that on the Grissom? Where did this bureaucratic mind-set of yours come from?"

Celeste's unchanging face finally sagged. She kept staring, her face grim. Chu watched her for ten heartbeats before he realized that she wasn't going to speak again, that she was waiting for him to suggest something better.

"These alien nanotech machines"—he jabbed at his chest—"could take us apart in a few seconds if they wanted to. At least let us do something useful, dammit. What else have we got to lose?"

"Specifics, Bernard. What do you want to do?"

Chu settled down and got a grip on his emotions. He felt like a man dying of lung cancer who was about to volunteer to smoke two packs a day.

"The entire moonbase is infected, too, thanks to Typhoid Mary. Dvorak has confirmed that. So it doesn't matter if we come into contact with them. I propose that we abandon the Collins and go down to Columbus. We can load up in the LTV and head for the Moon before anything happens."

"Convince me. What advantage is there?"

Chu shrugged. "They've got more resources down there. You just hauled the biostatistics equipment up here when you transferred my command. I'm a biochemist—maybe I can do some work on this, too."

"What do you propose doing differently?" Celeste's questions seemed to be pro forma, as if she wanted to see if his answers matched her own ideas.

"First off, I'd start taking care of things Dvorak should have done a long time ago. This is the perfect time to send a scouting party out to Daedalus Crater, explore the artifact. Since everyone is infected, why should we be afraid of the nanomachines now?"

"You'll be disassembled if you do that." Her voice sounded cold.

"We should have been disassembled hours ago! Something has happened, a mutation maybe, and we need to take advantage of it! Our death sentence is already signed."

Celeste pondered this for some moments, but Chu could not tell what she was thinking, could not read her body language. Her voice came as a near whisper transmitted across cislunar space. "What about the rest of the Collins crew? Do they agree? Are all fourteen of them willing to go along with this?"

Chu thought of the two astronomers and one tech locked up and sedated in the loading pod bay, how they had broken down and started raving when told of their infection.

He also thought of Bryan Zimmerman, who still did not know of their situation, though he too was infected. Chu had decided that with so much riding on the pilot shuttling everyone down to the surface, it was best not to tell him yet.

Chu whispered, "Yes, everyone agrees—we need to expedite leaving the Collins."

Celeste glanced down at her watch. "We can't postpone the Rising Sun longer than seven hours before they have to abort and return to Earth orbit. Can you leave your station before then?"

"Of course." Chu felt confident in that much. He had checked already in the LTV specs; if everyone took only minimal items with them, the Lunar Transfer Vehicle was rated to carry the full complement down to the lunar surface, though Bryan Zed might have a tough time piloting the heavy craft. And Chu wanted to bring as much of his biostatistics equipment as he could.

"Very well, now listen to me carefully." Celeste's voice became hard. "Once everyone has departed, we will remotely initiate the station shutdown sequence."

Chu frowned. *Shutdown sequence?* "That doesn't sound familiar. I was supposed to have been fully briefed before I took over command up here—"

Celeste waved a hand. "General Simon Pritchard is working with me to oversee a new instruction uplink to your onboard computers. We're writing the program as we speak."

"But what does it do? What's going to happen to my station?"

"Once we get you to the Moon, the uplink instructions will sterilize the Collins. No one—including that Japanese tug or any hotshot salvage artists—can be allowed access to the L-1 staging area anymore. Any contact could bring the infestation down to Earth. Do you agree?"

Bernard found a lump growing in his throat, but he couldn't swallow it away. "So what exactly is going to happen?"

"The instructions will cause your power plant's shielding to open; the reactor will then run up to maximum. This will irradiate the entire waystation and kill any of the nanotech machines that remain." She paused. "We hope."

Chu pushed back against the chair netting, then nodded to himself as the words sank in. That would make the L-1 station unusable for years due to primary and induced radioactivity, not to mention all the damage it would do to sensitive diagnostic equipment. Without the L-1 rendezvous station, returning to Earth would be more difficult—if Earth ever decided to lift the quarantine.

A thought raced through his mind: *Did Celeste already know that we'd vacate the station ... or did she plan to shut it down with us still onboard?*

He forced a frightened smile. Maybe the station would be an orbiting monument to their sacrifice, just like the proposed Grissom memorial that kept troubling Celeste all these years. At last the Collins would live up to its namesake, keeping vigil alone in orbit while everything else happened on the Moon.

If any of them survived the nanotech infestation.

That was their first big problem.

Bryan Zimmerman kept his thoughts to himself as the last of the Collins crew loaded the Lunar Transfer Vehicle. *Seventeen people in a space for ten,* he thought, *not including all the equipment Chu had stuffed into the cargo bay.* Nobody would give him any details about this "emergency temporary evacuation," but they had kept him on the Collins for a full day and a half after delivering Erika Trace. He was already running behind schedule.

The LTV was overdesigned as it was—the specs allowed for a fifty percent increase in passenger weight, and he had carried twice that amount in supplies without breaking into a sweat.

But supplies weren't on the verge of panic, as were at least half the passengers here. He never understood why others couldn't keep their cool. He always did.

As Zimmerman punched up the outside aft view from the lunar shuttle, he saw the Collins grow smaller in the viewscreen. Evacuating the waystation for the Moon without even leaving a skeleton crew behind seemed really crazy—but orders were orders. He had seen Director McConnell's authentication himself.

He stole a glance at Erika Trace as she settled in behind him. She looked really frightened now, withdrawn, not as pretty as she had appeared during the first trip to the Moon. But the weightlessness still caused her breasts to swell out more than they should have. Before he punched the orbital-transfer rockets, he sighed.

Erika watched the Collins recede as they moved away from her stepping-stone to home. Nobody was ever going to go back. Not until they found a surefire cure to the nanocritter infestation.

We're probably all going to die soon, she thought. Yet most of the people were taking it so coolly . . . until it struck her that this was just exactly what the astronauts had been selected for in the first place, why the initial and follow-on screening had been so rigorous. She was the only one who had been rushed through a condensed version of the training.

Erika looked up. All the passengers kept to themselves, their heads down, or just looking toward the viewscreen, watching the Collins drop away behind them as the pockmarked surface of the Moon rose up on the other side.

She lifted her own hand. Opening and closing her fist, she studied her fingers. She felt no different, but inside she knew she was swarming with nanomachines. *How soon—when will they disassemble me? Why haven't I died already?* The thought of an alien invasion within her body made her feel violated.

A human voice, transmitted from Earth, came over the radio. "We have you five hundred kilometers away, Zed."

A synthesized voice broke in. "Collins reactor doors are opening."

Erika frowned, looked at the videoscreen.

Moments passed, and again the synthesized voice spoke. "The station has been flooded for ninety seconds. Approaching critical temperature."

A pause, then, "Detonation sequence initiated."

"Detonation!" Bernard Chu burst out, sitting up against his acceleration restraints. "What detonation? How?"

Zimmerman's face held an expression of surprise, but he merely grunted his reply. "Please confirm last transmission. Detonation sequence?"

"Confirmed."

"I never agreed to this!" Chu cried.

Erika sat blinking in surprise, unable to believe any of this was happening. The other Collins refugees began to jabber among themselves.

"Please specify detonation—" the pilot started to say, but the waystation suddenly grew bright onscreen, overwhelming the stereochip's brightness monitor. The superheated reactor breached its containment and ignited all the fuel tanks. Rainbow colors danced silently on the viewscreen in the nonnuclear explosion.

An instant later Erika saw nothing but the black blanket of space filled with stars and twinkling bits of molten debris. Millions of incandescent pieces of metal—all that remained of the Collins—flew radially out from L-1.

Erika prayed that the radiation burst from the nuclear reactor had killed all the nanocritters left onboard—and not hurled them through space toward other targets.

17

antarctica—
nanotechnology isolation laboratory

The cliché of having the rug pulled out from under your feet applied to Jordan Parvu in the Nanotech Isolation Lab. He had been in a near panic since learning of Erika's contamination and the destruction of the Collins. *How could this have happened?*

He felt so helpless, stuck at the bottom of the world, cut out of the loop completely. Shouldn't he be there, working side by side with his assistant to find a solution to the automata invasion in their bloodstreams? He briefly thought about taking the Emergency Overland Vehicle, driving to McMurdo Sound, just to get out of here . . . but what would that accomplish? He had tested his own blood, sick with fear that he, too, might be contaminated by the supposedly dormant automata he had sifted out of the Antarctic snow. And if he was infected himself, then everyone on the planet might be as well.

But the blood under the high-resolution analyzer showed no contamination at all, no alien machines invading his cells. Whatever had caused them to spread through Erika and everyone else at the moonbase had kept them inert here.

He tried to call Erika, just to see her face and to give her a long-distance shoulder to cry on. The static-gray holoscreen in front of him blinked, with a maddeningly calm "STILL TRYING . . ." message flashing at the bottom. Finally, it informed him "ALL LINKS IN USE. PLEASE TRY AGAIN LATER."

He muttered expletives in four different languages. No doubt everyone who had any relatives at all on the moonbase, or on the Collins, would be trying to get through. He imagined families dipping into savings accounts just to pay for the transmissions. He wondered if Erika's own family would bother to call—certainly not her father or brother, but possibly her mother would make the attempt.

His emotions warred within him, and the intensity frightened him. He had always been calm, too calm sometimes according to his wife Sinda.

Why had the Sim-Mars sterilization precautions not been sufficient? What if the ever-present dust on the lunar surface was itself a vector, transporting alien automata from one place to another? And what did it matter how they had gotten loose? The question of what to do about the infestation remained.

Parvu felt guilty for having sent her to the Moon, for pushing her into an assignment she did not want. He had felt confident and proud of Erika, but now she would never be able to come home . . . if she managed to survive the contamination at all.

As he paced inside the living area, listening to the Antarctic storm outside, Parvu turned his anger toward Celeste McConnell for having given Erika inadequate facilities to work with, not enough assistants, an unproven lab, and primitive equipment for sophisticated work. And now no one else would be coming to help her.

But most of all he turned his confused anger on the faceless aliens themselves who had the gall to indiscriminately fire their destructive mechanisms across the Galaxy—without regard to the ecosystems they might disturb, to the lives they might ruin. Like Erika's.

Shuffling around his living quarters in his slippers, Parvu stared at the stockpile of freeze-dried food, but nothing looked appetizing. He couldn't remember the last time he had eaten or slept. He needed to make sure he had fed the white rats recently. In the perpetual darkness of Antarctic night, it was difficult to keep a routine. Especially alone.

He wondered if he should go back out to the lab dome, to study the prototype specimens in the nanocore again. Or the inert alien automata Kent Woodward had scooped up.

Parvu had found a total of twelve specimens in the remaining snowpack samples. All twelve were dormant. He hadn't the slightest idea what had happened to switch them off.

As he pondered, he made the connection between the inert automata he had found in the snow and the dormant machines in Erika's bloodstream. *Why had they shut down— especially those that had been taken from the Daedalus array on the Moon?* Those automata had already proven themselves to be exceptionally active—and destructive.

What had Erika done to deactivate them, if indeed she had done anything? Parvu had gone over her logs, all the experiments she had accomplished. What could possibly be in common between Erika's blood and Antarctic snow? How had she managed not to be destroyed?

He paced the room. Back in his own quarters, he changed the CD, sifting through his stacks to select better "thinking music." On the walls, his videoloops of family members still went through their motions, maddeningly reminding him of happier times.

Come on, think! There had to be something there, some small similarity. Why was it that Erika had been so much luckier than the three astronauts who had been killed. . . .

Then it occurred to Parvu that the automata had not directly killed the three people on the Farside of the Moon. The tiny machines had merely begun to disassemble the pressurized hopper, Waite's and Snow's spacesuits. Explosive decompression had done the rest. What would have happened if the automata had actually reached the living bodies of the three astronauts? Would they have shut themselves down, just as they seemed to have done in Erika's bloodstream, and in the Antarctic snow?

Was it something to do with living things . . . *organic* material? Antarctica seemed about as dead as anyplace on the Moon. In the center of the continent, across the vast wasteland, it was indeed the most sterile place on Earth. But Parvu remembered reading something about the failed search for life on Mars from the Viking probes, how the soil tests had showed little activity—and how a similar test performed in the most barren Antarctic core sample would have gone off like firecrackers. Even here, in this inhospitable climate, Earth had enough bacteria and left-over organic material that the automata could not have gone far without bumping into some signs of life.

He drew in a quick breath. Had the aliens perhaps included a fail-safe system that caused the self-replicating machines to terminate their programming if they encountered life? Parvu frowned. *Aliens with a conscience?* That changed everything.

He thought about contacting the United Space Agency, telling them that it was no use quarantining the Moon, because the nanomachines had already reached Earth. Humans would not be able to stop them from doing whatever they had been programmed to do, and so it made no sense to keep Erika up there as a hostage. They might just as well let her come back home so she could work with him here to solve the problem!

But he did not want to tell McConnell about his discovery. Not yet. Her reactionary tactics—such as ordering the destruction of the Collins—frightened him. What would she do upon learning that automata had landed on Earth? What would the rest of the population do? Already, signs of panic manifested themselves across the world, fear of the invisible enemy approaching too closely. The terror would only increase once people learned that the enemy was already here, that it was already too late.

At MIT, that egotist Taylor had refused to go to work for a week and he had assigned all his grad students to different duties. Maia Compton-Reasor had spent money out of her own pocket to hire security guards around her labs at Stanford.

The contamination of the moonbase had already proven that research precautions were not sufficient against such sophisticated automata. Parvu could never be completely assured of his own safety, no matter how many preventive steps he might take. Certainly, no one would ever come to work with him now. He wondered how long it would take before radical activists came plodding across the snowpack to wave signs around in front of the NIL—or perhaps they would do more damage than that.

Soon, Parvu would probably receive orders to shut down his work in Antarctica and come home—after obliterating the viable prototypes in the nanocore. It would be such a waste, after their tremendous success.

He didn't have much time. Erika didn't have much time. Perhaps, the Earth didn't have much time. But he had to do something to help Erika first, to find a way to get rid of the mechanical organisms in her bloodstream. The image of her dissolving into a disassembled pool of fluids and protoplasm made him wince. He stumbled toward the double airlock doors. He had to get back into the lab.

Parvu had twelve specimens of the dormant alien automata to work with. And he had only one tool with which to study them.

His own prototype assemblers had been tremendous successes in their own small way. They had been designed to study samples for microstructure, to disassemble and analyze test objects, and to transmit information back out to the nanocore's collating computers. He would let them study the inert alien machines. There was no telling what they might find.

Somehow it seemed fitting. He would use his own clumsy prototypes to study those far more efficient ones.

Suddenly it seemed brash to him, exciting. But he would be doing it for Erika. It was his only hope. And besides, what was the NIL for—with all its drastic containment precautions—if not risky work like this?

He increased the volume on Rimsky-Korsakov's "Scheherazade" and went to dress for the clean-room. As the music swept him up and away into imaginary places, he thought it appropriate for the wonderland he might now be encountering.

He could see the nanocore pillar in the center of the lab. The nutrient solution was murky from the population of self-replicating prototypes he had been testing for weeks. Now he was going to introduce them to something much more sophisticated.

He only prayed he would not concoct some sort of monstrous changeling.

moonbase columbus

Jason Dvorak watched the last evacuee from the Collins struggle through the moonbase airlock. Though the lunar gravity was only one sixth of Earth normal, it seemed overpowering to the crewmembers who had spent the last four months in zero-G. Normally all personnel would have been gradually acclimated for a return to a gravity environment, but the nanotech infestation had not allowed any time for that.

Now, in the Columbus receiving area, all seventeen evacuees cycled through the electrostatic dust-suppression unit as they entered the base. Lunar dust hung in the air, and the filtration system couldn't cleanse the receiving complex fast enough. Everyone began coughing as soon as their helmets came off. As one of the first to be processed, Bernard Chu stood silently beside Jason like a conquering hero returning to reclaim the land that was rightfully his.

But the matter of Erika Trace burned foremost in Jason's mind. The sandy-haired young woman had seemed to light up Columbus when she had first appeared ... what, two weeks ago? She had been so fresh, so nervous, so out of place among the other crewmembers. Her youth and naivete had reminded everyone of normal life back on Earth, and hinted at the tourists and adventure seekers that were to come when the moonbase became a full-fledged outpost. Her attitude was a welcome change to the matter-of-fact professionalism that permeated the colony.

But this fresh-faced woman had brought the terrible nanotech infestation right into their homes. Through her incompetence, she had cut them off from any possibility of returning to Earth.

They would probably all be dead in a few days, because of her mistake. Jason would never again see his children. He would never learn exactly what the Daedalus construction was meant to represent. He felt like a jackrabbit on the road at night, frozen by approaching headlights.

How many centuries had it taken humans to reach the Moon? To establish a precarious toehold on a bit of lunar rock that still demanded the utmost of combined technology for simple survival? Yet the whole effort—billions of dollars, trillions of rubles and yen—were now wasted because of an alien infection caused by what must have been a moment of carelessness on the part of this young woman.

Watching Erika as she struggled out of her spacesuit in the receiving dock, Jason felt anger well up inside. He had liked her a lot, but now his jaw involuntarily tightened. She had ruined everything for them.

But yet—

What did they have to gain by lynching Erika Trace?

Jason knew deep down that it was not her fault. She hadn't done anything not demanded of her by Director McConnell. Erika had never wanted to come up in the first place. But Jason couldn't bring himself to transfer the blame completely, not now. He had to have a scapegoat, someone that he could shake a finger at, didn't he? For a disaster of this magnitude!

Everyone else felt the same way, from the grumbling he had heard in the tunnels. He wondered who would get Erika first—the alien nanomachines or the angry moonbase inhabitants.

The last evacuee stumbled into the airlock. The woman removed her helmet and started coughing from the floating dust. Newellen squeezed through the lock behind her.

The dust shield around Newellen's mouth looked like a button on an oversize clown, but at least it kept him from coughing like the others. When he spoke to Jason, the filter muffled his voice. "Have you heard the word from Earth? We didn't catch the latest on the riots."

"Riots?" Jason lifted an eyebrow. *With all that was going on, who would think to listen in on any of the Earth channels?* "We've only kept in contact with the Agency the last few days, and they didn't mention anything like that."

Newellen rolled his eyes. "Surprise, surprise."

"What is going on, Big Daddy?" asked Chu. Jason wondered if McConnell would give Chu his command back . . . and if he himself really cared.

Newellen rubbed his hands along his coveralls, then snorted as none of the dust went away. He looked at Jason, then Chu. "Well, since nothing's left of the Collins, I trained the directional antenna back to Earth, picked up the newsnet broadcasts relayed up to geosynchronous sats. It was a little weak, but I'm sure we could pick up the sidelobes here—"

"The news, Big Daddy," said Jason in exasperation. "What's going on?"

"You mean the riots? Earth seems to be going absolutely apeshit—marches, riots, protests, all that type of thing."

Jason turned to Chu. "Did you hear anything about this before you abandoned the Collins?"

Chu merely shrugged. "We had an open line to the Space Agency, but they indicated nothing for us to worry about. Of course, they didn't bother to consult me about blowing up my station either. 'We can never afford to have anyone set foot on the Collins again,' Celeste says. She made damn sure of that!"

Jason looked around. The evacuees had been ushered off to the infirmary for checkups and monitoring. Jason didn't know how they were going to fit seventeen more people into the limited quarters! Crowding would make tensions rise even higher, but there were going to be some mighty close friends before this was over. If anybody survived.

Chu nodded in the direction of the control center. His face looked flat and tight, his skin stretched like a drumhead over his cheekbones. "Let us find out what is going on. If Celeste is feeling a great deal of pressure, she may decide to do something . . . drastic."

As they started for the control center, Chu held out a hand to steady himself against the wall, but once he got his step, he seemed to be all right. They passed through two airlocks and a series of interconnecting tunnels through the buried modules to reach the domed control center. The tunnels were constructed of inflatable foil, made rigid by an interlocking agent.

Once in the control center, Jason called to Cyndi Salito, sitting at one of the duty stations. "Anything unusual over the link to the Agency?"

"Nothing out of the ordinary," she said. Salito had been scheduled to go home on the next rotation of crewmembers to Earth; now she would be stranded on Columbus with the rest of them.

"No news flashes, public unrest?"

"Should there be?"

Chu stepped up. "Have you been monitoring anything other than the Agency channels?"

"Just listening in on Agency Select." The semiofficial channel carried news items, human interest stories, and some of the more popular shows that highlighted the United Space Agency's efforts. Jason knew that the crewmen didn't have the time or inclination to call up and pay for commercial video, and the Select channel normally did an outstanding job of distilling what was important out of the hundreds of drivel newsnets. It was generally hard to pick up the commercial nets anyway with sufficient resolution to make them worth watching.

"I suggest we try some other frequency. Tune in one of the commercial channels," Chu said to Salito.

Jason felt embarrassed to be caught so much off guard in front of his predecessor. He had never thought the Select newsnet would turn out to be a one-way propaganda filter.

Seconds later the talking head of one of the commercial networks appeared in a cube, worms of purple and gray static lacing through his 3-D image. "Locked on," said

Newellen. Standing next to Salito's station, he munched on a sandwich, probably retrieved from a hiding place in the control center.

"—since the startling video transmission of astronauts dissolving on the Farside of the Moon and the discovery of an enormous alien construction being built there. The United Space Agency still vehemently denies that the phenomenon has spread to anywhere else on the lunar surface."

The announcer's head faded out to show footage from one of the flyovers of the growing Daedalus construction, looking like a gigantic diamond water lily sprawling across the crater floor.

"We switch now to Julia Falbring, our science corre-spondent with Dr. Maia Compton-Reasor, a prominent researcher in nanotechnology at Stanford University in California. Julia?"

"Thank you, Tom." The image resolved to show a curvaceous blonde. Besides the fact that she wore a minimum of clothing, Julia Falbring's skin, hair, and even voice were so perfect Jason thought she must be a com-puter-generated sim-person, living only in some cyberworld.

"Here at Stanford, Dr. Compton-Reasor heads a group of researchers at the cutting edge of technology." A short African American woman appeared beside her; red-rimmed glasses slid down her nose.

Jason found his mind wandering as the holotank filled with an artist's conception of a tiny molecular construct. He looked around. The control center was crowded with more than the normal number of people. Most of the Collins crew would still be checking through the infir-mary.

Erika was not among those who had come to the control center, though she would not have been much affected by the change in gravity. He wondered if she would hide herself away at the Sim-Mars lab again, keep working with the nanomachine specimens. Jason considered calling her to his office, but thought better of it. If *he* had been responsible for infecting the crew, he'd want to hide as

167

well. Jason turned back to the holotank and the commercial newscaster.

"—and with that in mind, I think we all have something to ponder, Tom."

"Thank you, Julia." The newscaster swung around in his chair as a corner camera took the shot from another angle. "And finally, we have live in our studio Major General Simon Pritchard, special assistant to the director of the United Space Agency. General?"

"Thank you, Tom." The view drew back to encompass the features of General Pritchard. He sat back in his seat, relaxed, with one leg crossed over the other. His Air Force uniform looked immaculate. It was plain, blue, and not overladen with the medals or emblems so popular with the other military services. Jason remembered Pritchard as the man who had been with Director McConnell when Columbus sent the first telepresence explorer to Daedalus.

"General, just how seriously is the Agency taking this threat of alien technology? We've just seen through our special-effects studios how an entire planet might be devoured if nanotechnology is allowed to run rampant. Is there anything we can do?"

"Well, first Tom, we're not sure this is *alien* nanotechnology. That's all conjecture right now, though the Daedalus artifact is indeed being built by microscopic machines.

"We still have no idea what the big construction will turn out to be or when it will be finished. Because of the extremely hazardous environment surrounding the site, we cannot even send remote vehicles to explore it directly. We're working with very limited information." Pritchard folded his hands in his lap.

"We're trying to cover all our bases. An eminent team of life science specialists manning the Lagrange waystation Collins has been shipped to the Moon, to assist in the examination of this phenomenon. They even recommended destroying the Collins so there would be absolutely no chance of infestation—"

"What?" interrupted Newellen in the control center. He looked around the room. Chu stood mute. Jason scowled at the screen.

"—in fact if this were a runaway nanotech threat, all the experts agree that the entire Moon would have disassembled days ago. So really the situation has been blown out of proportion. Granted that the unfortunate accident to Trevor Waite and his companions was widely disseminated, some evidence suggests that all three of them merely had a case of massive micropuncture, perhaps from an anomalous meteor shower. And, yes, the destruction of the Collins was costly . . . but it shows how far our astronauts are willing to go to ensure Earth's safety."

"I can't believe it!" The Columbus control center filled with a storm of response.

"Quiet!" yelled Jason. "He's trying to build a cover story. Let's just see how the hell this turns out."

Newellen grumbled as he waved up the volume.

The newscaster nodded sagely. "But suppose this is something out of sci-fi—you know, what if the Andromeda strain were to really exist, an alien robot virus that could wipe out our world? What would we do then?"

Pritchard's face went stone-cold. "That is why the United Space Agency appointed me as their military deputy, Tom. If anything ever arose that would harm the sovereignty of the United Space Agency's signatory countries, we are prepared to deal with it in the swiftest, most decisive manner. The old methods of using conventional procedures would simply not work against such an insidious threat. Thus, we are prepared to do all we can, if need be."

The video took a close-up of the general. Jason could see muscles working in Pritchard's jaw.

"Swiftest, most decisive manner?" the newscaster asked. "What precisely can we do to prevent this thing from getting to Earth? After all, we've got a crew of what, seventy or so people on the Moon, including those from the Collins?"

Pritchard waited a beat before answering. "Let me make myself perfectly clear. The military has many options that will prevent the contamination of Earth. We may have to make some tough choices."

"Exactly what types of choices, General?"

"Let's hope it never comes to that," Pritchard said with an edge to his voice. "And you must remember that everyone on Moonbase Columbus is aware of the consequences and the risks they accepted when going up there. *We cannot risk contaminating Earth*—that is the paramount concern."

Newellen shouted over the buzz that started to rise around the control center. "What the hell is he talking about? Has he written us off, or what?"

"Switch back to Select," said Jason quietly.

"What?"

"I said switch to Agency Select." Few grumbled when a second image slid into the cube, sharing space in the cube with Pritchard's interview. An old video of a space shuttle shot filled the cube. The hushed voice of the narrator described what an awesome task it was to be in space to stay.

"They're not even covering the news conference," Jason said.

Chu snorted. "They're interviewing McConnell's deputy about leaving us high and dry on the moonbase, and Select is showing reruns."

Jason thought for a moment before speaking. "Does that tell you how much Director McConnell really cares about what happens to us up here?" In his mind he saw an image of the abandoned Collins self-destructing in a silent fireball. "What does she have in mind?"

sim-mars

Back at the Sim-Mars lab module, Erika felt as if she were the only sane person remaining on the Moon. There was really no need for her to continue her investigation in isolation; Columbus certainly had enough laboratory space, equipment, and experts in the life sciences to assist her.

But Erika didn't want their help as much as she wanted to be alone. She had to get away from all the angry glares. The people blamed her for releasing the samples, for infecting everyone on Columbus.

She went over and over her procedures, trying to discover where she had slipped, where she had breached her own rigid experimental protocol. Even Parvu couldn't see what she had done wrong. But the nanocritters were so resourceful that they could have gotten through any barrier she tried to erect. She had been foolish to think otherwise.

So what were the nanocritters waiting for? Something must have changed inside of them. Did it have anything to do with the Disassemblers vanishing from the regolith samples? How had the nanocritters modified their programming to know not to disassemble people?

Nanocritters. The half-whimsical nickname didn't seem humorous anymore. Not when she had billions of them coursing through her bloodstream, waiting for some signal to destroy her. If indeed that was what they were waiting for.

171

Compton-Reasor's group at Stanford, Taylor's at MIT, Sommerveld in Belgium, and even Parvu had offered every assistance from afar. Some pondered the problem with computer models, others configured mock experiments. But simple suggestions were worth only so much, and working over the 240,000-mile telepresence link was far too cumbersome, even with slow test procedures.

Erika pulled back from the holographic monitor and stared at the nanomachines swimming through the sample of her blood. Small enough to assemble viruses, the nanocritters were not even noticed by normal human immune-response systems.

She rubbed her eyes and concentrated on the holotank display. She had to find some answers. Her fingers skimmed over the controls, programming the computerized scanner to run another analysis of the blood sample, this time sorting for any nanomachine that did not explicitly match the known configurations of Assemblers, Quality Checkers, Reprogrammers, or Controllers.

The disappearance of the Disassemblers was the crux of the matter, she felt. They had vanished from the regolith samples contained in the Sim-Mars chamber, and they had not appeared in any of the infected blood samples, though all the other types of nanocritters had been passed on.

As far as Erika knew, the Disassemblers could be hiding, massing for an attack. And if that happened, there would be no warning. Everyone on the Moon would dissolve in an instant. She couldn't imagine how it would feel—like being eaten alive by billions of hungry ants?

Erika activated the scanner, setting the computerized machinery in motion. The scanner initiated a shape-matching algorithm of the nanotech machines in Erika's blood against the stored templates. The microwaldoes and their imaging sensors traversed the drop of blood like a giant ocean liner plowing across a pond. On the holotank's screen, nanocritters were caught up in the microwaldoes' wake, twirled around in the turbulent flow.

She glanced at the backup telepresence units. Identical to the sealed infection chamber at which she now worked, the three other units displayed similar statistics on their flatscreen panels. Each of the Earthbound teams was conducting separate and independent investigations, but no one had suggested what to do about the infestation. Because of the light delay in the feedback loop, their telepresent microwaldoes moved unsteadily though their samples.

Even as the millions upon millions of nanocritters were examined, cataloged, and discarded, Erika knew that it would take hours to completely analyze the sample. She pushed away from the station and stood, stretching.

She padded to the coffee machine at the back of the lab and circled back to the holotanks. Tucking her legs beneath her, she made herself comfortable and waved on the communications tank. "Jordan Parvu, please."

The screen blinked, waited for the signal and response from the NIL, then Parvu's face filled the holotank. It took a second, but the sleepiness in his eyes disappeared as he recognized Erika. "I hoped it was you, Erika! I was wondering if you had made any progress."

"No." She shook her head. "Still no luck." The light delay made Parvu's expression seem frozen in the tank.

Erika sipped at her coffee. "How are things going down there? I haven't heard how the rest of the world is taking this. And the Agency Select channel is worthless as far as critical information."

"I'm afraid I do not know much more than you. Remember, I am pretty isolated myself. But from what I have heard talking with my son and his wife, people aren't taking this too well. I hear there has been a resurgence in all the old threat-from-space films—*War of the Worlds, Alien, Earth vs. the Flying Saucers*. I have been far too busy trying to think of a way to help you."

Erika sighed. "I wish you were here. What can you do for us down there?"

Parvu hesitated for a moment. He seemed to be uncomfortable with the subject. "I would rather not say at this moment, okay? I have several ideas I am pursuing." He folded his hands in front of him. "How do *you* feel?"

Erika answered carefully. "I'm tired and scared, a little weak, but that can all be explained by my circumstances.

No need to invoke some external agency. As far as I know, no one who's been infected has experienced any . . . changes."

"Perhaps the automata are working on something in your body that you do not know about. How would you know, for example, if they disassembled your appendix?"

"I had mine removed when I was ten."

Parvu waved at the air, then smiled. "Then how would you know if they rebuilt it? Anyway, that was just an example." He shrugged his narrow shoulders.

"I'm having another one of those microcameras sent over to Daedalus today. Still no progress on why the Disassemblers vanished from our samples. That's the key, I think. What if all the Disassemblers have stopped taking material apart and are now finishing up their construction?"

Parvu tapped his fingers together. "I have a different idea. Do you think it has anything to do with the presence of organic material?"

"You mean can the nanocritters tell if they're inside a living organism?"

Parvu placed a thin brown finger on his lips. "I have other evidence I may need to share with you. At this moment, my suspicion is that the automata can indeed determine the difference between organic and inorganic material. And they have instructions not to disassemble living substances."

Erika shook her head. "Even if that were true, they should have disassembled the skin of this lab, my spacesuit, all of our life-support equipment."

Parvu's answer came quietly after the two-second delay. "Perhaps they know to switch themselves off, or at least do nothing more than collect data and replicate themselves inside a living organism without causing damage. You may have been given a reprieve by the alien minds that programmed their scouts."

Erika frowned at the implications. Even the problem of mass communication between the billions of nanocritters seemed too difficult to overcome.

Parvu suddenly looked impatient. "I've got to get back

and rethink a few of these ideas. Tomorrow perhaps we can make further progress. I will contact you soon, Erika."

As Parvu switched off, she couldn't help but wonder if he had a working hypothesis already mapped out. And he had never before refused to tell her what he was doing.

antarctica—
nanotechnology isolation laboratory

Jordan Parvu paced back and forth in the outer ring of the NIL, looking at the glass walls of the nanocore and the sophisticated experimental equipment inside the inner clean-room. He spoke into a voice pickup receiver as he studied the micro-scanning analysis. For future researchers who might need to follow on to his work, he had to make sure he documented everything properly.

Normally his assistant would have done all this for him.

"Playback," he said to the computer. His words came back at him. *"Basic morphology of assay six."*

"Stop!" He hadn't been listening to the words; he had been hearing Prokofiev's *Kijé Suite* in the background. Muttering to himself, he shut down the stereo pipe-in from the living quarters and stood up again. Why was it getting so difficult to perform normal day-to-day activities?

He would have felt comical kicking himself, but that was what he deserved at the moment. He hadn't been paying attention. He had always been meticulous and careful, but now he seemed distracted all the time. Absentminded, wasn't that the stereotype?

He forced his concentration back to the task at hand. "Begin description again," he told the computer. He repeated the date and the assay number once more as he called up images to display what the microwaldoes and scanning optical microscopes were seeing inside the nanocore.

"Link to hypertext file of images," he said. "Begin. The results of my hybrid experiment continue to be fascinating. Somehow, together, the two automata 'species' have . . . combined. My crude prototypes have done their duty of inspecting and studying the few extraterrestrial samples gathered from the snowpack. But they went much further, far beyond a simple analysis.

"The prototypes have somehow incorporated certain design features from the dormant automata—or perhaps their analytical routines managed to switch the dormant automata back on, which then adopted some of the characteristics of my prototypes. It happened very quickly, and we—" He stopped himself. He was the only one now; there was no we. "*I* was unable to take samples rapidly enough to study the exact course of evolution."

He paused to scratch his head. "The two types of machines have become something very new. Something that seems to take the best characteristics of both." He smiled to himself. That was how sophisticated nanotechnology was supposed to work, to seek out design improvements and to incorporate them.

With the music off, he could hear the wind outside howl louder, constant now, hour after hour. Parvu sat up straight as he hissed in surprise. He had forgotten to feed the lab rats again! It had probably been two days. He got up from his chair. How could he keep forgetting?

Despite the progress he had made in creating the hybrid automata, none of that would benefit him—or Erika—unless he could understand what his new toys would do inside the bloodstream. That was the next step.

And it was a very large step.

"Old Gimp" seemed the healthiest of the three rats they kept in the NIL. As he held the animal in the palm of his hand, Parvu remembered that Erika had named the rat because of the two missing toes on its forepaw. Neither Parvu nor Erika could discern whether it was merely a

177

birth defect—not unusual for a lab rat—or whether it had somehow gotten its digits snipped off in the cage door.

Without care for two days, the three rats' food dishes and water bottles had been completely empty. Parvu let Old Gimp eat in peace for a few minutes before taking the rat out of its cage. Now the rat trembled in Parvu's hands. It looked hungry, but none the worse for wear.

Parvu washed the rat with water and disinfectant soap several times. Old Gimp squirmed and fought in his hands, but he needed to make it as clean as possible, to remove the loose white fur.

"This is going to be havoc in my clean-room," Parvu said, speaking to Old Gimp. "But it is all part of the experiment, okay?"

And, he thought to himself, *the Agency is going to shut me down soon. If I do not take chances now, no one else will make the appropriate attempt to find the answers for Erika.*

Parvu returned the rat to its cage, and he dressed up in his clean-room garb. He had no one else to check with, needed no further approvals. He was in charge of everything here, and he had no one to whom he must answer.

This was his show and he could take as many risks as he wished.

Parvu kept losing track of time. The stereo continued to play random musical selections, letting him work for hours with no interruption.

With the rat inside its cage breathing the filtered air of the clean-room, Parvu had no idea how long he had tinkered with the nanocore's fail-safe controls. He knew the passwords, the security interlocks—he had designed the system himself, after all. But he couldn't remember everything.

Finally, when the Klaxon screeched its warning for the fourth time, upsetting Old Gimp inside the cage, Parvu found the main power circuits and shorted across the wires.

The nanocore would allow him access now.

His hands shook as he worked. His actions, the inexcusably risky course he had decided to take by mixing the two types of automata, went completely against his lifetime of meticulousness and care, of rigid adherence to procedures and controls. He himself had been considered a roadblock to other researchers because he insisted on so many double checks.

And now he was sabotaging his own equipment. He, more than anyone else, understood the dangers of unleashing the nanotechnology demon. But he didn't have much time. Erika needed answers now! He couldn't wait.

Using the microwaldoes and tiny capillary pumps that had been intended for seeding analytical samples, Parvu managed to withdraw a small aliquot of the milky nutrient solution filled with billions of hybrids.

He stared down at the nanocore seals with his fingers trembling on the controls before he keyed in the long command sequence that would release the sample. It required three separate passwords. Each time, a warning message told him the peril of his actions. Each time, Parvu overrode it.

The Daedalus automata had already spread three kilometers across the lunar surface. They had already infected Erika and everyone else on the moonbase and on the Collins—but for some reason they had replicated but otherwise gone dormant in the human bloodstream.

He squeezed his eyes shut, driving back the panic. *What if he was wrong?* The clean-room dome was sealed and airtight, but by no means would it contain vigorous nanotech samples if they attempted to breach the walls. What if he was starting a chain reaction that would turn the planet into a ball of Drexler's infamous "gray goo?" Parvu himself would be responsible for bringing a nanotech plague to Earth.

However, he always had the x-ray burst inside the NIL as a last resort. That would disintegrate the hybrid automata, blast himself and everything else with an instantly fatal dose of radiation. It gave him small comfort.

For now, Parvu had to see what the machines would do when they encountered the rat's bloodstream.

Old Gimp squirmed and made a high-pitched noise as Parvu injected it with the sample fluid. "Hold still, please," he told the rat. "This is what you were brought down here for, after all. Did you not read your contract?"

He put the rat back in its cage, left it in the clean-room, and glanced at the chronometer on the wall. Now he would have to be very conscious of time. He had nothing else to do but wait.

Parvu tried to sleep, but it didn't work.

Out of desperation, he decided to call his family, but they didn't answer. Checking the time, he realized that it was the middle of their day; his son would be off to work, the four grandchildren at school.

He very much wanted to call Erika at the moonbase, but he couldn't talk to her about this yet. He did not want to confess the incredible risk he was taking for her sake, until he could be sure it would pay off.

Parvu observed the rat without a break for the first hour, but when nothing seemed to be happening to it, he came back and checked only every fifteen minutes. He couldn't see any change in Old Gimp, but he kept watching, muttering to himself "Come on, come on!" as if urging whatever was going to happen to hurry.

But Parvu realized he didn't want to see *anything* happen. He wanted the rat to remain unharmed by the hybrid automata. He wanted the test to be safe so that he could determine how to help Erika. Any gross change in the rat's body structure would be a step in the wrong direction.

He found he could wait no longer than three hours. Parvu entered the clean-room again, this time not bothering to put on the full outfit, merely the lab smock and booties. *What did it matter?* The rat would have contaminated the inside much more than what he was doing now, and Parvu had already let the hybrids out of their confinement. He had let the genie out of the bottle, and he had to pray that it was friendly.

Picking the rat out of the cage, he held Old Gimp in his hand. The rat seemed perfectly healthy. It didn't tremble or feel warm, but kept squirming in his grip as if it wanted to get down. Parvu stroked it behind the ears. He couldn't remember if the rat's tail had looked so pink and fresh before.

The rat squealed as Parvu stuck it again to withdraw a sample of blood. But Old Gimp seemed unperturbed when he put it back in the cage, as if it had grown used to being pricked and prodded.

He squirted the blood sample into the scanning optical microscope and called up displays on his screens as the apparatus went through its analysis sequence. The realtime images made him hold his breath in amazement.

The rat's blood cells looked like islands across the screen, and around them—like the swarming canoes of invading islanders—hybrid automata moved about. They had infiltrated the cells. They wandered in the proto-plasm, traversed the serum between the cells. Larger substations had been constructed inside the cell nuclei, like control centers. The external units were tiny, of several different designs, like scouts, workers, program-mers. They all had many arms vigorously moving, going about unfathomable tasks. The hybrids looked very different from the images Erika had sent him from the Sim-Mars lab. The automata were certainly no longer dormant.

And the rat did not seem harmed in the least.

Old Gimp scrabbled at the sides of its cage, making a racket. Parvu went over to it, grinning, and bent down to the rat's level. "We have done it, my friend. Though I am forced to confess that you did the most difficult part." He tapped his finger on the wires to stroke the side of the rat's head. Old Gimp raised itself to hold on to the cage, looking up and around with pink eyes.

Parvu blinked twice. All of the rat's digits were intact. The two missing toes had grown back.

Parvu took one step backward. He knew he wasn't imagining this. Then his grin widened farther. Of course! He had known all along about the theoretical reconstruc-tive abilities of properly programmed nanotechnology. Somehow, the sophisticated alien automata and his own prototypes had learned how to analyze the cellular struc-ture of the rat, to determine what was missing and what was wrong—and to fix it. It was just as Parvu had imagined, as he had dreamed.

To progress this far had seemed impossibly out of reach. He had never thought nanotechnology research would come to this point in his lifetime, or even Erika's. All Parvu's doubts were suddenly buried by a sense of wonder.

He found he couldn't keep himself from chuckling. "We will have to find a new name for you, Old Gimp!"

He considered telling Erika this much, at least, so she might have hope, so she might imagine her mentor coming to the rescue after all. But he needed to try one more thing before he could let himself rest. This was incredible!

He took Old Gimp out again and held on to it with one hand. "I believe you are not going to like this, my friend," Parvu said, keeping his voice to a whisper. "But you may be surprised as much as I, okay?"

The knife was thin and delicate, used for trimming wires and scraping deposits from old circuit boards, but it did the job. Parvu brought it down swiftly onto the end of Old Gimp's naked pink tail.

The thin blade snapped and pinged off the lab table. Old Gimp squeaked and whirled in Parvu's grip, trying to bite him, but Parvu held on to the bunched muscles in the rat's back. About an inch of the tail lay severed on the tabletop.

A tiny drop of thick red blood congealed on the end of the stump, but otherwise the tail did not bleed. Parvu had no idea whether that was normal or not. Lizards didn't bleed much when they shed their tails—what about mammals?

In the conference room, the chimes signaling an outside transmission suddenly rang out.

Parvu grumbled to himself, looked down at the rat without knowing what to do. No one made social calls to the Nanotech Isolation Lab, so every transmission had to be considered important. Parvu thrust the rat back into its cage.

Perhaps the caller was Erika.

He closed the cage door as the transmission chimes rang out again. He forced himself to be careful, to fasten the cage door so that Old Gimp could not escape, and ran to the double exit doors.

The chimes rang a third and fourth time before Parvu managed to answer them. Panting, he stared at the screen as a spacesuited image filled the field of view. A gloved hand reached up to flip up the faceplate.

"Hey, Doc!" Kent Woodward said. "Did I catch you napping or what?"

"Hello, Kent. I am very sorry. I was busy in the lab." Anxious to get back to his tests, he sighed. He wanted to waste no time on small talk, but he couldn't say anything, especially not to a hotshot like Kent. "And what can I help you with? Surely this is not a social call?"

"We're not allowed to make social calls, Doc. This is a serious mission we're on here." He grinned. "I got another bunch of snowpack samples, like the last ones I brought over."

Surprised, Parvu didn't know what to say for several seconds. "But I did not request these samples."

"I was bored." Kent shrugged in the bulky spacesuit. "I'm afraid these won't be from quite as undisturbed and pristine snow cover, though. That storm is really whipping things up."

"Storm? Ah, yes." The insulated plates showing the outside view displayed mostly Antarctic darkness, with white wind swirling across the landscape.

"You seem preoccupied, Doc. Better watch out you don't get a rep as an absentminded professor. Say, can you tell me what all this sample gathering is about, anyway?"

Parvu considered, then gave what he thought would be the best answer. "Something for Erika. And I am making great progress." Kent would be excited by that—surely, he must know of Erika's predicament and the quarantine of all those on Moonbase Columbus?

"Okay, uh, so I'm on my way over to drop these samples off. No time for a shower today though. Gotta get back to base before Bingham Grace has a bird. I shouldn't be out in this storm, but hey—there's dust storms on Mars, right? This is all part of the simulation! Good training!"

He switched off. Parvu had no idea how far Kent had to travel to reach him, but he could not wait for the young man. He had to see what was happening to Old Gimp.

Returning to the clean-room, Parvu pulled on rubber gloves, but took no other precautions. The gloves were important to him to keep the automata from contaminating his hands, though certainly the poreless rubber would not stop the machines from spreading, if they were so inclined.

The hybrids were loose in the environment now, escaping from the rat's skin, from its exhaled breath, from the droplets of blood exposed to the air when Parvu had cut off its tail. He had probably inhaled them already.

He had taken outrageous chances. It was stupid and extraordinarily risky. Inexcusable. In fact, he had gone past the point where he could ever regain his professional ethics—but that no longer mattered to him. He had gambled everything on his hybrids.

As he stared into the cage now, at the rat moving from corner to corner, as if looking for something to eat, *and saw its clean pink tail restored, good as new*—he knew that the desperate gamble had paid off.

The hybrid automata worked. They were not a threat—and now perhaps he could use them to save Erika. And the other contaminated people stranded on the moonbase, of course.

Many major questions remained—could he somehow find a way to use these "good" automata to eradicate the dormant ones in Erika's body? Could he replace or reprogram the ones inside Erika so that they would repair and maintain her body, just as they were doing to Old Gimp? All of Drexler's visions of perfect health, protection from injuries, lack of aging, possible immortality, flashed through his mind. Erika and the moonbase inhabitants could be the first.

Such a fantastic breakthrough would turn everything around. Regardless of what the Daedalus construction was, the alien nanotechnology had shown a way to help all of humanity. This could change the world's paranoia about nanotechnology into appreciation for the magical cures fallen from heaven.

Parvu had to contact the moonbase and let Erika and everyone else know. He had to give all the details to Maia

184

Compton-Reasor, and Celeste McConnell, and Maurice Taylor. He had to make some sort of statement for the newsnets, find a careful way to describe what he had done without making it look like he had taken so many inexcusable chances.

By doing so, he had perhaps single-handedly saved humanity.

Parvu felt like a schoolboy as he went to the teleconference room. He fidgeted in the chair and worked and reworked the words in his mind. He wondered what Erika's reaction would be. She had looked very frightened last time, her eyes sunken and withdrawn.

But Parvu could change her fear. He keyed in the proper access codes and commanded the optical transceivers to adjust to a different satellite pickup that would direct his communication to the moonbase. He had not used it in several days, keeping quiet and out of touch as he did his risky experiments. But now, when the optical transceivers tried to realign themselves, a message flashed on his screen. "ERROR—ABORT."

Parvu stared at the screen and tried again, but the monitor displayed the same message. "Inquiry," he said, requesting the reason for the error.

"UNABLE TO DIRECT ANTENNA."

Parvu stared. He didn't know much about how to fix the equipment, but he had the manuals on-line and in hypertext. Parvu canceled his command and then went back out to the living quarters. He would have to go outside and take a look first.

It would be tedious suiting up, but the wind and the Antarctic cold could do major damage to the human body in a very short time, especially in a storm like this. He didn't want to take chances, not now.

He opened the closet. Erika had left her spare parka inside. He felt a pang. Little landmines of memory like this kept popping up, small items she had forgotten, projects she had started but never finished. And she never would finish them, unless she came back home.

Parvu got the insulated flexible pants and tugged them

over his own loose trousers, then sealed them around his waist. He pulled on the parka cap, the gel-impregnated face-shield, then fitted the hood over his hair and sealed it tight against his cheeks. He tugged on his mittens and congratulated himself at finally having finished.

Outside, he took a deep breath of the knife-edged air, startled at how cold it was, and how fresh. He had not set foot outside the NIL for weeks, a month perhaps. Maybe not since he had bid Erika goodbye.

The steep crags bordering the NIL on two sides blocked off most of the wind, and jutting rock on the third side diverted it farther, all of which made the isolation laboratory nearly impossible to reach via overland long-distance helicopters. Now, the rough formations turned the wind into a vortex, blasting ice crystals and snow horizontally into an abrasive, stinging force that hissed against the hood of his parka.

Parvu stepped into the storm and sealed the door behind him. Just the look of the blizzard made Parvu shiver, though none of the cold had penetrated his layers of insulation. He trudged across the snow and rock toward the optical transceivers.

A pearly white light from the snow lit up the landscape. The optical transceivers stood like skeletal silhouettes glistening as he approached. He saw clods of ice that had fallen to the ground—and sheared-off scraps of metal.

Staring at the girders and the sheltered mirrors, Parvu needed only a moment to determine what had gone wrong. The storm had frozen up the hydraulic guiding mechanisms. Though every cranny had supposedly been protected from the onslaught of weather, the long barrage of the storm had penetrated even those defenses. When Parvu had attempted to adjust the pointing array from inside the NIL, something had snapped.

He would have to fix the mechanism before he could talk to anybody. He wasn't certain he could complete the repairs at all, and he certainly couldn't do it in this blizzard.

Worse, in his attempts to redirect the jammed pointing array, he had managed to move it out of alignment before the hydraulics had broken; now he couldn't even talk with the others in the United Space Agency or even the Mars practice base. Nobody would bother to check up on him until he had been silent for more than a week. He rarely made contact with the outside more frequently than that.

The NIL was effectively incommunicado except for whatever short-range radio transmissions came in, and none would with all the intervening rock outcroppings and the storm. He couldn't tell Erika his news. He couldn't find out what was happening to her. That would be the worst part. Damn all the other inconveniences!

He cursed as he staggered back to the NIL. He pulled off his thick gloves, but otherwise remained suited up. He felt cold to the bone, though not from the weather. Now what was he going to do?

Parvu stood inside for several moments before he finally recognized the insistent hum of the warning beacon inside the communications room. Another message? Who could be sending a warning, and how could he receive it without his optical transceivers on-line?

He unsealed his parka and hurried into the other room, activating the RECEIVE switch. It was an automatic Mayday beacon on a regular radio frequency—from one of the Mars rover vehicles.

It must be Kent Woodward. Something had happened to him in the storm.

Parvu touched the controls again. It would be a broad-spectrum Mayday; he didn't need to find the exact frequency Kent was transmitting. His answering radio message would be distorted by all the rocks in the vicinity of the NIL, but it might get through. If Kent was close enough.

"Kent, is that you? Please respond. I have received your Mayday. How can I help?"

A loud burst of static came back over the speakers. Parvu was unused to communicating in such a crude way, to listen to weak voice transmissions without video. "Kent! Is that you?"

Another burst of static, enough that he knew someone was trying to speak to him. Finally, deep within the buzzing static, he could make out words. *"Help . . . crevasse. . . ."*

"Kent! This is Dr. Parvu. I will attempt to help you, okay? Please hold on. I will do everything I possibly can, okay?"

He had no idea whether Kent could hear him or not. He switched off the TRANSMIT, then had the computer home in on the automatic beacon. Perhaps he could send the coordinates to the Mars base camp and Kent's astronaut comrades could dispatch a rescue mission.

But Parvu realized he could not accomplish that. If Kent's signal could barely reach him, his own transmission could not penetrate the obstacles to reach the distant habitation modules. Without the optical transceivers, Parvu was out of touch; he could not even ask for help for Kent.

The computer spat back coordinates of a line, projecting them on a topographical map of the area; there wasn't enough information for an exact triangulation of Kent's position. Parvu sat up, startled. Kent was somewhere on that line, still kilometers away from the NIL.

Forging ahead through the storm with those unwanted samples he had gathered for Parvu, Kent had made it most of the distance before plunging into a crevasse.

Parvu stared at the map. He had no training in Antarctic rescue operations—what could he do to help?

He felt a pang. Had he been floating with elation at the success of his hybrid automata only an hour ago? Now things couldn't have felt more different.

Parvu had to chip away ice around the seals of the outer storage cubicle before he could slide the door open. Battery-fed lamps shed low illumination into the darkened interior. He had to move, but he couldn't go fast enough. He felt very old suddenly. He kept pushing ahead, doing what he needed to do one step at a time, though everything threatened to overwhelm him. He could not allow himself to be distracted; he could not let helplessness slow him down.

Kent's life hung in the balance.

He shoved aside heavy boxes of canned and freeze-dried food. A quick check ensured that rope and spotlights were in the Emergency Overland Vehicle; the winch looked operable as well. Neither he nor Erika had ever seriously thought they would need to use the EOV, and he mistrusted the contraption as well. But as he fired up the engine and keyed in the coordinate line the computer had given him, Parvu blessed whatever regulation-chasing clerk had required it to be here.

Parvu left the crags surrounding the NIL behind as the vehicle engine thrust him forward over the bumpy surface. He picked up speed as the locator kept a lock on its position.

Parvu found himself gripping the wheel and squeezing his eyes shut, hoping he could trust the obstacle-avoidance computer. The vehicle rocked and jostled with the wind, and he felt as if he were riding a kayak down white-water rapids.

The journey seemed to take hours. If he hadn't already known it was there, and if he hadn't been watching Kent's homing beacon so closely, Parvu never would have seen the crevasse himself.

He pulled the EOV to a stop, slewing it sideways as it reached the crevasse. A wide lip of ice overhung an outcropping of rock. Kent would not have seen it from his own direction, but it covered a gaping maw in the ice below.

Parvu climbed out of the EOV into the blasting wind and grabbed the portable spotlights from the tool compartment. Ducking into the lee of the rock outcropping, he shone the beams out in search of the rover vehicle.

The massive machine had gone front-end first, rolling sideways and crushing the driver's compartment against the sharp ice boulders on the chasm wall. It had wedged about ten meters down. The sides of the metal were torn and gaping. All of the windowports were either spider-webbed or completely shattered from the shock of impact.

As he directed the bright spotlight into the front compartment of the rover, Parvu could see the dark form of a spacesuited body caught among the twisted controls.

He turned and reentered the EOV, his hands shaking from the tension. He drew in several breaths before starting the vehicle, trying to calm himself. Slowly, he backed the EOV up to the crevasse so he could use the winch.

Parvu grabbed all the equipment he could and tried to attack the problem, analyzing how he was going to get down to Kent and retrieve him—if he still lived. Panic and helplessness threatened to seize him again, but he managed to push them aside.

He anchored the EOV and secured himself with a cable to the winch. He thought briefly about allowing the winch to lower him to the rover, but decided instead to pound pitons into the ice wall to use as crude steps. He did one at a time, tying a rope onto each metal spike and praying as he dangled down to pound in another a few feet below.

He managed to work his way down, step by aching step, until at last the wreck was in reach. He uncoiled the rope. Even in the roar of the storm, he heard it slap against the caved-in side of the Mars rover. Parvu used the ice hammer to pry out the front window plate, since that looked to be the easiest access to Kent Woodward.

Kent's spacesuit had probably saved his life. The extra padding had protected him from what would otherwise have been a fatal fall. Parvu crouched with one boot on the buckled control panel and the other still outside on the front of the rover. He bent in, unsealed Kent's helmet, and pulled it off.

Blood had spattered the inside of the glass and streamed down to the young man's mouth. Both of his eyes were shut. As Parvu jostled him to remove the helmet, Kent winced with a sharp intake of breath.

He was alive.

All of Parvu's training suggested that he should leave Kent there and wait for professional help. But out of communications, and with the snowstorm roaring around them, they had no choice, no choice at all. Kent would likely die when Parvu took him back to the NIL—but he would certainly perish if Parvu left him out here any longer. He would have to haul him up with the winch.

The cold would soon get to Kent. Parvu put the helmet back on. He noted the torn portions of the spacesuit, the seeping blood as he wrapped the cable under Kent's arms, around his knees, and over his shoulders so that he could hoist the young man up.

Kent was definitely bleeding internally. There was no telling how many broken ribs he had suffered, and since he coughed blood, he had probably punctured a lung as well. Parvu hoped that the helmet was padded enough to have prevented Kent from suffering a fractured skull.

At least, Parvu thought, *the cold temperature probably helped.* The frigid air would have slowed Kent's metabolism, kept the bleeding in check.

Parvu felt his adrenaline flowing. His heartbeat pounded inside his head, right behind his eyes. Somehow, he found the energy to haul Kent out of the wrecked driver's seat and pull him from the rover. He left the astronaut dangling as he tied a rope onto the highest piton he could reach.

This is going to be a nightmare, an absolute nightmare. Parvu drove back the thoughts of panic again, and concentrated on hauling himself up to the next piton.

Piton after piton, he clawed up the ice wall. The ten meters seemed like a kilometer. Parvu hung there with the destroyed rover below and the EOV seemingly an infinite distance above.

It occurred to him just how alone he was now, stranded. Even when they got back to the NIL, Parvu had nothing more than a sophisticated first-aid kit.

Reaching the top, Parvu pulled himself over and staggered for the winch. He tried not to think about how tired he was, the aches from climbing in the punishing cold. The EOV's engine coughed as the machinery kicked in, but ever so slowly, the line started reeling in, pulling Kent up from the crevasse.

Kent's body bounced against the wall as Parvu hauled him up, leaving stains on the ancient ice. Though Parvu tried not to think of it, his mind kept shouting the thought at him—*Kent Woodward would never survive this.*

washington, d.c.

Major General Simon Pritchard had given many one-on-one interviews, but this was his first national press conference. Beside him, as she prepared to accompany him to the podium, Celeste McConnell squeezed his arm in support. He nodded to her. Though small in build, with a wiry frame and nonthreatening features, Pritchard had a no-nonsense look. His dress blouse was impressive, portraying a man of total authority, someone to be counted on in a time of crisis. That was the persona Celeste had asked him to project.

Pritchard's normal environment was scientific conferences, closed-door political meetings, and military briefings—nothing like this PR show. He was accustomed to his colleagues jetting in from across the country, all shoved into the same cookie-cutter hotels, meeting each other in restaurants and talking about advanced conventional weapons. The conference attendees wore business suits: the east coasters like a second skin, the west coasters like a hot blanket.

Pritchard was used to closed meeting halls, messed-up transfers of security clearances, boring multimedia presentations put together by scientists who should better have spent their time doing science than trying to concoct dog-and-pony shows. He thought of the stale coffee, the prepackaged breakfast pastries always provided during morning break, the evening receptions and required social engagements when he would rather have been back in his room curled up with a book.

Despite the complaints, Pritchard knew how to deal with such situations. This wasn't to be that type of conference, though. Today, he had to sway the public opinion of the entire nation, possibly the world.

Already, he could hear the press corps waiting to impale him with uncomfortable questions devised by digging into every detail of his life, while completely ignoring the point of the prepared multimedia statement. Pritchard should have warned his three brothers on their blue-collar jobs—they would probably be targeted for surprise interviews within a day or two.

He didn't dwell on what the newsnet reps might come up with—had anybody in his extended family done something appalling? Did his mother wear strange underwear? Did one of his brothers give financial contributions to South American regimes? No doubt he would find out in a few minutes. The newsnet reps would spring it on him.

"You'll do fine," Celeste whispered in his ear. "Just stick to the topic. They'll try to lead you around by the nose, but you must make sure you get our point across. We have to stand strong. I need your support." She squeezed his arm again.

"You're on!" the assistant called from offstage.

Pritchard heard the announcer introducing him and Celeste. The hounds would most likely be after her, since they were familiar with the director of the United Space Agency. He narrowed his eyes in a flash of protective instinct, but then washed it away. The petite, dark-haired Ice Lady could fend for herself better than he could help her.

Pritchard stepped up to the podium. He looked at the crowded people eagerly waiting to misquote him. He stood in silence for a moment, waiting for the right time.

"Gentlemen, ladies, because of the discovery of an alien infestation on the Moon, you have all heard a lot about nanotechnology in the past several weeks. You have covered that story from many angles already. Now it is time to ask the next question, a topic that seems more unthinkable even than the Daedalus discovery. What would happen if these microscopic alien robots got loose on Earth?"

Working the controls on the podium face, Pritchard illustrated his points with a slow-dissolve sequence of images from the Daedalus construction, which appeared to be approaching completion. The high-resolution flyby photos showed the emerging arches, the diamond-thread superstructure, the sloping petals of the main foundation, and the pit at the center of the complex.

Next, as Celeste had requested, Pritchard hit them with the invasion scenario. Aliens sending out an expeditionary force of nanomachines, building an outpost on the Moon and waiting for the main ships to follow at a slower speed.

Pritchard showed them scanning optical micrographs of the Daedalus nanomachines Erika Trace had investigated—and then subsequent micrographs of the same, or similar, nanomachines lying dormant in her bloodstream. The gathered people already knew the story, of course. Celeste had released the story after only a day of cover-up; it was difficult to downplay the abandonment and destruction of an entire space station. But this was the first the newsnet reps had seen of the actual comparison views.

Celeste stepped up beside him and leaned over the microphone amplifier. "When you look at these alien destructive devices, some of you may recall the old-time videogame of Pac Man." She waited, but no one seemed to know what she was talking about. Pritchard barely remembered it himself, and he had spent a great deal of time studying computer simulations.

Celeste continued, as if confident that everyone recognized her analogy; that way, the newsnet people felt inadequately informed, instead of Celeste having to admit a mistake. "Like Pac Man, the alien assemblers zip through their medium—whether it be lunar regolith or human tissue—gobbling up the raw materials they need to self-replicate, molecule by molecule, building copies of themselves or constructing whatever structure they were programmed to build."

She showed a montage of images from the Daedalus Crater. "Given free rein, these alien nanomachines will wipe out everything in their path. You have seen accounts of army ants on the march in South American rain forests, stirred up by the waves of construction going on down there." She smiled sardonically. "Well, think of that devastation covering this entire planet. We have to make sure the alien infestation never ever reaches Earth. That is why we took such extreme countermeasures once they were discovered on the Collins."

Pritchard summoned another series of images that made him uncomfortable. Celeste had insisted that he pull the heart strings, and this would certainly do it. But the tactic did not make him feel very admirable.

The face of a smiling man filled the screen, enlarged from an old personnel record that was never meant to be used for any high-profile purpose.

"This man was Trevor Waite. You probably recognize him from your first coverage of the Daedalus discovery. His colleagues called him 'Can't Wait' because he was always in a hurry to get his work done."

He advanced to the next frame. "Another familiar face. This man is Siegfried Lasserman. He remained in the hopper as the contact and MainOps. His service record is on file. It is truly exemplary."

Finally, he showed a slender young black woman who was smiling a great deal more than the first two men. "And this is Becky Snow. She had been on the Moon for only a few weeks. She was accompanying these other two out to Farside as part of her qualification requirements. The three of them had no warning, no indication that they were heading out for anything more than a simple repair mission."

Pritchard fixed his gaze on the newsnet corps in the room, as if demanding their silence and their respect. "Instead, they discovered the alien construction on Daedalus Crater." He paused for a beat. "They died for it. The alien nanomachines killed them."

Out in the audience, Pritchard could sense an uneasiness bordering on panic. He was certain that many—if not most—of their reports would be heavily slanted, thereby priming the world for drastic measures.

"We are not taking this threat lightly," Pritchard said, gripping the podium hard. "We have some very serious preventive measures that we are even now putting into place. Perhaps they will seem like desperate actions at first, but these are desperate times. One slip, and our entire planet could end up a seething mass of self-replicating machines."

He maintained his silence for several seconds longer than it felt comfortable. "Listen to me. This is our proposal to keep control of the situation. This is what we must do."

Beside him, Celeste nodded her encouragement again.

Simon Pritchard had just made everyone on the planet feel naked and vulnerable—and he was about to sell them clothes.

antarctica

On the day after the storm, Antarctica lay clear, with a star-filled night sky planetariums would envy. A subdued white blanket of moonlit snow covered everything.

The Mars rover tore across the pristine landscape, chewing tracks into the snow, moving on a beeline to its destination.

Inside the vehicle, Gunther Mosby kept shifting his gaze from the terrain to the pilot's seat, where Bingham Grace drove with fixed concentration, probably trying to mask hopelessness.

On the rover's instrument panel, Gunther saw the tracking grid showing their progress toward Kent Woodward's bleating distress beacon. The signal glitched a few times, then returned. The lost rover's battery would be running down, leached by the intense cold.

Kent had finally taken one too many chances. He had defied direct orders, failed to report his position at regular intervals, failed to request authorization before deviating from the daily schedule, failed to obtain approval for his extracurricular activities.

Commander Grace had flatly refused to allow volunteers to search for the lost astronaut in a Class 4 storm severe enough to jeopardize the rugged base camp itself; it was best that no one die searching.

Gunther and the rest of the Mars crew had listened soberly, flinching as the storm pressed against the living modules. He thought he saw a tremble in Grace's lips. Everybody knew that Kent could never survive out in this weather, even if the accident had been relatively minor. And Kent's weak initial transmissions had said something about a crevasse.

When the storm stopped hours later, Gunther began donning his suit. He was surprised to find Grace already suited up. "Woodward's under my command. The others will back us up. We'll go find him. I'm driving. You navigate."

Asking Gunther Mosby to navigate was equivalent to asking an ostrich to fly. But he didn't complain. He wanted to be there when they found Kent. If they found him at all.

The Antarctic night made the search eerie, like a ritual under a full Moon. The locator homed in on the last known position of the rover, leading them to where Kent should have been waiting. The astronauts had all been briefed time and again about survival measures. The Mars rover contained plenty of resources. Gunther imagined finding his friend next to the stalled vehicle, hunching over some jury-rigged heater, drinking reconstituted coffee, and waiting for them to rescue him. Gunther tried not to think of other, more realistic scenarios.

The rover's speed picked up; Grace was anxious to get the bad news over with. But when they lurched over an unseen outcropping of rock, the commander slowed their pace. "We're not going to join him at the bottom of that crevasse," he said. "I'll take it easy."

Gunther swallowed. "Kent would have had me say, 'Fuckin'-A,' I believe."

Commander Grace nodded his helmet slowly. "Yes, that's probably what he would have said."

When they came around a jagged ridge near the location of the lost rover, they suddenly began to receive the distress signal more clearly. Then the rover picked up speed, hurrying the last half kilometer.

Reaching the target point, Commander Grace brought the vehicle to a halt, then switched on the intense broad-beam searchlights to augment the headlights. The rover hissed and sighed as it settled onto its stabilizers.

Gunther didn't wait for Grace to secure the vehicle before he activated the sequence to open the external doors. He stepped down on snow that crunched under his boots. Though the winds had scoured the landscape with ice particles, very little new snow had actually fallen. The hardened surface near the edge of the crevasse had probably been there for decades, with only the topmost layer redistributed by seasonal storms.

Kent was down there somewhere, deep in the jaws of the crevasse.

Gunther peered down into the glaring splash of spotlights on the crevasse walls. He could see the twisted wreck of Kent's rover. Loose snow had settled onto the broken hull, obscuring the United Space Agency logo but showing jagged tears where split metal plates had popped loose.

His stomach sank, tempered by amazement that Kent had not been killed outright in the plunge, that he had survived long enough to activate the distress call and voice a few words into the radio.

Beside him, Bingham Grace spoke through the suit radio. "We need to go down there. Just to make sure." Gunther turned to see that the commander held a cable in his hand; one end had already been clipped to the front of the rover. "Do you want to go down or should I?" Grace asked.

"Me." Gunther took the cable in his gloved hand, looped it around his waist, and clipped it to the safety line on the back of his suit—just the way they had learned to do it in astronaut training. He pulled the cable taut, then backed toward the edge of the crevasse.

The yellow-white glare of the rover's spotlights washed over him. He saw Bingham Grace's silhouette giving him the high sign. Gunther gestured back to him, then eased himself over the lip of the ice shelf.

He felt as if he were falling into a giant jagged mouth. He grabbed the cable more tightly and walked down the rough wall, letting himself drop a few feet at a time. The spotlights glared down, drowning out the stars above. He kept his mind focused on the descent, finding each foothold, securing his weight before seeking another place to set his boot. It seemed a long way down, a long way to fall.

His boots struck the metal side of the rover. He caught his balance, eased his weight onto the wreck, then released the cable. Somehow, he expected Kent to jump out of the rover and wave. "Hey, what took you guys so long?" But he heard only his own muffled breathing in the stillness of the crevasse.

"Anything yet?" Grace's voice came over the suit radio.

"I am working my way forward now." Gunther stopped at the front. The windshield had been smashed out. The pilot compartment was empty. "Commander! He is not here."

"What?" Grace's silhouette came a step closer to the top of the ledge ten meters above.

Gunther made an exaggerated gesture down into the rover. "The pilot compartment is empty. The windshield has been smashed out." Shining his broad-beam light into the dark interior, he saw the bent control panels, the sharp edges that would have stabbed Kent as he sat in the pilot seat. He double-checked for the tangle of a frozen body crammed in a corner, hidden by shadows, but the rover cabin was empty. He saw blood on some of the sharp protrusions.

"Where did he go?" Grace asked.

Gunther stood up outside of the vehicle and turned around, playing his beam on the opposite wall. Something glinted.

"I see pitons. He must have managed to get himself out." Gunther edged his way over to the far wall of the crevasse. The pitons had been pounded into the ice wall at scattered intervals, as if Kent had not been able to think straight. Two of them had been pulled loose during the climb. Gunther's beam fell on patches of blood rubbed against the wall.

"He made it to the top. He was bleeding badly. It has been hours—he could barely walk, and he climbed right out into that terrible storm."

"Shit," Bingham Grace muttered.

Gunther reeled with disbelief and despair. He felt cold inside his suit, though the heaters were working to full capacity. He remembered his astronaut training with

Kent, sharing dorm quarters with him, listening to the other man's constant bragging about his plans for Mars.

On one of the first days at the training center, when Gunther had commented how much he enjoyed the cafeteria food they were being served, Kent had made a sour face, then changed to his 'friendly and helpful' expression. "Why don't you tell the server, then? I'm sure the cook would like to hear all the compliments he can get."

"But I do not know what to say—"

"*Ka-ka.* That's the American term for it. It means 'delicious.' I'll help you with your colloquialisms. Just go up there and tell the server that 'This food is ka-ka!' Really!"

Gunther had thanked him for his help—but the server had snarled at him when he repeated Kent's phrase. Gunther had not found out until weeks later how Kent had been pulling his leg.

Kent always did things like that, but somehow Gunther could not bring himself to resent his partner. Especially not now. Injured, Kent must have crawled to the top of the crevasse and stumbled out into the middle of a blizzard. Gunther knew that they would never find him.

"Come on back up," Commander Grace said.

Gunther grabbed the cable and began the ascent. When he reached the top, he turned and looked across the flat ocean of snow and ice and rock, lit by stars and the rover's searchlights. Somewhere out there, frozen, covered by snow, lay his friend. He recalled seeing the mummified carcasses of seals trapped where they had died a century before. The bodies of Robert Falcon Scott's disastrous expedition to Antarctica had remained preserved for months before another group had found them at their last camp.

Perhaps Kent Woodward would join them in folklore.

Bingham Grace opened his faceplate to the still Antarctic air. This shocked Gunther; the commander had always been the most strict adherent to the simulated nature of the mission, always dressing and behaving as if they were actually in the Martian environment. The mission had been his entire life. Now, he stood with his helmet open,

Kevin J. Anderson and Doug Beason

his face drowned in the shadows left by the rover's bright lights.

"Commander?"

Bingham Grace turned to him. Gunther saw a stunned, defeated look on the man's normally florid face. "It's over."

Gunther thought he was talking about the death of Kent, but the commander continued, "This has ended our mission. With the Moon quarantined, and the Sim-Mars base contaminated, and now the loss of one of our crewmembers—that alone will spark months of investigative hearings. We are finished. We will never set foot on Mars . . . not us, at least."

He turned and walked back to the waiting rover vehicle. His words continued to come through Gunther's suit speakers. "This is the end. The mission's over. All we can do now is wait for Director McConnell to call us back home."

23

sim-mars

Erika woke with a start. As she opened her eyes, she felt as if she were falling. She reached out to steady herself, and discovered that she was sliding off her chair in a dreamlike, low-gravity topple. Her stomach lurched as she suddenly knew that the disorientation, the buzzing in her head, the vertigo, were all from the nanocritters inside her body. They had finally decided to take her apart. *She was dissolving!* She struggled until the black tatters of sleep finally cleared from her mind.

It took a second until everything came back to her. She was on the Moon, in the Sim-Mars lab module. She must have dozed off while keeping watch on the interminable experiments. They needed some drastic action to get rid of the infection, and it was up to her. And she didn't have the courage, or the imagination, to figure out what she needed to do.

Erika glanced around the lab, blinking away the blur from her exhaustion. In the center of the module, the steel column holding the sterilization apparatus ran straight up from the floor; the holotank was built into the cylinder to save space. Four isolation chambers of varying sizes were set symmetrically throughout the room. She had tests running in two of them, with tandem telepresence verification tests in their counterparts.

Ordinarily, she should have sterilized the Sim-Mars lab two hours ago and requested a new sample from the

Farside crater. But it just didn't make sense to waste an important sample now. The nanomachines were already loose, contaminating everyone and everything on Columbus—what more access could they have? She just had to gamble now.

Especially if what Parvu had suggested was true. Had the Disassemblers really gone into a "fail-safe" mode because they had encountered a living organism? Had they mutated, perhaps, into something dormant . . . until something turned them on again? Some follow-up signal from the faceless aliens? And what other evidence did Parvu have, data he was reluctant to share with her?

Back at Columbus, Jason Dvorak continued to study the growing structure, attempting to second-guess what the nanocritters were building, hoping to find some clues to understand the purpose behind the aliens. By extension, that might provide some insight into how Erika could defeat the infestation in their own bodies. But so far, none of it had helped.

Fighting the stiffness and aches of a bad sleep, Erika picked up her cup of cold coffee from the control panel. Dumping it into the reclamation sink, she prepared a new cup from the dwindling supplies and studied the isolation tank experiments. Still nothing exciting, nothing helpful.

Inside Erika's body, her life was ticking away, dependent on microscopic machines. Even if the aliens had taken enormous precautions, with the sheer number of automata present, surely one of the robot memories would get zapped by a stray cosmic ray and "flip a bit," the electrical equivalent of a hiccup. And if that just happened to switch off the fail-safe mode . . .

Erika had to understand it before she could consider any solutions. She had to know what the Assemblers were doing in her bloodstream, besides multiplying. Were they gathering data—for later? The nanotech Controllers were running the show, giving their Assembler servants every instruction.

A thought came into her head. *If the Controllers can reprogram the nanocritters . . . if a cosmic ray might scramble their instructions . . . why can't I?* Because she didn't have the slightest idea where to start.

She mulled over the thought. Each nanocritter had a memory like that of an antique supercomputer. Altogether, they were very clever, very sophisticated. They had the capacity, but did they have the flexibility, the intelligence to understand?

What if there was a way to reprogram the existing Assemblers, to direct them not to replicate themselves? The population of nanocritters would exist in steady state.

What if she took the next step? What if she managed to program Assemblers to seek out other Assemblers, destroy them, then shut themselves down when they could find no other prey?

A new and improved multipurpose Assembler! Yes, that would be wonderful. But then it would really be a *Destroyer*, wouldn't it? It would cleanse her bloodstream, purge the entire moonbase of the nanotech infestation.

Erika grew excited at the prospect. The only problem was how to go about reprogramming the nanocritters. She had not learned the smallest detail about the operating system resident in the submicroscopic memory cube of each Assembler, nor in the larger controlling stations. Erika herself was no expert in machine languages, though she knew a little about basic programming.

Earth computers had become so intuitive and user-friendly that no one needed to know the nitty gritty details of code. You could tell the computer what you wanted, and it usually accomplished the task. You didn't have to dissect its circuitry to add a new program. And these nanocritters were vastly more complicated and sophisticated.

Erika stopped, flushed with excitement. She set her mouth, feeling as if she were back in grad school again and had stumbled onto the solution of her thesis problem. Except now, the stakes were much higher.

She almost had it. Her muscles were tense, cramping as she hunched over the holoscreen, gripping the microwaldo controls. She was afraid to move, afraid to do anything that might shatter the spell.

Reprogramming the Assemblers.

Instead of trying to induce an electronic or an even more cumbersome chemical change among the nanocritters, why couldn't she take advantage of their heuristic programming? If the Assemblers "learned" to adapt to their environment, why couldn't she modify that environment to produce the results she wanted?

First she had to scramble them, "reset" their rigid programming into something that might be amenable to modification. She had taken a large sample of the nanocritters and bombarded them with radiation—neutrons, charged particles—enough to destroy many of them, and alter the rest. Leave them open to suggestion.

She would try to . . . *train* them. Modify their behavior. Teach them what to do. She couldn't think of any other way to describe it.

She had huge numbers of the nanomachines to work with. Surely some of them would turn out the way she wanted. If she provided the right stimuli, some of them might get the hint.

Erika flipped through her on-line archives, skimming over how B. F. Skinner had set the wheels of behaviorism in motion back at Harvard years ago. The Assemblers had shown a remarkable tendency to learn. All she had to do now was shape their environment to get the intended response, nudge their behavior in the direction she wanted.

The response she wanted would switch the Assemblers to a "Destroyer" mode. But how to do it eluded her. What could she do to encourage them to kill each other?

A voice from the holotank jarred her out of her thoughts. "Dr. Trace?" A message window appeared in the holotank, overriding her background images. "Erika? This is Jason Dvorak."

"What?" She was surprised at the curtness of her response, but the irritation dug at her. *I almost had it!* As she turned to the holotank she pushed back her hair. She realized she must look haggard, a mess. "Yes, what is it?"

Dvorak was in a spacesuit, his helmet off. His image bounced as if he were riding in a vehicle. He looked apologetic. "Sorry if I disturbed you—"

"It's all right," she lied. "How can I help you?"

"I'm about ten minutes away from Sim-Mars. I've decided to come over and help you."

Ten minutes? Her instant reaction was that she didn't want him bothering her right now. She fought the urge to switch him off. Erika had no need for distractions. Now that she felt close to a solution, Dvorak thought it was tourist season. She frowned. But if he was offering to help, then she would put him to work.

"Thanks for the warning. Ten minutes." She smiled sweetly, turning on the southern charm that made everyone think she was a bimbo. *Right.* "Will you need any help getting in?"

He gave the hint of a smile. "No. I know the way."

After Dvorak switched off, Erika caught a glimpse of her reflection on the metallic surface of the sterilization cylinder. *No use being completely uncivil,* she thought. For no other reason than to freshen up, she slipped to the bathroom cubicle. And after washing her face, she decided to brush her hair.

"Hand me that milli, please," she said to him, not looking over her shoulder. When he didn't respond, she said, "The milliwaldo glove, over there." Erika nodded to the set of gloves that hung by the experimental table.

"Sure." Dvorak stood in front of the gloves. They were lined up in descending sequence, color coded with embossed words: DECI, MILLI, MICRO. Dvorak pulled a yellow glove and handed it to Erika.

"Thanks," she grunted. He genuinely seemed to want to help, to be supportive and offer whatever assistance he could give.

She used the glove to guide an array of milliwaldoes against each other, overlapping their splayed fingers to form an enclosed chamber. One by one she placed the milliwaldoes around the enclosure until she had formed a tiny cage only a millimeter in size. Closed, the claws of the milliwaldoes made bars too close-set for any of the nano-critters to push through. A high-voltage electrostatic charge along the surface would keep the nanomachines from disassembling the equipment itself.

Satisfied that her box was sealed and escape-proof, she zoomed the holotank view down by three orders of magnitude. The tiny cage now appeared to be an impenetrable wall.

Still wearing the milliwaldo glove to hold the cage in place, Erika used the microwaldo on her other hand to round up the Assemblers she had earlier bombarded with high-energy radiation. They looked like a horde of bubbling gnats as she herded them into the cage, then pushed a grain of regolith in after them. Sealing the box with another milliwaldo, she locked the waldoes in place before leaning back with a sigh.

Dvorak stood next to her, uncomfortable. After some moments had passed, he finally said, "So what next?"

Erika looked up. Dvorak waited, not pressing the issue. She had not explained her idea to him, though she had thought it would be obvious from her actions. But then she realized that Jason Dvorak was an architect, not a micro-engineer. To someone not versed in research methods, Erika might have been performing some sort of witch-doctor rite.

Erika nodded to the holotank that, at this magnification, still showed the immense expanse of the milliwaldo as a cage for the nanocritters. "We can't come up with some sort of quick purge to get rid of all those nanocritters in our bodies. At least I can't think of anything. We need to find some other way of going about the problem. Come up with a new weapon."

Dvorak's forehead creased with concentration. "So why enclose these things in a box?"

Erika grinned. "These nanotech machines are not dumb. But they're not very smart either, not intuitive. They have a limited amount of intelligence, if you want to call it that, with a whole bunch of sophisticated programming. Look at the Daedalus construction—each one of the Controller substations must carry a complete blueprint of the whole structure! So, I'm hoping they're smart enough to take a hint, if I can make the hint clear to them."

"So what's the hint?"

"I've scrambled them with high-energy particles. Maybe that'll knock out some of their old programming and leave them open to suggestions. I'm trying to teach them a different type of behavior."

Erika poked a finger at the box made up of milliwaldoes. "Here's my rationale: We already know the Assemblers power themselves by using energy from breaking chemical bonds—but they seem prohibited from using organic molecules. At least for now—that's why we haven't been gobbled up. But if they can't break down a few molecules every minute, they'll go dormant."

Dvorak nodded and smiled. But he obviously didn't get it.

"So, I've trapped a lot of those buggers inside my cage here. They can't get out because of the electrostatic fence I put up. I added a grain of regolith to keep them happy for the time being. But once that runs out, and since there's no organic material to cause them to switch off, they start getting hungry."

"So what next?"

"We sit back and wait."

"For what?"

Exasperated that Dvorak still didn't understand, Erika said, "Take an overpopulation of rats in a box and throw in a piece of cheese. If there's not enough cheese to go around, the rats learn a new behavior pattern—when they get hungry enough, they start eating each other."

Dvorak paced behind her chair, as if he were digesting the information. Now that he had shown a healthy interest in her work, she looked at him in a different light. Before, Dvorak had come across as a know-it-all, insisting that she get him some answers. But under the circumstances, with the sudden pressure and the relative newness of his command, and with her coming up to the moonbase requiring special treatment, Erika could understand his reactions.

He didn't look as distant as she had first thought either. Without the thinning spot on the top of his head, his dark curls gave him a youthful appearance. His persistent almost-smile made him appear good-natured, approachable. Even the faint lines around his dark eyes didn't seem threatening. . . .

Jason spoke softly. "So you're training some of these Assemblers to run amok?"

"Well, we can use them to attack the other Assemblers in the bloodstream. If Dr. Parvu's fail-safe theory is correct, they won't be able to do anything to the organic material in our bodies—they won't have any other source of energy, besides other Assemblers."

Jason snorted. "I never thought I'd be saved by cannibals."

Erika didn't mention the other possibility, the nagging fear that had almost made her stop the experiment entirely: She could just as well be training the nanocritters to devour organic material. She had to hope that the restriction was fundamental to their programming and could not be overridden so easily. Otherwise, the moonbase would be disassembled after all.

Tense, Erika trembled as she moved the milliwaldo. Under high magnification from the scanning optical microscopes, her motion made the cage door look like a giant wall grinding slowly to one side.

Seconds later, a flurry of small, dark shapes wiggled past her field of view, moving like bullets into the test solution and beyond the field of view. The rest of the cage was empty.

Jason's voice close behind her asked, "Well, did it work?"

Erika reached up to adjust the counter and ran a slow-motion replay in one of the holotank's cubes. "Watch."

The freed Assemblers sped out of the box, this time on a timescale a thousand times slower than what she had just observed. Something about them reminded her of a submicroscopic wolf pack. She counted only eleven of them—out of the thousands she had corralled.

"Did it work?" Jason asked, worried.

Erika flopped back in her chair and ran a hand through her hair. Her hand started trembling again. But this time she was grinning. "Yeah, I think so. In fact, I'm pretty sure."

Jason remained unconvinced. "You don't sound excited."

Erika cracked a smile. Suddenly she remembered Jordan Parvu hauling out his stash of caviar and celebrating their success with the crude prototypes in the NIL nanocore. "This is all the excitement you get. What am I supposed to do, get up and dance?"

On impulse she staggered to her feet. She hadn't stood up for hours, and even in the relatively low gravity the blood rushed from her head, making her feel dizzy. "If you insist." She grabbed Jason, lifted his arms, and began a clumsy twirl around the lab.

Jason looked shocked, but after a beat he managed to take the lead in a pantomimed ballroom dance that brought Erika to the front of the lab without breaking anything. Once stopped, she held a hand to her mouth and giggled. Jason looked bewildered.

Erika pushed back her hair and put out a hand to steady herself. She noticed her drawl coming back and tried to restrain it. "Ever since I came up here y'all thought I was some sort of wizard called in to save the world. And now I think I just did!" She stopped, at a loss for words.

Jason nodded with a bemused look. "I think I understand. I went through something like that when I first got here, too. I never planned on being put in command of the moonbase. I was just the architect. And now Chu's back."

Erika jumped when Jason placed a hand on her elbow. He steered her back to the holotank. "But we're not cured yet. What do we do next?"

Erika ignored that question as she sat back down. "Why did you come out here to Sim-Mars, anyway? Everyone else—"

"Is scared to death we're all going to die," Jason finished for her. He looked into her eyes and fell silent for a moment. He started to answer, hesitated, then said, "I thought you'd need some help, that's all. Like you said, everything is riding on your shoulders, and I figured you might appreciate another back to carry the load."

"But you're still the moonbase commander. What about your own responsibilities—"

Jason smiled wanly. "Bernard Chu is doing very well, thank you. But that's beside the point right now. You need to save us." He scooted his own chair closer to hers.

Erika blinked. "All right, let me take some blood. I'll inject the, uh, 'nanocannibals' into the sample. We'll use that as a first test."

Jason started rolling up the sleeve of his powder-blue jumpsuit. "I hope you take blood better than you dance!"

She gave the test half an hour longer to run than she had originally intended. This allowed more time for complications to set in, and it permitted her to record a full report of her procedures creating the modified Destroyers.

She preferred her nickname of "nanocannibals," but her peers on Earth would probably say she was being too flippant with a crucial problem. Prudence dictated that she follow a semblance of professional demeanor.

Jason peered over her shoulder as she prepared the solution of nanocannibals and displayed the results. "What's up?"

"Look for yourself. It worked. Every last one of those suckers is gone."

"You mean the nanomachines in my blood?"

"At least the ones in your blood sample. And the nanocannibals don't seem to have damaged any of the blood cells at all."

Jason beamed with relief, then frowned. "What about the last nanocannibal? They all ate each other, right? So the king of the mountain has to be left."

Erika thought for a moment. "Starved to death. Nothing else to eat, you know, and it's prohibited from breaking organic material. We hope."

Jason gestured toward the walls of the Sim-Mars lab. "I still don't understand why they didn't go after the non-organic stuff all around us."

"Why should they? Their behavior was modified to only go after other Destroyers, the only other 'food' they had. We weeded out all the other ones. The important thing is that it worked. Now I've got to test it on something that matters. We've got to see if it'll work in the human body."

"Don't we need to run some more tests first? Look for side effects, double-check the procedure—"

Erika flipped her hair behind her ear and frowned at him. "Look, every one of us is carrying a time bomb. What if the Controllers decide to circumvent the restriction on organic material? The Assemblers are still there—what if they decide to alter our DNA somehow? I'm not waiting around for that to happen, especially when I have something that might work."

"Point taken." Jason started to roll his sleeve back up again. "I've got nothing to lose. Let's get to it."

Erika shook her head as she eyed the hypodermic, now filled with a second generation of nanocannibals. The solution looked perfectly clear to her naked eye, but the liquid teemed with reprogrammed Destroyers, already devouring each other. "You're too important, Jason. You're the moonbase commander. I've already done everything I can."

"Don't be stupid. You can always try something different. Nobody else has your background. You can't give up."

Erika said, "I'm not giving up. I'm being practical."

As Jason took a step toward her, Erika considered warding him off with the filled hypodermic; but the thought nearly made her laugh. She thought of all those scenes from old plague movies, where the brilliant doctor comes up with a risky serum to cure the disease and decides to test it on himself first.

Before, Erika had always found those scenes ridiculous. But as Jason held out his hand to her, she quickly jabbed her arm and squeezed the hypo. "Ouch!"

It wouldn't really matter if she hit an artery or just muscle tissue. The nanocritters were inside her body. She could just as well have smeared the nutrient solution on her skin.

She felt Jason's arms around her. "Sit down, you idiot." He helped her to her seat.

"At least I'm an academically trained idiot," she said. Sitting back, she felt suddenly woozy. "Whatever's happening is going on a lot faster than it should."

"What does it feel like?" Jason's face swam in and out of focus. He held a hand to her forehead. "You're cool, but damp."

"Great. It's like they just got turned loose in a free-for-all banquet. Good God, what's going on?"

Erika fought to keep herself conscious. She felt dizzy, and the edges of her sight seemed to collapse inward, into a brown tunnel. Jason's voice became a buzz, growing louder, as if all she could hear was the chittering of millions of nanocannibals voraciously working their way through her body.

Chaotic, psychedelic nightmares faded into bursts of static and twinkling lights. When she opened her eyes, she felt as if she were falling, dissolving. . . . She reached out to steady herself and found that she was sliding from a padded couch. Back at . . . Moonbase Columbus?

Jason Dvorak's face appeared, wearing a ridiculous grin. "It's alive, Igor!"

"What?" Her mouth was dry, cottony, and tasted terrible. "Who's Igor?"

"About time you woke up. You've been out five hours."

Erika tried to struggle up from the couch, but he firmly pushed her back. "What happened to me?"

"Well, it worked—or at least everyone thinks it did. Once I got you on the couch, I managed to get hold of Compton-Reasor on Earth and Bernard Chu here. They led me through the procedure for keeping track of your vitals, and it looks like you were completely purged of the nanocannibals within fifteen minutes. I brought you back to Columbus for monitoring."

"What about Jordan? Dr. Parvu? Does he know what I did?"

He shook his head. "He's been off-line, but the weathersats showed a big storm over McMurdo Sound. Don't worry. We'll get back in touch with him." He squeezed her shoulder.

"You haven't heard the best news: remember how the Assemblers must have originally been transmitted to us, by touch? Well, your nanocannibals have done the same thing—Bernard Chu tested my blood, and he can't find any trace"—he grimaced at the pun—"I mean any evidence, of Assemblers there either. Transmitted through the skin, the nanocannibals are working their way through everyone who's infected."

Erika interrupted with a feeble wave. "You said I was out for a few hours. Weren't you affected yourself? What happened?"

"I was dizzy and feverish for a few minutes, but it passed. Chu thinks you suffered more from fatigue than from Destroyers."

Erika ran a tongue over her teeth. They felt as if they were covered with fur. "Could I get some water?" After she drank, she said, "You know, I'm not even sure what I did to create those things."

"Taylor's group is working to come up with a few theories. They'll probably milk dozens of journal articles out of it."

Erika sighed. "It still seems too easy."

Jason's expression grew more serious. "It's not over yet. The Agency thinks it was too easy themselves. They're not even going to consider letting us back to Earth for quite a while."

Erika sat up too fast and felt dizzy again. "Why not? If all of us check out clean, what are they worried about?"

"The Daedalus construction," he said. "They still don't know what it is, and they're terrified. It looks almost finished and they're afraid we've all been . . . well, *possessed* by the aliens. They don't know what the nanomachine infestation did to us. And neither do we."

24

antarctica—
nanotechnology isolation laboratory

When Kent Woodward woke up, he did so fully and completely, as if he were a machine suddenly switched on. With a blink of his eyes, the bright surroundings came to him like a slide projected on a dark screen. He felt no fatigue, no soreness, only a persistent buzzing in his head, a singing thunderstorm of white noise chewing at the back of his thoughts.

He blinked his eyes again and sat up. His entire body felt as if it were crawling with the pins-and-needles sensation of having circulation cut off during a deep sleep. Every one of Kent's nerve endings screamed.

He found himself in a clean white room, filled with glass surfaces, porcelain, stainless steel. *A UFO came down and kidnapped me!* he thought. He saw the worktables, a line of stereoscreen and flatscreen workstations, various pieces of analytical hardware. Rising through the center of the room like some high-tech Roman column stood a transparent cylinder filled with milky liquid; metal conduits and conduction strips lined the walls of the cylinder. A control bank sat at the bottom.

On one of the worktables rested a wire-mesh cage that held a white lab rat. Oblivious to Kent, the rat scuttled around and sniffed its food dish. He noticed cameras staring at him from the ceiling.

Everything clicked at once. He was in the Nanotech Isolation Lab. Alone.

The next chunk of information dropped into his mind. He remembered the blizzard, the unseen crevasse, the crash of the rover. He had been barely conscious, bleeding. Pain crushed him from the inside out, and impossible cold gnawed at him.

He had known he was going to die, but he sent out a distress call anyway. Someone, a garbled voice, had answered. But nobody could have rescued him. Not in that storm, not so far away, not with his injuries. He hadn't had a chance!

"So, Kent, I observe you are awake. Welcome back to us!"

Turning, he saw Jordan Parvu standing on the other side of the observation windows. Parvu fluttered his hands in the fidgety way that indicated how anxious he was. Relief washed over Kent as he saw the old scientist. The scenario did make sense now, at least a little bit. Everything was under control.

He remembered getting the extra set of snow samples for Parvu, though the doctor hadn't asked for them. Kent had done that on his own initiative, sure. He was bored. He wanted something to do—and gathering samples gave him a legitimate reason to poke around. He had ignored the increasing storm. Right now, even he had to admit it was a pretty stupid idea.

"So tell me, please—how do you feel?" Parvu placed his hands against the outer glass, as if to get a better view . . . or to steady himself.

How do you feel? That was a rather inane question. *Oh, I'm fine. How about yourself?* But then Kent began to wonder. He clearly recalled the pain deep inside as he tried to work the rover controls . . . the blood, the grinding ache of broken bones.

Now he felt no pain at all, not even the dull throb of healing—only the fizzing, crawly sensation running through his entire body, inside and out. Kent noticed a dozen or so RF electrode pads on his body, wirelessly transmitting his vital signs to sequencers and computer monitoring systems.

217

What had Dr. Parvu done to him?

He recalled Gunther Mosby's superstitious fear of the NIL and nanotechnology research—and he wasn't sure he wanted to know.

With fear biting his stomach, Parvu watched from the other side of the window, looking into the clean-room of the NIL. The walls appeared too thin, the observation window too weak to hold anything back. It seemed a very questionable membrane to protect him from the invisibly boiling environment inside.

None of these barriers could protect him—or the world—if the hybrids decided to break out. The alien automata had escaped much more rigid controls in the Sim-Mars lab and infected Erika. From what Parvu had seen at the Daedalus Crater, from what he knew about the theoretical possibilities of nanotechnology, he couldn't stop the hybrids from doing anything they decided to do.

Luckily, his hybrids had shown themselves to be completely benign miracle workers. As he watched Kent Woodward, amazingly alive, functioning as if nothing had gone wrong, Parvu waited—what was the English language cliché? He waited for the other shoe to drop.

He stared at the readings piped in from the electrodes attached to Kent's body. All readings looked normal, but that had changed drastically over the past day.

He had spent many sleepless hours watching Kent sealed in the inner chamber, unable to go to him to help. Electrodes traced Kent's huge temperature fluctuation, from near hypothermia up to a high fever. The fever had lasted a long time, brought about most likely from waste heat put out by the incredible number of hybrid automata working inside his body.

Kent had even died once, completely, as Parvu stared into the observation windows, helplessly pressing his palms against the glass and wondering what he should do. All of Kent's vital signs had been flat for more than thirty seconds, and then—with no intervention on Parvu's part—had jumped back up to human norms, as if someone had rebooted Kent Woodward. A true deadstart.

Now, as he observed the young astronaut sitting on the table and staring at his hands, Parvu wondered exactly how he was ever going to tell him the truth. Parvu had taken enormous liberties with Kent, but it had been the only way, hadn't it?

Kent spoke into Parvu's long silence. "So . . . can I get out of here? Why am I in this room, and how come you're staying out there?"

Kent swung his feet off the table, standing up. He lost his balance, reached out to grab the edge of the table. He overestimated and ended up stumbling to the floor. He slowly climbed back to his feet, his eyes wide. "Feels like I'm drunk."

Avoiding Kent's gaze, Parvu looked down at the heavily caulked doors, at the sealed vents. Only the autoclave would allow him to pass food and other items in and out. Parvu realized he hadn't thought this through very well. He hadn't had the time. And now he had to keep patching up repairs as he thought of things he hadn't considered before.

"I am afraid you are in quarantine, Kent."

Kent looked at Parvu fixedly. "Quarantine? From what?" His voice slowed, as if he were selecting his words carefully. "I got hurt in an accident, didn't I? Did I . . . get exposed to something?"

Parvu folded his hands together in a praying position. "You were mortally wounded in that accident, Kent. In fact, you did die for over thirty seconds. I have all the readings to prove it to you, if you should doubt me."

As Kent had lain near death on the clean-room table, Parvu had taken a few of the active hybrids from the nanocore. When he had injected the hybrids into Kent's body, Parvu had no idea if it would work, or how long it would take. Just because they had worked with a rat suffering a minor wound did not mean they could do anything for a human being.

Parvu also did not know what the consequences might be for the young man. But he had no choice.

It had taken a day and a half for Kent to wake up, apparently fully healed. Now Kent touched his chest, flexed his fingers, dubious about what Parvu was saying. He could see no injuries at all. "Then how—?"

Parvu swallowed before taking a deep breath. "My nanotechnology prototypes . . . saved you."

Kent's mouth worked, but no words came out. Finally he said, "You put those nanothings in me! Like the ones that infected all those people on the moonbase?" Kent raised his hands and stared at them. "Is that why I feel so strange? Are they crawling all over inside me?"

"Kent, please calm yourself. They saved your life, okay? You must remember that. They repaired your damage on a level no surgeon could have done." Parvu tried to sound reassuring. Maybe he should play some calming music for Kent. Maybe if Erika were there, she could make him relax and accept the situation.

"To tell you the truth, the rat in the cage beside you has also been treated with my . . . automata. He is fine. In fact, he has never been healthier. All of the little things that had been bothering him are now fixed. You, too, will be fine. It was a risk I had to take to save your life. Do you understand?"

Kent turned to stare at the rat in the cage. His shoulders slumped.

Parvu couldn't stop himself from justifying his actions, though Kent didn't seem to be listening. "Believe me, I would not have taken such a chance, but it was the only way."

He drew another shuddering breath. "And perhaps this will provide the information we need to help Erika! That is the most important thing, is it not? We can find out how to get rid of her infection, too. If we learn how to treat you, perhaps we can free her from the quarantine and let her come back to us."

He hoped that would suit Kent, who he knew had always had a deep crush on Erika—but instead the young astronaut kept rubbing his arms and legs, as if trying to brush away ants. "No, it is not the most important thing. Everyone up on the Moon is in their mess because of Erika's screwup. And now Sim-Mars is ruined for the Mars mission, too."

Parvu blinked in total shock. Surely he had misunderstood something. "But, Kent, how can you say that? I thought you . . . do you not love Erika?"

"*Love* her? Where did you get that idea? She hardly ever said a word to me, and she's been gone for weeks!"

Parvu felt his body stiffen and he pressed his lips together. "I see I was greatly mistaken." His voice was brittle.

Kent stood up. His face was flushed and desperate, his expression suddenly plaintive. The RF electrodes showed his body temperature shooting up. "They can solve their own problems up on the moonbase, Doc. They've got all the facilities of Sim-Mars and the Columbus research centers. Forget about Erika for a minute. What are you going to do about me? You can't just leave me locked up here in this lab—like a rat!"

He paused, as if suddenly realizing something. "Have you told Commander Grace or the Agency yet? What did they say? Did McConnell give you permission to do this crazy experiment on me?"

Parvu felt himself becoming angry. He didn't want to lose control. He needed to think about this some more. "Right now, I am going to turn out the lights and let you rest. You are too distraught to continue a meaningful discussion at this moment."

Without looking back, Parvu dimmed the lights in the clean-room until the room was lit only by a glow from the instrument panels and the nanocore.

"Hey!" Kent shouted. His voice sounded hoarse and distorted through the speakers. "Hey! Don't just walk away!"

Parvu stopped, out of sight from the observation windows. He waited, half wincing.

"Come back here, dammit!"

Suddenly a high-pitched alarm squealed from the diagnostic panels. All of Kent's RF electrodes had flat-lined.

Parvu scrambled back to the observation window, only to find Kent tearing off his electrodes and throwing them at the window. Kent kept shouting at him. "You infected me just so you could figure out what to do for her, didn't you? I never volunteered to be your guinea pig!"

"Kent!"

But the young astronaut did not hear. With no more electrodes to throw, he knocked over a chair, then moved to tip one of the worktables. The cage holding Old Gimp clattered to the floor, bouncing and rolling on its side. The rat squealed in terror.

"Kent, stop this!" Parvu flicked the lights back on in the quarantine chamber. Kent stopped for a moment to glare at him, then moved over to the workstation terminals. He grabbed the keyboards and jerked out their cables. He tossed one against the thick glass of the observation window.

Kent picked up the chair he had toppled, held it over his head, and ran toward the nanocore.

"Kent! If you don't stop, you will trigger the self-destruct systems!" Parvu shouted into the microphone pad and turned up the volume so that his words thundered into the clean-room. Kent hesitated for just a moment, the chair ready to swing.

"Do you not remember the fail-safe systems here? Your friend Gunther was always afraid of them. If you trigger the sterilization sequence, you will flood the entire NIL with x rays. Do you want this? I think not! Now, *calm down*!"

Kent heaved the chair at the other side of the room instead, then collapsed to the floor. He crossed his legs under him and stared at his knees.

Parvu gnawed at his fingernails, frightened by Kent's tantrum. Had he done such a poor job explaining the necessity to him? Didn't Kent understand?

Inside the clean-room, Kent crawled over to Old Gimp's cage, righted it, and looked inside. The rat appeared agitated, but otherwise unharmed. Ignoring Parvu, Kent opened the cage and pulled the rat out. The rat squirmed, trying to escape, but Kent stroked the back of its head, scratching its ears. Eventually, Old Gimp resigned itself to the manhandling and relaxed, sniffing Kent's fingers with its vibrant pink nose.

Parvu narrowed his eyes as he watched the young astronaut. Perhaps Kent had not recovered as completely as he had hoped. What if the automata had somehow unbalanced his hormones, thrown the delicate ballet of human bodily chemicals out of equilibrium? That might make Kent prone to fits of anger and irrationality, turning him into a Mr. Hyde.

Or could he really be so furious at Parvu's method of saving him? He didn't know. Parvu watched in turmoil as Kent continued to stroke the rat, shutting out everything else around him.

Parvu left without saying goodbye.

25

moonbase columbus

With Newellen sitting beside him in the surface transport, Bernard Chu watched the autopiloted supply shuttle come in low across the cratered horizon. They both craned their necks to look through the slanted front window of the vehicle.

Like a satellite racing across the black sky, the shuttle first appeared as a gleaming white dot. The dot grew until Chu could discern ragged edges at crazy angles with no aerodynamic constraints, gangly antennas, and landing pods.

The Agency hadn't written them off yet. The sheer presence of the shuttle showed they had some sympathy for the people under lunar quarantine. At least Celeste was still sending them food.

As the shuttle grew closer, Chu could imagine the rumble it would send across the lunar plain if there had been an atmosphere. The shuttle approached the surface quickly, kicking up a cloud of dust that obscured the distant landing area.

"Robotic landing worked like a charm," said Newellen. "Better not rub Zimmerman's nose in it. He hates that autopilot stuff."

"Let's get going." Chu indicated the transport vehicle's controls. It felt good to be outside working again on the Moon. He could hear Newellen's breathing over the suit radio as the other man eased the vehicle forward to meet the shuttle.

His thoughts turned to the supply shuttle and all that it meant. Though the automated piloting systems had always been in place for emergency telepresent landings, all regular shuttles required a human in the loop. Though it would have been vastly cheaper for many missions to send a bare-bones ship without the frills a human pilot required, United Space Agency policy insisted on it. But now Celeste refused to send any more people into the plague site.

But they had all been cured. *Cured, dammit!* They were clean, not a nanomachine showed up on any test. Celeste should let them run back to safety on Earth. What was she waiting for?

It was that nightmarish construction out at Daedalus. Dvorak had been spending more and more time going over the analyses, trying to second-guess the builders, to no avail. Flybys documented the inexorable progress, but they still knew nothing more about what its purpose was. Celeste wanted to keep them there as guinea pigs, an expendable investigation team. He was tempted to send somebody out to Daedalus to poke around.

Of course, he would have to get Dvorak's approval to try something like that. Or maybe he wouldn't. Dvorak didn't seem too interested in keeping his command, now that Chu had returned. Dvorak had never struck him as someone who really cared about power or responsibility, but seemed more wrapped up in his own interests.

"Hey, watch out for that depression." He gestured out the window.

Newellen nodded curtly inside his helmet. "I see it, plenty of time. I can ride a bicycle almost as fast as this thing moves."

Now that the landing area dust had settled, drifting to the surface like grains of sand through water, the shuttle stood in the raw sunlight.

Chu wondered what it would take to refurbish it. What would stop them from adding some more fuel, disabling the telepresent autopilot, and having Bryan Zed haul them all back to Earth? Zed's L-1 shuttle used volatile liquid hydrogen, impossible to produce at this point on the Moon.

These shuttles used methane, which they had plenty of.

Somebody could calculate an appropriate orbit, even without the Collins transfer station. They would survive the trip—they'd need to worry only about being blasted out of the skies by Earth-based defenses. Just how serious was Celeste after all?

As Newellen brought the flatbed transport up to the shuttle, Chu worried that the craft might have landed poorly on its pods. But it looked stable enough. He clicked his chin mike. "Can you get a relay to base?"

Newellen leaned forward and fiddled with the communications port. Ever since the Collins had been destroyed, they couldn't bounce their communications off L-1 anymore; since the L-2 relay was on the other side of the Moon, they were limited to line-of-sight transmissions. They had had to place backup K-band relays around the crater walls to communicate when out of sight.

"Link's up."

Chu cleared his throat. "The shuttle made it, Columbus. Our pantries are full again for the time being."

"Make sure the bastards didn't booby trap it when you enter," said Cyndi Salito's voice. Chu grunted, but didn't reply to her bitter warning.

They climbed down off the flatbed rover and trudged toward the shuttle, keeping away from its still-hot engines. A ladder unfolded as Newellen pressed the actuator. The single door slid open and seemed to beckon them forward. The interior had not been pressurized.

Newellen waved Chu forward. "I told you we should have brought the lift. We didn't know what design they were sending down." He looked at the legs, the ladder. "Boy, I wonder where they got this ancient wreck."

"It's an old Russian job, probably scheduled for dismantling," Chu said. "Not human-rated anymore. Expendable." The word "expendable" made them both fall silent for a few seconds, but Chu set foot on the ladder to climb up.

"It's all yours," Newellen said, not mentioning the fact that he might have difficulty squeezing his beefy frame through the shuttle door.

Chu worked his way up the aluminum ladder, making sure he positioned his foot firmly on each rung before shifting his weight. The ladder was a relic from old days that didn't make sense—spend a couple of billion getting to the Moon, and then as an afterthought strap on a couple of rungs and vertical bars that cost a few bucks and change.

By the time he reached the top, he was out of breath. He didn't weigh much on the Moon, but compared to the last month he had spent in zero-G aboard the Collins, he felt as if he weighed a ton. He didn't know how well he would ever readjust to full gravity—but it no longer looked as though he would have the chance to find out.

"You okay up there?"

"Yeah," returned Chu.

The door to the supply shuttle opened directly into the control room—there was no airlock, just like the old lunar landers. It saved weight and was much easier to engineer. The craft's inside was not pretty, but high in utility. The Russians had done a good job outfitting the emergency craft. Low-current LEDs were set above old-fashioned mechanical switches; the control panel jutted out at an odd angle, put together with welding technology instead of melded composites. Extra controls were jammed next to the main systems, relying on redundancy instead of computerized heuristic fault-finding for backup.

Chu stepped forward. A sheet of plastic was taped to the control panel, directly in front of the empty pilot's seat. Inside the plastic, a piece of paper read:

Food and medical supplies are located in the hold. We included a 5% surplus of fuel for landing only--fuel for takeoff is not, repeat NOT, available.

Additionally, a biological agent was released into the remaining fuel precisely two (2) minutes after pump shutdown--the fuel line and tanks should be entirely corroded by the time you read this. Don't worry. We'll find some way to bring you home. Your well-being is our highest priority.

--DIRECTOR CELESTE MCCONNELL

She hadn't even signed it herself. A *"Sorry, hang in there guys!"* was scribbled at the bottom of the note, obviously put on by the crew that had sealed the craft.

Chu reached forward, and after searching for a moment joggled the pump switch. The LED blinked from amber to green, then burned a bright red. Directly above the PUMP STATUS indicator, another row of LEDs burned red.

"You bitch." Chu slammed his hand down against the control panel. He barely felt it through the thick glove.

The whole thing sucked. Of course McConnell wouldn't risk sending a shuttle that could return to Earth—there was too great a chance that one of the Columbus people would defy her quarantine and try to get back. As he himself had been contemplating. And with no fuel for Zed's L-1 shuttle, that left only the low-velocity methane-fueled hoppers—and they barely had enough thrust to reach lunar orbit, and nowhere near the delta-vee required to reach Earth.

That was fine logic if you were back on Earth. But the fact that Celeste obviously didn't trust them—didn't trust her long-time supporter Bernard Chu of all people!—made him seethe inside.

He recalled the precautions taken before the Apollo 10 shot. Tom Stafford, one of the fly-by-the-seat-of-your-pants astronauts back in the 1960s, had been assigned to pilot a lunar module to within nine kilometers of the Moon's surface. Traveling across space from Earth to the Moon to be brought up short by only nine kilometers sounded a bit too tempting, or that's what the NASA administrators thought. How could they be sure Stafford wouldn't suffer "transmission difficulties" and "accidentally" land the craft after all, becoming the first human to set down on the Moon?

So before lift-off, knowing just how cocky some astronauts were, NASA officials had taken Stafford to the contractors who had built the lunar module. There, Stafford was personally shown how much the module weighed, how much fuel it carried. They took him step-by-step through all the calculations that proved the module was absolutely, positively a thousand pounds too heavy to leave the lunar surface if he broke orders and landed the craft. No matter how much he might want to land, Stafford would know in his gut that the lunar module would never fly again if he did.

Chu felt the same way now. He touched on the idea of trying to clean out the fuel tank, patch it, and try to rocket off the Moon, just to spite the Agency—but he, too, was no fool.

Chu tore the plastic-covered note from the panel. The people stranded on the base had been bitter before. This would be like another slap in the face. *See what Earth thinks about you now?* He stuffed the note in his patch before opening the doors to the hold below him.

At least they had plenty of food.

The Columbus inhabitants greeted the flatbed transport and supplies with little enthusiasm, but they helped bring in the packets of food and medicine. Inside the receiving bay, Cyndi Salito pawed through a heap of dehydrated foodstuff, then scowled. "What, no dairy products? What the hell are they expecting us to do, live on calcium pills?"

She handed off a bag of the stuff to Bryan Zimmerman, who was standing next to her. A line of crewmen extended the length of the inner corridor, helping to stuff the extra supplies into overhead nets and storage cubicles.

Zimmerman answered her in a deadpan voice. "They want us to keep our cholesterol down. It's bad for the arteries. Otherwise, we might die of a heart attack."

Salito's eyes widened at the remark. Bernard Chu held back a laugh. It was the first humorous thing he had ever heard the shuttle pilot say. If it had indeed been meant as a joke.

Once the supplies were stowed, Chu walked among the people, offering words of encouragement, feeling like the moonbase commander again. Jason Dvorak couldn't be bothered to be there, instead spending his time back over at the Sim-Mars lab. What did Erika Trace have left to do over there anyway? Weren't they all purged of their contamination?

229

Kevin J. Anderson and Doug Beason

As he patted Salito on the back, she stared grimly at him. Most of the crew spoke in low murmurs to each other, if at all. Depression had descended again—quite a difference from just a few days ago, when Erika Trace's "cure" for the alien infestation had been announced. Everyone should be out dancing on the regolith right now, but they—like himself—did not trust the Agency to lift the quarantine anytime soon, and most of them wanted to flee for home *now*.

Chu would have to provide a good example, strong leadership. Perhaps he would even take official command of the moonbase from Dvorak. Somehow, he doubted Dvorak would mind.

Chu had been forced to follow orders and go up to the Collins. Just as Dvorak had been thrust into his place. Now, Dvorak must realize that the only right thing to do was to give up his unwanted command here. Leave it in more experienced hands. It was time to push whatever buttons he could with Celeste McConnell—her friendship seemed to be fading fast.

He squeezed past Newellen and the others in the tunnel and made his way to the control center. "Someone bring up Agency HQ. I need to speak with Director McConnell."

The technician—someone Chu did not recognize, probably one of the new people brought in on the last rotation—turned, a question written on his face.

"Well?" Chu asked.

The tech searched for words. "It's eight o'clock in the evening there. Twenty hundred hours."

"Well, then try her at home. You do have the access code, don't you? If not, I'll give it to you myself."

Five minutes passed before the tech could track her down. Celeste wore a neon sweatsuit, and tendrils of damp hair stuck to her forehead. In the background, her two big dogs barked and played with each other. She gave Chu a bland look that was tight at the lips. She nodded into the stereochip. "Hello, Bernard. Is everything going all right?"

"We just unloaded the supply shuttle, Celeste."

"We were waiting for your confirmation. Shouldn't you have called through the official line to Mission Control? I

230

assume that everything came through in good shape."

"Except for the fuel tanks." He made his voice sound bewildered and sarcastic at the same time. "Someone using your name played a terrible joke on us. They wrote us a letter, typed your name on the bottom, saying they sabotaged the fuel tanks so that the shuttle is useless now. Now, I know you wouldn't have had anything to do with such an action—"

She set her mouth, showing impatience. "You know why we had to do that, Bernard. Same thing as with the Collins. We can't take chances, no matter how many tests show that you are not infected. Give it a little time for confirmation. Dr. Taylor at MIT has publicly said that there is a small chance that the infestation has only grown dormant, like a retrovirus. No one knows what might stimulate the nanomachines. And only one of them needs to get to Earth, maybe brought down by some hotdog hero from the moonbase. I don't want to take that risk."

"If you can't trust the people you sent up here, who can you trust, Celeste? You handpicked each and every one of us."

She moved her head back and forth. "You know I'm sorry. But until we can find out exactly what is going on, and what that damned thing is at Daedalus, we . . ." She stopped herself in midsentence and straightened. "I won't get into that any further. Is there anything else I can help you with?"

"No compromise on the quarantine?"

"None. That is closed for discussion. For now. If the situation changes, we will reconsider."

"If the situation changes! How can it change? We're all clean."

"Bernard. Stop it."

He stared at her. "Is there anything we can do then?"

She looked momentarily surprised. It was the only chink in her armor he had seen for some time now. "Your orders remain unchanged: take any action you think necessary to ensure the survival of your crew—without jeopardizing Earth, of course."

Chu studied her for a long time. The light delay added to the effect that she was staying still. More sweat stood out on her forehead than he had seen a moment ago.

He saw in front of him the woman that had saved his life onboard the Grissom. Whatever her sixth sense was, he owed his life to it. He should know better than to argue with it.

"Okay then—give me command back of Moonbase Columbus."

She pursed her lips. "Bernard—"

"You heard me, Celeste. I'm practically in charge now. Just make it official."

She waited several beats, finally lowering her eyes. "All right. I was considering that anyway. I'll inform Dvorak."

Chu nodded. Celeste had pulled him out of this job just to let him be a station keeper, but that had had its place, too. *Who else could have discovered Erika Trace's nanotech infestation, if he himself had not been doing biomedical studies on the Collins?* He had brought the microgravity research up there, started taking baseline data. If he had not caught Erika's infection right there, the alien plague would be spreading like fire through all of humanity, making AIDS look like a minor cold in comparison.

With all that Celeste had done, with all of her proven insight, he knew he shouldn't be so angry at her. She just might be the one person responsible for ensuring the survival of mankind.

But as Chu switched off, he still cursed her for abandoning them.

antarctica—
nanotechnology isolation laboratory

Parvu watched Kent Woodward pace inside the NIL's sealed clean-room. So far Kent had not bothered to acknowledge the scientist's presence.

Old Gimp rode on Kent's shoulder. The young man had been stroking the rat obsessively for the past day. The lab videocameras recorded every move he made.

Parvu had crammed as much food as he could into the autoclave and told Kent he had only to open the other side if he wanted something to eat. He hoped the food would last at least a week, because once the autoclave's interior had been exposed to the air swarming with automata, he did not want to open it to the outside again. Perhaps by the time Kent's food ran out, he would have some ideas, some solutions.

But so far Kent had eaten nothing.

The young astronaut suddenly whirled to face Parvu. The rat on his shoulder scrabbled to keep its grip on the smooth cloth of Kent's jumpsuit. "So why don't you just turn this nanoshit inside me off, Doc? What's wrong with your design?"

Parvu fought down an urge to flee, then put his hands on his hips. "I do not know what your question means, Kent." He kept his voice calm. Any conversation at all had to be helpful at this point.

Since Kent had removed his RF electrodes, Parvu had no way of knowing anything about the other man's health. Despite Parvu's cajoling, Kent refused to cooperate. And Parvu needed that data if he was ever going to be able to interpret any information to help Erika, even if Kent did not care about her.

Kent sat down in his chair and took the rat in his hands, scratching its ears. "You sold McConnell this grand plan of seeding Mars with nanomachines to liberate the oxygen and water trapped in the rocks. And once they had done their job, you were going to transmit a satellite signal that would shut down all the devices. Well, your nanomachines have done their work inside me. It's finished. So shut them down!"

Kent stood up, livid. He was visibly trembling all over, as if he were about to go into convulsions. The rat dropped to the floor and scrambled into hiding under the chair.

"Kent, I did not design these hybrids," Parvu said. "My own technology is not sophisticated enough to program them—we were just . . . lucky, you and I, that the hybrids were intuitive enough to understand your cell structure, your injuries. I do not know how to turn them off. I wish I did."

"Then you need some help," Kent said.

"I have no assistants."

"Have you requested any more? Now that I'm stuck here, maybe the Agency will be a bit more interested."

Parvu shook his head. "More likely they will decide to sterilize the entire NIL, with you and me inside it, as an unacceptable threat. They will fly over with bombs and think they are safe when it is all over."

"So you still haven't told anybody I'm here, have you?"

"My optical transmitter remains out of alignment." Parvu felt as if he were being interrogated.

"Haven't you even tried to fix it yet? The storm's been over for two days! What have you been sitting around here for?"

"I have been monitoring you." Annoyance crept into his voice, making him sound stern and paternal. "You are the most important problem at the moment."

"Well, I'm fine now. Go out and fix the transmitter."

Parvu tapped his fingers against the glass. "I will make a bargain with you, Kent. If you put the RF electrodes back on your body, then I can be assured of continued monitoring, even while I am outside. Without the data only you can provide, I can find no way to help anybody, including yourself."

"Go to hell."

Parvu waited a moment. "I need that data . . . and you need to be free again. How much trouble is that for you?"

Kent clenched his hands together. Parvu sighed. It was no use. The young astronaut was too headstrong to agree.

As he turned to go, Kent slowly shuffled to the worktable, bent over, and picked up one of the discarded electrodes that lay against a table leg. Grudgingly he stuck it to his chest. "All right already." He searched around for another electrode. "I know how to put these on. Just go outside and fix the damned thing."

Two hours later, inside the NIL's teleconference room, Parvu squirmed like a teenager about to ask someone to the prom. After replacing the hydraulic cables and working with the computer to iterate and realign the optical uplink outside, he had showered, changed his clothes, combed his steel-gray hair, made sure his appearance was professional. Now he could talk to Erika again. Now he could communicate with the rest of the world.

Now he had to break the news of exactly what he had done.

The computer processed the sequence, requesting a connect.

Parvu swallowed the lump in his throat. After his break in communications, he should have called the simulated Mars base camp to inform Bingham Grace that Kent was not dead after all. Or he should have contacted his wife Sinda, to let her know that he was all right. He should have gotten in touch with United Space Agency headquarters, to see if they had sent any urgent instructions, since they were bound to order him to shut down the NIL. Everything was falling to pieces.

Instead, what Parvu chose to do first—what he needed to do first—was contact Erika Trace.

When the Moonbase Columbus receivers accepted his transmission and relayed it to the Sim-Mars substation, the screen flashed to tell him he was waiting for someone to answer. When the image of Erika resolved itself, she appeared thinner, tired, harried—but she smiled upon recognizing him.

"Jordan!" she cried. "We've been trying to reach you for days, but you've been off-line. What happened?"

Parvu blinked, momentarily at a loss for words. "We had a storm here. Some of the cables from the optical uplinks became fouled. I just got them fixed." He smiled. "But what has happened to you? I too have received no information in days."

She took a deep breath. "We're clean, Jordan. All the nanocritters are gone. We're not infected anymore."

Parvu sat back in his chair and folded his hands together in his lap, just to grip something. "But how? How can you be sure? Was it spontaneous?"

Erika said, "I did it myself. I . . . modified the nanocritters."

Beside her, a man whom Parvu recognized as moonbase commander Dvorak pushed into the field of view. "She created nanocannibals!" he said, then turned to grin at her.

It took Erika several minutes to tell the entire story, but by the time she had finished, Parvu was standing up, barely controlling his delight.

"Celeste McConnell still doesn't believe we're clean," Dvorak said. "She won't let us come home."

Parvu waved his hands to dismiss Dvorak's concern. "That will come soon. You have nothing to worry about now! That was ingenious, Erika, to use behavioral modifications while I had grown stagnant thinking of direct reprogramming." He of all people should not have underestimated the adaptive abilities of the alien automata.

Suddenly the screen flashed. Erika squinted offscreen. "We've got an incoming message from the moonbase.

Bernard Chu, I think. Can we talk to you later? I have a lot of things we should discuss."

Parvu sighed with a bittersweet feeling. He had learned so much in this conversation that he could be happy for now. True, he had not been able to tell her about Kent Woodward and his situation there at the NIL, but that was no longer so important. Erika had saved herself, and Parvu could perhaps use the same techniques to purge Kent of his automata. It would be difficult, and he was working with a different breed of automata entirely, but the light at the end of the tunnel had reappeared, brighter than ever before!

"Goodbye, Erika. I will call you back as soon as I am able. I must check on several things now that you have given me this new information. My congratulations. I am very, very proud of you."

She beamed at that, and he saw Jason Dvorak clap a congratulatory hand on her shoulder. The transmission ended and the picture winked out.

Less than five seconds later, Kent Woodward began screaming from the quarantine chamber.

Parvu ran down the curved corridor and stopped in front of the observation window.

Inside, Kent Woodward was scrambling backward. He had knocked a chair over and stood up against the nano-core, screaming. His eyes remained fixed on something that looked like Old Gimp convulsing on the floor.

"Kent!" Parvu shouted. He turned up the volume on the intercom. "Kent, what has happened?"

"I was holding it right in my hands! Right in my hands!" He extended his palms, staring at them and then at the floor.

Then Parvu noticed that the rat looked fluid, bumpy, and *flowed* over the floor.

Suddenly its legs convulsed, sticking straight out. Bulges pulsed on its sides, bending the rib cage outward. Its mouth opened wider, wider, until the skin parted, and still the rat's jaws folded backward even more.

The seams split as the rat writhed and thrashed. Blood oozed out, then sealed up. Something squirmed inside the yawning mouth of Old Gimp, a lump, a pinkish gray shape thrust out—a second head, with blue-black eyes buried beneath a film of wet skin. Two more legs protruded from its sides.

The rat's ears elongated, folded back again. The whole body shuddered, split, and rolled over. A dozen more limbs protruded from its rib cage. Something that might have been a . . . wing thrust upward, flapped once, and then curled over to melt like cellular wax back into the seething main body.

Kent was screaming now. But Parvu could watch nothing but the rat as it began to lose all bodily definition. It flowed together into a sizzling mass as eyeballs and bones and teeth bubbled upward and came back down.

White fur suddenly sprouted like tall feathers, turning the lump into a mound of hair—but then the strands, too, rippled and flattened out. The thing changed to a uniform brown-red consistency, like protoplasm oozing in a formless mass, adjusting its contours to the shape of least structure.

Then the whole thing slowly moved, extending a tiny pseudopod forward.

Parvu opened and closed his mouth, gaping. He felt a cold deeper than the Antarctic storm running through his veins. What had he done? "Kent," he said. "Kent!" But he had no idea what he should say. Inside the quarantine chamber, Kent was not listening anyway. His screams had continued to rise in pitch until his own eyes rolled backward, white.

He stretched out his hands in front of him. He screamed and stared at his fingers. They visibly elongated, stretching out like pencils.

As Parvu watched, the skin sloughed off Kent's finger bones like melting grease, red and pink and yellow crayons oozing down into his cupped hands.

"Oh . . . God . . ." Kent gurgled, then he toppled backward. His knees seemed to turn to jelly as he fell onto the floor, convulsing.

27

moonbase columbus

Take any action necessary to ensure the survival of your crew.
McConnell's words rang in Bernard Chu's ears. He hadn't spent all that time in astronaut training and periodic refresher courses learning how to roll over and die. He knew how to find options, to determine what he could do and how he could fight back. Now it was for real.

The ordeal on the Grissom seven years ago had taught him that he might not always get a second chance. Celeste wasn't giving him any second chances. She had dumped it all back in his lap. Okay then, she had no right to complain if she didn't agree with his tactics from now on. He was going to make her pay attention. He had to convince Celeste to let them all come home.

Rubbing his jaw, Chu wandered into the commissary, which was kept open to accommodate the different working hours of the crew. Since days and nights on the Moon were two weeks long, Earthbound work schedules meant little.

Tables and chairs fashioned of scrap metal from the original cargo landers made up the decor. Only a third of the fifty-meter-long cylinder was used for eating; the galley and food storage areas were hidden behind a sectional curtain of plastic blankets. Some crewmembers had scrawled sarcastic but generally good-natured graffiti over the walls; others had pinned pictures of home to the plastic blanket.

Lon Newellen and Bryan Zimmerman were the only two people in the commissary. When Chu entered, Newellen held up what appeared to be a slice of pizza. "Come on in, Dr. Chu. Care for a piece?"

Chu glanced at the food in disbelief. "Is that what it looks like?" Their diets had always been rigidly controlled by the Agency. "Whatever happened to all that high-protein, low-fat stuff the dieticians require you to eat?"

"Here." Newellen pushed a plate holding the last slice of pizza. "Take a bite."

Chu pulled a chair across from the two men, trying to decide if he wanted to be sociable or be annoyed. His eyes lit up as he tasted the slice. "This is good. Very good. What in the world did you do?"

Newellen slapped Zimmerman on the back. The pilot grinned weakly, then returned to his flat expression. "Zimmerbuddy, here, is our secret weapon." Newellen's bulging frame and Zimmerman's straight-backed posture made them look like Laurel and Hardy. "Oregano, basil, bay leaf. You know—spices. Just like Marco effing Polo! Zimmerbuddy brought it with him. All that stuff the Agency said would be bad for our metabolism."

"Personal items," Bryan Zimmerman said. "I am allowed five kilograms on each flight."

"Ever since they decided we were going to be part of the life-sciences database, Zimmerbuddy has been stashing this stuff away and bringing it with him," Newellen said. "You'd be amazed at the trades you can make with the Japanese."

Chu ran his tongue around the inside of his mouth, tasting the pizza again. First the years on Columbus, then months up on the Collins—it had been a long time since he had tasted food that wasn't overly bland and healthful.

Chu said, "This has been going on underneath my nose the whole time?" He should have known that some type of smuggling would occur, but cold-fish Bryan Zed as the perpetrator? The thought of these supposed straight arrows circumventing the Agency's stormtrooper dietary plans nearly made Chu laugh. The overriding purpose of the long-range life sciences experiments was to control the entire colony's diet, to ensure with a strict accounting of intake and caloric expenditure that real differences in the human metabolism might finally be understood. Not only would the results have benefited the upcoming Mars mission, but it would have helped the medical community as a whole. Now all the data had to be questioned.

Zimmerman shrugged. "Life's got to go on."

Newellen scrunched up his face. "Now that the Agency has put us on permanent hold, why should we keep suffering for their stupid nutritional experiments? Maybe one reason we were infected by those nanocritters was because of our bland diet. A little bit of cayenne pepper might be the perfect antidote."

Bryan Zed smiled innocently. "Personally, I like the idea of thumbing my nose at the Agency, for stranding us here."

Chu narrowed his eyes. That insipid letter Celeste had placed in the robot supply shuttle had made him feel betrayed, written off by the one person he always thought he could count on. Chu couldn't depend on her to come to the rescue anymore; he had to try something of his own before they all died, before that alien construction was completed and triggered itself.

And Chu decided he wouldn't mind throwing a wrench in Celeste's works right now, either.

He suddenly stood, knocking his chair backward to the module floor. Newellen and Zimmerman blinked at him in astonishment. Chu gathered his thoughts before he turned to them. "What can we salvage from the dead supply shuttle to get to Farside? Can we patch the fuel tanks long enough to get it that far?"

Newellen looked puzzled. "The shuttle's engines are fueled with a LOX-hydrogen mixture, same as Zed's. The hoppers used on the moonbase are methane based. We can crack methane on the surface, but there's no way we can make liquid hydrogen."

Chu shook his head. "That's not what I mean. Perhaps between the two shuttles and a hopper, we can deliver a . . . bomb to Daedalus."

Zimmerman raised his eyebrows, then shrugged his shoulders. "If my shuttle can't go anywhere, then let's cannibalize it so we can do something about that construction before it gets finished."

"He wants to do *what*?"

Jason gently pushed Erika back into her chair at Sim-Mars. "You've got to understand where he's coming from before raising a stink."

"I understand. He's come back from the Collins and has taken over your job—"

"He's much better suited for command than I am." Jason sounded too defensive.

"He's taken over your job and now he feels like he's got to prove something."

Jason ran a hand through his dark sweaty hair. He could hear her South Carolina accent much more clearly when she was upset. "Erika . . . it's an option. There's no reason not to try it. At least we'll go down swinging." He knew he didn't sound convincing.

"But what's it going to accomplish? Even you haven't been able to figure out what the construction is supposed to be." Her eyes narrowed. "You don't believe this dormancy theory that Taylor is pushing, do you? That the nanocannibals are still hiding in our muscle tissue and waiting to surge back once they receive some signal?"

Jason held up his hands. "All I know is that Chu thinks he can use one of the hoppers to drop a bomb on that structure. We might be able to wipe them out. Or at least wreck that thing they're building. I doubt if he can, but have you seen the flyover images? It's not changing much—so the aliens must be nearly finished, and we still don't know what the hell they're building. This just might get rid of them."

"How?" She flipped her blond hair behind one ear. "My God, Jase, there are billions upon billions of nanocritters at Daedalus! What happens if that bomb just scatters them across the surface?"

Jason shook his head. Somehow it didn't bother him when Erika called him "Jase." Not like Margaret at all. "I don't know." He didn't have an answer.

She stood. "Well, we've got to do something then. To protect ourselves in case Chu's plan doesn't work!"

The hopper sat a good five kilometers from the landing pad; if anything went wrong and the hopper or the shuttle hulk blew up on the pad, nothing else could be damaged. Only one other hopper remained at the moonbase.

Bernard Chu watched as the modified refueler filled the shuttle's salvaged hydrogen tank, now mounted inside the hopper. It had been a tight fit, but by removing all of the fixtures intended for human use, Cyndi Salito had managed to force the shuttle's cryogenic H$_2$ tank inside the hopper. Bryan Zed had watched stony-faced—as usual—as they dismantled his shuttle for the scheme.

Salito's voice came over Chu's headset. "We've got a steady flow rate now. I don't want to increase it more than this. I just don't have any experience with this stuff."

"Neither does anybody else," said Chu. *Which is why we're lucky as hell being able to tap informational resources back on Earth,* he thought.

He had contacted Celeste, pulled as many strings of guilt as he could manage, and gotten her to promise him several things. It had taken only a matter of hours to dig up the appropriate explosives experts who could explain how a minor change in the regeneration equipment would produce a supply of nitrogen and oxygen; chemical stores had provided glycerol as well as concentrated nitric and sulfuric acids. As an unappreciated joke, Celeste had even transmitted an on-line copy of the *Anarchist's Cookbook.*

Cyndi Salito had set to work adding the glycerol to the acids, drawing off the top layer of the mixture and then washing it with water and sodium carbonate. When she had finished, Salito had managed to cook up several drums of old-fashioned nitroglycerin. They added that to containers of all the explosive rocket fuel they could scavenge from Bryan Zed's shuttle as well as the useless supply ship.

"We're going to blow the hell out of that sucker," Cyndi said over the suit mike. "I sure hope it's a good idea."

243

As he watched, Chu wondered to himself why such a relatively simple idea had fallen to him. Why hadn't the people back on Earth thought of delivering an explosive out to Daedalus if they were so frightened of the nanotech construction?

No matter. The important thing was that they had the hopper available now, and with Salito's change to the refueler, the ton and a half of nitro was being pumped into the tank of Zimmerman's shuttle along with about five thousand gallons of rocket fuel.

"We've got three quarters of the tank full now, Dr. Chu." He saw a spacesuited figure bounding his way from out of the fringes of his suit faceplate. Cyndi Salito. She said, "No topping off, though. I don't want the whole shebang blowing up in our face."

"And you still think it can take the lift-off okay?"

She probably would have shrugged if the bulky spacesuit would have allowed her that much freedom of movement. "I still insist we get the hell out of Dodge when this thing launches. Lift-offs are a bit bumpy, you know—even with quaint little methane engines. This safety distance of five kilometers is for the birds once the hopper gets off the ground—if it explodes then, the blast could send pieces everywhere."

Cyndi looked up from the data screens. Her station was set away from the main holotank and depended on solid-state readouts rather than holograms projected into the central tank. The room was darkened, packed with most of the moonbase crew. "Ready when you are, Dr. Chu," she said.

Newellen glanced around at the crew. "Hey, has anyone notified Jason at Sim-Mars?"

Chu scowled, not wanting to think about the former commander hiding in the isolation lab, as if there wasn't more important work to be done here.

"We've got him hooked up through the secondary relay," Salito said. "He should be getting the feed along with us."

"Let's do it, then," said Chu. "No use waiting for Earth

to okay it. We're the ones on the line, here, and this is our show."

Working the virtual joysticks with his massive hands, Newellen paused. "Uh, you don't want a countdown or anything like that, do you?"

Bryan Zimmerman hovered beside him, watching the sequence of events; Cyndi Salito stood close to him, looking as if she were going to explode. "Come on! The longer you let that nitro wait, the more likely something could go wrong!"

"Okay, okay. Don't be so touchy."

Chu motioned with his head. "You heard her."

Newellen jabbed at the virtual controls. An instant later the image of the hopper in the holotank shuddered. Dust flew up, obscuring the lower part of the view. The holotank seemed to vibrate. Suddenly the hopper shot up and out of view.

"She's off, and no explosion," said Salito. She leaned into the projected diagnostics. Green lights from the controls reflected off her face. "Looks like we've got a good trajectory, and she's holding together. Good job on those patch-up welds."

"Does this mean it'll make it?" asked Newellen.

Salito straightened. "We'll know in half an hour. Max G loading was at takeoff. Since the nitro survived that, there's no reason to worry. None at all."

"I'm going to start worrying as soon as it prangs into the artifact!" Newellen said. "Then we'll see what the aliens decide to do. What if they get pissed?"

"Three . . . two . . . one," Salito said. "And . . . now!"

The control room became dead quiet. Every diagnostic on Salito's panel showed no activity. Chu wet his lips before speaking. "Did it work?"

"Give us another minute for the S wave to get here, boss," Newellen said. "We'll be able to tell from the seismic shock if it was merely an impact or if the nitro detonated. Thud or thunder."

He twisted his large frame in the chair and read off the seismographs that fluttered beneath their glass-enclosed cage. "I've got two stations reporting now and it looks good, as far as magnitude goes. Big boom. Once the S wave gets here I'll have a fix on the exact location."

Chu merely nodded. It would have been so much easier if the satellite at L-2 had monitoring capability, rather than just the bare instrumentation necessary for a relay station.

"Got it, got it, got it!" Newellen announced. He stood and scanned the seismograph. "A direct hit, smack in the middle of the artifact! And it made a big kaboom."

Salito folded her arms and looked smug. "That much nitro should have taken out more than the entire structure! There's probably a crater within the crater."

Chu spoke rapidly, snapping his fingers. "Launch the javelin probe. I want a look at it now. As soon as it gets a chance to cool down, we need to validate via IR that we've stopped all nanotech activity."

As he stepped back, Chu watched the team swing into action. Even though no confirmation had yet come through, the morale of the entire base had lifted. At least now they had something to look forward to. They had struck a blow. They had done something instead of sitting around and playing victim.

Chu prayed that he hadn't made things worse. What if the alien nanocritters decided to strike back?

The control room had only a skeleton crew when Newellen approached Bernard Chu with a handful of further results. "Take a look."

Newellen used a chubby finger to set up a playback cube, calling his own files. As the image appeared, Chu felt a sudden sense of vertigo. "Walk me through this, if you please."

Newellen set the playback to slow motion and pushed a finger into the holotank. "The javelin is coming down off its ballistic trajectory, here, and has rotated so the ground is 'down.'" The view swung around, moving from a backdrop of stars to the mottled black-on-gray of lunar regolith. Everything looked eerie in the infra-red spectrum; most of the nightside surface was cold, showing no heat being emanated. "Any second now it will pass directly over the artifact."

Chu watched, half expecting to see no change in the mysterious structure, half wanting to see it leveled to the crater floor. As the javelin approached, he sucked in a breath.

Portions of the Daedalus complex were down, disconnected. The superstrong diamond-woven fibers comprising the structure seemed unharmed, but tangled, with all the foundation and support knocked out from under them. The perfectly symmetric hole from which the artifact had sprung now showed irregular features as part of the surface had collapsed, revealing an extensive network of unexpected catacombs beneath the crater floor.

But the main image that stayed with Bernard Chu was that the area glowed a brilliant white in the IR, brighter than it had ever been before—showing that nanotech activity had increased over an order of magnitude since the explosion.

"That's not just residual heat from the blast, is it?" Chu asked, already suspecting the answer.

"No way! That stuff permeates everything. They're swarming all over the place like ants after a rainstorm."

Chu watched the transmissions as the javelin went over, then impacted the regolith, cutting off the image. He whispered, "We didn't do a thing, did we? All we did was to give them a minor setback. And spread them out farther."

"Yeah," said Newellen, "we sure stirred them up good." He waited a beat. "Now they seem to be in even more of a hurry."

28

washington, d.c.

Compared to this, a war would have been a piece of cake, Major General Pritchard thought.

Lips drawn tight, Pritchard looked out his office window toward the Air and Space Museum. At times like these, Pritchard envied his military classmates, still on active duty at the Pentagon some three miles away. The Pentagon types only had to worry about smashing the hell out of whomever the president told them to—a fast, clean job. And no president had given such orders for years.

Pritchard, on the other hand, had to deal with a threat that was anything but certain. Nothing about the alien construction was certain. Was it even a threat at all?

An old flatscreen-television played quietly in his office. Pritchard watched the Cable NewsNet from the corner of his eye, though he concentrated mainly on the Smithsonian complex across the street. The National Air and Space Museum contained relics of other times mankind had found ways to solve seemingly insurmountable problems. Maybe someday there would also be a model of the Daedalus structure on exhibit. If the human race survived.

For the past year the Air and Space Museum had been negotiating with Pritchard as the Space Agency liaison for new material to display: lunar hoppers taken out of service, prototypes of the stegosauruslike He-3 mining rovers, Jason Dvorak's blueprints for a remodeled Columbus.

248

Within six months, a new wing of the museum would open, devoted entirely to the Moon-Mars initiative.

By that time, Pritchard thought, *there might not even be a lunar colony in existence!* The Farside construction had put everything in question. Could the Agency continue setting priorities on a manned Mars mission without knowing the true nature of the alien race behind the nanomachines?

As Pritchard's gaze lingered on the white marble buildings, he heard a chanting crowd on the television set. He swung around in his chair. The camera panned over thousands of people. Some held up signs, many shook their fists in the air. All of them were chanting something Pritchard could not make out.

"Where is this?" he asked.

The screen displayed a slugline: STANFORD UNIVERSITY.

The voice of the news commentator came up over the noise. "The crowd is estimated to be over thirty thousand by the police, and a hundred thousand by the protest organizers. Their spokespeople claim they are very concerned about the threat of nanotechnology, whether it be from the Farside of the Moon, or closer at home here in California. Researchers at Stanford have refused to come out and meet with the demonstrators—"

The scene switched to the Daedalus construction—an image two weeks old, Pritchard noticed. The newsnets had played similar stories two or three times an evening for the past month or so. With the destruction of the Collins, public interest and panic had soared.

Suddenly, an unknown threat had fallen in everyone's lap. The security they had felt from years of peace now wavered with paranoia. "ALIEN INVASION!" screamed the tabloids.

As Pritchard watched the protesting crowd, he knew that this nanotech menace seemed more threatening even than "radioactivity," which had caused unreasoning panic among the stubborn and uneducated for generations. At least people could explain what radioactivity was, and they could take precautions against it. But the self-replicating nanotech menace was something no one had a handle on.

Some people had cheered yesterday's attempt by Bernard Chu to blow up the construction, while others screamed bloody murder about provoking the alien presence, about giving the wrong message to another technological civilization. Pritchard knew it had been a hotdog act by Chu, more to spite Celeste than to protect the moonbase, and Pritchard didn't approve of such drastic actions. The setback to the Daedalus construction should have calmed the world somewhat, though. Now they had a little more breathing room.

But the public would not be reassured so easily.

He turned away from the CNN televised images of chanting crowds and swung his gaze across downtown Washington. It seemed so peaceful out there: humid air, tourists, fountains spraying. Agency Headquarters hadn't yet been the focus of many protests—but the nanotech labs would only be the first place people would hit.

Anti-war demonstrators took their anger to the defense contractors, the laboratories that produced the weapons, and even the soldiers themselves. But after a while, they lashed out at the people responsible for making the policy. It was only a matter of time.

If Pritchard could just find a way to make them feel safe again while the Agency worked on the real solution. If he could show the public the Agency was taking decisive action, lull them into a sense of security. . . .

Pritchard leaned forward and slapped at the intercom on his desk. "Jeff?"

His aide's voice came back within seconds. "Yes, sir?"

"I need some information, as soon as you can trace it for me. The International Verification Initiative watchdog team—what can you get me on it? What devices have they got available, and how can I get my hands on them? What authority do I need?"

After a pause, Jeff responded, "I've sent the electronic servant through our combined databases. It should have all the information on your terminal in a few minutes. You have the authority to contact the IVI directly on an Undersecretary level. Even Director McConnell can't get any higher because of diplomatic protocol. Shall I initiate a contact for you?"

250

Pritchard thought fast. Dealing with an agency not within the U.S. government made things tricky. The United Space Agency could supposedly get around those barriers, being an "international" agency itself. But because they were housed, staffed, and mostly underwritten by the U.S., the Agency carried only "lip-service" diplomatic credentials. The Verification Initiative, on the other hand, was a true international commission. But the IVI was the key to what he had in mind.

Pritchard said, "I need to speak with Director McConnell first. Is she in?"

Two heartbeats passed. "She's over at the Hill. Do you want me to raise her?"

Pritchard thought briefly. He was a big boy, and things were changing too damned fast to worry about covering his butt every time. No one had thought up anything better yet, so he decided to go ahead with his decision. He drew in a breath.

"No, but I need to put in a call for a press conference. Wait, make that a video statement instead. We'll issue it to the newsnets and do a conference to answer their questions another time." He glanced at the Stanford mob scene on the television, then at his watch. "Make sure the studio room is open. I want to go on in an hour."

"Very well, General. Ready in forty-five minutes."

As his aide clicked off, Pritchard thought, *I sure the hell hope I know what I'm doing.*

The technician pointed at Pritchard and mouthed, "Three, two, one . . . you're on." A red light came on over the tri-D cameras mounted at 120-degree intervals around the studio.

Simon Pritchard tried not to look at the cameras, but instead stared into the stereochip that showed his features on the wallscreen. Minutes earlier he had finished combing his hair, and had checked to make sure his military jacket was immaculate. He didn't have as many medals, pins, or insignia as his contemporaries, but that was the price he paid for being a scholar in a warrior's world.

Kevin J. Anderson and Doug Beason

Pritchard said, "Good afternoon. As I have said before, the United Space Agency will keep you updated during this time of crisis. After yesterday's attempt to use explosives against the alien construction on the Moon, we now know that conventional methods of eradicating the nanotechnological phenomenon will not work. Though we believe the explosion has set back the work of the machines for a time, they seem to be recovering rapidly. We still don't know what it is they are building, nor do we seem able to stop it—even if we wanted to.

"The United Space Agency believes it is imperative to keep this alien technology at bay until we know its purpose, until we can be sure it is not a threat. We need some ace in the hole, a defense we can count on if—and I repeat, *if*—the Daedalus construction turns out to be something we should fear."

He concentrated on maintaining a grave expression. "Exactly one half hour ago, the United Space Agency formally sent a petition to the International Verification Initiative, the sole international organization tasked with the accounting of nuclear weapons. Since they are headquartered in Washington, D.C., we expect a response from them shortly. A go-ahead from the IVI would allow the United Space Agency to remove up to six nuclear devices from this nation's last nuclear stockpile."

He paused long enough for that to sink in. He wondered, when this was broadcast, how many home viewers would stand up and cheer, and how many would scream in outrage?

"We plan to transport these devices onboard a robotically controlled ship in the safest manner possible to Daedalus Crater on the lunar Farside. Once the shipment has been delivered, it is our plan to have Columbus personnel install these six devices in a ring around the crater—as a safety measure only. We must make the alien presence know we are serious. We must be prepared, in the event that the construction turns out to be a weapon of some kind directed against Earth.

"We will install a total chemical equivalent of over twenty million tons of TNT, with each device capable of

252

producing a crater over a mile in diameter. In case of an emergency, we will detonate the devices to ensure that the alien artifact is completely destroyed."

For a moment he let himself feel immensely relieved that he had not allowed any of the newsnet reps into the studio room. He couldn't handle the questions right now. Pritchard nodded at the camera and said, "We will keep you updated. Thank you."

He continued to stare toward the stereochip until a red light above the unit blinked out. Pritchard relaxed his shoulders for the first time in what seemed like hours. The technicians scrambled around to straighten up the room. Someone else was already passing the tape through the classification people, but Pritchard could veto anything they complained about. He was more worried about what Celeste would say. But somehow, he knew she would approve.

The Agency would soon be inundated with protests from all sides. It was bad enough to have the anti-nanotech freaks upset at him. Now he'd be bringing the old anti-nuke protesters out of the woodwork, too.

It would have been a lot easier to fight a war, he thought again.

sim-mars

For the second time in his life, Jason Dvorak knew what it was like to be run over by a truck.

The first time had been when Margaret demanded a divorce. The second time was the helpless feeling after having this unwanted command snatched away from him. Jason could feel it eating at him, making him want to do something instead of letting the bureaucracy and the circumstances jerk him around.

Jason hadn't particularly resented it when McConnell placed Bernard Chu back in command—the other man was much better suited to the task, by any measure. But watching Chu's bombing of the Daedalus construction made Jason have second thoughts.

Chu was a biochemist, not an architect. He had not bothered to figure out how best to damage the Daedalus artifact with conventional explosives. Jason wondered if he should have been more outspoken. Their instruments showed the thing was made with diamond fiber and diamond foam—it wasn't a house of straw that could be blown down with a huff and a puff.

True, the nitroglycerine and rocket fuel explosion had knocked out much of the support structure under the regolith, fractured and collapsed some hefty catacombs— lava tubes, maybe?—which had made the alien structure unstable. No one had even known the tunnels existed before this. Was there more nanotech excavation? How much of the alien complex was actually hidden from view underground? Chu's explosion had also spewed the Daedalus nanocritters far and wide.

Watching the IR flyover afterward, Jason found it painfully clear that the pace of the nanocritters' activity had tripled to repair the damage done. The scattered hot zone had shrunk visibly in an hour, showing that the nanocritters were regrouping at the construction site.

Jason felt safe out at the Sim-Mars lab module with Erika, but he didn't trust his temper around the new commander right now. He turned his back on the main holotank. Erika was on the stool next to him, looking exhausted. Jason said, "Okay, I give up. What do we do next?"

"What?" Erika raised her eyes. She looked wrung out, as if it didn't matter to her anymore.

Jason dropped his hands to his side. "I mean, what else can they expect us to do?"

Erika's sandy hair clung to the perspiration dotting her forehead. "Now that somebody's decided the safest course of action is to knock out the construction, Chu was just trying to get rid of it—"

"Nobody decided that! Chu just wanted to show off. He could have left the whole damn site alone! Just look at what the explosion did!" He gestured to the infrared view of Daedalus in the holotank behind him. Though the alien structure was in ruins, hot spots of activity showed clearly, reconstructing the damaged framework in the rubble.

"What if we've pissed off the construction boss in charge of your nanocritters? What will they do now? What if they come back here to take apart every scrap of metal on Columbus?"

She shook her head. "These are machines working in some kind of programmed way on a preset blueprint. *Programmed*, Jase. These things don't hold grudges, they don't have a penchant for getting even. What just happened to them could have been a random meteor strike, for all they know. They're machines, not Saberhagen's Berserkers."

"Bronco busters?"

255

"Berserkers ... never mind." She stood and walked to the holotank, tapping her finger on its base. "They've just looped back to another part of their construction program, assembling whatever they were supposed to except at an accelerated pace to make up for lost time. Before long, you won't be able to find a scratch from our home-made bomb." Erika sighed. "I don't know what to do now."

"So let's put our heads together." Jason forced a smile for her. "New challenges and all that. You've already found a way to cure us. Come to think of it, would it be too difficult to send some of your nanocannibals over there to stop the construction process?"

Erika's greenish eyes grew wide. "Jase—my God, we've had the answer all along! Why didn't we think of this before?"

"I thought it only worked in our bodies."

"If it works on us, why wouldn't it work on Farside? It'll be like a vaccine for the whole construction site!"

Erika was already speaking to the holotank controller. "Computer, bring up Bernard Chu at Moonbase Columbus immediately! Priority one, or whatever the urgent category is."

"Priority A," Jason said.

"Priority A!"

Jason moved closer to Erika. In front of him, she had turned to the experimentation chamber, preparing the enclosed crucible to accept more nanocritter samples. She grabbed Jason by the ears and pulled his face to hers for a quick peck on the lips.

"I have to make a new batch of Destroyers," she said. "Once we've stopped the near-term threat of that construction—if it is a threat—we'll have more than enough time to find out what makes those nanocritters tick."

Chu appeared in the holotank, bleary-eyed in front of the transceiver. Grinning, Erika knew she was going to give him something that would really wake him up.

The first IR overflight showed images exactly as Erika had expected.

Five hours earlier, Moonbase Columbus had launched another projectile at the alien construction site, filled with an electrostatically contained sample of Erika's modified Destroyers. Comparing it to a vaccine against an infection on the Moon's surface, she had convinced Chu that the Destroyers would self-replicate and defeat the rest of the alien nanomachines. Within twenty-four hours the nanotech activity should have decreased by about ninety-five percent, with only a few nanocannibals left to clean up the rest.

Standing again in the control center of Moonbase Columbus, Erika felt immense relief as the infrared map from the first flyover javelin displayed pockets of intense activity—but the overall concentration of alien nanomachines had decreased dramatically. A few people in the control center applauded. Agency Select broadcast it all live. Celeste McConnell sent her personal congratulations.

All indications were that Erika's Destroyers were slaughtering the critters swarming around the gossamer construction. The nanocannibals wouldn't tear down the structure itself, merely "disinfect" it. It would be like an entomologist cleaning out a wasp nest before studying its structure. Somebody—maybe even Erika herself—could safely go to the site to get an up-close view of what the extraterrestrial blueprint carried. Who could tell what might be buried under those new catacombs Chu's bomb had cracked open?

Upon seeing the decreased IR activity, Chu immediately broadcast a new videoloop to Earth. He no longer used Erika as a spokesperson though—the idea seemed to be working, so he didn't need her as a potential scapegoat anymore.

With her legs trembling even in the low lunar gravity, Erika went back to the moonbase room she shared with Cyndi Salito. Up and down the module quarters, other exiles from the Collins crowded in with moonbase personnel. With Erika gone to Sim-Mars most of the time, and with Salito working odd hours, they had crossed paths only a few times. This time, the dim underground room was empty. With a sigh, Erika lay back on the flex-polymer bunk and closed her eyes to take a nap. Next javelin in five hours. By that time the nanocannibals should be halfway through mopping up. . . .

Erika hurried into the control center, nearly late for the arrival of the second probe. She had fallen asleep to uneasy dreams and had awakened with only time enough to wipe a cold towel across her face. Jason had met her in the halls, coming to fetch her before she was late.

When they entered the bustling room, Newellen brought up several cubes showing perspectives of the incoming javelin. Chu, sitting in the prime focus of the holocameras, was already broadcasting live. From the side, Cyndi called up an image of the previous extent of the nanocritters' IR hot zone, then the much dimmer mapping of the infestation five hours earlier. The hot spots still showed areas of intense nanomachine activity.

"We expect to see a similar reduction in population," Chu was saying to his unseen audience. "We'll confirm this in just a moment."

The IR image speckled and resolved into grainier colors. Using the morphologies Erika had determined from her first work, Newellen had developed image enhancement techniques that could determine the gross characteristics of large congregations of a particular type of nanocritter; "packs" he called them. Yellow indicated the standard Assemblers clustered over the structure of the construction itself; green showed the packs of Disassemblers, combing the regolith for raw materials they would ship molecule by molecule to the waiting Assemblers. Not shown, but scattered throughout the population were the much larger Controllers, information substations that directed the operations, as well as the courier Programmers that carried messages and instructions through the entire population.

Erika's nanocannibals were coded red. The processed image from the first flyover showed bright red sweeping over the site like a tidal wave, consuming all the nanomachines it encountered. She expected the color coding of the rest of the area to be overwhelmingly red after ten hours.

The javelin soared over the lunar surface as Daedalus Crater came into view. "Here we are," Chu said. "Images coming in now. We are processing them realtime."

The view in the holotank rotated and grew to take up the entire volume. It took on the garish colors of the data-massaged infrared signal. But the colors did not look right. Not at all.

"Oh, no," Erika said, at a loss for any other words.

The image glowed in sharp relief. A mosaic of colors glittered in the tank. Black areas covered the regolith, the construction, the entire crater floor, swallowing up most of the red—the red that signified the nano-Destroyers. Bright blots of yellow and green—Assemblers and Disassemblers—had resurged, filling areas that the red had dominated only five hours before.

Jason moved next to Salito. "Is the contrast adjusted properly?"

"That's a real image we're getting back," she said, looking bewildered.

The diamond thread spires holding up the alien structure burned bright in the infrared from nanomachines swarming over the columns. Everywhere the alien complex stood out in vivid detail: the parabolic curves of the "petal" segments, humplike structures that lay off to the side, bright cracks showing where immense tunnels branched away from the central pit.

Chu seemed to have forgotten he was transmitting. "What are all the black areas?"

Newellen said, "We color-encoded with black to signify an unknown morphology of nanocritter. We're seeing something new. Completely new."

Erika whispered, "This can't be true."

She sensed Jason moving close to her. The control center became too quiet. "What do you mean?" he asked. "What is all this about?"

"An unknown species of nanocritter." She looked at Jason, her eyes wide. Her words were probably being picked up by Agency Select and broadcast everywhere.

"They can't replicate that fast. Those are my nano-cannibals, I think. They've been reprogrammed. Or the other nanocritters have been. Daedalus set up a classic immune-system response—they sent out a new form of machines like white corpuscles."

She stared at the image of the Daedalus construction. "This is much more aggressive, and I don't think they'll tolerate any more attacks from us. They're learning to protect themselves."

30

alpha base—
wendover air force base, utah

"Got your bearings yet, General?"

"What?" Simon Pritchard cupped a hand to his ear and leaned close to the young black major sitting next to him. Wind whipped through the backseat of the helicopter, making it difficult to hear. Up front, the pilot didn't even try to speak, circling the restricted airspace.

Major Felowmate yelled out, "I said, do you know where we are, sir?"

"Not sure—first time I've been to Alpha Base."

The major gestured over the seat in front of them. "We're heading west—Nevada state line is two miles in front of us. I-80 is twenty miles to the north, and Wendover is just behind us. We're sitting on top of Alpha Base right now. I'm in charge of this whole sandbox."

"Sure got here fast!" Pritchard shouted. He looked down at the gaping crater called Alpha Base. He could see bunkers set into the ground and dotting the crater walls like shacks in a strip mine. "Why aren't we landing yet?"

"Getting final approval, sir. Priority one restricted airspace! We'd be shot down if we didn't have special electronic equipment onboard to identify us as 'friendly.'"

Pritchard snorted and leaned back into his jump seat. As a scientific officer, he had never had to live in close quarters with operational military men.

Felowmate turned around in his seat as the pilot made a sudden motion in front of them and pointed out the cockpit. Felowmate gave the woman a thumbs-up, then turned back to Pritchard. "Just been cleared to land."

Pritchard nodded and turned to look back at the ground. Desert stretched out on either side, broken only by the four barbed-wire fences that encircled Alpha Base. To the west lay the mountain ranges of Nevada; he could see Wendover AFB to their left, and the long runway where the Agency plane had landed him only twenty minutes before.

Built a good forty years before as a nuclear weapons storage site, Alpha Base held the majority of America's remaining warheads. Most had been dismantled, but a few of the "safest" devices remained here, watched over by an extensive International Verification Initiative team.

As the helicopter bumped to the ground, Major Felowmate ducked, jumped from the craft, and motioned for Pritchard to follow. The pilot remained in her seat, saluting Pritchard as he climbed out.

The hot, dry air hit him like a blast from an oven. He and the major scuttled away from the Blackhawk helicopter toward a caravan of waiting cars. The helicopter's rotor blades whipped dust up into the air, making Pritchard's eyes sting.

As they approached the cars, uniformed guards on either side of the lead vehicle snapped to attention. Both carried automatic rifles. A woman in a white dress got out of the car. Her blond hair braided into a bun and her white stockings made her look like a bizarre hallucination in the bleak wasteland. She held one hand to her hair and the other shielded her eyes.

Pritchard heard the helicopter roar back into the air toward Wendover AFB. After a few seconds the thrumming noise had faded enough for him to hear and think clearly for the first time since he had landed in Utah.

Major Felowmate made the introductions as they walked up to the waiting group. "General, this is Francine Helschmidt. She's our International Verification Initiative liaison officer out of Salt Lake City."

262

"General." Her grip was firm and her eyes hard as volcanic rock. "Glad to be of help."

"Thank you." Pritchard looked around at the rest of the caravan. Now that the dust from the helicopter had dissipated, he could see that the four-wheel-drive vehicles were painted Air Force blue. Each held a military driver, several civilians, and what appeared to be an armed guard. Pritchard nodded toward the other people. "These are the IVI observers, I take it?" His voice rang in his ears, still vibrating from the helicopter ride.

"That's right, General." Francine Helschmidt handed him a list of names. "They've been cleared through appropriate channels. We have assured them that once the seals are broken on the storage bunkers, they will watch your every move. We need to make sure you get only the specific warheads to which you have been authorized."

Pritchard did not like Helschmidt's cool tone. He cocked an eyebrow at her. "You mean 'nuclear devices,' don't you? I'm not going to use them as warheads. We're not going to war. They are a protective measure against an extraterrestrial threat."

Helschmidt stood with her feet apart and her hands stiff at her side. "We might as well call a spade a spade, General—there was no reason to have produced these things other than for going to war."

"Really?" Pritchard drew his lips tight. He had met people like her before, and at times he found it amusing to push their all-too-obvious buttons. In this case, though, he had no time to play games.

"Yes, really, General," Helschmidt said. "But that appears to be a moot point, doesn't it? You have received your approval. Whether you call them warheads or not, we've been instructed to ensure that only six 'devices' are removed from the storage bunkers. I have already studied your security plan for transporting the weapons, and I believe it might be effective, provided you run into no unforeseen difficulties."

Pritchard refused to react to her comments. He had run the security plan through expert sabotage teams, challenging anyone to come up with an ambush scenario that would successfully divert the devices from their intended delivery point. Now he understood her—Helschmidt didn't know what the hell she was talking about, but wanted everyone to think she was important. He wondered how she had managed to reach her present position.

"Thanks for reminding me, Ms. Helschmidt. Now, if we could go about our business?" Pritchard turned to Major Felowmate, who gestured to the lead vehicle. Opening the front door for her, Pritchard nodded to Helschmidt. "Please have a seat."

"I'll sit in the back, General."

"I insist."

Helschmidt stepped up into the vehicle. Pritchard slammed the door and moved to the rear seat, where Major Felowmate held open the door, then climbed in beside him.

The caravan of vehicles lurched into motion along the dirt road as soon as Pritchard had buckled his seat belt. The road was dusty and full of potholes and scrub brush.

Helschmidt turned in her seat. "Major Felowmate, I assume you have the secondary holo-key."

Felowmate patted his chest. "I've got it." To Pritchard, the major explained, "The storage bunkers need two holographic keys to produce the interference pattern necessary to open them. One key is kept by the IVI Institute while Alpha Base holds the other. Without both, it is impossible to open any bunker."

Pritchard had heard of such keys. Lasers could produce a nearly infinite number of interference patterns. Without the exact sequence of spatial frequencies, no one could break the code to open the bunker.

The vehicle bounced as the driver tried to find the smoothest part of the road. Pritchard watched the landscape for a few moments before he spoke again. "So, how long have you been with the IVI, Ms. Helschmidt?"

She brushed back her hair. "This is my second year. I was appointed by the Administration to this post after the election."

"So you've had experience in disarmament before, I take it?"

"Actually, no. I headed a small PR firm in Washington before this. I was part of the advance team for the president's campaign. I was on the road for most of a year and a half, visiting every small town on the map, getting people inspired for the president's visit."

Pritchard nodded, but forced himself not to speak. He had learned to put up with a lot during his fast-track Air Force career, where politics always made the job more difficult. Yet most of Pritchard's own assignments had grown out of being in the right place at the right time. He thought of Celeste McConnell and the positions she herself had held. *Now that was definitely luck*, he thought. Everything from escaping the Grissom destruction to her promotion at the Agency.

Major Felowmate leaned to the front of his seat and directed the driver around to the front of an array of white concrete bunkers. "Those are the ones."

Behind them, the caravan pulled into a semicircle. Three storage bunkers faced each other, 120 degrees apart. The bunkers stood twenty feet high, fifty feet across, and a hundred feet long, covered with a dirt berm. At least five hundred bunkers dotted the crater, each one with metal searchlights affixed to the top, each one displaying the three-bladed international radiation symbol painted in magenta and yellow.

Felowmate nodded toward the closest bunker. "Here we are, General."

Pritchard joined Francine Helschmidt out on the concrete apron in front of the nearest bunker. She smoothed her skirt, though wind continued to flick it around her knees. Pritchard noticed a half-dozen modified Sikorsky helicopters hovering at various points around Alpha Base. Watchdogs. He turned to Felowmate and pointed at the choppers. "Are they providing security for us?"

"And against you," Francine Helschmidt said. "Just in case anything goes wrong."

Felowmate answered Pritchard. "Three of them are, sir. The other three will land to take you and the devices back to Wendover, where you'll load them on the transport plane."

"Those three helicopters aren't to carry only six devices, are they? I requested tactical nukes, not something that needs a crane to lift."

The major nodded. "I added two other copters as decoys, sir. We don't want anyone to know which one actually has possession until the last possible moment—terrorists, you know."

Escorted by security policemen, three men walked up to them from the other vehicles. In the lead strode an overweight man who carried his jacket over one arm; dark semicircles of sweat seeped from his armpits as he wiped at his face with a handkerchief. Beside him, a small, thin man also sweated, but he seemed determined not to make an effort to cool down; his suit looked two sizes too big for him. The third man wore a loose-fitting short-sleeved shirt. Swarthy and with a medium build, the man looked comfortable in the desert. Of the three, only he grinned at Pritchard. He held out a hand and spoke with a British accent. "Major General Pritchard, pleased to meet you. Francine has briefed us on what to expect. I look forward to expediting matters."

"Thank you," said Pritchard. He turned to the other two men but they merely nodded.

Helschmidt said, "Well, General. This is the rest of the IVI on-site verification team. Are you ready?"

"Let's get moving."

Major Felowmate stepped to the bunker door, unbuttoning the top of his khaki shirt. He pulled on a chain around his neck to withdraw a squat rod that looked like a tiny flashlight with bumps dotting the base. "Ms. Helschmidt?" She fumbled with a chain about her neck and withdrew an identical-looking rod.

The major motioned to the security policemen to stand aside. The guards stood around the bunker in a semicircle, facing outward with weapons ready. Pritchard glanced around the empty desert, trying to find any evidence of a threat.

At first it seemed ludicrous to Pritchard that such precautions were being taken deep inside of Alpha Base, already past four barbed-wire fences and dozens of intruder-prevention measures. Perhaps the extra show of security was to impress either himself or the IVI team.

Major Felowmate escorted Francine Helschmidt and Pritchard around to the side of the bunker. A shoebox-sized panel protruded from the wall at shoulder height. Felowmate motioned for Pritchard to step back. "Stand outside of the red lines, sir. That's where the bunker doors will swing open."

Pritchard took a step back to be completely away from the semicircle only half-visible on the dirt-covered concrete slab.

Felowmate wiped dust from the top of the box and squinted at a number engraved on its surface. "SK-3452," he said. He checked a number written on a small card he withdrew from his pocket. "This is it. Double-checked." Both he and Helschmidt made some sort of adjustment to their keys.

Pritchard fidgeted on his feet in the desert sun. He should have delegated the tedious retrieval task to someone else—but he wanted to keep this under his own close supervision.

"Bunker number is keyed in," said Helschmidt.

"Have you done this before?" Felowmate asked her.

Helschmidt hesitated. "No." She seemed embarrassed, but Felowmate ignored it. "I'll go first. You'll have ten seconds to insert your key or every alarm on base will go off. Ready? Here goes."

Felowmate inserted the squat rod into the box. Beside him, Helschmidt added her holo-key to an adjacent receptacle. Inside the shielded box, lasers scanned the keys' interference patterns. A green light glowed at the bottom of the box.

"Please wait until the doors stop moving," Felowmate said as the two massive doors began to crawl open, like the gaping entrance to some ancient tomb.

Felowmate said, "Each one of these steel doors weighs somewhere around twenty tons. They're five inches thick and reinforced with rebar—built to withstand a twenty-thousand-pound bomb going off right next to them."

When the doors stopped moving, they looked like the giant jaws of some behemoth, waiting to swallow anything that came too close. "General, Ms. Helschmidt?" Felowmate motioned to them, then pointed toward the waiting security policemen. "Smitty—you, Witz, and Dardanelle follow us in. You know the drill."

"Yes, sir," all three answered at once. They drew up their weapons.

Felowmate said, "They've got orders to shoot, General, if anyone tries anything."

Pritchard smiled to himself. "Don't worry, I won't."

"We are waiting, Major," said Helschmidt. She stood by the entrance with the other three members of the verification team.

When they stepped into the shadows, a hint of coolness along with a musty smell wafted from the bunker. The small man in the big suit pulled out a computerized notepad. He made notes with a stylus as they entered the bunker. Stark screened-in lights cast shadows across the floor. Yellow lines were painted on the rough-surfaced concrete.

Felowmate pointed to a yellow band. "Follow the yellow brick road, please—we need you to stay inside the path." He turned to Pritchard. "The devices are dispersed here inside the bunker. Can't risk having too many nukes too close together, otherwise the probability of spontaneous fission goes up. Too many stray neutrons in the air."

As his eyes adjusted to the light, Pritchard could see corridors running off in different directions. After walking past two intersections, Felowmate stopped and pointed toward the right. "This is the chamber we want. Ms. Helschmidt?"

They approached another steel vault door. A second shoebox-sized panel, identical to the one outside, was embedded in the wall. Felowmate extracted his holo-key. "Same procedure as before."

After inserting their keys, he and Francine Helschmidt stepped back and allowed the vault door to open. Felowmate said, "This is it, General. Here's your nukes."

If the alien artifact on the Moon turned out to be an immediate threat, and if Pritchard had to jump through

268

this many interlocks and double-checks before they could use their defenses, they might just as well kiss Earth goodbye. He would have to speak with Celeste about streamlining the command and control process.

Pritchard waited for the major to enter the chamber first. When no one moved to accompany him, Pritchard stepped inside the vault himself. He saw ten white cans the size of oil drums, each inside a yellow barrier circle painted on the floor.

"Storage containers, sir," said Felowmate. "They're equipped with PALs—Permissive Action Links—a device that can disable the warheads if they're stolen. There's also some other nasty protective things embedded in the containers in case somebody tries to screw around with them, but we can't talk about that."

Helschmidt and her team stepped into the chamber. They walked around the containers, using a micro-barcode reader to verify each device. Satisfied that the right warheads were where they should be, Helschmidt pointed to six of the containers. "These are yours, General."

Pritchard nodded in silence. If the alien nanomachines became a threat, he thought, those weapons might be their last hope. If he needed to wrestle red tape to get a quarantine ring in place, he would put up with it.

"Good luck, General," Felowmate said.

"Save your luck for the people up on the Moon. They need it more than I do."

Felowmate nodded to the security policemen still standing guard outside the vault door. "Smitty, get a crew in here to take these away. General Pritchard will give you instructions."

Francine Helschmidt stepped forward and spoke to Pritchard in a low voice. "Don't make us regret this, General."

31

daedalus crater, farside

Bryan Zed would look right at home chewing on a stalk of grass,
Jason thought. Even in a spacesuit, the silent shuttle pilot
gave the appearance of a good-old-boy as he went alone
on his mission across the desolate Farside terrain—not
quite a redneck, just someone who was honest and straight-
forward to the point of parody.

After Zimmerman lay down in the rover bed to keep
himself from being seen, the vehicle sped away. Agency
Mission Control and everyone watching on the newsnets
thought the rover was simply a telepresent inspection
vehicle commandeered by Newellen. But Zimmerman
had volunteered to try something on his own. A long shot,
of course, but the people on Columbus really had nothing
else to try. Or to lose.

Jason stood with Big Daddy Newellen and Cyndi Salito
on a small rise ten kilometers from Daedalus. Even from this
distance, Jason could make out details of the sprawling
weblike construction, like a spun-glass sculpture in the
middle of the VLF array. The huge flowerlike central structure—some sort of receiving dish?—glistened in the harsh
sunlight along with humps of support buildings. The entire
thing was opaque and well defined now. Within the last few
days the complex had taken on a new look of solidness.

"That sucker looks almost finished," Newellen said into
the suit radio. "And to think it's been only six weeks since
we found it."

From their position, the three spacesuited people also had a good view of where the Agency's shuttle would land. The ship would be carrying six nuclear warheads for them to deploy around the alien construction. To destroy it as a last resort.

This certainly isn't the reason I came up to the Moon, Jason thought. He glanced at the chronometer projected onto his faceplate by the heads-up display. "Five minutes," he said.

"Right on time," came Cyndi's voice over the radio. "I just hope they land in the right place."

Newellen snorted in the suit radio. "I'd hate to think what six atomic bombs will do if they miss the mark and slam into us."

"Bad for you, lucky for me," said Zimmerman from the rover. Jason wondered if he had caught a trace of humor in the man's transmission.

"They're not armed yet," Cyndi said. "We have to activate the PALs when we bury the devices."

"Shut up, you guys," said Jason. "We're going live any minute now. We don't want them hearing Cyndi's voice." Salito had worn Zimmerman's namepatch, just in case any remote cameras happened to catch the ID.

Jason heard a click over his earphones, then Bernard Chu's filtered voice. "Jason, Columbus here. We show the L-2 link has been established. We've got an updated vector on the robotic ship. They're pegged to land right on schedule."

Chu still sounded nervous about setting the warheads in place. He had changed his attitude dramatically after the first bomb had not caused as much damage as he had hoped, and Erika's nanocannibal "purge" of the site had failed. Jason couldn't blame him—what if the nanocritters decided to retaliate? They had certainly received enough provocation. Or was Chu perhaps more concerned with Celeste McConnell's agenda, resenting that she was running the show while sitting safe on Earth?

Jason clicked his chin mike. It would take about three seconds for his voice to travel up to the L-2 relay station, all the way to Earth, then back up to Moonbase Columbus.

"We're ready out here, Columbus. If anything goes wrong with the landing, you'll know when we do. You'll just be around to enjoy it longer."

Jason remembered reading about catastrophes that had occurred transporting nukes during the Cold War days—bombers crashing on takeoff, weapons inexplicably "dropping" from bomb bays, mid-air collisions where some warheads had actually been lost. . . .

Intellectually, he knew that the probability of an accident was vanishingly small. But standing out on the surface of the Moon and waiting for an autopiloted machine to bring down the equivalent of more than twenty million tons of high explosive only a kilometer away from him, he felt weak in the knees.

The nanotech threat ten kilometers away didn't make him feel any better.

He didn't know how Zimmerman could find the guts to be there when the robotic shuttle landed. Especially when he claimed to distrust autopiloted systems.

"One minute," said Chu.

Jason turned away from Daedalus and looked up. He scanned the star-sparse sky. The Sun was still up, glaring down on the landscape, though the sky remained black with no atmosphere to scatter light. Farside had another three days before the Sun would set for two weeks.

Cyndi Salito's voice broke the silence over the radio. "Got it!" Then she abruptly silenced herself, remembering that she wasn't supposed to be saying anything. She pointed due north of Daedalus, thirty degrees up from the horizon.

Jason could see a patchwork of stars, fighting the glow from the Sun. He caught a movement out of the corner of his eye. There, just below Corona Borealis, a light grew brighter every second. The ship had already passed through the L-1 point and descended through a quick polar trajectory.

The giant alien construction towered over the floor of the crater in perfect silence, motionless. On Agency Select and the other channels Moonbase Columbus could tap, Jason had seen signs of the fierce debate still going on back

ASSEMBLERS OF INFINITY

on Earth about the purpose of the structure. Was it some sort of antenna for communication? A giant solar collector? A docking port? A work of art, like Alexandre Eiffel's tower on Earth?

The whys bothered Jason even more now than before. He himself was helping to set in motion the destruction of the artifact, and whatever purpose the alien structure had in store. As an architect, it offended him to knock down something so spectacular out of paranoia. As an inhabitant of Moonbase Columbus, though, the thing scared the bejesus out of him.

The bright spot of the incoming shuttle grew quickly enough that Jason could discern features. *What if it misses the landing site and hits the artifact itself?* What would happen if the nanomachines got to the warheads before someone had a chance to detonate them? Surely, the Disassemblers could render all the electronics inert in only a few minutes. Would Director McConnell have the warheads already primed and ready for immediate remote detonation, just in case that happened?

He recalled McConnell's skepticism that the nanocritters had really been purged from the bodies of the moonbase inhabitants. Had McConnell intended to detonate the warheads all along, to wipe out the artifact—and most of her problems—while claiming it had been an accident?

Sweat broke out over his body, forcing the spacesuit systems to work overtime. The possibility sounded so reasonable to him that he could not shake the idea. Jason started to speak his doubts, then decided not to voice them on open line. He barely had time to make out the spindly legs of the shuttle's landing pods as it came down, right on target, right on schedule.

Jason closed his eyes and let out a silent sigh of relief.

"Another perfect landing," Newellen said, raising his suited arm high in the air. "All hail the autopilot." The sudden movement in the constant-volume suit caused his other arm to cock back.

A rude noise came over the radio, most likely from Zimmerman.

273

Jason clicked his chin mike. "We've got a visual on the landing, Columbus. The rover will reach it shortly to unload the warheads." On cue, he saw the rover bouncing along out to the landing site.

They still had the task to unload the nukes and deploy them around Daedalus, just outside the hot zone. Six warheads, each equivalent to over three million tons of TNT. If this didn't finish off the "gigathreat via nano-technology," nothing would.

Once they had the defensive ring in place, the next move would be up to the alien artifact.

Lon Newellen sat hunched over the controls of the telerobotic rover. "Easy now," Cyndi whispered, looking over his shoulder.

A thin sheet of sweat glistened on Newellen's chubby face. He didn't look up from the controls. "No shit."

Jason joined them at the aft of the hopper that had taken them to the Farside. All three had taken off their helmets to breathe freely in the sealed cabin.

"Sorry." Cyndi stepped back and flashed Jason a nervous smile. Jason nodded wordlessly. Newellen was doing fine.

Newellen used the rover's robotic arms to reach inside the shuttle. Zimmerman was nowhere in the rover's narrow field of view—just as planned.

The shuttle's hatch slid open. *What if the Agency had booby-trapped it?* Jason thought of the "To Whom It May Concern" letter Chu had found in the last supply shuttle. Would they have thought to do the same thing here?

The six weapons were contained in the white storage barrels from Alpha Base. Everyone had watched the tapes of Major General Pritchard supervising the loading of the nukes onboard the transfer rocket from Cape Canaveral. Everyone knew that the weapon cores were supposed to be harmless until armed by the Permissive Action Links but Jason still felt nervous. He couldn't imagine what Zimmerman must be feeling as he scrambled to keep out of sight.

Newellen worked the robotic arms. Once he had managed to stand the first on the back of the flatbed rover, a second white container came quickly out of the hold. He was getting the hang of it.

At one point, Jason caught a flash of a white suit at the fringe of the field of view—Bryan Zed trying to keep out of the way—but Newellen quickly swiveled the robot's viewer and focused on hauling the remaining warheads out of the cargo bay.

Newellen withdrew his hands from the virtual controls and mopped his forehead. "Cyndi, get me a bag of apple chips out of the emergency stash. Then I'm ready to deliver these babies."

Munching, he took the controls again. Ahead of him on the area map, they watched the blip of the flatbed rover move away from the shuttle's landing site. In bright colors, the map showed the edge of the Daedalus hot zone, along with bright spots to indicate where the warheads should be placed. "It'll take me about an hour to drop off all six."

"Gives Zimmerman plenty of time," Jason said.

As Newellen drove the predetermined path around Daedalus, he stopped at each designated spot. He seemed a lot less nervous now, stopping for only a few minutes at each point, reaching in back of the flatbed with the robotic arm, and depositing one of the white canisters on the lunar surface. There was no need to place them with any finesse. If the nuclear ring were detonated by Earth command and control, a few feet of powdery regolith would make no difference.

Jason remained tense as the operation continued. They had heard no word from Zimmerman, nor did they expect to for at least another fifteen minutes.

One after another, Newellen deployed all six warheads. "I deserve a pizza when we get back to the base," he said.

Finally finished, he had encircled the three-kilometer-wide danger zone of Daedalus and returned to the remote shuttle. He motioned Salito to silence, then leaned closer to the intercom. "Columbus, mission accomplished and we're about ready to bring the rover on back."

"Rog. Have you taken care of everything?" said Bernard Chu. They all knew what he really meant.

"Just about. We're dropping the L-2 link while we remotely service the rover. Be back up shortly."

"Good luck."

As soon as Chu's voice stopped, Newellen flicked off the link. He threw a glance back at Cyndi. "Any luck?"

She fumbled with her equipment. "I'm trying a direct line of sight now."

Jason leaned toward the controls. Newellen tapped the panel. "Come on," he growled. He glanced at the clock. "They'll only believe us being out of touch for a few minutes."

Salito looked up. "Got him." She ran a hand over an array of lights. Bryan Zed's voice came over the new radio link. "—as well forget it. The bastards have done it again."

Jason leaned into the intercom. "Sabotaged the fuel tank?"

"That and worse. They have a shitload full of explosives wired up to the controls. I could probably get around it in a few hours, but who knows how happy their trigger finger is? I guess they figured if we found a way to get around the fuel tank being sabotaged, they would just blow the whole thing up."

With a sinking feeling in his stomach, Jason took in a breath. "Okay, Bryan. Get the hell back here. Hop in the rover and get on board before Earth suspects something's up."

"Rog," said Zimmerman.

Jason slumped in his chair. They had hoped to make off with the shuttle after they unloaded the nukes. Once brought back to Columbus and given enough time, they could have found some way to fly it back to Earth. They would have at least had an option.

But who would have figured that McConnell still wouldn't trust them?

32

antarctica—
nanotechnology isolation laboratory

In his wildest nightmares, Jordan Parvu could not have imagined the things he saw inside the NIL's quarantine room.

Under harsh lights, the sprawling amorphous mass covered most of the floor, viscous and writhing. It seemed to be curious, but it had not yet breached the sealed walls. Parvu knew that the billions of automata could chew through any obstacle in a few moments, once they made up their minds to. But right now they seemed to be reassessing—plotting?

The automata had disassembled Kent Woodward the way they had the rat, cell by cell. His bones had turned to jelly, his skin split and re-formed. Parvu had closed his eyes and shut off the speakers to silence Kent's screams.

Parvu had caused this himself. He bore the blame. It would have been better to let the young astronaut die in peace, frozen at the bottom of the crevasse in an empty sleep. His companions would have found him eventually, given him a proper burial.

Instead, Parvu had offered him a few more days of life—at what cost? The hybrids had mutated, turned into destructive monsters. And if they got loose—

Parvu uncovered his eyes to see the shapeless mass of Kent Woodward oozing across the floor to fuse with the much smaller smear of material that had been the body of the rat. They combined totally. The automata, the white lab rat, and the young astronaut were all one organism now.

The mass burbled on the floor of the clean-room, simmering like a pot of too-thick pudding. Somewhere inside of it remained what had been Kent.

Reaching forward, fighting off panic, Parvu found the intercom switch. He stopped, trying to rationalize what he was doing, but it did no good. It made no sense, but he had to make the attempt. It gave him something that might provide a solution.

"Kent? Kent Woodward, can you hear me in there?"

The surface of the blob rippled. It swelled and strained upward.

"Kent, I—"

The formless mass flowed toward the wall speaker. It bumped against the smooth vertical surface, waiting.

Startled and frightened, Parvu switched off the intercom and held his breath. Through the observation window he could see the brownish mass hanging there, pulsating. What if it decided to chew through the wall?

Sweat dribbled down his temples, plastering his gray hair against his head. He did not want to move—what if his motion attracted the mass, made it want to disassemble the window and plow through the NIL? The entire room seemed oppressively quiet, with only a distant creak from the wind that had picked up outside. He had not put on any music; silence seemed more appropriate anyway. The entire place was like a tomb, death waiting to happen.

Parvu sat watching the motionless mass for half an hour. His eyes stung from not blinking, his throat hurt from not swallowing. He wanted the thing to make the next move—but he was terrified at what it might do.

Finally, the blob dribbled down the wall and flowed to the center of the room, swelling up and over a toppled lab stool like a blanket of mucus. The shapeless entity engulfed the stool, disassembling it like a snake swallowing a mouse. It destroyed the leg of an adjacent lab table as well, bringing the table crashing to the floor.

The impact and the resulting noise startled the thing, and it sent splatters of itself in different directions, like outlying guards until they drew together again into the large main body. Parvu saw that the organism had increased its mass, growing as it incorporated new material. The stool was completely gone.

With wraithlike pseudopods, the thing reached out to touch objects that had been on top of the table—an RF electrode, a broken keyboard, some tools, a laptop flatscreen, and the empty cage that had held Old Gimp. As tendrils of the entity touched each object, the item dissolved, like a powerful funnel sucking material away and cataloging what it found.

It waited a few more moments, as if gathering its energy, and then in a rush it bulged, redistributed its mass, mounded its center up, and extruded from its own body a newly created stool, standing upright this time, as if the thing remembered what a stool was for and how it was supposed to stand.

But this stool had nine spindly legs, curving away from the seat like stems from a flower petal. It had been assembled in a flash, molecule by molecule, with the resources the hybrids had available. It seemed to be made of a mixture of metallic and organic compounds.

Parvu shuddered as a thought occurred to him—could this possibly be an attempt to communicate?

Terrified, Parvu ran out of the observation area.

Out of the corner of his eyes, he saw a rapid motion, as the mass swarmed to the window to get a better look at him. He did not look back as he pulled open the double doors that gave him access to the NIL living quarters.

Squeezing his eyes shut, Parvu huddled on his narrow bed. He tried to remember ways to calm himself, but they seemed silly and ineffectual. He finally managed to hum to himself, to count to fifty, and reached the point where he could open his eyes again.

Part of him expected to see the escaping mass swallowing the NIL whole, digesting the walls, the windows, the doors, to create one enormous hive organism that would engulf the Earth. Instead, he saw the perpetual videoloop on the wall, showing his grandson's birthday party.

The boy laughed and smeared chocolate ice cream on his face. Timothy and his wife applauded. A younger Parvu stood off to one side, looking immensely pleased with himself. Idyllic times, in an unreal universe where nightmares like what he had created in the clean-room could never exist.

Compared to what he had done, Erika's mistake of letting the alien nanocritters infect them was trivial.

He moaned Sinda's name. He had not talked to her in months. She was out of touch, off in the wilds some-where—could it be possible that she didn't even know about the Daedalus construction?

Parvu could not face the thought of confessing the magnitude of what he had done—he had successfully avoided doing that for days. Perhaps if he destroyed every-thing thoroughly enough, no one would have to know. He had had a full and admirable career. He need not ruin it at the end because of a single mistake, no matter how large.

He had seen colleagues with distinguished credentials follow the wrong ideas, use their long-earned fame to publicize crackpot theories, with the result that their life's work was dismissed as "lucky guesses." Parvu did not want to leave that legacy behind for his family.

But everything had gotten out of control. He couldn't understand how it had turned so bad. He felt sobs rising up again.

If Parvu informed Celeste McConnell, she would de-stroy the NIL and its surrounding areas. No question about that—she would have no other choice. She would do it without warning, for what good would a warning do? She would send flyers with napalm, or more likely she would drop one of the long-stored nuclear warheads and annihilate the entire site. It was the deepest wasteland of Antarctica—no one but himself and perhaps a few of those still at the Mars base camp would be killed.

But Parvu couldn't be sure the flyers would do a thorough enough job. More likely, McConnell would send in a team to arrest him and take his research as evidence, charging him with unleashing the hybrids from whatever meager confinement he had managed to erect.

Perhaps the devastating fail-safe systems could be rigged with a time delay to trigger the x rays after he had fled outside to where he could be rescued. But that, too, would be useless.

With his clumsy precautions, Parvu almost certainly carried some of the first hybrids in his own body, much like Erika's contamination. He had handled Old Gimp after the rat had been infested with the automata. Any number of hybrids could have escaped the first time he breached the nanocore containment—which was by far his most appalling mistake.

The worst part was, he could not even check his own blood for infection! All of the analytical apparatus was in the central lab, the quarantine section.

Unlike Erika, Parvu would never come up with a miracle cure to purge himself and erase the thing he had created. He had taken too many inexcusable chances already. He could not afford another one. . . .

Walking on leaden legs, he returned to the observation window. He thought he heard strange buzzing sounds permeating the NIL, and the air seemed oppressively warm. He held his breath before looking into the quarantine chamber.

The reconstructed stool remained standing inside its churning pool of automata and organic matter. Squirming up the legs of the stool, pulsing on the bowed surface of the seat, writhing lumps appeared, hints of something without quite enough information to assemble itself. Yet.

Kneading his knuckles, Parvu knew exactly what he had to do. Soon. And he was much too frightened to do it.

33

moonbase columbus

"We left the stereochip right there so we could watch every detail," Newellen said, paying no attention to where he was driving the rover. "But if somebody decides to trigger those nukes, we won't see a thing. The prompt gamma rays from the nuclear explosions will fry the chip's circuits before we see any of the really cool stuff."

"They aren't supposed to just push the button from Earth," Cyndi Salito objected. "We're the ones in danger up here."

"Uh huh," Bryan Zed said. No one could tell if he intended any emotional undertone to his remark. The rover continued to follow the dim starlit path leading from the hopper's landing pad toward Columbus.

"Wait a second," Jason said, "that's all just a last resort measure, a fail-safe in case the Daedalus thing takes some aggressive action. Nobody's just going to blow it up."

"Uh huh," Bryan Zed said again.

"Jase, who do you think has the say on activating those warheads?" Newellen asked. "The president, sure, and probably Director McConnell, since she's in charge of all this mess, maybe even General Pritchard. But can anybody tell me why it is that we—you know, us folks who have our butts right on the line—don't happen to be in the loop?"

Jason had no answer. He knew only that McConnell had seen fit to sabotage the warhead delivery shuttle—and he

couldn't even complain because then she would know they had tried to go behind her back and retrieve the spacecraft.

"Just pay attention to the drive, Big Daddy," Jason said. "It's too dark to see where you're going." It was nightside back at Columbus, and Newellen had already barely missed several boulders large enough to ruin the vehicle.

They had been quiet nearly the whole trip back in the hopper, lifting off from Farside and returning to the landing area twenty kilometers out from the moonbase. It was Columbus's last hopper, and Jason felt uncomfortable using it too frequently.

The crew's silence had been caused by pondering the nuclear noose around Daedalus. Or maybe it had been their last view of that shuttle lying like a beached metallic whale—intentionally crippled by the Agency just so the moonbase crew would have no chance to escape.

The lights of Columbus shone out from the half-buried modules and the shielded dome of the control center. Jason spotted a spacesuited figure emerging from the main airlock under a mound of regolith. "Looks like we've got a welcoming party."

"Or the bearer of bad news."

Newellen slowed the rover to pull under the sunshade near the airlock opening. "Here we are folks, back from saving the world. Please feel free to throw money, wine, or women," he said.

"Big Daddy, shut up," Salito said as she climbed down from the rover. She brushed dust from the vehicle. "You're starting to drive me crazy."

Newellen made a rude noise. "Risk your life for all mankind and look at the respect you get."

As if they had rehearsed the action, the smaller forms of Bryan Zed and Cyndi Salito picked up Newellen's hulking suit in the low gravity and carried him struggling to the airlock station. Jason blinked at their sudden exit, as the other spacesuited figure activated and shut the airlock door for them.

"Hi, Jase."

Jason turned at the voice. The figure now stood next to him, assisting him in wiping black lunar dust off of the rover's more delicate components. He read Erika's name-patch on her suit. He brightened, happy that she would come out to see him.

"Hi, yourself."

Erika laughed. "Glad y'all are back." She hesitated, then looked around. "It's kind of hard chatting in a spacesuit."

"Especially with everybody listening in." Jason imagined he could see her blush, even behind her visor, lit by status lights inside her helmet. Line-of-sight communication might be private enough, but . . .

He turned off his radio with his chin control and stepped up to her. He touched his helmet against hers and said loudly, "Turn off your radio." He made a pantomiming sign with his hand.

She looked puzzled, then moved her chin against the lower part of her helmet. Jason took a step back and glanced at her suit status display—the LED marked RADIO burned red. They clicked helmets again. "Now you've got your privacy."

"You sound like you're shouting from the bottom of a fish tank, but I can understand you fine. Low-tech conquers all."

Jason waited for her to say something, but she remained quiet. "Anything the matter? Why did you come out here in person? Just to greet me?"

She paused for a long moment. "I guess I needed someone to talk to."

Jason smiled to himself. "Thanks. I guess." He touched a gloved hand to her spacesuited arm. The silver fabric felt rigid even to his padded hands. "So, why don't you give Parvu a call? Might make you homesick, but it'll do you some good."

Erika moved her hand up as if to brush back her hair, but stopped when her glove hit her helmet. "That's why I wanted to talk with you."

Jason felt warm inside that under all this pressure Erika wanted to be close to him, that she could talk to him. They had spent a great deal of time together at Sim-Mars. Why did she insist on being alone most of the time? She was so intelligent, attractive, but tough—her South Carolina accent and her demure attitude sometimes made her appear soft and helpless, but Jason knew better. Being around Erika made his breath quicken.

Compared to her, Margaret was the Wicked Witch of the West. He wondered what his wife, his ex-wife-to-be, was telling young Lacy and Lawrence. Since Jason couldn't be there to show them love on his own, the children had no choice but to listen to her anger and her bitterness. Margaret had obtained an unnecessary legal separation. Just how much more separated could they be, with her on Earth and him quarantined on the Moon? Or maybe Margaret just wanted to keep the legal work nice and tidy so she wouldn't have any complications about seeing her "friend" Perry.

He stopped his mind from wandering into more self-pity. Right now Erika was more concerned with her old mentor. "Is something wrong with Dr. Parvu?" he asked.

She hesitated, seeming to swallow away tension. "I can't raise him, Jase. He refuses to answer any calls."

"Did you try an emergency override?"

"His communications link isn't even up. It's like he turned it off, or maybe something happened to it." She paused. "They're having riots back on Earth, you know."

"He's kind of out of the way for any mob to bother him."

She pulled her helmet back, breaking audio contact. All Jason could hear now was his own breathing. A moment later he could hear the pounding of blood in his ear.

He pulled her toward him, touching helmets again. "Hey, I'm sorry for even suggesting that. Only a joke. It's just that sometimes people get tired of interacting with the outside world. Sometimes they shut themselves off from it if they're really under pressure. Other people go and take walks alone on the Moon. Like someone I know, for example."

She snorted. "Yuk, yuk."

"Come on. Let's get inside. They're going to get a new IR scan of the crater." He tugged at her arm. "After that, I'll help you raise Parvu."

■ — ■

They were alone in the ready room as they hung up their gear, going through the meticulous motions of detaching all the suit-component interlinks, "dismounting" from the main body core. Air whooshed around them, trying to remove lunar dust that might have escaped the electrostatic curtain. As they left for the main corridor, Jason glanced up at the SAFETY FIRST sign that glowed above the inflatable airlock. He shook his head—the quiet reminder seemed ironic with everything that had happened.

Making their way to the control center, Jason felt clammy in the moonbase's air-conditioning. His light-blue jumpsuit was sweaty. When they stepped into the central dome, Chu nodded to them. He said nothing about the sabotaged shuttle. Chu turned his attention back to the holotank and said, "We've got an estimated TOA of three point six minutes for the next javelin."

It took a full two seconds for the reply to come back from Earth, confirming the javelin's journey to the Daedalus Crater. "Rog, Columbus. This flyby will serve as a benchmark and double-check to see if anything's happened since deploying the safeguard ring. Have you initiated your diagnostics?"

Chu swung his gaze around the control center. Two of the crew manning the seismographs, radiation detectors, and the rest of the monitoring equipment gave a thumbs-up. Chu said, "All diagnostics seem to be working."

Seconds passed. Albert Fukumitsu, the Earthbound Mission Control supervisor, responded on the audio-only channel. "Very well, Columbus. We read you in at two minutes. Please switch to the javelin's IR display."

Chu stood stiffly. Jason could see how much he resented having Earthbound Mission Control directing his every action. *What ever happened to the Agency's all-important local command philosophy?* he thought. *That's what happens when the bean-counters get control.*

The holotank blinked, then displayed the image of the lunar surface speeding underneath the javelin's trajectory. The long tungsten projectile was still relatively high above the Moon's surface, broadcasting images up to the

L-2 relay station where they were bounced toward Earth. Soon, the IR images would arrive in a super-high-resolution mode, enabling detailed playback as the javelin passed over the alien artifact.

Chu sidled up to Jason and Erika, speaking in a low tone outside the broadcast locus for Agency Mission Control. "Glad you could make it for the fireworks."

"Thanks."

Chu nodded to Erika. "It's going to be interesting to see how active your little nanotech machines have been, Dr. Trace. They could just march out and dismantle those warheads."

Jason saw her eyes widen at the reference to *her* nanomachines—as if the entire Daedalus construction were somehow her fault. He said, "I was just out there, Bernard. From what I could see, the artifact looks about finished."

Chu glanced to the holotank, then lowered his voice. "If that's true, then Celeste isn't going to wait terribly long to detonate those nukes."

Erika stared at the IR javelin's transmissions as she spoke. "We can't say for sure whether or not the construction is finished if we don't even know what it is."

"Thirty seconds," came the voice from the holotank.

Chu turned away, focusing his attention on the activity again. "Max magnification." He rubbed his hands together. "Enhance surface-temperature contrast. Use false-color imaging."

In the holotank, the ground below the javelin rushed by, a strange dark gray with patches of barely discernible light. Sudden splotches of primary colors burst in, showing subtle differences of the sun-washed regolith.

The crater lip appeared, roared behind them, then left the huge alien construction glistening in reflected sunlight, smeared by faint color changes of temperature fluctuations. But otherwise the structure remained at ambient temperature. The hot zone that had previously been glowing in intense colors from the nanocritters' waste heat now showed only the same as the average dayside lunar temperature.

The dipole antennas of the Very Low Frequency array appeared on the floor of the crater as the javelin continued its flight. A good fifteen seconds passed before the holotank turned fuzzy white on gray as the signal went dead. "Gone," said Newellen.

From Mission Control, Fukumitsu's voice said, "Looks like we didn't get good data on that one, Columbus. Malfunction in the IR instruments?"

Chu frowned and spoke to the crew in the rear of the control center. "How does the javelin check out?"

"Infrared instruments functioning normally."

"Okay." Chu fell silent, then turned and searched the room. "Newellen, get on the playback controls and try the backup camera. Run back those last fifteen seconds— pump it as low out of the visible as you can."

"Right." Newellen waddled over to the side and slid behind the panel. "I think I can get down to near-IR with that filter."

A minute later they watched the ghostly image of the Daedalus artifact, fuzzed out by the hampered resolution of infrared in the blazing sunlight. The alien structure showed no temperature differential from the surrounding regolith.

"Well I'll be dipped," Newellen said. He twisted around in his chair. "Ambient temperature. If I didn't know better, I'd say the artifact is stone-cold."

"What's going on?" Jason asked. "How could the nanomachines stop radiating heat? Is it something in response to our planting the defensive ring?"

"No," Erika said. Her green-brown eyes had widened and her voice dropped to an awed whisper. "It means they've stopped. All of the nanocritters. They're shut down."

"What are you talking about?"

"No more activity. They switched themselves off." She turned to the image on Newellen's holotank. "And that means they must be finished! The structure at Daedalus is completed. Whatever it is."

Albert Fukumitsu's voice broke in from Earth, agitated. "Columbus, what the hell is going on up there? Should I contact Director McConnell?"

Chu waved a hand at the back. "Turn those clowns off so I can think."

Newellen grinned and spoke into the link, "Ah, having some trouble up here, Mission Control. We'll have to deadstart the link." He switched off communications with Earth.

Chu stepped up to the holotank. He stared at it for a long time. "Launch one of Newellen's supercameras. I want to see the regolith close up. If the nanomachines have indeed shut down, then the camera will keep broadcasting images." He scratched his dark hair. "This way we can see exactly what those aliens are up to over there."

Three cubes displayed test-pattern images from the incoming supercamera; tags identifying them as IR, VISIBLE, and UV glowed beneath each of the respective cubes. After a splash of static as the images reassessed themselves, they began to show high-resolution micrographs of regolith grains. Nothing else.

"Nothing. Just plain nothing," said Newellen. He stared intently at the three cubes.

The camera's sampling end had penetrated several meters into the regolith; it should have been swarming with the nanomachines that had taken apart Waite, his companions, and their hopper. Instead, they saw only regolith.

The view from the probe's upper stereochips looked out over the crater from a canted angle. The glistening alien structure stood waiting.

"But why now?" Chu swung around in his chair. "It doesn't make any sense."

Newellen sat up straighter. "Do you think they might have caught on that we're going to blow the hell out of them? Maybe they're holding their breath to see what we'll do. Maybe they're massing right now to take out the nukes."

Salito snorted. "They would have shown up in the IR."

"It had to happen," Erika said. "When they're finished with the preprogrammed construction, they would have to shut off."

Again, silence. The images in the holotank hadn't changed. If anything, the IR cube had grown darker, less patchy.

"One minute," announced Newellen.

Erika moved away from Jason and approached the holotank. She stood next to Chu and with her finger followed the outline of the distant structure in the holotank.

Jason watched her for a moment, then said, "Okay, what now?"

"Cut it," said Chu. "We'd better decide fast what we should do—otherwise the Agency is going to make up our minds for us. They'll get spooked and push the button."

Erika's voice came out stronger than the murmuring comments in the control center. "There's something we have to do. Something we can finally do. It's been impossible before."

Jason saw that all eyes in the control center had turned to her. Even Bernard Chu watched her with eyebrows raised, waiting.

Erika spoke as if she were saying the most obvious thing in the world. "We have to go out there in person. We can finally see what this thing really is."

34

washington, d.c.

Celeste woke up screaming. She couldn't breathe. The sweat-drenched sheets tangled around her like ghostly assailants trying to hold her down and rape her.

Chuck and Yeager leaped off the bed and started barking, as if to protect her from some unseen threat. The bed rocked as they sniffed and placed their paws on the mattress, craning their heads to find the enemy that had somehow come into the house without them noticing.

Beside Celeste, Simon Pritchard sat up wide eyed and blinking. He couldn't seem to form words after his startled awakening. Instead, he wrapped his arms around her, pulling her against him. "Shhh," he said.

Celeste shivered, fighting back the visions clamoring out of her subconscious. She nestled back against Pritchard's chest, feeling the warmth of his body, the press of his skin, the strength of his arms as he held on to her.

Her nightmare was like a shadow of something terrible unleashed across the Earth, so great that it would swallow up the stars. Another facet of the dream, bright light and blinding cold. Someone had let the demon out of the bottle, or someone would. Celeste felt tiny and weak, smothered by the dreaded foreknowledge.

She had no idea how she could stop something so immense.

"It's okay," Pritchard whispered in her ear. He gripped her arms, kissed the back of her shoulder.

She couldn't drive the blackness of terror from her mind. Her heart pounded, trying to catch up to her panic. She knew her breathing had stopped during the vision— she had barely survived the nightmare.

She squirmed out of Pritchard's grasp, reluctant to leave his encircling arms but needing something to wash down the screams in her throat. Trembling, she gulped some lukewarm water from the glass on the bedside table.

Beside the bed, the black Lab and the German shepherd both whined, anxious for reassurance. Celeste squeezed her eyes shut to stop another gush of panic. No, it wouldn't be all right. Nothing would ever be all right again.

Unless she could do something to stop it. She had failed many times to interpret her dreams correctly—but she had succeeded with the Grissom. This time, she must get it right.

Tears stung her eyes, but she blinked them away, keeping her back turned to Pritchard. He remained sitting behind her, baffled and helpless, unaware of what she needed him to do.

Reaching out, she let the two dogs lick her fingers. Her gut-level reaction kept telling her to run. But Celeste McConnell, director of the United Space Agency, could not surrender without a fight.

She and Simon Pritchard had intended to have a few quiet hours to themselves after weeks of unrelenting scrutiny and too little sleep. They had enjoyed a quick candlelight dinner of take-out barbecue ribs and cole slaw, eaten in the screened-in porch of her house. When she had excused herself and returned a few moments later wearing a new glittersilk negligee, Pritchard had laughed before standing up to wrap his arms around her, pushing his hips against hers.

When they made love on the floor, listening to the hum of thousands of insects outside, Celeste could taste the spicy barbecue sauce on Pritchard's lips.

Afterward, lethargic, she had shut off all the household communications systems before leading Pritchard to the bedroom. Just to get some peace, some much-needed sleep. The two of them deserved that much of an escape. They had kissed for a while, holding each other's sweat-slick bodies in the humid air before drifting off to quiet dreams.

And nightmares. A thousand times worse than the Grissom dream, worse than her feelings of dread when an accident was about to happen. Whatever was now unfolding would shake the entire world.

Pritchard tried to comfort her again. He squeezed her shoulders, massaging her neck and her back. Normally she would have purred with contentment at his touch, but now the muscles felt as if they might snap rather than relax. She had not turned to look at him in nearly a full minute.

"It's okay," he said again. "It's just a nightmare."

"No," she said in a brittle voice. Pritchard did not understand, nor would he. How could she ever explain her dreams? "No, it isn't 'just' a nightmare, Simon. Never 'just' a nightmare."

Without waiting for him to respond, Celeste went into the living room. The fireplace sat black and cold. In the screened-in porch, the table where they had eaten lay strewn with smeared napkins.

On the main screen in the den, an insistent red message light flashed. Though it did not surprise her, seeing the light filled her with dread. This was it. Last time, the communication had been Bernard Chu telling her of the contamination on the Collins. This time the nightmare had been infinitely worse.

She heard the rustle of a robe as Pritchard came up behind her, still perplexed. With him there, she spoke to the receiver. "Play message." She felt her anxiety surge as the image formed.

Albert Fukumitsu, the manager of Mission Control, stared out at her, appearing both exhausted and annoyed. His black hair looked even shaggier than usual. He pursed his lips, then frowned before speaking. "Director McConnell, I wish I could find you. I've tried your office, your vehicle phone, now home." He sighed.

"I hope you get my messages. You really should be here." Behind him several technicians in the nerve center were busy, more agitated than they should have been at such a dead hour. She could see spacesuited figures on the holoscreens in the background, but she knew of no special EVA activities on the schedule.

"The alien nanomachines at Daedalus site have shut down. All at once. Whatever that alien construction is, it must be completed, ready to go. Jason Dvorak and Erika Trace have taken Columbus's last hopper over there. You really should be here, Director McConnell. The whole world is watching. Please get in touch with me as soon as possible." He signed off.

In the dim room, Celeste stood naked and shivering. Everything had gone cold within her body. Outside, in the thick forests overlooking the Potomac, she could hear the buzzing of insects, who seemed to be whispering to each other about the impending end of the world.

The two dogs paced the den, bumping her legs in an effort to get a casual pat from her. Celeste felt sick with fear. The pieces were starting to fall into place.

The Daedalus construction was complete. Any moment now it would fulfill its purpose—or Dvorak and Trace would trigger something. Either way, all of humanity was threatened.

"This is fantastic," Pritchard said, startling her. She turned and saw his eyes wide with childlike wonder. "Now we can finally see what's out there."

For a moment Celeste wanted to scream at him for being so stupid. How could he express delight and curiosity when the construction might be a planetary-sized weapon that could crack Earth open to the core? She controlled herself and marshaled her thoughts. If she was going to have a chance at saving humanity, she would have to call on every scrap of ability she possessed.

"Simon," she said, turning to him, "this is a crisis. I need you now more than ever. Get dressed. You'd better make it your dress uniform. The whole world is watching, as Albert said. We have to make this good." She checked the time of Fukumitsu's message and glanced at the chronometer on the wall. "Damn it all to hell! Why couldn't I have more time?"

She glared at Pritchard who still stood in his robe, wide awake but stunned. "Simon!" She hustled him back to the bedroom, to his clothes. "We've got to stop them before they destroy all of us!"

35

daedalus crater

"You two going to be all right staying in the hopper?" Jason finished checking the chest panel of his spacesuit. He flexed his gloves before looking up to Bryan Zimmerman and Cyndi Salito by the cramped controls.

"Give me a break," Cyndi said, grinning. "Right, Zed?"

Zimmerman grunted. He didn't appear interested in anything except disabling the Agency's coded radio links with the nuclear weapons encircling the crater. He tried to key in a hack that would scramble the detonation sequence.

As they looked at the towering alien superstructures, Jason felt like kicking himself for agreeing to place the ring of warheads—it had seemed like a safe option at the time, a comforting defense against the unknown. But now he and three others were sitting ducks if someone back on Earth got itchy fingers.

Not to mention the threat from the supposedly dormant nanomachines inside the hot zone. They were about to go trudging across the regolith where Waite, Snow, and Lasserman had gotten chewed to pieces.

The hopper's IR sensors were hooked up to alarms designed to yammer like crazy if they detected any telltale waste heat indicating a surge in nanotech activity. Inside the helmets, Bitchin' Betsy chips would squawk at them to get out of there.

Jason glanced at Erika. "About ready to go?"

296

She smoothed back the headcap that held her sandy hair out of her eyes. "Time's a'wasting." She turned to the hopper's airlock. "You're holding up my Nobel Prize."

Jason picked up his helmet to follow her. "We'll keep in contact, Cyndi. Hey, Zed, any luck with the links to the nukes?"

"Not yet," Zimmerman said.

Jason tried to squelch his panic. "Keep trying. If there's any way you can cripple the detonation links—"

"He's trying the best he can," said Cyndi. "We've got just as much incentive to stop those things from going off." She leaned over and kissed Jason on the cheek. "Be careful out there." She spoke softly and threw a glance at Erika. "And take care of her, too. She's good for you."

"Thanks." Was his attraction to Erika so obvious? Of course it was.

After sealing his helmet, Jason squeezed into the airlock with Erika. When the pressure began to drop, his suit stiffened as the trapped air redistributed itself to push against the vacuum, like a thousand tiny palms.

Emerging from the hopper, they climbed down the ladder. A few stars burned in the lunar sky, though it was Farside's daytime. As soon as they touched the crumbly ground, Jason could see the fine dust kicked up by their landing. Outcroppings of lava rocks were draped on the crater wall, highlighting the access road Waite had taken in his rover, before anyone had known of the alien construction. In the distance, sprawled across the flat pan of the crater like a madman's twisted glass sculpture, the Daedalus artifact stood out against the backdrop of space.

Knock knock. Anybody home?

Jason bumped his chin mike and spoke to Erika. "Get as many pictures as you can with the additional stereochips. Keep them interested Earthside."

Erika finished taking a panoramic shot of Daedalus Crater and the disassembled portion of the VLF array. The gaping pit beneath the giant weblike struts looked bottomless.

Beside the hopper, the inflatable lunar rover unfolded and swelled to size. Jason scanned the rover's controls. As his own breathing echoed inside his helmet, he was re-minded of snorkeling on the reefs in Hawaii. Only this time there wouldn't be pretty fish to see—only dormant Disassemblers ready to switch to new, more destructive programming.

Three videoscreens with touch-driven menus took up most of the control panel. Powering every system on, Jason brought up the forward-looking IR sensor as well as the surface-scanning radar to warn of obstacles washed out by the glare of sunlight.

On another display screen he brought up a digitized map of the construction. The whole crater had been well mapped out by now, watched almost daily as the alien complex grew in size. Inside the hot zone plunged a deep pit from which rose the main arches of the structure. Low-slung objects that resembled buildings were suspended all around the edge. Nine causeways—roads?—connected the buildings to the area outside the hole.

With his eyes on the map, Jason traced a path to the pit, then to an access way that might allow them to enter the complex. The printout gave a running estimate of the probable material strength of the construction. Nano-machines locking crystals together one molecule at a time could create substances with enormously greater flex-ibility and strength than even the best zero-G materials Jason himself had used in his Earthbound architectural designs.

"Well, are we gonna get going?" Erika asked.

Jason stopped reviewing the map. "Right now." He brought the rover up to its maximum speed. They approached the Daedalus artifact.

Cyndi's voice came over the radio. "You'll hit the hot zone in about seventy seconds."

"Former hot zone," Jason corrected.

Erika broke in, "Still no activity?"

"You'd be the first to know," said Cyndi. She clicked her mike.

"Thanks," said Jason. On the suit radio Erika sounded scared, but amazed to be setting foot in the place she had studied for so long.

Jason kept his attention riveted to the blasted ground in front of him. The crater floor was smooth, and even at the rover's speed, there was little jarring. Somewhere beneath the dust, uncountable millions of nanocritters had been swarming only hours ago. He hoped they would remain sleeping. The image of Trevor Waite dissolving kept replaying itself in his mind.

He glanced at the IR scope in front of him and saw no activity. Newellen's supercamera was still transmitting in perfect health. As they trundled along the access road, the radar scan showed no obstacles bigger than five centimeters—except for the artifact.

"Ten seconds."

Jason looked to Erika. She stared straight ahead, intently watching the alien artifact grow closer.

Cyndi said, "Congratulations, guys. Let me be the first to welcome you to nanotech neighborhood. Please keep your seat belts fastened until the Moon has come to a full and complete stop."

"Dr. Salito, please restrain your sense of humor," Bernard Chu's voice broke in through the suit radio, reminding them that all of the Moonbase, and Agency Mission Control too, were watching every move they made.

"Roger, sir," clicked Cyndi.

Oh, well, Jason thought. *This isn't supposed to be fun anyway.* Another minute or so and they would be at the rim of the pit. Jason clenched the steering controls, ignoring how the gloves bit into his fingers.

Cyndi's voice came over the radio. "Careful you don't go flying over the edge, Jase. No safety rails, you know."

Jason pulled back on the throttle and paid more attention to the radar images on the flatscreen. The rover slowed to a more reasonable fifteen klicks. Jason decided to get in as much sightseeing as he could—this was one of the biggest firsts in the history of humankind.

The radar screen turned black at the edge, showing the rim of the nanocritter-excavated hole. Jason looked out over the horizon, and suddenly the hole grew enormous in front of them.

"That came up pretty fast," said Erika.

"I keep forgetting about how close the Moon's horizon is. And that's one big mother of a hole!" Jason looked down at the computerized map, then across the flat plain of Daedalus. "We might as well cut across, use those bridges if they'll hold us. We'll reach the access roads faster than trying to go around the circumference of the hole."

"Go ahead," said Erika. "I'm trying to get in as many shots as I can." She kept scanning the artifact. "Stop when you get to the access way. I want to drop off a package of instruments for Big Daddy and a portable relay dish."

Jason concentrated on getting the rover safely to the access way, alternately using his computerized map, radar, and line of sight to guide him along the deep pit. All around them rose the solid arches, like gossamer confections stronger than steel.

The support struts and the main walls of the structure rose cleanly out of the regolith, with no footprints, no signs of disturbance. Even though he knew the nanocritters were responsible for the assembly, he still felt shivers looking at the tall, milky structure.

Bernard Chu's voice broke in. "Please give us a running account, Dr. Trace, Mr. Dvorak. We can't see all the details from the visuals you're sending us."

Erika cleared her throat. "Jason is approaching the edge of the pit now, directly next to one of nine causeways that extends to a complex of secondary structures that surround the lobed construction in the middle."

Jason anchored the rover with the emergency brake. He turned to Erika. "Well, should we get out and look?"

The two of them dismounted from the low vehicle and cautiously stepped toward the edge of the sheer pit. Behind them they left footprints on the regolith that seemed glaringly obvious on the otherwise untouched crater floor.

The giant dish structure lay before him not half a mile away, like a glass water lily a thousand meters high. The diamond-thread arches came up from the hole to a point at the base of the petals. On either side of the path leading to the antenna, the hole dropped off into deep blackness, where even the Sun's unfiltered rays could not penetrate.

"This is simply incredible," Jason said, shining his lamp down into the dark. "We've found the network of catacombs. No telling how deep or how far they go. As ambitious as those nanocritters were, the Moon could be Swiss cheese all the way to the center." He turned to Erika. "Got a close-up of this?"

Erika finished setting up a package of instruments on the ground next to the rover. "I've got the magnification up high, but there may not be enough contrast. Kind of hard to focus."

Jason stepped forward to touch one of the towering milky-glass pillars. Not long before, every molecule here had been assembled by swarming nanocritters. He hesitated only a moment before he stroked the smooth surface. "Columbus, looks like everything in the alien complex is made up of long, unbroken fibers. Primary structural elements are all wound together, and each winding is surrounded by another winding, making a bigger winding, and so on up the hierarchy." He shook his head. "Far away, it looks smooth, but not up close."

Seconds later, words bounced from Mission Control on Earth came to them. Jason recognized the voice of Albert Fukumitsu. "All our channels are open and active. We're recording everything here. No way are we going to lose any of this. And by the way, we've got an accurate measurement of the former hot zone from Erika's sounder—it's 2.99944 kilometers." The excitement in Fukumitsu's voice made Jason breathe a little easier. Nobody was going to push the button right now at least.

Jason felt pressure on his arm, Erika tugging him onward. After the two of them climbed back into the rover, he turned the vehicle toward the nearest pathway that arched across the seemingly bottomless pit. He took a deep breath. "Columbus, we're moving onto the causeway. Approaching with extreme caution. Seems sturdy enough."

"Roger."

Under the starry black sky Jason couldn't make out the other eight symmetrical pathways that he remembered from the maps. The unsupported path was a good five meters wide, rising up in a steep fifteen degree slope to a point halfway across the chasm before coming back down onto the main complex.

With the foreshortened perspective, it looked like only a hundred meters to the other side, but as Jason started driving across, the distance seemed to get longer.

He kept his attention on the rover while Erika continued her commentary. "The causeway—a bridge, really—seems to be comprised of the same twisted fibers that make up the arches. There is one large bundle I can make out, along with finer and finer strands down as far as I can see."

The steep slope of the glassy bridge made Jason feel like they were about to fall to the side, ready to plunge into the pit. But the rover tires held, and he maintained a meter of clearance on each side.

Jason peered over the edge, unable to see the bottom. It seemed to go on forever. "How are we ever going to find out how deep this guy goes?" The depths had not reflected any of the electromagnetic signals sent out by the javelins.

Erika shifted in her seat. "My EM sounder isn't giving a reading. Somebody would have to go down there, I guess."

They rolled to the top of the cleanly rounded summit and paused to survey their dizzying position, before beginning to roll down the slope to the other side of the pit. In another few minutes they would reach the complex.

Jason felt a drop of sweat work its way down his back, seeping through the tight inner garment he wore.

Ahead of the rover, the Daedalus construction looked enormous. The glassy pathway sloped down to the top of one of the secondary structures. The "roof" was flat and approximately square. He couldn't judge distance, but it had to be more than a hundred meters on a side. And this was one of the smaller buildings!

The overhanging translucent petals of the kilometer-wide dish sprawled over them, blocking out the stars and casting blurred shadows on the floor of the crater. On the flat rooftop of the secondary structure, Jason eased the rover to a halt.

Erika pulled another instrument package from the rear compartment and stepped out. She placed her bulky boot gingerly on the structure's roof. She set her package down, then brushed her gloved fingers over the construction material. "I can't tell what it's made of, but it's unyielding."

On sudden impulse, Jason rummaged through the emergency toolbox and withdrew a long bar meant to be used as a lever. "Erika, get a picture of this." He placed a foot on the building, took a swing and hit the alien material with the bar. His own inertia lifted him up into the air, then practically tossed him flat on his back. The bar recoiled violently, hurting his hands.

"It's solid all right," he said. "I can feel this bar vibrating like crazy."

With a crackle of static, Newellen's voice came to them, relayed from L-2. "Let's just hope nothing comes out of the door now that you've knocked."

Erika turned back to the instrument package. "I don't detect any motion that might point to heavy machinery inside." She paused. "I did pick up your hit, though."

Jason said, "Let's keep going then. Look at all these access paths. There has to be a way to get inside."

"Follow the nano-brick road," said Erika.

"Very funny." He drove on. He watched the base of the antenna construction approach as the rover crept over the top of the secondary structure. As an architect, everything he saw amazed him. He wondered what his old hero Eiffel would have thought about all this.

"It occurs to me that we haven't seen any type of ground support for this thing."

"Aren't those diamond arches holding up the petals?"

"Yeah, but how are *they* being held up? And what about this building we're driving on? Where's its base? The only visible means of support are these pathways extending over the hole."

Jason kept his eyes straight ahead and his hands on the wheel. "We're looking at something truly alien, designed by minds that didn't develop architecture the same way humans did. I mean, even on our own planet, different cultures developed different ways of accomplishing the same tasks. Look at the pyramids of Egypt and then in

Central America. The Mayans never developed the arch—they used trapezoids instead of squares. Who knows what a completely alien brain on a completely alien planet could have cooked up?"

He paused to ponder longer. "If this whole thing is being supported by just those pathways—my God, the entire structure could be 'floating' suspended in this gigantic hole. And how far down does it go into the pit—miles?"

The base of the giant flower was a hundred meters away. The diamond arches gathered at a point at the base, keeping the huge dish off the surface of the building.

Erika indicated a point just under the arches. "I see a bulge on the surface, where everything converges. Maybe it's an access port, some kind of doorway."

Jason turned to look at the base. The thing looked impossibly delicate—too elegant—to have been constructed on Earth, or even conceived by a human mind.

He whispered, "Suppose this whole construction wasn't meant to stay in place? If it's floating, then maybe this is some sort of spaceship . . . maybe this wasn't meant to remain here, but to go on to Earth?"

36

washington, d.c.—mission control

Simon Pritchard held on to the passenger side of the car as Celeste drove at breakneck speed toward Washington, D.C. They wound down the narrow lanes from her home on the Potomac, sliding on fallen leaves dampened by dew, then got onto the George Washington Turnpike.

Pritchard did not dare to say a word. The street lamps glowing at 3:14 A.M. flashed across her face like strobe lights. She increased speed. Pritchard kept stomping an imaginary brake pedal on the passenger-side floor.

Glaring headlights from late-night drivers splashed across their view. Celeste wheeled along the road, going around anyone in her way. Exit signs flashed by, unread. They both knew the way to Mission Control.

By the time Celeste reached Agency headquarters, Pritchard had grown numb with uneasiness. Something had terrified Celeste, and he could not get her to talk about it. But he saw how much it disturbed her. She parked, and Pritchard squeezed her arm to show his support, whatever she might need. By now he had learned not to ask questions.

She gave him a distracted mumble of acknowledgment and got out of the car, motioning him to do the same. She ran up the walk, up the wide syn-granite steps, and Pritchard hurried after her, stiff in his confining dress blouse.

Pulling the glass doors open, Celeste darted past the two outer-perimeter guards, waving her badge but not giving them time to inspect it. The guards stood up, startled, intent on watching their own screens of Mission Control, where something important seemed to be happening.

Celeste ranged ahead of him down the halls, and Pritchard walked briskly to catch up. She paused for him at the access doors of Mission Control, then pulled open the alarmed gate, slipping her ID card into the reader as they both crammed inside. As soon as the outer gate closed, the inner door unlocked, and they squeezed out of the booth into the bustling control center.

By this time Celeste was so out of breath that she could not even speak. Pritchard felt his heart pounding as he steadied himself against the wall. Adrenaline gushed through his bloodstream, and he made ready to help in any way, though he still did not understand what was going on.

Some of the technicians turned to look at their arrival, but the others remained enraptured by what they saw on the screens, even the two armed guards standing by the entry, a Japanese man and woman. The head of Mission Control, Albert Fukumitsu, was too wrapped up in the events to give them more than a cursory glance. A hush blanketed the whole room.

On the big holoscreens, Jason Dvorak and Erika Trace were exploring the alien artifact.

Celeste panted and tried several times before she finally managed to push words out of her throat. "Mission Control internal cameras off!"

Albert Fukumitsu turned to her, ready to mouth "Why?" but she snapped, "Cameras off! This is a security matter!" Celeste had grown livid. It frightened Pritchard to see her this way, transformed into a stranger by her unexplained terror.

The techs looked at her with stunned expressions, as if too many things had happened in too short a time. Several turned to Fukumitsu for guidance. One reached across to an unoccupied console and keyed in a command string.

The tiny red lamps above the implanted videocameras on the wall winked out.

"Okay, cameras are off," the tech said.

Fukumitsu strode over, wearing bell-bottom jeans that had already gone out of style for the second time. He wore a harried, concerned look. "You got my message, Ms. McConnell? The Columbus team has been at the Daedalus site now for about half an hour. Do you need a full report?"

"Get them out of there!" she shouted. "We don't have much time!"

Pritchard narrowed his eyes. Fukumitsu squinted as if to doublecheck her identity. "It appeared safe over there. They volunteered. I thought you would want someone to explore—"

"Get them out! You don't understand what they're going to cause! We're all in very grave danger!" Her black eyes glistened.

Pritchard stepped forward to support her, as he had mentally promised to do. "Please listen to the director, Mr. Fukumitsu. Order those people to return to Columbus immediately."

Fukumitsu froze for a moment, and Pritchard could sense the wheels turning inside his mind. The head of Mission Control chose to be passive. He shrugged helplessly. "These are images being transmitted from atop Dr. Salito's hopper, taken from long distance. We can't communicate directly with Mr. Dvorak or Dr. Trace—Dr. Chu has complete operational control from Columbus, so Trace and Dvorak are cut off." He shrugged a second time.

"Get hold of Chu then!"

Fukumitsu spoke slowly, "Every newsnet in the world is picking up these transmissions. You can't cut them off... like you did us."

Celeste looked at Pritchard, then pressed her palms to her temples. She appeared much older than he had ever seen her. Her black irises looked as deep as the pit on Daedalus. Her desperation began to rub off on Pritchard.

"Then we're going to have to take some drastic measures," she said. Her voice sounded very cold. "Right now. We may only have a few minutes left."

Pritchard sensed the situation was careening out of control. He hesitated for a moment, then decided to get one more piece of leverage. He strode over to the pair of Japanese guards, walking straight. He remembered them from the first time Celeste had taken him to Mission Control.

Pritchard chose the closest guard, the one who looked more uncertain. If these two were anything like the Agency security in the outside lobby, his task would be simple. "Sergeant, please hand me your side arm. Now."

Confused, the man hesitated.

"Sergeant, do you hear me?"

The female guard intervened. "I am sorry, sir. We cannot surrender our weapons without proper authorization."

Pritchard raised his voice, knowing that everyone's attention was now fixed on him. Thank God Celeste had thought to shut down the cameras. "Do you see these?" He pointed to the two stars on his right shoulder. "I am the top of your chain of command! What more authorization do you need?"

Then he lowered his voice. "This is a crisis situation, Sergeant. You are supposed to follow orders, particularly now. Can't you see that world-shattering events are taking place here? You"—he turned to the woman guard who had interrupted him—"may keep your own weapon as my backup."

He returned his attention to the first guard. "Your side arm! Now!"

Reluctantly the man handed over his service pistol. Pritchard took the weapon, trying to hide his own over-whelming tension. He wondered if he looked sufficiently threatening.

"So what do we do now?" one of the technicians mut-tered. Albert Fukumitsu shuffled his feet and stared at the floor. His lips moved, as if he were holding back a dozen different outbursts.

Celeste looked at the pistol in Pritchard's hand, and her shoulders slumped with relief. Her expression changed from inner terror to determination. He saw her swallow hard.

On the big stereoscreen, the images of Jason Dvorak and Erika Trace shuffled forward in a dream walk. They started their descent into the alien pit.

Pritchard prayed to God that Celeste knew what she was doing.

37

antarctica —
nanotechnology isolation laboratory

Parvu dictated his farewell message to Sinda and his family, then stored it along with the video and textual-comment records of what had happened in the quarantine chamber . . . what he had done to Kent . . . how he had risked every life on the planet.

He had come clean, explaining everything, leaving the excuses out. History would have to worry about that. The final memory cubes were sealed and shielded. They would survive any disaster now, short of nanotech disassembly of the entire facility.

He had never gotten around to detailing the procedures he had used with the hybrids, with Old Gimp. The monitoring systems had automatically recorded the actions, but he had added no explanations. Parvu's records would be incomplete and confusing. And there was not enough time to fix them.

When he had spoken into the recorders, addressing his wife and family, he had kept his voice from trembling, though tears streamed unhindered down his cheeks. He had not shaved in days, and he felt unclean and ashamed for leaving them such a pitiful last impression.

After saying for the seventh time that he loved them, Parvu realized he was babbling, that he had said nothing new in some time. He recalled Sinda's image, thought of

Timothy and his wife and their children before he reached out to end the recording.

He wiped his forehead and his hand came away hot and sweat-filmed. His head pounded, and he felt dizzy. He had not slept in days. He could no longer think straight. He had not been thinking straight since the moment he mixed his innocent prototypes with the dormant alien automata.

The alien creators had known what their scout machines would do to a living world if the devices happened to touch down there, and so the aliens—far wiser than Parvu—had incorporated a fail-safe routine into their programming. If an alien nanomachine encountered organic molecules during its initial attempts to assemble the primary blueprint in their Controllers' computers, the Disassemblers would shut down entirely. The Programmers, Quality Checkers, and Controllers would continue gathering data while waiting for further instructions. But they would not threaten any living world.

Parvu had sabotaged those precautions with his clumsy prototypes.

He reentered the NIL's main lab complex, then shuffled off to the storage area. His slippers felt too tight on his feet. His balance seemed to be gone, and he stumbled several times, holding himself up by leaning against a curved wall until most of the dizziness had passed. He thought he could hear the roaring passage of blood in his head.

In the storage area, Parvu encountered a smell and a stillness that should not have been there. Boxes of backup equipment and components still sat where they had been stacked, wrapped in bioplastic film. But the cages holding the other two white rats—Old Gimp's companions—were accusingly still. Wire-mesh coffins.

Inside, the two rats lay dead, bloated mounds of white fur.

Parvu shrank back, for an instant terrified that the automata had broken free of their containment and had come to kill the other life-forms in the NIL. But then he saw the rats' emaciation, their gas-swollen stomachs. Their food trays were empty. The metal edges had been scalloped and dented by tiny teeth as they gnawed in desperate appeal for food.

Parvu had not remembered to feed them for days. *Days.* The two rats had pushed themselves against the wire mesh, clawing in a frantic attempt to tear each other apart for food. Both of their small wedge heads had flopped toward Parvu, glassy pink eyes now filmed and grayish with death. They seemed to be accusing him of betraying everything he had ever known, from his family and his world to his helpless laboratory animals.

Parvu stumbled out of the storage room. Unable to focus his vision, Parvu saw the screen swimming in front of his eyes. Images appeared in it from his mind, the solid form of Maia Compton-Reasor shaking a finger at him. Her glasses kept sliding down her nose. When Parvu tried to see the rest of her, he noticed that she was blocked, her other arm wrapped around the burly form of Maurice Taylor.

Taylor looked like a tough football player, not the highly paid MIT research head. Taylor's brow was furrowed and accusing. "I knew we should have kept running computer simulations," he said. "Real nanotech research is too dangerous."

As Parvu bumped against one of the self-conforming chairs, the forms of Compton-Reasor and Taylor merged into a tall, blond, cadaverous shape that he recognized as Piter Sommerveld, the head of the Belgian research group long suspected of doing unethical nanotech experiments. Sommerveld extended a finger out of the screen. He wore a tarnished silver ring set with a massive opal. "You should have let us tinker with it first, Jordan Parvu!"

Parvu's skin felt like lava, seething and hot. The fever was eating him up—could he have gotten sick from lack of sleep, from working too hard, from the stress? Or was this a sign of waste heat from madly replicating automata inside his body, eating him from the inside out as they swarmed through his cells, collecting data, analyzing, trying to communicate with their brethren inside the clean-room, getting ready to disassemble him!

Rounding the corner in the outer labs, he saw the observation window and stared into a snapshot of hell, rippling with living rivers of flesh. The walls themselves seemed to be pulsing.

The blobs of the enormous composite organism seemed to sense his approach and flowed away from the window, allowing him to look inside. A membrane of organic and metallic sludge had draped itself over the computer terminals like spiderwebs, over the toppled table, over the equipment. It had covered the control console at the seat of the nanocore, but the hybrids left the glistening cylinder intact. Perhaps some memory of Kent's had warned them of triggering the fail-safe sterilization systems that would slag the chamber with x rays if anything breached the containment.

The emergency override—the "panic button" Erika had called it—sat key-locked and encased in glass below the panel that housed the recording and data-entry flatscreens. Parvu prayed the rampant automata had not been smart enough to subtly reconfigure the electronics from the other side.

As he stared through the window, the surface of the sea of disassembled flesh swelled and pulled itself together, rising up in a cylindrical shape. It became taller, spread out, grew protrusions as it drew more mass from the main organism. The hive of automata built something else, molecule by molecule, cell by cell.

It was a body. Humanoid, but stylized, streamlined and smooth.

Then it grew Kent Woodward's face, in a pulsating, ever-changing flow of psychedelic colors.

Around the quarantine chamber, small colonies detached themselves from the primary mass and crawled about on the ceiling, moved over the smooth sections of walls, and fixed on the seals of the autoclave, on the blocked ventilation systems. The edges of the observation windows bubbled as a thin smear of automata chewed through the epoxies holding the thick glass in place.

Trying to look both places at once and moving as fast as his fingers would allow, Jordan Parvu withdrew the small red-enameled key from his jumpsuit pocket.

On the other side of the window, Kent Woodward's reconstructed body flinched, as if all the muscles had not yet been put back into place, as if the controllers did not yet know how to operate the vast and complex machine of a human being.

Parvu's hand shook violently. He had to hold his arm steady with his other hand to find the slot, to slip the key into the lock-box around the panic button. He twisted it, then opened the glass covering.

A dagger of pain shot up through his stomach, up his spine, and into his head. He had never felt anything like it before. A warning jab from the automata trying to gain control of his own body—or just terror of dying?

Inside the chamber, the Kent reconstruction moved one leg, but its foot was still fused to the gelatinous mass on the floor. With slow precision, one cell at a time, a seam appeared, freeing a naked, perfectly formed foot.

Parvu punched the priming button. Even now the underground capacitors would be charging.

Kent opened his mouth as if to say something. Then his lips opened wider. His teeth looked very white and blocky, but then they sharpened. His face twitched, puckered, as his mouth and nose and cheeks elongated, stretching out into a long snout. His mouth opened again, this time showing sharp fangs that pierced upward, growing into tusks. His entire head contorted, cramming into a wedge shape, like a rat. Pointy ears protruded. White fur thick as spines poked out from his pores.

Both of his arms extended. His hands flexed and grasped at air. They became claws, curved and sharp enough to rip through the wall of the quarantine chamber. Behind the mask of the monstrosity showed the clear, human eyes of Kent Woodward, filled with pain.

Parvu's own skin seemed to be burning, his muscles knotting and rearranging themselves, crippling him. But he could still move.

He felt something bump his feet, something small and moving. Instinctively he flinched away, glanced downward. He could not keep himself from screaming.

He saw a rat, a white lab rat. Old Gimp. Or an exact replica. It had been reassembled right at his feet.

The automata were loose! They had finally broken out

of their holding tank to burst free upon the entire Earth. He could see the seals around all the windows boiling, falling away.

Parvu heard singing in his head, a million chittering voices all screaming *NO!* But he exerted control of his own body for one last time as he brought his finger down on the second button.

Beneath the floor of the NIL, a seven-armed array of capacitor banks dumped their charge at once, seven electrical cannonballs slamming together in the center of the star to create a plasma toroid that roared up the conducting path of the nanocore. Colliding with the depleted uranium slab set in the ceiling, the plasma spewed a shower of deadly x rays, sterilizing everything inside the laboratory. Not even a virus could survive, nor a single nanomachine.

Jordan Parvu felt a blinding white light behind his eyes, inside and out.

Bright, bright . . . *very bright.*

38

the daedalus construction

"It's an entrance."

Jason looked down the ramp that descended into the secondary structure. The corners of the arches were delicate and rounded, highly elongated. Each detail added to his guess of what the alien "builders" must have looked like. "How big is it?"

Plodding in her cumbersome suit, Erika circled the ramp, taking measurements of the yawning hole with the electromagnetic sounder. "About three meters in diameter—big enough to take the rover down. How about a Sunday drive?"

Jason craned his neck and looked around. The ramp was set into the top of the building, directly beneath where the nine diamond-fiber arches came together at the base of the giant water-lily structure. He pulled the rover to where the ramp plunged under the lunar surface. Blackness swallowed the headlights. "That damned material makes it hard to see how far down it goes."

He flicked up both the radar and IR sensors. The IR showed heat radiating from inside, but not enough to let him see any features—and not enough to make him fear a nanocritter resurgence. The source of this warmth seemed to be something else entirely. "I guess the only thing to do is go down and see for ourselves."

"You're getting pretty cavalier, Jase. What about sending the rover down telerobotically?"

316

"We could have done that from the hopper." Erika still seemed skeptical, but Jason felt numbed by the grandeur around him. Somehow, he didn't think the "builders" would intentionally hurt them. "Where's your sense of adventure?"

Erika rummaged in the rover's cargo bin and pulled out a portable relay antenna. Setting the parabolic dish on the top of the building, she tried to find a place to anchor it, but the pneumatic punch had no effect on the alien material. She finally stretched out the tripod and eyeballed it to the L-2 point above.

"I want to keep everybody informed of what we're doing." She pulled out a winding of fine fiberoptic line, plugged it into the relay dish, and started unreeling it toward the ramp. "I've got a few kilometers of this stuff. At the very least, it'll help us not to get lost."

"Hansel and Gretel on the Moon?"

"Yeah. Ready to go?"

"Just a minute. Cyndi, you been following this?"

"Just be careful down there," came Cyndi's voice.

Another cold shiver pulsed through him. It was a weird feeling, surrounded by a deserted alien complex as large as a small city. Craning his head back, he glanced up. A thousand meters overhead, the base of the kilometer-wide parabolic dish fused with the diamond-thread arches. This point seemed to be the central nexus for the whole complex. And the doorway led inside.

Jason swallowed and turned back to the rover. As he watched Erika smooth the loop of fiberoptics to reel out behind them, he spoke into his mike, "Okay, Columbus— we're going in."

The ramp was steep, about a fifteen percent slope. Jason had to bend backward to keep from stumbling with the massive sensor package he carried. High above, near the opening, they had been forced to abandon the rover in the first tight turns of the catacombs.

Even worse, they almost turned back when Jason discovered they could transmit signals out through the fiberoptic connection, but they couldn't *receive* anything.

Returning to the surface, they discussed the problem with Columbus.

"The cavity must be a one-way membrane for radio waves," Newellen conjectured. After a brief consultation, Chu had directed them to continuously transmit their journey via the fiberoptic link.

Erika used a cluster of lights to light the way along the sloping tunnel. The passage was tall and narrow and inclined to one side in a claustrophobic helical turn.

"Like a parking ramp in Augusta," said Erika. She directed the stereochip cameras in front of her, piping the signals out the optical fibers to the relay dish, hoping that Columbus could still pick it up.

Jason laughed. "I bet the Disney Corporation is already designing a new rover, complete with fiber optics, so people can explore this place. Imagine the ticket prices."

"And the lines!"

Erika played her light up and down the walls of the corkscrew as they descended. The walls were black-speckled with a faint blue glow. The fibrous windings-within-windings continued to appear in the walls and floors. Otherwise, they saw no markings, warning signs, or even instructions.

"Your nanocritters aren't much for interior decorating," he said, trudging after her.

She hesitated. "Maybe they don't care about such things. We shouldn't assume the builders think like we do."

Jason quickly lost count of the turns as they descended. He had abandoned all sense of direction; his inner ear was useless to him. He saw only Erika's light in front of him as it splashed against the weirdly textured wall.

She captured everything on the stereochips. Beams pierced the darkness, showing the walls opening into wider passages. She shone her light around to the right. The corkscrew had stopped and was flush with the floor. "Looks like we've hit bottom," she said.

"Great." Jason placed the diagnostic package on the hard ground. He took care to lower the box by bending his knees. "This thing feels like it's gained weight."

Grunting in her unwieldy suit, Erika knelt in front of the package. Powering up the unit, she ran through a series of self-calibrations. "Stop breathing so hard, Jason. You're biasing the seismic sensors."

Jason took the light away from her and looked around, but most of the illumination was either absorbed or scattered by the alien material, reflecting barely enough for him to see in the large chamber.

Everything had a fuzzy blue look to it, as if Jason could see the walls better without his illumination. He handed the light back to Erika. She knelt on one knee in front of the diagnostic package.

"Did you bump this against anything bringing it down here, Jase?" she asked. "You sure you didn't prang it against a wall?"

"No, why?"

Jason squinted at the box on the floor. LED readouts, touch-sensitive controls, and a few hard-switches made up most of the exterior control panel.

Erika straightened. "I'm getting an anomalous reading on some of the instruments. Really anomalous. UV photons are at a hundred watts per square meter— enough to give you a bad sunburn if you weren't in your suit. The second number is the neutrino flux. It's way too high."

Jason frowned. *Neutrinos?* They were notoriously difficult to capture in instruments, needing about a hundred *light-years* of lead to be sure of catching one; their superconductor-based detectors were good, but still not completely reliable. "Neutrino measurements aren't too accurate anyway," he said.

"We're not trying to be exact to a bunch of decimal points—but look at that exponent! Five orders of magnitude higher than what we saw up top. The detector can't be that far off."

Erika pondered, then keyed in a query, moving clumsily with her gloved fingers. "It's about the flux of neutrinos you'd expect from a fission reactor."

He studied the perimeter of the chamber again, searching for telltale signs of any kind of machinery.

319

"No neutrons, though," Erika continued. "No charged particles. Nothing else except a UV flux." She stood up. "Don't ask me to figure it. Should we go on?"

"We don't know a damn bit more about the place," Jason said. He recalled sitting in front of his holo-dais, while Eiffel stared down at him. He had pondered the arches, the secondary structures, trying to infer something about the alien builders, a hint as to their mind-set, their purpose, or their home world.

"Wait, maybe that UV flux does give us a little hint. What if it's their illumination? Maybe that's the alien equivalent of visible light, the frequency they see in. If their star is a UV radiator, then it makes sense."

Jason swung the lights behind them to where the complex opened up, deeper beneath the lunar surface. Handing the lights back to Erika, he picked up the massive diagnostic package with a grunt. "I feel like a pack mule." He followed Erika cautiously into the dark, not sure where they were going.

"Follow your nose," Erika said.

"Nothing else around here to navigate by."

With each footstep they took, it felt as if the darkness opened around them in an ever-expanding circle. Erika moved the illumination back and forth. Looking down, Jason could see only the indicator lights from the diagnostics package. The walls, the floor, and the ceiling of the alien structure seemed to swallow up photons as they struck, leaving only the windings-within-windings material glowing a cool purple.

They trudged on in silence, growing more tense each moment. Waiting for something to jump out at them. Every step Jason took seemed lighter than the last, which didn't make sense.

"This is weird, like one of those House of Mystery tourist traps with slanted floors and trapezoidal archways."

Erika finally pointed the beam to the top of the ceiling. "The ceiling is sloping up, too. Everything is focused on where the corkscrew started."

The chamber kept getting larger around them. The downward slope increased again. Jason took two steps in front of her, as if he were walking into the mouth of something terrifying.

"Holy shit!" He felt himself starting to slip. His booted feet couldn't find a grip on the floor—because the floor was no longer there. It had suddenly lurched beneath him, dropping away like a fun-house gimmick. A surge of gravity grabbed at him. "I'm falling!"

He flailed his arms, trying to keep his balance; he pushed the diagnostic unit away from him. Every second seemed to take an eternity. Jason twisted his body as he fell, trying to prevent his helmet from cracking against the hard ground. All the time he kept his arms moving. The loose light twirled beside him, making crazy patterns as it spun through the vacuum.

He heard Erika's shouts, but couldn't make sense of them through his own yelling.

Even through the bulky padding of the suit and the slow-motion fall in low gravity, Jason felt the breath go out of him as he struck bottom. He had landed on his back-pack; the heating and oxygen unit had softened the fall. He struggled to breathe, and only after the first sharp pain had gone away was he able to gasp for air. Sounds came over his radio, but they were distant, someone calling. . . .

His heart continued to beat fast. He tried to take slow breaths, to keep from hyperventilating. He didn't hear any telltale sounds of air hissing in his ears. Checking his life-system parameters with the heads-up display, he saw that his suit pressure was stable.

He heard a low moan. He struggled to an elbow. His backpack kept him from bending forward. Jason shoved hard with one hand and rolled to the front. Pushing up with both hands, he straightened. *You sure weren't meant to fall down in a bulky spacesuit,* he thought. "Erika?"

"Yeah." Her voice sounded weak. "Right here."

The light was off to the side, illuminating a distant wall. Jason stepped to the light, reaching out to ensure that he wouldn't hit anything. "You okay?"

"Yeah. I didn't even move, and I still came tumbling after you!" Her voice took a second to come back. "What happened?"

"Besides falling? I don't know." Jason bent to pick up the dropped light. He found Erika lying not far from where he had fallen. "How's your suit pressure?"

She took a minute to reply. "Steady." She reached behind herself. "And the optical fiber's still attached. Think we're still transmitting out?"

"We can't be sure if we ever were."

He stepped carefully to her. Walls of alien material rose up around them, glowing with the edge-of-vision blue color. He couldn't see how far they had fallen, or what had become of the hole they had walked through.

"Jase," Erika said. She had just finished struggling up from the ground. "Behind us. Is it my imagination, or is there a passageway back there?"

At first Jason could see only more of the alien material, then he caught a glimpse of something darker. "You're right." He turned the light back toward her. "How could you see that?"

"No blue glow. The light in your hand was blinding you."

Jason pondered that. "Let me try something. Stay still." He switched off the light. The entire chamber plunged into darkness.

It took a minute, but shortly Jason began to notice the faint outlines of several square entrances into the chamber. The squares were deep black, while the walls and floor around them glowed a bluish violet. He felt his eyes getting used to the darkness about as much as they ever would to the edge of the spectrum; to a different set of eyes, the chamber might be blazing with light.

"This place looks like a train station. I can count seven, no eight tunnels coming in here."

"Nine," corrected Erika. "Think about it—nine arches outside, nine pathways, now nine tunnels." Jason stood by and watched as Erika measured all the entrances to the tunnels and the chamber they were in.

"Sounds like they've got a thing for nines, or threes." Jason took another deep breath, felt his heartbeat slowing down. "Well, do we try to go back outside? Everybody must be worried about us. Or do we go on?"

"Go on, of course." He had never heard Erika sound so determined. "We might not get another chance to come out here, if somebody blows it all up. All we've seen are tunnels so far. There's got to be something more."

Jason swallowed again, knowing she was right. "Then let's find it." He switched the brilliant light back on, breaking the spell. "So which way?"

"Your call," said Erika. "Pick a tunnel, any tunnel."

He hesitated for a moment, then struck out for the first corridor. He lifted the heavy diagnostic pack, hoping it would be worth their while to lug the thing along. They walked in silence on a level floor.

After many minutes of plodding, they stopped as Erika's light splashed on something large ahead of them. Jason could just discern the outline of a multifaceted building constructed of panels placed at odd angles. An architect's bad dream. The structure was a lighter color than the surrounding floor and walls; it appeared to be made from a different material. Some of the panels were adorned with an ordered array of circles parallel to each other, all pointing back down the tunnel.

Erika said, "What do you think?"

Jason wet his lips. The recirculated air in his suit seemed even drier than usual. "I don't know." He felt at a loss to communicate; this overwhelmed his sense of architectural insight. It looked as if an autistic child had tried to build something and had parts left over. Thin panels, wedges of material at every angle, a snapshot of a house of cards in midcollapse. The structure didn't look as if it could support itself.

Erika started toward the exotic building. She kept the light trained on the structure, lighting up the panels covered with aligned circles. As Jason approached, the building seemed to rotate. It was all in the perspective, like walking through a painting. No matter where they viewed the structure, the circles pointed straight at them.

As if it were trying to tell them something.

moonbase columbus

Big Daddy Newellen shifted behind the virtual display panel in the moonbase control center. It took him a moment before he could piece together words enough to speak out loud. Damned harebrained theory—but it all checked out. Everything.

Bernard Chu and the other crewmembers stared at the images transmitted back from Jason and Erika's exploration of Daedalus. At times, bursts of static interrupted the foreshortened images piped through the fiber-optic cable Erika had laid down, but they missed little.

An exterior view of the whole structure came from the hopper's cameras, sent by Cyndi Salito and Bryan Zed. At least those two were still in two-way touch, and antsy to do something. Three separate times, Salito had requested permission to go in after Jason and Erika, but Bernard Chu had flatly denied her.

Zimmerman had not been able to disarm the nukes in the fail-safe ring. Personally, Newellen couldn't imagine McConnell setting off the warheads now, not with people over at Daedalus—but Mission Control on Earth had fallen mysteriously silent, without even Fukumitsu's insistent questions. Chu had called it good riddance to distractions. But it made Newellen uneasy.

This new idea of his made him uneasier still.

"Hey, Bernard, I've got to show you something."

Startled, Chu turned from the command podium. "What?"

Newellen gestured. "Come here. You're not going to believe me unless you see the calculations yourself."

Chu sighed and moved over to Newellen's station, keeping his gaze toward the holotank showing 2-D images transmitted by Jason and Erika. "Is it good news or bad?"

"Depends. Good, in the sense that I might have figured out a reason for a big part of that structure. Bad, in that it means all four of our people at Daedalus are in deep poop."

Chu's pinched face focused on Newellen now. "Tell me."

"Well, let's assume that that flowerlike main structure is some sort of wonky dish antenna. It has to have a purpose, and that seems likely. If it's to transmit EM waves, then there has to be a way to get the electromagnetic energy to the antenna. Amateur electronics stuff."

"Okay . . . " said Chu, "remember, I'm a biochemist."

"Basically, I've run some antenna design calculations and I think the passageway Jason and Erika are walking in is a mode converter. Giant size."

Newellen waited for some shocked reaction. Chu looked at him with a puzzled expression. "A what?"

Newellen sighed. "Mode convertors take electromagnetic energy in one spatial form and convert it to another. It's usually more efficient to produce EM waves in one mode, but to actually transmit the signals, they have to be converted to another mode, or pattern. I'm pretty sure from the measurements that those catacombs are mode converters."

"But what for?"

"It may be a way to phase-conjugate the waves, if they're coherent." He paused. "Our people might be walking through a giant radio amplifier. When you think about it, that one-way radio membrane makes sense: radio waves can only come out, not in. Since there are no incoming waves, it cuts down on losses in the cavity. It's a true diffraction-limited amplifier."

Chu grew alert, still not understanding but concerned. "And if it's turned on? While they're still inside?"

Ah, now the man was getting it! "Depending on the intensity, there's a good chance they might be cooked. The suits will protect them some—but radio-frequency waves will still couple to the human body. It's not a very healthy place to stand."

Chu drew in a breath. He glanced around the control center, as if hoping for an inspiration.

Newellen kept stating his case. He felt suddenly hungry. "From what I can tell in the last batch of transmitted pictures, those circles on that gadget are some sort of solid-state devices, probably used for creating the EM waves. It's a simple matter of phase-conjugating them—and the measurements work out." He shrugged. "But this is all theory, of course."

"Of course." Chu scowled, as if finally realizing that he wanted to pass this one off to Mission Control on Earth—but they had cut him off without any explanation. "Anything else I should know?"

Newellen worked his pudgy fingers along the controls, calling up another set of calculations. "Well, I was really puzzled by the energy source for this stuff. First, I thought, with the neutrino flux so high there might be some sort of fusion reactor inside. Neutrino detectors are quirky things, but they're not that bad. Erika's readings were a thousand times higher than they should have been for a fusion reactor, though. Outside the error bars by a mile."

Chu stared down at the stream of numbers, but they obviously didn't mean anything to him. "And?"

"The only energy source I know of that produces a neutrino flux that high is a matter-antimatter reactor."

Someone in the control center whistled. "Isn't that impossible?" said Chu.

"So are alien nanotech machines on the Moon," Newellen answered dryly.

Chu swallowed and regained his composure. "So that device they've found is probably a matter-antimatter reactor?"

Newellen was suddenly struck by a thought. "And if each of those tunnels is supposed to act as a waveguide, then there must be eight more reactors just like this, one at the end of each tunnel. That signal's going to pack one hell of a punch when it goes."

Bernard Chu fidgeted, as if forcing himself to swallow something he found extremely unpalatable. "So Dvorak and Trace are sitting in the middle of a giant alien microwave oven."

"That's basically right." Newellen nodded. "And they don't even know it. Worse, since the nanocritters shut down and the complex is completed, that transmitter could go off at any time."

washington, d.c.—mission control

Major General Simon Pritchard felt his hand grow slick with sweat on the textured handle of the service pistol. Everything came to a stop as tension thickened the air.

In the Mission Control center, all attention flicked back and forth between himself, the transmitted images of Dvorak and Trace exploring the Daedalus catacombs, and Celeste in her barely controlled state of panic.

Petite and coiled to spring, Celeste turned her back on Albert Fukumitsu and marched toward one of the Mission Control flatscreen terminals. The tech sitting there swiveled in his chair as if poised to run.

"Punch up the command sequence for setting off the nuclear quarantine ring," she said. "I have the access codes. We've got no alternative but to detonate the warheads and end this once and for all."

Pritchard felt his skin crawl. He had been stupid not to realize what she intended to do, and now he didn't know which course to take. *How could he let her go through with this?* He trusted Celeste implicitly. Or did he?

Several of the techs leaped to their feet in outrage. "Wait a minute—" Fukumitsu cried. He sputtered before he finally found words. "On what basis do you make that decision? I've been here every second of the exploration and I've seen no evidence of a threat! Exactly the opposite—the aliens could have killed all the people on Columbus during the infection if they wanted to. They could

328

have retaliated when Chu sent his home-made bomb. But they've made no aggressive move. None.

"Instead, look at what they've done—" He gestured to the screen where Dvorak and Trace stood inspecting the glimmering matter-antimatter reactor. "We still don't have a clue what any of this is. How can you just push the button—"

She shouted at him. "Because I *know*! I always know. That's how I knew about the Grissom, how I knew something bad was going to happen on the Collins—" Celeste caught herself before explaining any further. Pritchard furrowed his brow, trying to understand what she was implying.

Celeste lowered her voice. "You are out of line, Mr. Fukumitsu. It is not part of your job to question my orders. You are relieved, as of now."

Fukumitsu flinched as if he had been slapped in the face. But he refused to move. Celeste turned her anger instead to the tech by the console in front of her. "Punch up the command sequence, I said!" She pushed him aside and crouched over the panel, working with the interface to pull up a set of menus.

Pritchard shifted the service pistol to his other hand, trying to keep himself motionless as the turmoil churned within him. What the hell was she doing? Now that more pieces were falling together, it made even less sense to him.

He remembered the night of Bernard Chu's communication from the Collins, how Celeste had wakened from a deep sleep full of nightmares. Then he recalled the uncanny story of how she alone had managed to rescue the people on the Grissom by somehow knowing to get them into the only safe place on the entire station. She had once told him how interested she would be in hearing about his dreams—had she been speaking literally?

Pritchard experienced the sudden, sinking certainty that Celeste McConnell, the powerful director of the United Space Agency, was making her major, often-questionable decisions on the basis of *dreams*.

Pritchard recalled making love to her earlier that night. Celeste had seemed so desperate, clinging and grabbing at him. She had been full of erotic energy, wrapping herself around him like raw electric wires. Now, she wanted to use half a dozen warheads to blow up Daedalus and all traces of the alien artifact.

Perhaps she had been planning this all along. Because these were old-style warheads from a secure stockpile, they didn't retain all of the attendant checks and balances, bureaucratic stalling devices that would have made it impossible for anyone to set them off in a timely fashion if something disastrous did happen at the alien construction site.

Since the quarantine ring was not to be triggered anywhere on Earth, and on the opposite side of the Moon from Columbus, they had managed to ramrod approvals through, to streamline an emergency detonation process. Pritchard himself had helped.

The U.S. President had one set of access codes, and so did the director of the United Space Agency. Celeste did have the power to detonate them—legitimately. In an emergency only.

But was this an emergency?

Prickles of sweat appeared on his forehead. Pritchard had not comprehended the magnitude of what they were doing. He had been swept along with his newfound glory, press conferences, important decisions that affected the whole world, sudden prestige for his lifelong dedication to a military that had fallen on weaker times. Somehow this did not seem to be the proper culmination of his life's work: to destroy mankind's first link with an advanced alien race . . . because of a bad dream.

On the screen, Dvorak and Trace moved deeper into the alien hall of wonders beneath the lunar surface. *There were supposed to be no people present when the warheads went off,* Pritchard thought. No risk to human life! But now two people had gone to explore, daring to do something no one else would do. And look at everything they had discovered. . . .

How could he let Celeste wipe that away because of a nightmare? A blot of mustard, a fragment of underdone potato, as Dickens would have said. And if she had only a vague feeling of impending disaster, how could Celeste know that she wouldn't cause the disaster herself? What if the nightmare were warning her of a completely un-related threat? Even if her dreams were somehow truly prescient, how could he be sure Celeste was interpreting them correctly?

Then Pritchard recalled seeing her sit up screaming in the middle of the night, sweat-drenched, with terror on her face. She did seem to know something. And she had been absolutely right about the Grissom. . . .

Hunched over the flatscreen, Celeste called up the warhead command sequence. The technician stood be-side her, his face the color of wallpaper paste. No one was willing to challenge the director's orders, especially not with Major General Pritchard standing there with the guard's service pistol ready.

"This is the only way. We'll be safe," Celeste kept whispering. "Trust me."

Rigid and formal, the second guard pulled her gun out of its holster. "I'm afraid I cannot allow you to do that, Director McConnell," she said. "Please step away from the console. Immediately."

Livid, Celeste whirled to glare at her. Her lips curled back. Pritchard thought for a moment she was going to hurl herself at the guard and try to wrest the weapon away.

On the screen in front of Celeste, a schematic of Daedalus Crater showed red circles at the locations of the deployed warheads. A blinking string of letters on the screen requested the access code, holding on a thirty-second time to detonation.

Pritchard pointed his own gun toward the guard, hold-ing it steady. He did not let his own gaze waver. "Sergeant, please drop your weapon. Now."

The guard froze. She turned to meet Pritchard's gaze, but the major general could read nothing in her eyes. Would she shoot? How deep were her convictions? How deep were his own?

Pritchard cocked the pistol. "Drop it."

After a blistering pause, the guard set her gun down on the floor.

Celeste threw herself at the keyboard again and began entering the complicated access code that would trigger the ring of nuclear weapons.

In the holotanks, Dvorak and Trace stopped at a towering crystalline structure that pulsed with deep blue lights. Trace reached up to point at something.

Calmly Simon Pritchard turned toward Celeste's console and pulled the trigger, aiming into the controls. Then he pulled the trigger a second time, and a third.

Glass, plastic, and metal shards flew into the air as the flatscreen burst and the covering of the control panels shattered. Splinters of debris sprayed out, cutting Celeste's cheeks and arms as she staggered backward.

"No!" she screamed in frustration and despair. "Don't you understand!" She glared at him in stunned fury.

Then, a low buzz came from the speakers, unnoticed for a moment with the echoes of gunshots. Within seconds, it built to a roar that screeched out on all wavelengths.

"It's coming in on every receiver!" Fukumitsu shouted.

The enormous signal continued to increase, deep and rumbling like a thunderstorm in a bottle. Something of immense power had been transmitted from the great petals of the Daedalus complex.

"Blocking all channels!" one of the technicians shouted.

Pritchard wavered. On one of the wall holoscreens, he saw the image of the completed bowl of the Daedalus structure like a gigantic antenna. A transmitter. The enormous construction was designed to broadcast back to its creators and the whole Galaxy that it was finished. It was ready.

But ready for what?

"Like an all-clear signal," Pritchard whispered to himself. "Now all we've got to do is wait for a response."

Everyone fell silent in Mission Control. Pritchard found a seat and slumped into it. He flicked the gun's safety back on, and let the pistol drop to a shelf on one of the consoles. He closed his eyes. He did not want to have to look at Celeste. Not right now. He could not face her.

The air around him stank of burned gunpowder. He wondered if history would paint him as a hero or a traitor.

It would all depend on how the aliens answered the call.

Celeste paid no attention to him. She had fallen to her knees on the floor, bleeding from a handful of minor cuts. She stared at the red on her hands. "Now it's too late," she said, over and over. "It's too late. . . ."

41

moonbase columbus

Bernard Chu had blocked out the communications channel to Earth as the roar rumbled through the speakers in the control center. The technicians stood in their places.

"Get me Salito's hopper over on Farside! Now! Get a confirmation that Salito and Zimmerman are all right." He raised his voice to break through the chatter in the control center.

"Uh, Bernard—" Newellen said, trying to interrupt.

"I've got an answer from Salito!" one of the other techs said.

"Put her on! I want to know what just happened over at Daedalus!"

"Bernard," Newellen said again, more insistent, "that transmission didn't come from Farside. The L-2 relay is ringing as much as all our other instruments, but not from Daedalus."

"What are you talking about, Lon?"

Cyndi Salito's voice burst through the open channel. "Holy shit, Columbus, what was that?"

"Are you all right?" Chu demanded, turning back and forth as everyone shouted at him in the same moment.

"Sure—nothing happened here. Other than that transmission we heard."

"Bernard," Newellen interrupted. "I've got it pinpointed. That signal did not come from here at all. It's Mars! It was broadcast from Mars!"

Chu could not find words to respond as chilling thoughts winked into his mind. Of course, how could they have been so parochial? If, as Erika Trace and Jordan Parvu had suggested, the alien builders were indiscriminately beaming automata across the Galaxy, looking for any place to land and begin construction, how could they hit Earth's Moon and nothing else? Why wasn't Earth itself hit? The Daedalus construction must not be the only such alien monument being built in the solar system, nor was it even the first completed.

The Daedalus nanomachines had been working double-time to repair the damage caused by his nitro and rocket-fuel bomb. It wouldn't be long before the Daedalus transmitter sent its own message. He thought of Newellen's idea of a giant microwave oven—and then he wondered if Celeste was going to push the nuclear button after all.

He clapped his hands. "All right, listen up. Salito and Zimmerman, I want you to take off. Get away from the crater. Now! Get to a safe distance."

Salito broke in. "Ooops, something's happening here. Seismic sensor just started dancing."

"A moonquake?" Bryan Zimmerman's voice crowded over hers.

"I think the antenna is moving!"

Chu scowled with impatience. "Cyndi and Zed, did you copy? Lift off, now. Safe distance."

The people in the control center milled around, staring at Chu. Finally, after too long a pause, Salito's voice came back.

"Uh, we're not too keen on leaving Erika and Jason abandoned inside there. We know they're still alive."

Chu crossed his thin arms over his chest. "Dr. Salito, if they are inside the radio cavity when a signal of that magnitude is broadcast, they will be fried by the radiant energy. If you are not shielded, you will also be killed. At the very least, all systems on your hopper will be shorted from the EM interference. And we don't have another hopper to come rescue you. Do you understand me?"

Bryan Zed's voice remained flat. "Sir, don't you think we should go in after them?"

335

Dammit, Chu was getting tired of everyone trying to be a hero. "No! Four stupid deaths are worse than two. Get going. That's an order!"

"All right," Bryan Zed finally replied.

Moments later, when the hopper lifted off and turned its panoramic cameras down across the alien complex on Daedalus Crater, they all watched as the huge glassy petals of the transmitter dish began to slowly swing around.

42

the daedalus construction

Jason scanned the dim tunnels and the flashing, exotic structure embellished with the matrix of circles.

Then the fireworks started.

Ripples of blue light streamed along the tunnel walls, like annular waves of energy spewed from the strange machine. A flash of brighter intensity burst out, followed rapidly by a third.

"What's happening?" Erika whispered.

Jason stared. The first thought that came to his head seemed the most likely and the most frightening. "Powering up, I think."

The tunnels behind them held nothing, just conduits streaming to the surface, toward the gossamer bridges that connected the deep catacombs to the giant Daedalus antenna. It would take a long time for them to get back to the hopper, following Erika's fiberoptic thread—if they could even manage to get back up from where they had fallen. Somehow, he didn't think they would have time for that.

Another burst of light rippled along the translucent walls. "This doesn't seem like a good place to be, whatever is about to happen," he said.

"There's only one place to go," she said. "And that's down."

"Come on, then." Jason stumbled forward. "Hurry! No telling how far we have to go before it's safe." He

337

stooped to set down the heavy diagnostic pack. No way was he going to carry that thing at a dead run.

On the surface, he knew Cyndi Salito and Bryan Zimmerman were sitting on ground zero—in more ways than one—but he knew of no way to warn them. They would have to fend for themselves.

The two of them bounded around the panels behind the weird building, through an intersection, to the tunnel beyond. Erika's illumination bobbed through the murky catacombs. She pointed the light to a series of openings in the wall. The beam skipped from entrance to entrance. "Which direction?"

"The lady or the tiger," muttered Jason. "Maybe it doesn't matter." He looked behind them, but he could not see through the darkness. He turned back to Erika, then on impulse, he headed into the middle opening. "Only one way to find out."

Erika entered the tunnel beside Jason and stopped. "Wait!" She reached behind her to where the fiber-optic line was attached to her suit, disconnected it, then let the end drop to the floor. "I hate to do this, but if there's going to be some big energy surge through the tunnels, I don't want to be wearing an antenna hooked up to my suit!"

Jason hesitated. They would now be cut off entirely from the outside world, unable even to transmit out. And they wouldn't be able to follow the strand back to the surface like a lifeline. He shivered at the thought of being lost down here in the dark.

"Oh, well, it didn't work for Hansel and Gretel either." Leaving everything behind, they hurried onward.

The next opening turned out to be an archway, tall and narrow. As they passed under it, Jason heard static clicking over his suit radio, then his suit suddenly grew slack and more comfortable. "What the—?" He checked the heads-up display beamed on the inside of his faceplate.

"That sounded like your electrostatic curtain back at Columbus," Erika said. "Snap, crackle, and pop."

Jason studied his suit display. The readings confirmed his suspicions. "I'll be damned! We just entered an atmosphere. That must have been some kind of screen to hold in gases."

Erika took a moment to answer. "I wish you hadn't left the diagnostic unit. We could tell what the atmosphere consists of."

Jason checked his air gauge. "I'm not taking off my helmet to check. We've got plenty of reserve in our tanks for a while." He drew a deep breath, pumping up his courage.

They entered a sprawling chamber, vaster than anything else they had seen under Daedalus. Erika's light never quite illuminated any one object, but showed enough to leave them both awestruck. Jason couldn't tell the scale of what he saw—the ceiling and walls were too far away for him to judge distance.

He tried to make sense of incomprehensible images: soaring buildings that twisted in odd helixes, glittering crystalline structures taken from a distorted Escher woodcut, rectangular plates that extended at random angles from the floor, arches that looped unsymmetrically.

They stood trying to absorb the sight, made even more difficult by Erika's tiny exploratory light. Finally Jason whispered into the suit radio, "Sensory overload." He swept out a spacesuited arm that moved freely now in the pressurized environment. "My brain can't comprehend any of this stuff."

Erika switched off the light. The dull UV glow had increased enough for them to make out hazy forms. "Much brighter here. I can almost see."

"So what does that mean?" he asked.

"With the atmosphere? I bet this is where the aliens live."

Jason's first reaction was to turn tail and run. But the only path that they had found led back to the unprotected corridors—and something was going to happen out there. He could feel it. Not that the Rube Goldberg contraptions here made him feel any calmer.

It took a few seconds for his heart to stop pounding, but when no bug-eyed creatures came swarming out of the buildings, he calmed down. He tried not to let his voice crack when he spoke through the helmet radio. "So where do you think the aliens would be? Or is this just a staging area, waiting for a colony ship to arrive?"

"How can there be any aliens yet? They just sent their nanocritters to build this place."

"But what about this atmosphere? Why else would your nanocritters fill this place with gas—presumably breathable to the aliens—and keep it enclosed with some sort of barrier if it isn't meant to house living things for a few decades yet?"

"I don't know." She was quiet for a while as their eyes grew used to the dark. "Hey, Jase, see that building over there?"

Jason squinted through the darkness. He couldn't see as well as Erika. "I only see one thing that looks anything like a building—kind of low, flat-roofed?"

"That's it."

Erika switched her light back on, driving back the deep purple haze. Under harsh white light, the place appeared no friendlier. She moved the light slowly over the underground metropolis.

Visions of old "sci-fi" movies flashed through his mind—long tentacles protruding from flying saucers, death rays smoking the ground, scantily clad women gasping in horror as they were kidnapped from Earth. Fighting back the paranoid snapshots from his imagination, Jason took hold of Erika's arm. "Come on. Let's finish looking around."

They moved to the low-slung building, passing weirdly shaped objects on the way. The things reminded Jason of displays in modern art museums, conceptual sculptures that had meaning to the artist and little else. For all Jason could tell, the objects might have been anything from street signs to water closets. Erika's light scattered off the objects, making the curves and shadows look even more exotic.

After skirting a gnarled tower that twisted up from the floor, they arrived at the building.

"Okay," said Erika, "how do we get in?" The walls appeared to be one continuous flow of black-speckled weave. As they looked closer, the building's edges appeared more rounded than sharp, as if extruded upward from the floor.

Jason stepped forward. "If it's really sophisticated, maybe it'll let us inside when we approach. You know, less work for the users. At least that's the way I'd design things." He walked up to the building, but nothing happened. He touched his helmet against the wall. No opening appeared.

He kept close to the building and moved along the wall. "The door could have a sensor that prevents anything other than the builders from entering. To keep out alien dogs and cats."

"Maybe it isn't even a building," said Erika. "How about a water tank? Or a humongous footrest. Who knows?"

Just as Jason reached the end of the building, an opening dilated, melting outward in a plastic flow. "There," he said. "I knew I'd find it."

Erika flashed the light around as she joined him at the opening. "Should we go in?"

"What have we got to lose now?"

When they stepped into the building, the bluish tinge increased in intensity, as if they had stepped into some kind of greenhouse. Row after row of bubble-covered boxes filled the area—each item presumably assembled where it stood by the nanocritters. The translucent boxes were crowded next to each other, basking in the UV.

He stepped up to the nearest bubble-box and extended a gloved hand. Erika held the light steady; Jason could hear her rapid breathing over the radio. "Careful, Jase."

As he got closer to the bubble, he said, "What do you think is in here—plants? A mineral bath?" He bent closer, then froze, suddenly recalling a vision of hideous Hollywood alien parasites hiding in eggs, waiting to latch on to the faceplates of hapless space explorers.

"Can you see inside?" Erika didn't offer to look herself.

Jason's glove touched, then passed through the surface of the bubble. He jerked his hand back. "What the hell?"

"Hey, look!" Erika directed the light over the tops of the bubbles in the room. As the beam of light hit them, they glowed brightly, became more transparent. "I bet our light is too far down in the spectrum for the aliens to see, so maybe this is their equivalent of an infrared image to us."

Not touching the bubble, Jason bent over to see into the box through the bubble field. "Give me a little more light here?"

Erika brought the light closer. "My God. . . ."

The box held a pale gray thing, not more than a few centimeters long and a centimeter wide. At first it looked like a plant, a mutated piece of asparagus, but as Jason watched in horror, the thing twisted in its box.

"It's an incubator," breathed Erika. "These things are alive."

Jason watched wordlessly. It took a few seconds, but he could make out signs that the thing in the incubator was being nurtured—tiny black threads ran across the bottom of the box, connected to the creature's outer membranes; black fluid ran from a minuscule tube to the bud at one end of the creature's length; the box jittered, keeping the creature constantly in motion.

Erika took a step back. She flashed the light into the rows of incubator boxes around her. Jason drew in several breaths, recalling how many similar buildings they had seen inside the enormous cavern. How many embryos were being grown here?

His next thought was that the creatures' parents might be somewhere around, giant versions of the same entity ready to charge in and devour the two of them for disturbing the . . . nursery. He looked around the place; nothing moved, nothing seemed different from when they had first come in.

"What are they doing—growing, feeding, or what?" Erika's voice sounded shrill inside his helmet. "What if we set off some sort of alarm? What if they know we're here?"

Jason tried to comfort himself at the same time. "If there are any aliens, they should have noticed us a long time ago."

Erika edged toward the opening. "Let's go," she said. They backed out of the building, leaving the incubators behind. "Back up to the surface, see if Columbus got any of our transmissions."

As they stepped back into the primary chamber, Jason felt more and more uneasy. They were still surrounded by silent, UV-laced darkness. He somehow sensed that they had violated a growing ground.

Erika flashed her light from side to side in jerky spurts. Nothing had changed, as far as they could tell. Everything remained quiet. "I don't like this. I don't have a good feeling about this anymore," she said. Jason could hear the sound of her breathing grow quicker.

"Don't make it any worse," said Jason.

"Let's get out of here." Her words sent a chill running through Jason, like an ice-cold razor that sliced across his skin. He knew they were just getting jumpy, feeding on each other's growing panic.

After what they had been through, why would something just be hiding out there, waiting, when it could have sprung at them long ago? Unless they had set some kind of machinery in motion, some kind of robotic guards. . . .

A loud crack rolled through Jason's helmet. The sound came in a sudden pop and a high thrumming, as if something had smacked against his helmet. The sound went on and on, a lightning of white noise that rattled through his head, roaring like a tangible force over the coatings of his suit. His heads-up displays swirled colors and meaningless numbers across the viewing area of his faceplate.

Somewhere in the suit radio, he heard Erika scream, drowned out by a high shriek of static. He felt everything growing blacker around him, cutting off every thought in his head.

The Daedalus construction was sending its own transmission across the Galaxy, back to the builders' home world.

43

the daedalus construction

Jason could barely hear himself speak. "Erika?" His voice sounded far away, as if his helmet were filled with old socks. The suit radio crackled and hummed with static.

No answer.

"Erika? Can you hear me?" He had a sudden thought that the suit transmitter was dead. His heads-up display confirmed that he had blown two solid-state fuses in the control pack, but everything should be up and working. Good thing the life supports hadn't fried from the pounding of the alien signal. But what if Erika's suit—

"What was that?" Erika's voice sounded as if it had been transmitted through a layer of cotton.

"A signal," Jason answered after fumbling to reroute the radio fuses to their backups. "A new alien base declaring itself ready." It was the only thing that made sense.

"My God, what would have happened if we had been in the chamber? At least here we were shielded—"

Jason worked his jaw and tried to pop his ears until the muffled feeling faded. "The relay station we left up top was probably knocked into orbit."

"Do you think Cyndi and Bryan are all right? If they were in the hopper waiting for us . . . " her voice trailed off.

Jason felt his stomach muscles knot. "Let's just hope they had some warning and got to shelter. Maybe they're asking the same questions about us right now."

Erika turned away. She panned the light over the alien construction, pausing at the building from which they had exited. Neither of them knew what to say.

Jason could see strange architectural shapes rising from the floor. Some looked grotesque in the shadows; others seemed frail and spindly, as if they were designed on a planet with gravity much lower than Earth's.

"None of this makes any sense to me yet," Jason finally said. "There's a whole city down here and no . . . *adults*. Where are the builders? Why aren't they here? Where did those embryos come from? Is there some sort of a ship or projectile we haven't found yet?"

Behind her faceplate, Erika shook her head. "No, Jase. No macro-sized projectile. If the theory is right, the Builders fired off automata across the cosmos like shot-gun pellets. Swarms of them. You can accelerate nanomachines near to the speed of light. No macroscopic projectile could accelerate that fast without damaging itself, without hauling tons of fuel behind it. That doesn't seem to be the way the alien Builders think. The nanocritters did all the work for them here."

"So how did the embryos get to the Moon?" he asked. "They had to come from somewhere. Are you suggesting that nanocritters built them, too?" He paused, shocked at his own suggestion. "It seems like black magic to me, Erika—nanotechnology assembling things on a molecular level. Bridges, transmitter dishes, or power plants is one thing—I can do that, given the proper materials and equipment. But living, breathing organisms with functional cells? DNA information is a billion times more complicated."

Jason watched her as she swung the light around. From the back he couldn't decipher her body language, insulated by the suit. She took a few steps away from the incubator building and toward a series of towers.

The floor of the grand chamber was scattered with a plethora of objects that seemed to have no purpose or order. Wispy crystalline gardens, mechanical trees, half-formed arches that stopped in midplunge to dangle in the air.

Kevin J. Anderson and Doug Beason

They walked among shapes that grew out of the ground. Solid triangles tipped on their sides, large spheres crowning slender poles, and panels that jutted out at crazy angles from the main structures.

Erika finally stopped before a tall trapezoidal arch flared with bright purple arcs. It led into another gallery that seemed to go on forever. After hesitating, she stepped through the arch.

Inside the gallery they roamed along a parkway of columns built of the same diamond-hard material, stretching as far as their light could reach. It reminded Jason of the ancient Parthenon.

Erika pointed at what appeared to be many-sided datacubes protruding from each tall column. Jason touched one of the fist-sized objects and it detached easily. He turned it over in his glove. "Buckyball, I think. Buckminster Fullerene, a humongous carbon molecule. Our biggest ones are barely large enough to see under magnification. Look at this sucker." Jason stuffed the object in his suit's sample pouch. "Used for information storage, maybe? I wonder if this place is a library."

Jason no longer felt the fear that had grabbed at them just before the radio burst. There was a sense of serenity now . . . of knowing that whatever happened next, they couldn't be overwhelmed by events. Not after what they had already seen.

They poked into other buildings, always finding the self-dilating opening on one wall. In one structure they discovered what appeared to be exercise equipment. An assembly hall? A classroom?

Finally Erika spoke. "I'm not sure we can even guess what the purpose is. But it looks like those embryos have absolutely everything ready-made for them when they grow up."

From beyond the rim of the crater, Cyndi Salito sighed into the hopper's radio link as Bryan Zed replaced another fuse. She had been right in the middle of an argument with Bernard Chu when the last fuse had blown, but now they should be all fixed.

"Dr. Salito, are you there again?" Chu's voice crackled back at her. Zimmerman hadn't even tried to restore the video circuits yet.

"Look, Bernard—we're going to go in after them, no matter what you say, right, Zed?"

"Right."

"So why don't you just give us your blessing? If we have to defy your orders in front of everybody, you're going to look pretty stupid."

She tapped her fingers on the control panel. When Chu finally responded, she could almost see his livid expression. "One hour, maximum. Keep in constant contact. One of you remain with the hopper while the other goes down. Follow the fiber-optic cable as far as you can. And be sure you listen for another movement of the antenna, just in case it decides to transmit a second signal. You might not be so lucky next time." Then his voice sounded calmer. "We all hope you find them."

"Gotcha." Cyndi turned to Zimmerman. "So who goes in? Do you have a coin to toss?"

He merely grunted. Cyndi grinned. Any other answer would have told her something was wrong.

Jason was startled to hear Cyndi Salito's voice over the radio when she had descended far enough into the catacombs. Her suit radio waves must have reflected through the tunnel to the alien city. Together, he and Erika worked their way back to the force field trapping the atmosphere inside the main chamber. Cyndi had followed the fiber-optic line along the main catacombs past the matter-antimatter reactors until she reached them.

Cyndi's eyes were wide when Jason pulled her through the field into the self-contained environment of the builders' outpost. "We didn't get any images once you dropped your line," she said. "Wait until Columbus sees this!"

"It's just the beginning," said Jason. "Wait until you see *this*."

Erika led Cyndi over to the incubator building, talking quickly, her voice sparkling with excitement. "We couldn't understand why an entire city would have been built without the aliens. Who was going to live in it? There's everything here, ready to occupy—a library, classrooms, power plants, communications facilities—"

"At least we think that's what most of the stuff is for," Jason interrupted.

"If the nanocritters were building this complex because another civilization wanted to colonize the Moon, then where are the aliens? Are they traveling by slow ship? If so, why would the nanomachines be programmed to build the entire complex right away, rather than just the trans-mitter to report back to the alien home world and ask for further instructions? I mean, the nanocritters could finish up any sort of construction long before aliens ever got here in person. So why do everything now?"

"Did a ship get here first and set off all this stuff?" asked Cyndi.

Jason led Cyndi down one of the sweeping arched corridors. "You told us yourself that another signal was broadcast from Mars, so we have to assume the nano-critters got there, too, and built the same sort of construc-tion. Not very discriminating, are they? How would they know if their 'accidental colony' was in a good location or not? They don't even seem to care."

Cyndi laughed. "My mind is spinning as much from these crazy ideas as it is from these crazy artifacts!"

Jason gripped her suited arm as they turned toward the incubator building. The soft door dilated and poured open, revealing the brighter purple light inside. "Now it's time for you to meet the aliens."

"What!"

Inside the chamber with rows of bubble-boxes, Cyndi was speechless, peering through the walls at the slowly squirming alien infants protected in their incubators. They appeared soft and gelatinous, with changing details across their skin. Jason tried to imagine what an adult might look like.

"But how did they get here? You said there wasn't any ship. And how could little organisms like this have sur-vived such a long trip? Cosmic rays alone would have destroyed most of them. Even if they had been frozen, they wouldn't have survived the impact."

"Nanocritters again," said Jason.

"We figured it out, I think," Erika continued. "With all those regolith samples I took back to Sim-Mars, I always found a 'species' of nanomachine that didn't seem to have a purpose. It just sat there waiting, while all the others did the disassembly, assembly, controlling, reprogramming.

"Now, I believe those tiny machines were the genetic carriers. Their entire memories were filled with instructions of how to assemble alien DNA, atom by atom. Building a complete organism would be impossible, I think— and then how do you make it come alive? No, but with a single strand of DNA, checked and double-checked by quality control nanomachines, they could effectively grow clones of whatever alien individuals provided the genetic blueprint."

Cyndi was breathing hard. "This is getting too tough for my brain to handle all at once."

Jason pointed to the incubator machinery. "Look at this equipment! It's built to nurture the growing clones. Look how far they have come in only the few months this complex has been available. The datacubes, the buildings, the living facilities here—it's a complete colony, ready-made."

Erika kept turning around, shining her light on the bubble-boxes. "Once the whole complex was completed and the embryos started growing successfully, the necessary systems determined that this place could indeed support the alien life. So they transmitted a signal back to the home planet, informing them the colony was completed. Even if the aliens only come by slow ship, they already have a skeleton colony here—buildings, facilities, and more importantly some of their own kind, brought up by machines, to help populate the place."

"But why would they want their children here alone, just waiting for them?" asked Cyndi.

Erika sounded grim. "Maybe this first wave of clones was considered disposable. Maybe they're being brought up as slaves for when the Builders get here."

They were all silent for a moment.

"So that means whenever the signal is received by those

aliens, we can expect some visitors—coming to our solar system to colonize?" Salito whispered.

"There's plenty of room in our solar system for a lot of things," Jason said.

"Not if those aliens are shotgunning out colonies this way. I must admit, it's a nifty way to populate the Galaxy, but we still don't know what they're like," Salito said. "How are we ever going to find out enough, in time?"

Jason drew in a breath and looked around. "They can teach us themselves. If all this equipment is to instruct the embryos, then we can be here to listen in, maybe even befriend these clones, influence them to be sympathetic to us poor Earthlings when the rest of the gang comes along."

"Reminds me of Tarzan," Salito said. "Raised by apes, he was more sympathetic to the jungle than he was to humans."

"Remember, there's another pristine colony on Mars," Erika said. "Judging by that first signal."

"At least we'll have some time to study their culture before the parent aliens arrive," Jason said. "The only question is, how long do we have?"

epilogue

The holotank displayed a representation of the Galactic neighborhood. Bright points of stars scattered out in three dimensions, showing how vast the spiral arm actually was, how far apart the individual stars were in the Milky Way, and how insignificant Earth's Sun was in the whole array.

"We've traced it to here," said Lieutenant General Simon Pritchard, reaching up to indicate with one finger. The white point he selected grew brighter to call attention to itself.

"This star is L145-141, a 'DA' white dwarf. The Daedalus transmission was directed there. L145-141 is a 30,000-degree UV radiator, located in Centaurus. Also, that star emits a Fraunhofer 't' iron line at 2.99944 angstroms, exactly ten billion times smaller than the diameter of the Daedalus construction. It's our 'smoking gun' evidence. L145-141 is only seventeen light years from Earth, practically right next door in the scheme of things, as you can see. Nothing particularly exciting about it, except that we now know the 'Builders' live there."

In the big simulations room, the new director of the United Space Agency nodded. Newly promoted General Pritchard was reminded of the time so long ago—or at least it seemed so long ago—when he had first met Celeste McConnell in here, showing off his simulation of an Icarus asteroid impact.

Forget about Icarus, General, Celeste had told him back then. *Let me show you exactly how interesting Daedalus has become.* And she had been right, but neither of them could have guessed how so many unexpected things would happen.

Agency Director Bernard Chu sat back down in his chair and frowned. His face looked pinched; lines of weariness surrounded his eyes. Pritchard knew the wiry man was having trouble adjusting to Earth's normal gravity. Chu had been away from it for six years; no wonder he had to rest frequently and sit down when most other people could stand. His muscles would take a while to build back up. Calcium supplements would restore what his bones had lost. Chu was on Earth to stay now.

"So what you are saying," he said, "is that the . . . person who receives the Daedalus transmission must wait seventeen years before he can even pick up the phone and say hello?"

"Yes," Pritchard said, "and another seventeen years with a response traveling at the speed of light before we can hear it back here."

E.T. phone home! he thought. The movie had just been re-released in a new three-dimensionalized version, despite the aged director's strenuous objections. A month ago, Pritchard had asked Celeste to see it with him, but they were no longer exactly on speaking terms.

When she had learned of the mysterious disaster at the Nanotech Isolation Lab in Antarctica, Celeste had clutched her head as if to fend off a migraine. "That was it!" she kept insisting. She had misinterpreted the warning, the threat to Earth. She had explained everything to Pritchard, but he wasn't sure he believed it.

The Agency had struggled to keep the details of her attempt at destroying the Daedalus artifact away from the newsnets, and had for the most part succeeded. Celeste had been removed from her position quietly and transferred to a minor post in a little-seen and little-heard department in the administration.

"I thought stars like that were too hot and too fast-burning to allow the development of life," Chu said.

Pritchard shrugged. "Nobody's saying that's where the Builders originated. They could be hopscotching across the Galaxy in waves, wherever their nanoscouts happen to land and set up a transmitter. But it makes sense, since it appears they see in the UV."

He pulled up an image of L145-141, taken with the optical interferometer on the lunar surface. The picture had a resolution a million times that of any Earth-based telescope.

Bernard Chu rubbed his temples. Pritchard canceled the image of the local star map and wondered if there was anything he could do. "I'm here to assist you, Dr. Chu. Please let me help if I can."

Chu sighed and looked at him, forcing a smile. "I am still acclimating to Earth, and I feel tired all the time. I cannot drink coffee, though I believe I could stand some weak tea. I don't know how I ever tolerated this gravity before! It's like wearing clothes made of bricks."

Pritchard laughed. "Would you like anything in your tea?" He touched the intercom panel. Chu shook his head.

While they waited for the tea, Chu tapped his fingers together. "I am not certain we can afford to restart Bingham Grace's mission, but it is imperative that we go to the site of the other signal on Mars. Even with thirty-four years before we can expect an answer from that star, it's going to require all of our resources to find out everything we can about the Builders. I am also putting Erika Trace in charge of the investigation team at Daedalus. She and Dvorak seem to work well together, and neither of them wants to come back to Earth."

"By the time we get a response from that signal, we'd better make sure that we know everything we can," Pritchard said. "It's in our best interests."

Chu nodded. "The United Nations has already agreed to issue a statement announcing that the primary mission of the United Space Agency is to do just that."

Pritchard agreed, "From now on, it has to be the primary mission of the human race."

Jason Dvorak sat back in the transmission booth on Moonbase Columbus. He couldn't keep himself from grinning. His two children, Lacy and Lawrence, pushed their way into the field of view, giggling. Both had dark, curly hair; Margaret had dressed them in identical tie-dyed tunics.

"We saw you on the newsnets, Daddy," Lawrence said, bouncing with excitement.

Lacy stuttered her sentence several times before she finally managed the words. "Did you really go out there to that place? Were you scared?"

"Yes, I did go there, and yes I was a little bit scared. That's where I'll be working for quite a while. There's a lot of things we still need to see."

"Say goodbye to your father now," Margaret said, standing behind them and placing protective hands on both of their shoulders. They waved at him before Margaret scooted them out of the field of view. She stared at Jason in silence for a moment, much longer than the transmission delay made necessary.

Margaret looked like a stranger to him. He recalled with a detached portion of his mind how attractive he still found her, but he could not summon up the feelings he thought he had once had. How could anyone go from love to apathy in such a short time? He didn't understand it himself.

"For what it's worth, Jase . . . Jason . . . you did do something important up there. I can see that." Then she set her mouth in the way that made her look ten years older. "It's too bad you set your priorities that way instead of with us."

Jason froze his expression, refusing to let any emotion show. That was probably what she wanted, just to jerk his chain. There was no winning with Margaret. He had to accept that. His best escape would be to let it drop. Drop entirely.

And so he did.

Erika kept up with Jason as they jogged around the Columbus track. She had finally begun to feel exhausted, and sweat made her running suit cling to her skin. She still hadn't started panting from a real workout, though she and Jason had run a full ten kilometers already.

They seemed to glide in the low gravity. She felt a sudden pang inside as she thought of the unfolding wonders at Daedalus. "It's too bad Jordan couldn't see this. I just don't understand what happened down there. Do you think they'll ever release his records?"

"Probably," Jason said through his dust mask, "as soon as the Agency figures it out for themselves. For now, though, you've got plenty of work here, being in charge of the Daedalus investigation."

Erika flicked a glance to her left to catch his expression. She could tell he was thinking about his ex-wife again, not Daedalus. In a way, she couldn't blame him. She was still getting over the shock of what had happened to Parvu, but she had placed it all behind her. There was too much to look forward to doing now.

Jason said, "At least my kids were impressed by what I'm doing up here."

"I'm impressed," Erika said. She put on a spurt of speed, catching him by surprise. Jason increased his stride to keep up with her.

He kept talking. Sometimes, he just needed to get his thoughts out into the open. "I don't know what to do about Margaret. I've tried everything. Should I care?"

Erika shrugged. "Some people just don't like to be challenged. She seems to be one of them. But you and I—we have a heck of a challenge at Daedalus."

Jason nodded. "And a lot of waiting."

"That's okay. That's why I like older men."

"Oh? Why's that?"

Erika smiled to herself. "Because they're patient." She pulled ahead of him.

Laughing, they sprinted toward the finish line.

about the authors

KEVIN J. ANDERSON and DOUG BEASON are remarkably well qualified to write about nanotechnology and the space program. Trained physicists working on the cutting edge of technology, they have also won recognition as two of the most talented new writers of hard SF.

Kevin J. Anderson holds a degree in physics and astronomy and for the past ten years has been a technical editor at the Lawrence Livermore National Laboratory. He is the author of ten previous novels and numerous short stories. His most recent novels are three adventures set in the STAR WARS® universe—*Jedi Search, Dark Apprentice,* and *Champions of the Force*—published by Bantam Spectra.

Doug Beason is a lieutenant colonel in the U.S. Air Force. He holds a Ph.D. in physics, and served on Lt. Gen. Stafford's *Synthesis Group* appointed by President Bush to study proposals for a manned mission to Mars. He worked for the President's Science Advisor at the White House under both Presidents Clinton and Bush, and is currently an Associate Professor of Physics and Director of research at the U.S. Air Force Academy in Colorado Springs, Colorado. He is also the author of three solo high-tech thrillers.

Their previous collaborations for Bantam Spectra include the highly acclaimed *The Trinity Paradox* and *Lifeline*; they are currently at work on a new novel.

▰▰▰ The Jedi Academy Trilogy ▰▰▰

Star Wars®

Jedi Search
by Kevin J. Anderson

As the war between the Republic and the remnants of the Empire continues, two children—Jedi twins—will come into their powers in a universe on the brink of vast changes and challenges. In this time of turmoil and discovery, an extraordinary new *Star Wars* saga begins....

While Luke Skywalker takes the first step towards setting up an academy to train a new order of Jedi Knights, Han Solo and Chewbacca are taken prisoner on the planet Kessel. But when Han and Chewie escape, their flight leads to a secret Imperial research laboratory—and from one danger to a far greater one....Luke picks up their trail only to come face-to-face with a weapon so awesome, it can wipe out an entire solar system. It is a death ship called the Sun Crusher, invented by a reclusive genius and piloted by none other than Han himself....